P9-DBK-340

RED TIGRESS

BOOKS BY AMÉLIE WEN ZHAO

Blood Heir

Red Tigress

RED TIGRESS

AMÉLIE WEN ZHAO

DELACORTE PRESS

This is a work of fiction. Names, characters, places, and incidents either are the product of the author's imagination or are used fictitiously. Any resemblance to actual persons, living or dead, events, or locales is entirely coincidental.

 Published in the United States by Delacorte Press, an imprint of Random House Children's Books, a division of Penguin Random House LLC, New York.

Delacorte Press is a registered trademark and the colophon is a trademark of Penguin Random House LLC.

Visit us on the Web! GetUnderlined.com

Educators and librarians, for a variety of teaching tools, visit us at RHTeachersLibrarians.com

Library of Congress Cataloging-in-Publication Data
Names: Zhao, Amélie Wen, author.
Title: Red Tigress / Amélie Wen Zhao.
Description: First edition. | New York : Delacorte Press, [2021] | Series: Blood heir ; book 2 | Audience: Ages 14 and up. | Audience: Grades 10–12. | Summary: Exiled princess and Affinite, Ana Mikhailov, partners with conman Ramson Quicktongue to take back the throne and stop the current empress, Morganya, from killing all the Affinites.
Identifiers: LCCN 2020025332 (print) | LCCN 2020025333 (ebook) |
ISBN 978-0-525-70783-7 (hardcover) | ISBN 978-0-525-70786-8 (trade paperback) |
ISBN 978-0-593-37693-5 (intl. tr. pbk.) | ISBN 978-0-525-70784-4 (library binding) |
ISBN 978-0-525-70785-1 (ebook)
Subjects: CYAC: Ability—Fiction. | Magic—Fiction. | Government, Resistance to—Fiction. | Fantasy.
Classification: LCC PZ7.1.Z5125 Re 2021 (print) | LCC PZ7.1.Z5125 (ebook) |
DDC [Fic]—dc23

Printed in the United States of America
10 9 8 7 6 5 4 3 2 1
First Edition

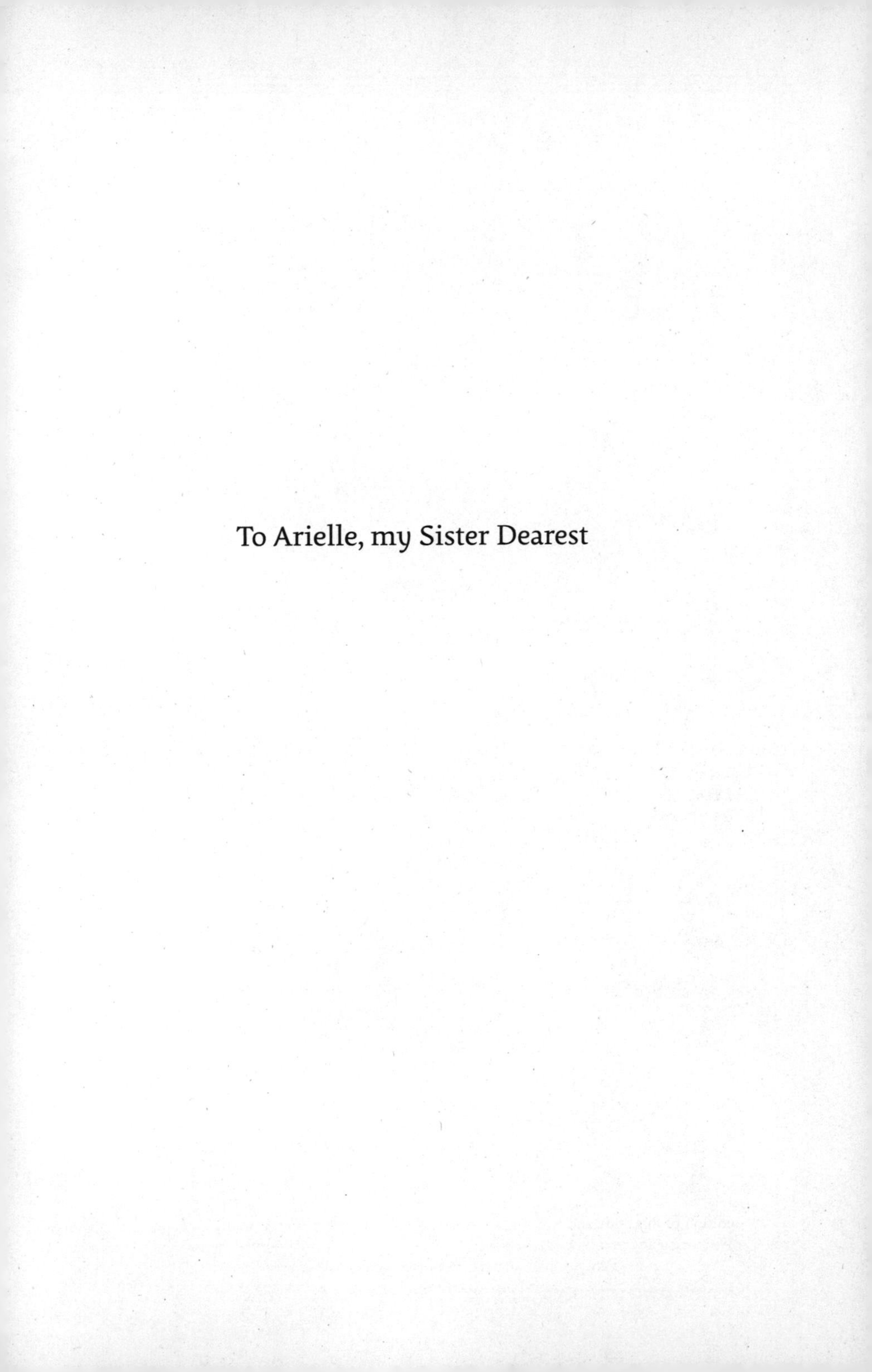

To Arielle, my Sister Dearest

N
W
E
S
The Silent Sea
The Kemeiran Empire
The Jade Trail
Sapph
Por
Blue Fort
Kingdoms of the Eastern Isles
Kingdom of Bregon

KRAZYAST TRIANGLE

SYVERN TAIGA

IGER'S
TAIL

Salskoff

Ghost Falls

THE
CYRILIAN
EMPIRE

he
hitewaves

Kyrov

Novo Mynsk

GOLDWATER
PORT

DZHYVEKHA MOUNTAINS

ARAMABI DESERT

CROWN
OF NANDJI

RED TIGRESS

1

Novo Mynsk reeked of death.

It always had, but to Ramson Quicktongue, the city had also held the stench of power and corruption, of murder and survival, swirling together in an intoxicating redolence that corroded one's soul. It was no different now, save for the eerie darkness and silent snow that blanketed it.

Ramson navigated the narrow alleyways of his childhood haunts with quick, precise steps. The last time he'd been here had been with Anastacya Mikhailov during the Fyrva'snezh at his former master's mansion. It had only been a little over one moon since the celebration of the First Snows, but now, that world felt almost utterly unrecognizable.

In just four weeks, Novo Mynsk had transformed into a ghost town, abandoned by most of its residents as they sought to flee the new regime. Streets that had once shimmered with torchlight and writhed with bejeweled bodies and raucous revelers had been replaced by shuttered stores and empty windows. Bodies littered the streets in areas where gangs had scrapped over bits of food, and snow had blanketed them, leaving only glimpses of clothing or a protruding boot as macabre grave markers.

It was not an unfamiliar sight over his travels from town to ravaged town with Ana. Since Morganya had ascended the throne, much of Northern Cyrilia had fallen to her control. From newspaper pieces and torn posters in abandoned villages, Ramson and Ana had learned of the Imperial Inquisition, a wide-scale hunt for non-Affinites who were accused of any affiliation with Affinite trafficking. Led by Affinites fiercely loyal to the Empress, it was a movement that had come to define Morganya's regime.

The south, though, remained free from the tightening grasp of Morganya's rule. That included Goldwater Port. According to Ana, the Redcloaks had established their base there, as it remained one of the last standing free havens for Affinites and non-Affinites alike. It was there that Ana traveled to begin her resistance movement with the Redcloaks.

And it was there, Ramson had slowly begun to think, he could fight for some semblance of a life again after all this was over. He'd once been the Portmaster; under his former master Alaric Kerlan's rule, he'd built a city teeming with commerce and crime and underground networks, the kind of place he'd dreamt of calling his own one day.

He hadn't told Ana explicitly where he was going tonight, because it wasn't *explicitly* a task for her—their—mission. Rather, Ramson had felt the silent call of this place as soon as he'd set foot in Novo Mynsk, the phantom pull of a connection he hadn't quite managed to sever yet.

He'd come to find out, for himself, what had happened to Alaric Kerlan and the Order of the Lily. And he'd come to bid the torn wreckages of his past good-bye, once and for all, as he turned down a new path.

The tapping of his freshly sharpened misericord against his hip came to an abrupt stop when Ramson turned the last corner and slowed. He found that he was suddenly glad for the sharp knife at his waist.

The Kerlan Estate stood alone in the middle of a snow-covered street, half-buried by the snow, its battered golden gates yawning wide. Gone were the rows of liveried guards; gone were the diamond-glass lamps spilling haloes of light onto lush lawns; gone were the brightly lit windows burning into the darkest nights.

Ramson touched a leather-gloved hand on the broken railing of the gate and hesitated.

Even now, the sight of the Kerlan Estate did not fail to elicit a muddy swirl of emotions in him. He'd known pain here—so much pain, still seared into his flesh in the shape of the brand of the Order of the Lily. He'd seen growth, sharpened by that hunger and fear and driven by the knowledge that he had to do whatever he needed to in order to survive. And he'd tasted happiness, fleeting as bursts of color in the Empire's gray skies, in the blood trades he'd made and the honors he'd gained, paid for with the lives of other men as he upheld Alaric Kerlan's rule.

Ramson's heart pounded in his throat as he hurried up the snow-covered path. When he reached the mansion, he saw that one handle of the giant mahogany double doors had broken; the other seemed to have been hacked clean off by a serrated blade of some sort. The wood creaked as he pushed them open and stepped inside, the mansion yawning wide like a dark, silent trap.

The Kerlan Estate looked as though it had been mauled. The marble walls had been stripped of the gold-framed paintings, and the lapis lazuli vases had disappeared along with the many other items Kerlan had deemed "exotic." Someone had shattered the glass ceiling, and one of the crystal chandeliers had plunged into the middle of the banquet hall, creating a mess of glass and crystal that glinted in the moonlight. Drifts of snow carpeted the hallways, and Ramson's breath plumed before him in the subzero temperature.

When Ramson turned a corner and almost tripped over the dead man, his alertness pricked.

The body was covered by the snow; he could make out only a sleeve and a blackened hand sticking out. Ramson knelt by the corpse, sweeping off the freshly fallen snow to unearth the man's left arm. Just as he'd suspected, a tattoo of a lily of the valley was inked on the inside of the man's left wrist.

He had been a member of the Order.

Instead of fear or grief or even pity, Ramson examined the frozen hand with a clinical curiosity. Skin, blackened evenly, suggested internal bleeding. Farther up, on the forearm, raised flesh—evidence of a rash.

He had been poisoned.

Ramson pushed away more snow, revealing the dead man's face.

It was twisted in pain, bruised to a hideous purple and sunken with time, yet perfectly preserved by the cold. Ramson studied the face for several more seconds before deciding it wasn't a man he'd known in the Order. The corpse of a low-ranking grunt, a nobody, left to rot once winter swept its snows away.

And though their common master was nowhere to be seen, his voice tided over Ramson in phantom echoes.

I suppose you'll die unknown and irrelevant, your unmarked body rotting along the sewage of the Dams.

Ramson stood sharply to his feet, the whispers dissipating as his senses picked up on something else.

In one motion, he drew his blade, swung his arm out, and pivoted.

A startled cry; his blade connected with soft flesh, exposed throat. And . . . long, wavy hair.

Ramson closed his fist around a handful of hair and pulled the intruder's face into the moonlight. His apprehension turned to surprise. "Olyusha," he said as the woman struggled against his grip. "Damn hells."

"Let me go," she gasped, but Ramson only drew her closer, angling the misericord against her delicate neck.

"I don't think so," he said. Hells, he hadn't been planning on running into anyone here—but as Ramson Quicktongue well knew, things rarely went according to plan. "Should've known this was your handiwork. Nightshade?"

"Oleander," she rasped. "You've gotten rusty, Quicktongue."

"Try anything and we'll see just how rusty my skills are with a blade."

He'd first known of Olyusha as an Affinite working at the Playpen, specializing in poisons and needles tipped with toxins. And though she didn't know this, he'd used her as a bargaining chip against Bogdan, the affable yet stupid Penmaster of the Playpen, the infamous club where Alaric Kerlan had run shows with indentured Affinites.

That she was here, amid buried corpses showing signs of poisoning . . . Ramson had an inkling he was very close to sniffing out the truth of what had happened to the Order.

Olyusha hissed, but he felt her swallow against his blade. "Then perhaps we'll both join the corpses at our feet," she sneered. "Let me go. I didn't come here to kill you."

"So why *are* you here?" Ramson asked pleasantly, digging his blade into her skin in a way that he knew would be uncomfortable but would not cut.

"To warn you. Kerlan wants you dead, and he's set a high price on your head. The whole Order's probably out for your blood, Quicktongue." She paused. "What's left of them, anyway."

At that, he glanced up, a thread of caution tightening inside him. The hallways stretched empty in front of and behind them. "And why would you want to warn me? We're cut from the same cloth, Olyusha, so spare me the 'out of the goodness of your heart' act."

"Because I need you." The sharpness to her tone became tinged with desperation at her next words: "Bogdan is gone."

This was news to Ramson. "What do you mean?"

The few times he'd run into Olyusha after her stint at the Playpen, she had been soft-spoken and doe-eyed, clinging to the gold-emblazoned sleeve of Bogdan. The Penmaster had rescued her from a lifetime of performances served under a forced contract—and he'd married her. It was Ramson who had helped cook Kerlan's books so that Kerlan would never find out.

"He's missing. That's why I came here to find you." Olyusha's throat bobbed against his blade. "Now, let me go, and I can explain."

So, there *was* something she needed from him. Ramson shifted tactic in an instant. "A Trade, then," he said. "You know I never give without taking, Olyusha."

"Fine," she said, and he stepped back, pushing her far enough from him so that he was out of range of any needles or sharp, poison-laced objects she might try on him. She straightened, massaging her throat, and he noticed that her hands shook as she swept back her tresses. She suddenly looked small, tucked into her coat, which had lost some of its sheen and was now covered in a layer of gray. Ramson had remembered her dressed in the finest of furs and silks, pearls glittering in her hair as she turned her head and laughed.

Ramson tapped his misericord on the marble floor. It echoed hollowly. "You can start by telling me what happened to the Order," he said. "What you mean by 'what's left of them.'"

Olyusha sniffed. "I forget how long you've been out of it all, Quicktongue. After Morganya took the throne, Kerlan forced me to kill everyone associated with his trafficking business. He is intent on burying proof that it ever existed, for fear of the Inquisition." Her eyes flashed. "Then he left with a handful of top-ranking members. He's decided to refocus his efforts on his new Trade with Bregon."

The name of Ramson's birth kingdom sent a shock wave through him, even as his ears perked at the news. "What Trade? And why Bregon?"

"He said it was a new development with Affinites. Besides that, I don't know. Probably to escape the Imperial Inquisition and the new Empress's purge on Affinite traffickers."

Ramson took a moment to digest this information. Morganya had hired Kerlan for a hit job—to kill the Crown Prince, Ana's brother—before, but since her Coronation, she had turned with zealous fervor against Affinite traffickers. It was

likely that Kerlan had caught wind of this two steps ahead, as always, and turned tail and fled. And now he was going to establish a new criminal empire . . . in Bregon.

That was the part that didn't make sense. Bregon had never shown interest in its Affinites—magen, they were called—who, in Ramson's memory, had been largely left alone and unidentified. "And how do you know this?"

"Because," Olyusha said, "he took Bogdan with him. I haven't heard from him in weeks."

Her voice had grown quiet; her large eyes shone wet in the dark. At last, Ramson connected the dots. "You want my help to find him."

"He promised it would be a quick job. He told me he'd be back within the moon." Olyusha swallowed. "I think . . . I think something went wrong."

He was getting sidetracked—he'd only come here out of an old habit, to find out what had happened to the Order and his former master. Perhaps it was indeed better to let sleeping wolves lie.

Ramson began to turn away. "I'd love to help, Olyusha, really," he said, "but with Kerlan demanding my head, I think I have better things—"

"He's in Goldwater Port." The words froze him, reeled him back. Slowly, Ramson turned to face her again. She was looking at him closely; at his reaction, she continued, "He told Bogdan that he would take it over, rebuild from there. No doubt he's leveraging the trade routes to Bregon that you've established."

Liquid cold spread through his veins, and suddenly, all the plans he'd been spinning for himself the past few weeks seemed

to dissipate into smoke before him. Goldwater Port had been center to any prospects of a future he'd dreamt up for himself.

Only, Kerlan had gotten there first.

He heard Olyusha speaking as though from very far away. "I thought that would get your attention. Here's my proposal: an alliance to take down Alaric Kerlan together, once and for all. Find him, find Bogdan, and bring my husband home to me. And in return, you'll have my protection. Someone watching your back from the enemy's side. Whoever from the Order is looking for you, I'll get to them first."

Ramson was silent as he considered, his thoughts already running ahead, weaving situations and possibilities and weighing the pros and cons of it all. He'd wanted to leave Kerlan alone, to let the Order fade away as a part of his past that he'd wished to bury—but it seemed they had come looking for him, instead. And by taking Goldwater Port, Kerlan had seized the most valuable asset between them, backing Ramson into a corner.

Through the broken windows, moonlight spilled onto the floor. Even in the empty house, Ramson thought he could feel his old master's presence, like a cold shadow looming behind him.

This was all a game to Kerlan; it was Ramson's turn to make a move.

He was tired of playing the pawn.

"Well?" he heard Olyusha say at last. "Do we have a Trade?"

"I'm inclined to say so," he said. "Though don't expect me to shake with you on it." He'd witnessed the tricks she hid up her sleeves, how one drop of her poison could paralyze a man entirely.

Olyusha's smile didn't meet her eyes. "I knew from the start that you wouldn't save Bogdan out of the goodness of your heart unless there was something in it for you. Seems I was right."

"Am I really that predictable?"

Olyusha shrugged. "I'm not one to lay any claims as to how well I know you, Quicktongue," she said, picking at one of her nails, "but Bogdan and I would not have survived for so long in Kerlan's Order without someone watching over us. Of course, you might have done those things to buy yourself insurance . . . but I do think that, despite everything about you, you have the propensity to be good, in your own terrible ways."

The words stirred an echo of a memory. A girl, standing beneath the softly falling snow of a new winter, her eyes brighter than the moon. *You could be good. Make the right choice, Ramson.*

Olyusha's voice dragged him from the memory. "Before we part, I have one more gift for you," she said. "I know someone in Goldwater Port. Kerlan hired her for a few shipping jobs before, specific to Bregon. She'll have more information."

Ramson listened carefully to the name Olyusha gave. It didn't ring a bell, which surprised him. Perhaps there were still secrets that Goldwater Port carried, buried deep beneath its sands by the man who'd made Ramson the person he had been: the person he still was.

It was time for Ramson to carve his own path.

He turned, tipping his cap at Olyusha. "Well met, Olyusha," he said. "You sit pretty and focus on murdering our excolleagues. By the time you're done, I'll be back with your idiot husband."

He heard her give a throaty laugh, the sound echoing over the clip of his boots as he walked away. "I'm not giving up on you just yet, Quicktongue." A pause, and then: "When you do find Kerlan, promise me you'll send him my regards."

"I don't make promises," Ramson replied. "That way, I can't break them."

Yet even as he spoke, he could feel the sharp edges of a vow burying deep into his heart.

Jonah had once told him to live for himself. *Thing is, Ramson,* he'd said, his raven-black eyes sharp with intelligence and uncanny wisdom for his twelve years of age, *you can achieve everything in this world, but if it's for someone else, it's pointless.*

Yet as Ramson walked through the snow, the Kerlan Estate hovering behind him with its empty-eyed windows and broken, gaping mouth of a door, he realized that the path in front of him was still far out of reach, blocked by a shadow that grew larger and clearer with every step he took.

Alaric Kerlan represented everything he despised about himself, his life, and this world. As long as Kerlan lived, he could never be free.

And right now, if Kerlan was establishing a new criminal empire in Goldwater Port, using the trade routes Ramson had built to get to Bregon, then he was the obstacle that stood in the way of the glimpse of the future Ramson had hoped for.

One that involved planting the roots of the resistance in the south with Ana, and then making some semblance of a life for himself after the war was won.

Ramson tilted his face to the starless sky, his breath unfurling before him in a cloud as he spoke. "I'll find my own path, Jonah," he said aloud. "But first, I'm going to hunt down Alaric Kerlan. And I'm going to kill him."

2

Winter held its breath over the city of Novo Mynsk, the bladed silence of night shrouding Anastacya Mikhailov as she searched the streets for blood. Here and there, her Affinity picked up faint traces of it: a splash, soaking the ground like paint; a handprint on a broken streetlamp, faded to a smear.

She hadn't imagined she would return to this place again, where she'd experienced loss and seen the cruelty of her empire firsthand. But several weeks earlier, on the run after Morganya had almost killed her, Ana had sent a snowhawk to her old friend Yuri, leader of the Redcloaks, requesting a meeting.

The response had come, cryptic in case of interception: *Meet at the ninth hour on the twenty-sixth day of the first moon of Winter, at the location where we last met. Search for my contact in the shadows.*

In just one moon, Novo Mynsk had been reduced to a husk of what it been back when she and Yuri had been reunited. Dachas had been left abandoned as the wealthy fled south from Morganya's regime; those remaining stayed indoors, their blood flickering faintly beyond thin walls as Ana passed by.

It wasn't an unfamiliar sight.

Many times throughout Ana's travels in the past few weeks, she and Ramson had found empty towns, the wind whistling through smashed windows and half-shuttered shops. Through glimpses of announcements and flyers scattered on streets, they'd pieced together Morganya's plans for her new regime.

Newly Crowned Empress Morganya Mikhailov Rules by Justice and *Imperial Court Reforms Spawn New Era for Cyrilia,* one headline had blared; others had declared *Non-Affinite Registration Required; Identification Papers to Be Carried at All Times.*

Slowly but surely, Morganya was reversing the fates of Affinites and non-Affinites. But the specifics of it, Ana had yet to find out.

When she turned the next corner, Ana drew a sharp breath. Her steps faltered.

Where the Playpen once was sat a charred skeleton of a building. The farcical imitation of a Cyrilian cathedral was burned black, the stained-glass windows once depicting scantily clad women now shattered. Gaping holes were left in their wake like empty eye sockets staring out from a ruined face.

It was hard to imagine the Playpen as it had been over a moon ago, when she had encountered Yuri in the midst of an Affinite trafficking ring: raucous, crowded with writhing bodies, and hot with the pungent smell of sweat and cloying perfume. Now, the gilded mahogany doors had been smashed through. Debris cracked beneath her boots as she entered, her steps echoing loudly in the silence. Beaded curtains littered the floor like pearls from a broken necklace, and the love seats were overturned, stuffing spilling from them.

Ana cast her Affinity before her like a torch, sensing the outline of the place through the blood splattered on the walls around her and the steps leading to the room below.

Gradually, she picked up on a single flicker somewhere beneath her.

Her contact.

With a gloved hand she retrieved a globefire from the inner pocket of her new cloak—a dark red this time, the color of blood. It was one she'd chosen in a remote village in a rare act of self-indulgence.

Ana shook it. The chemicals inside rattled and then, within seconds, crackled to life in the form of a small, persistent fire, throwing light onto her surroundings.

Holding the globefire before her, she descended the staircase and made her way down the long corridor that led to the auditorium. Ana's Affinity pulled taut, tuned in to the flicker of blood that grew closer with every step.

She entered the room that just weeks ago had been alive with torchlight and laughter and the thrum of drums.

The performance dome now resembled a graveyard. Stone pillars were in pieces and covered the floor, the silk and ribbons once clinging to them now half-buried among the rubble. Here and there, the walls were scorched with burn marks, and people had toppled the statues of the Deities that once guarded the stage. A sorrowful stone face stared up at her as she picked her way across the room.

Ana stopped before the stage. It was still littered with flowers and bits of whatever elements had been used to perform before it was destroyed. The blackstone-infused glass that May had brought down glittered like snow. No one had even bothered to clean up this place. Kerlan must have left it like this after the rebellion.

For a moment, a ghost of a memory flickered in her mind, and she saw a child standing on the stage, nursing a flower to life. The child looked up, her ocean-eyes bright, her hair a soft tangle around her face.

We are but dust and stars.

Ana turned away abruptly. Tears ached, deep in her chest.

But there was something else. In the torrent of her emotions, Ana almost—*almost*—missed the flicker of movement at the edges of her Affinity.

The light of her globefire suddenly vanished, plunging the auditorium into darkness.

Ana could hear her own breathing, the stuttering of her heartbeats . . . and the slightest shuffling sound from somewhere beyond the wreckage of the stage. She shook her globefire; the chemicals rattled, the glass was warm, as though the flame still burned . . . but there was no light.

She could sense the person standing about a dozen paces from her.

Ana drew a sharp breath. "Show yourself," she said.

A spark of light flickered in the globefire, between her fingers. And then the light flared again, filling the chamber.

On the stage, by the statue of a weeping Deity, stood a young man. He'd appeared as suddenly as an illusion, and as he gazed at her intensely, she had the distinct impression that he was less illuminated by the light than carved out by an absence of shadows.

"Apologies if I frightened you." His voice was smooth, cold, dark as velvet night. "It is necessary that we take the utmost precautions when meeting with strangers."

She considered him, thinking of the way the light of her globefire had been stolen, watching how the shadows seemed to drape him like a cloak.

Search for my contact in the shadows.

An Affinite, then. A shadow Affinite.

"I'm a friend," Ana replied, "of Yuri's."

"I highly doubt that." He began to walk toward her, debris cracking beneath his polished shoes. His outline flickered, shadows licking at his edges, and as he drew near, she began to make out his features. He looked to be around Ramson's age, just a few years older than she. A crop of straight, ink-black hair fell with casual neatness over his forehead, framing a startlingly beautiful face with the features of the Aseatic kingdoms. He was clad in an all-white tunic, silver buttons fastened tightly at his pale throat. Lithe and elegant, he resembled a fairy-tale prince.

Only, his eyes held a wild darkness.

Briefly, she wondered whether he had been trafficked into the Empire at a young age, like her friend Linn; like May.

The boy paused at the edge of the stage. With a light hop, he stepped off. "Seyin, Second-in-Command."

So *this* was the Redcloaks' Second-in-Command.

Ana noted how he didn't bow. Determined to show him proper courtesy, she dipped her head. "Anastacya Mikhailov. Heir to the Cyrilian Empire."

She thought she caught Seyin's eyes narrowing for a fraction of a second, but she blinked and his face was expressionless again. "Well, meya dama," he said, and once again, she noticed that he didn't address her with any honorifics. "I am here by request of our Commander."

It was easy to derive a second layer of meaning to his words. *I am not here of my own will.*

Everything he said, every move he made, was done with deliberation, and she was beginning to sense a subtle hostility beneath his cool diplomacy.

She suddenly wondered what Yuri had said to his Second to invoke the distant coolness with which he regarded her. It had been over a moon since she'd last seen Yuri, back at Shamaïra's when their paths had crossed briefly, then separated again.

When you're ready, send a snowhawk to Goldwater Port, he'd told her. His eyes had brimmed with warmth back then.

She looked into the cold, dark gaze of his Second. Had something changed? "Thank you for your time," she said. "I'll get to the point: I'm here to take up an alliance with the Redcloaks."

There was a pause, and she had the strangest sense of the shadows around her deepening, pulsing, as though they were alive. Seyin watched her impassively. "And why," he said slowly, "would the Redcloaks agree to an alliance with you?"

The question caught her off guard. An alliance with the Redcloaks had seemed only natural after her parting exchange with Yuri.

Ana met Seyin's gaze. "Have you spoken with Yuri?"

"I have" was all Seyin said in response.

"Then you know that we are fighting on the same side, to bring down Morganya. I want to make a safe world, for Affinites and non-Affinites alike." Her breath unfurled in an icy mist. "I can defeat Morganya. I can take back the throne."

Seyin stepped forward, pulling back the darkness around them. Moonlight spilled over them in a silver pool. "You must realize that is precisely why we are not, and cannot be, allies."

The sentence robbed her of breath. "No, I *don't* understand. Is it not the wish of the Redcloaks to make an equal world?"

Seyin's smile was cold. "It is."

"Then why—"

"But it is not yours," Seyin interrupted, his eyes glittering. "Tell me, what is the difference between you and Morganya? You are, after all, both Affinite empresses promising a better world for your people."

Shock burned through her, followed closely by disgust. What game was he playing with her? "Seyin," Ana said, grappling for calm. "You've seen the charred villages, the burnt corpses, the trail of blood left behind by Morganya's forces. She is not creating equality. She is using violence to upend the social order of the Empire while cementing her own rule."

"And isn't that what you, too, will do once you take the throne?" Seyin spread his hands in a careless shrug, then brought them together. "I see two Affinites fighting for the throne, both promising better futures to the vulnerable and exploited."

Fury licked up her chest, hot and searing. "Morganya is *slaughtering* the innocents—"

"She is purging those who were affiliated with Affinite trafficking and exploitation."

"And that isn't equality or freedom! That's *massacre.*"

A twisted little smile played at Seyin's lips. "But isn't that what history tells us? The path to becoming a ruler is painted in blood. In the death of thousands of innocent lives. Morganya, too, promised us equality and freedom. What makes you so different, that we should throw our forces behind you? You're just a girl born to a silver spoon and a golden crown. That says nothing of whether you are capable of ruling."

The fire that had been building inside her flickered out, leaving her cold.

"You see," Seyin continued, "the issue that I have isn't whether you or Morganya will make for the better ruler, Anastacya." She flinched at the way he spoke her name, with dominance, as though he'd suddenly stripped her naked. "It is with the system itself. The last emperor, and the one before him, and the one before him . . . they all promised the people wonderful things. Yet letting a monarch go unchecked means there is nothing to protect the people should that monarch fail." He looked somber now, spreading his hands. "Suppose you are merciful. Suppose you are gracious, and that you rule with justice. What happens after you die? What about the next ruler, or the next, or the ones after that? Can you guarantee that they, too, will carry the benevolence and sense of justice that you claim to have?"

Ana struggled to think of a rebuttal and found that she had none. She thought of the first time she'd run into Imperial Patrols, of how they'd treated her and May like criminals, of how she'd seen, with her own eyes, the inequities that her father had allowed to bloom like a sickness in their empire.

All along, she'd sought the throne because she trusted herself to change it all, because she knew with a conviction greater than her own life that she would bring equality to her empire once again.

Yet never had she thought to question the system of rule

itself. What Seyin was saying . . . was unthinkable to her in the moment.

"You say you fight against Empress Morganya," Seyin continued quietly. "You say you wish to create an equal world under a monarchy. But it is the monarchy itself that is the fault here. The people—Affinites and non-Affinites alike—have suffered for too long under the theory of a benevolent ruler. It is time we had a say in the way our lives are ruled." Seyin spread his hands. "The future is in the hands of the people. *That* is the mission of the Redcloaks."

It felt as though her world were shifting, signs she had missed earlier blazing to life. Yuri loved her, but he had never promised her anything—not a throne, not an alliance, not even a common goal. She'd hinged all her hopes on him and his revolution. In her own creed for justice, for equality, she had never paused to question whether they were even on the same path.

But she had experienced life both privileged and oppressed; she had been a princess and an Affinite. Surely . . . "I'm not like the other monarchs," she said, her voice raw. "I know how it feels to be an Affinite, to be told that you're unwanted and to be reviled by society. I've seen what happens to the weak and the vulnerable in the darkest corners of this empire. I want to change the system."

"Simply changing the system isn't sufficient," Seyin said. "We need to *break* the system." He paused and lowered his hands, almost apologetically. "But, enough of grand political philosophies. You see now why the Redcloaks cannot and will not ally with you. You are the heir to the monarchy, Anastacya. You are the antithesis to our movement."

She thought back to a moment that felt like a long time ago, standing back in the moonlight with only the Syvern Taiga and the silhouette of the fire-hearted boy she'd known.

The Redcloaks were her only possibility for an alliance, and Yuri one of the only people left whom she loved—yet the reality was, they were far from fighting on the same side of the war.

The Redcloaks sought a revolution.

She sought the throne.

But—no. They faced a greater threat right now than who ruled and how they ruled. Morganya's grasp was tightening all along the Empire, and it was only a matter of time before she reached them, too, snuffing out any possibilities of resistance.

They *were* on the same side, for now. She had learned that the enemy of her enemy was her friend.

Yuri would see that. They'd bring down Morganya together first, and they'd work out their differences after. Because, Ana thought, if they didn't unite now, there would be no *after* at all.

That night in the Syvern Taiga, Yuri had sought her out to ask her to return. He'd said, *And remember that I love you, no matter what you choose.*

She needed to speak with him. She was wasting time with his Second.

In the whirl of her thoughts, she suddenly noticed that a hungry look had seeped into Seyin's features. His hands were at his hips, resting on the hilt of a sheathed dagger.

"The monarchy must die, Anastacya," Seyin said quietly.

The shadows around them deepened. Cold crept up Ana's back. Instinctively, she awakened her Affinity.

Seyin stepped forward.

And then, out of the stillness, a second flare of blood appeared. Fast approaching.

Seyin's eyes flicked to the entrance of the dome, his expression shifting again. The light emanating from Ana's globefire dimmed; the shadows held their breath.

Ana turned, her Affinity poised.

A figure burst through the double doors: a girl, hair disheveled, eyes wide. She wore a dark cloak, the insides of which flashed red.

Seyin frowned. "Yesenya."

Another Redcloak, then, Ana thought, watching as the girl came to a stop a dozen steps from them. "Seyin," she panted. "The Imperial Inquisition is here."

A chill ran down Ana's spine. She'd fled many ravaged villages since she'd been on the run; the Imperial Inquisition wasn't supposed to have arrived so quickly.

"Deploy the units," Seyin said. "We lie low, continue our reconnaissance."

Seyin's tone was sharp, commanding, and in that moment, Ana understood why Yuri had chosen him as the Second-in-Command of the Redcloaks. She disagreed with him on the path forward, but there was no doubt Seyin was an effective leader.

A leader who had begun to draw together a plan, starting with understanding exactly what Morganya was doing.

Ana watched him, a plan beginning to take shape in her head. Up to now, she'd been focused on surviving day-to-day, on eluding Morganya's forces. But she couldn't fight an enemy that she didn't even know.

If she were to speak to Yuri, if she were to try to convince him that she was fit to lead in the fight against Morganya . . . then she needed a concrete plan.

And that always began, as Ramson would say, with knowing the lay of the land. *Reconnaissance.*

Seyin turned to her, his eyes black and impenetrable. "Perhaps our paths will cross again," he said. "But for now, I have nothing more to say to a girl who thinks this war is but a game for kings and queens."

Without another word, the Second of the Redcloaks strode past Ana as though she were no more than one of the broken statues of the Deities. Ana watched his and Yesenya's outlines grow fainter and fainter until they disappeared into the shadows.

Alone in the darkness, Ana leaned against the wall. Seyin's words had cut like knives in the deepest corners of her heart, her fears and insecurities bleeding bright.

You're just a girl born to a silver spoon and a golden crown.

For so long, she had been focused on regaining her title and her right to rule, she hadn't considered *how* she would rule. She'd thought justice and tenacity and equality would be enough—but Seyin had taken every one of the tenets she held fiercely and shattered them.

She had no army. No power. No allies. Her plan—her *only* plan—had utterly unraveled in the course of an hour. Of all the failures she had anticipated, she hadn't expected this.

Ana forced herself to steady her breathing and her mind. If there was one thing she had gained from the meeting tonight, it was that Seyin had directed her to her next move.

She needed to understand her enemy, enough so that she had a plan when she faced Yuri again. Not only that—she needed to see, with her own two eyes, what made her different, and what made her the good choice, the right choice, for her empire.

That began right now, with the Imperial Inquisition.

There was just one problem.

Ramson, Ana thought, and for a moment, she imagined him leaning against a broken pillar, arms crossed, regarding her with that smirk. They'd agreed to meet at a pub named the Broken Arrow after their respective meetings, but that was in the opposite direction of the town square, where she needed to be.

Ana hesitated, glancing down the hallway where Seyin had disappeared. Instantly, all other thoughts dissipated. Ramson Quicktongue was not—could not be—a priority. Her empire and her people were her responsibility.

They should be the only things that mattered.

Ramson could wait.

Ana turned and ran after Seyin, her steps reverberating in the empty chamber. The blackened walls, the empty torch sconces, the stairs and crushed glass beneath her feet—it all blended together as the exit of the Playpen came into view, a destination brighter and more certain than the darkness around her: the Imperial Inquisition.

3

Outside, the streets were still empty, silence lingering in the darkness between alleyways. Toward the center of Novo Mynsk, though, right above where the town square should be, plumes of smoke choked the night sky, gilding it a bloody orange.

Ana focused on that, settling into the rhythmic sound of her boots against the snow.

Several more turns and streets and her Affinity swept over a cluster of blood down the next street.

She slowed and came to a stop behind a dacha. Drawing a tight breath, Ana peered around the corner.

To her surprise, a group of Whitecloaks stood in the middle of the street ahead. Their signature capes fluttered white beneath the light that spilled from a streetlamp, and the pommels of their swords glinted gold at their hips.

There were four of them. Their armor glittered with the telltale gray hue of infused blackstone, the natural inhibitor to Affinities.

But there was something different about one. He stood in front, an air of authority to his stance, the tilt of his chin and the angle of his shoulders. Ana frowned, her Affinity hovering against the bright glow of his blood. And then it hit her.

She had never been able to fully grasp the blood of other Imperial Patrols before because of the blackstone in their armor. There wasn't a hint of it in the livery the first Whitecloak wore. Upon a closer look, his armor was different—it lacked the telltale gray, glittering hue of blackstone, and embossed on the plate at his chest was also a different insignia, one she didn't recognize: a Deities' circle, carved into the quadrants to represent the Four Deities, in the center of which sat a crown.

Morganya's new sigil.

As she watched, the Whitecloak angled his head toward the dacha and raised his hands.

There was a *crack,* and the wooden door before them tore visibly from its hinges. The Whitecloak gave another flick of his fingers, and before their eyes, the door crumbled into sawdust.

An Affinite. Ana's stomach tightened in recognition. She'd read about Morganya recruiting Affinites into her army, specifically to carry out these Inquisitions. They were to lead missions across the Empire, eliminating anyone accused of crimes against Affinites and rooting out dissent against the new Empress. The "Inquisitors," they were called.

Historically, Affinites had always been barred from the Imperial Army—all but for yaegers, who were able to subdue Affinites. The Imperial Patrols had been assigned to patrol the lands to quell any unrest between Affinites and non-Affinites.

Within weeks, Morganya had reversed a core law of the Cyrilian Empire with little resistance, it seemed, from the Imperial Council.

In front of the dacha, the pile of sawdust was rising, twining itself into threads, and twisting those into ropes. They moved through the air like snakes. With a sudden gesture from the Inquisitor, the ropes shot into the dacha.

There were screams from inside, and several thuds. And then a man was dragged out, his wrists bound by the sawdust ropes.

The Inquisitor twirled his hand, and the man was lifted to his knees. He was pleading with them. "Please, mesyrs, I'm just a cobbler—I haven't done anything wrong—"

"Show me your identification papers," the Inquisitor ordered.

Ana's stomach turned. Suddenly, she was no longer in Novo Mynsk. She was in another town, in another market square, and a squad of Whitecloaks looked down at her, their cloaks glistening crimson in the setting sun. *Your employment or identification papers.*

"I—I can go fetch them, if you'll allow me," the cobbler begged. "They're inside, just not on me right now—"

"By the Imperial Decree of Her Majesty, anyone caught without identification papers must be brought in for further investigation." The Inquisitor paused, and even from here, Ana could see the white slice of a smile parting his lips. "Besides . . . we received a tip that you might be hiding dissenters of the regime." He motioned at the other Whitecloaks behind him. "Search the dacha."

This was the true purpose of their visit. Ana watched in horror as the remaining three Whitecloaks burst into the dacha. There were muffled shouts, and moments later, a group of people emerged, the Whitecloaks' swords at their backs.

The Inquisitor's smile widened. "Harboring fugitives, are we?"

In the group of people, though, Ana's gaze caught on one: a little girl, barely taller than her captor's waist. She shivered against the grasp of a Whitecloak.

"Please, mesyr," the cobbler begged. "There's been a misunderstanding. None of us ever trafficked Affinites—we were simply afraid—"

"Are you aware that resisting the Imperial Inquisition is against the law?" The Inquisitor's voice bore the force of a man with power.

"Please, mesyr—"

"In the absence of papers and without an Affinity, we do not have sufficient proof that *any* of you did not participate in the trafficking and oppression of Affinites," the Inquisitor continued, raising his voice. "Hence, we place you under arrest for violating Her Majesty's Imperial Decree for Affinite Equality."

Ana's hands clenched. This was not promoting equality. This was mistreatment of the law, and abuse of power. Morganya was using her forces to quell any disobedience under new, arbitrary laws. She was cementing her power, stamping out any possible form of resistance before it even began.

Ana couldn't just stand there and watch.

"Papa," the little girl cried as the Whitecloaks began to haul the cobbler away. She stumbled after him. "Papa—"

One of the Whitecloaks turned and backhanded her across her face.

The slap echoed across the streets. The child fell to the ground, blood welling in her mouth. Red bled into Ana's vision. She was once again in the dusty square at Kyrov, watching as a

Whitecloak aimed his arrow toward May. Back then, she'd been helpless to stop it.

Before she knew it, she had stepped out and was walking steadily toward the group, toward the little girl kneeling in the snow at the Whitecloaks' feet.

The Whitecloak looked up, his gaze locking on her. She sensed it then, a hint of a cold and unyielding touch brushing against her Affinity.

Yaeger.

She'd encountered one before: an Affinite with the power to control other Affinities. Back then, he'd snuffed out her Affinity as easily as a candle.

She'd learned her lesson from that.

Ana plunged her Affinity through his power before he could get a proper grip. Without blackstone in his armor to protect him, she seized his blood easily, lifting him bodily into the air, and hurled him forward with all her strength.

His body cracked against the brick wall of a dacha.

The rest of the Imperial Patrols slowed to a halt. For a moment, they stared at the wall, where the yaeger slumped, the pool of blood beneath him reflecting the streetlamps above.

And then their attention turned to Ana.

The Inquisitor extracted his sawdust ropes, leaving the cobbler standing in the snow, and lashed out, ropes whistling—

They fell limply to the snow.

The Inquisitor doubled over, falling to his knees. Blood poured down his chin, dribbling out from his nose and mouth. Ana gritted her teeth, and with another sharp twist of her power, the man collapsed.

She turned her Affinity on the two remaining Whitecloaks and focused on where their bodies were unprotected by their blackstone armor. With a flick of her will they dropped to the ground, blood pooling warm and sticky beneath them.

The world grew still.

Exhaustion washed over her. The world wove in and out of focus as she sank into a crouch and squeezed her eyes shut.

Something tugged at her cloak.

Willing herself not to throw up, Ana opened her eyes.

For a moment, in the blur of her vision, she saw someone impossible. A slip of a girl, eyes the warm blue of the sea.

The face swam into view: watery green eyes and scattered gold locks. It was the young girl, the cobbler's daughter. Their eyes met; Ana saw the shock in the girl's face, and recalled, a moment too late, the unnatural crimson of her own eyes that came with using her Affinity.

Ana recoiled, instinctively snapping her head down and grasping for her hood to cover her face. She was all too aware of the bulge of her veins against the skin of her gloved hands—a mark of when she used her Affinity.

But from the darkness came a whisper. "Thank you."

Ana slowly looked up. For a moment, a heartbeat, they looked at each other, the child's gaze uncertain yet unwavering.

"Dorotya!" The cobbler had pulled himself to his feet. The group of civilians watched, faces pinched with fear as they took in the scene around them.

The little girl let go and ran to them. As the cobbler gathered her into his arms, he cast Ana another frightened glance. They regarded each other for several moments from opposite sides of the street.

And then, to Ana's astonishment, the father raised a tentative hand and dipped his head. He turned quickly and, with an arm around his child, began to walk away. The others in the group followed suit, several inclining their heads toward Ana as, one by one, they stole away into the night.

Ana stayed where she was, kneeling in the snow. She could feel it now, the ache in her hands and fingers with her veins swollen against her flesh. Her Affinity was still warm with the blood of the four lives she had taken, bodies cooling all around her.

One moon ago, she might have shrunk back at what she had done. Now, she heard, again, the whispered thank-you from the little girl; saw the father nod his head in tentative gratitude.

They were her people. And, instead of balking in disgust and fear at the sight of her, they had thanked her for saving them.

A spark of hope blazed into resolve in her heart. Her people had signaled to her, through those small acts of gratitude, that they needed her. That she was utterly different from Morganya, and that she was not the monster Seyin had made her out to be.

Somehow, she hoisted herself to her feet. Somehow, she slid her hand from the wall and lifted her chin. Raised her gaze to the blood-soaked streets before her, and the flickering orange glow reflecting on the clouds ahead like flames from the depths of hell.

Red seeped back into her vision. The veins on her hands rose again.

She was Anastacya Mikhailov, blood Affinite and rightful Empress of Cyrilia.

And she would fight for her people.

4

Ramson lay stretched out on the cot in his room in the Broken Arrow. Moonlight filtered through the cracked window on one side of the wall, but he preferred to remain swathed in the shadows.

It was nearing midnight now, an entire hour past the time when he and Ana had agreed to rendezvous back here. Even as he flicked a silverleaf to the ceiling, watching its belly flash pale, he couldn't help the pricklings of panic.

Where was she?

He'd grown so used to her presence in the past moon that her absence had begun to make him uneasy. Traveling together, he'd whiled his days away bickering with her, delighting in the moments when his comments elicited a fierce glare or an irritated snarl.

And then there were the nights, when he graciously left her the bed and she accepted as though it were her right. Ramson hadn't minded. He'd looked up at her from his vantage point on the floor, taking in the delicate curve of her neck, the soft flutter of her lashes, the stern curve to her mouth even as she dreamt.

He shook those thoughts loose. The silver timepiece at his chest ticked away the minutes. It had been too long.

Ramson had just stood, when a noise gave him pause. It was faint, so faint that it might have been the groan of the old inn beneath the brush of the wind outside.

But Ramson's senses tightened. He moved to the door and flattened himself to the wall behind it, the moonlight cutting just beyond the tips of his boots. Slowly, so as to not make a sound, he drew his misericord.

Another muffled footstep, and this time, a loud creak from the trick stair at the base of the second-floor landing. Ramson had chosen this room specifically for this reason: He would hear any intruders coming his way.

The smallest sound of a pin jiggling in the lock on his door, and then with a *click,* the handle turned.

The door opened and two men burst inside. They wore thick furs and dark padded coats, stitched through with patches. Their movements were lumbering, clumsy, and a quick look at their faces, necks, and hands yielded no markings to reveal an underground gang association.

They were likely low-ranking brutes scavenging for prizes in the Dams. And they'd hit gold with him.

Ramson cleared his throat. "Looking for me?" he said, and as they spun to face him, he lashed out.

He flicked the silverleaf he'd been playing with and it shot out like a projectile, hitting one of the men square in the eye. As the man stumbled back, hand to his face, howling in pain, the second leapt forward.

Ramson dodged easily, the arc of his opponent's sword

cutting a hairsbreadth from his nose. He pivoted and let out a breath. "My nose is my most handsome feature," he said. "I mislike your attempts to sever it."

The man gave him a growl and lunged, but Ramson had him all figured out. These brutes fought street-style: dirty, with no technique. Ramson fought dirty, too, but he was highly trained.

He easily undercut the brute's swipe. By the time the man regained his sense of balance, it was too late.

Ramson's blade pierced his throat. "Now you see why it's called a misericord," he muttered as he kicked the man's body aside.

A shuffle of footsteps behind him. Ramson ducked just as the other brute struck out. His sword thumped to the floor, biting into the wood with the force of his swing.

"Ah, ah, ah." Ramson clucked his tongue. "Clumsy. I could hear you coming from a mile away."

In a flash, his sword was at his opponent's neck, digging into the softness of the man's flesh. "Tell me who you work for," Ramson growled. "Tell me how you found me."

The man resisted—they all did, at first—but Ramson tightened his grip into a choke hold, cutting off the man's air. Drops of blood warmed Ramson's fingers.

"Each time you make me ask, I slice a little more of your throat," Ramson crooned. "Now, let me ask again—"

"We're . . . for hire," the brute gasped. "Saw . . . Kerlan's . . . kill order . . ."

Ramson hummed. Olyusha would need to do better if she wanted to protect his—and therefore her precious, stupid husband's—life.

At the same time, these brutes were so amateur, Ramson

could imagine her rolling her eyes at him. *I leave the small fries to you,* she'd say. *I take the big fish.*

At least her information had been accurate.

"P-please," the mercenary was choking out. "Hard . . . times . . ."

"I understand," Ramson said, and then slit the man's throat anyway.

The second body thumped to the ground. Ordinarily, he might have given more thought to letting these men live, but his mind was focused on one thing.

Ana.

Their meeting place was clearly compromised, and Ramson didn't even want to think about what would happen if any mercenaries or gang members lingering around the Dams got to her first. Hells, he cursed to himself, he should've considered that first, before he picked an inn in the middle of what used to be the most dangerous district in Novo Mynsk. He'd thought that, with the fall of Kerlan, the entire Cyrilian criminal underground had collapsed, too.

It turned out that wasn't the case.

His heart beat in a drumroll, and he wiped his misericord on one of the dead men's shirts, then sheathed it. He needed to find her . . . he needed to get to her first.

Because he couldn't bear the thought of anything happening to her.

Ramson threw on his cloak and stepped neatly over the two bodies, making for the stairs. He didn't bother shutting the door behind him.

5

In the time it took her to cross the city, Novo Mynsk lit up like a rack of coals. The glow of torches colored the winding streets red, and the cloud-heavy sky was afire with shades of corals and crimsons. People had gathered in the streets, some groggy with sleep and some terrified. They shuffled forward together, papers in hand.

Whitecloaks were present on almost every street. They pounded on doors, barking orders at civilians, directing them to the town square. Most of them wore the blackstone-infused mail, rendering their bodies well out of Ana's Affinity's reach.

Yet some were outfitted in the newer armor, Morganya's insignia blaring out from the plates on their chests. Ana focused on them, observing as one melted a door with nothing but a flick of their hands while another broke down an entire stone wall of a dacha with the touch of a finger. The number of Inquisitors was few, peppered among the vast majority of non-Affinite Whitecloaks, but the effect of their presence, coupled with unbridled power and violence, was chilling.

The crowds thickened the closer she drew to the center of

town. The stench of smoke and fear rose thick in the air, choking the skies. The dachas around them were jagged against the night, reflecting the color of blood from the torches that blazed.

Ana turned and the town square of Novo Mynsk unfolded before her.

The entire town seemed to have gathered. Torches were staked in the ground, the square awash in crimson and shadows. And in the very center of it all, a wooden scaffolding had been set up, lit in the light of the torches surrounding it. On the cobblestone ground, Imperial Patrols formed a ring around the stage, the whites of their cloaks tinted red from the flames. About half wore the lighter gray of the Inquisitors' uniform.

Fluttering above it all in the middle of the scaffold was the silver-blue flag of Cyrilia, now bearing Morganya's sigil. And chained to its pole, shivering in nightclothes, was a group of civilians.

The image cut through Ana's exhaustion, bright and sharp.

A hush rippled through the square as a Whitecloak made his way to the center of the platform. His breastplate bore the new insignia of the crown and the Deys'krug, labeling him as an Inquisitor. As he unfurled a scroll and began to speak, the prisoners tied to the pole behind him shivered in the cold.

"Citizens of Cyrilia, we are gathered here today in the spirit of Kolst Imperatorya Morganya, our Glorious Empress, to dispense justice upon the land and carry out the will of the Deities."

The ashes of Ana's anger stirred, deep inside.

"These prisoners gathered before you today have been accused of heinous crimes against the Empire and Her Glorious

Empress," the Inquisitor continued, and as he spoke, there was movement on the stage.

Two Whitecloaks dragged a woman onto the scaffold. She was dressed in a silk nightgown, one sleeve torn, her hair falling out of a disheveled bun. She was crying and clutching a bundle to her chest.

One Whitecloak shoved her to the ground. The woman cried out, but her body curled around the small bundle. Protecting it.

From inside the layers of cloth came a thin, high-pitched keening.

A baby, Ana thought. Her head grew light with horror. There was nothing in what she had seen tonight that indicated justice, not in the way that Cyrilia had always enforced it: with a court, with a trial, and with evidence.

No, this was uninhibited cruelty, dictated by a monarch who now served as judge, jury, and executioner.

"All those who oppose our Glorious Empress oppose divine goodness and rightful justice and must be punished." The Inquisitor looked up, his eyes burning fever-bright. "We will purge this empire of unholy beings and criminals. From the *root*!" His voice rose into a shout.

Cold crept up Ana's veins. She could see what these Whitecloaks were doing, using words such as *divine goodness* and *rightful justice* to justify Morganya's actions. Morganya was using the Imperial Inquisition to steel her rule with an iron fist, and to spread the message that her will represented the Deities' will.

In Cyrilia, the emperors sought the blessing of the Deities

before each coronation. But none had ever dared to equate their actions with the wishes of the gods.

Seyin's voice whispered to her again. *The people have suffered for too long under the theory of a benevolent ruler.*

Sweat slicked Ana's palms. Onstage, one of the Whitecloaks crouched and began to drag the woman by her hair. The other wrapped his silver-gloved hands around the tiny bundle.

"No!" In the utter silence, the mother's scream was jarring. She lurched back, shielding her child with her body. Her pleas echoed through the square. "Please, mesyr, I beg you, my baby is innocent—we are both innocent—"

"You would deny that you kept indentured Affinites in your household?" the Inquisitor roared.

"Employed, mesyr, we gave them wages and food and boarding—"

"Under a criminal contract!" the Inquisitor shouted, drawing his sword. It sliced through the air, flashing red in the torchlight. "You and your family are condemned to death for these crimes."

"Not my baby, mesyr, please—spare my baby—"

The Whitecloak began to pull the bundle away, but the woman clung on, dragging herself from the floor, her dress ripping as the other Whitecloak grasped at her feet. From inside the bundle came the thinnest keening noise, threading through the crackle of the torches and the commotion onstage.

It happened so quickly.

The Whitecloak gave another pull and slammed his boot into the woman's stomach. She slipped.

The sound of her fall cracked across the square like the

whip of a lash. Blood seeped crimson across the platform, twisting serpentine through Ana's Affinity. The woman's body lay motionless.

Across the silent square, there was only the wailing sound of the baby as the Whitecloak carried it away.

Ana closed her eyes. Her thoughts were fragmenting, splintered by the blood of the dead mother and the cries of the child.

She'd come here to seek information on Morganya's new regime, and for what? So that she was able to form a long-term plan, slowly build herself up to take down the enemy? But wasn't the end goal of it all to create a better world? One that kept its people safe?

What kind of a sovereign was she if she simply stood here now, letting her people die as she watched? She might not have the answers to everything just yet, but there was one principle that she had always held fiercely—that she'd use her power to fight, to protect the innocent and vulnerable.

Your Affinity does not define you, her brother, Luka, had once told her. *What defines you is how you choose to wield it.*

Ana's eyes opened with clarity. Her Affinity bloomed. Red clouded her vision.

She targeted the Inquisitors first. Whoever had designed their uniforms had forgotten that while the removal of blackstone made these Affinites able to use their gifts, it also made them utterly vulnerable to enemies whose Affinity was to the very makeup of their bodies.

Ana hooked her Affinity around the bright, warm pulse of their blood and shoved.

There were shouts of alarm from the other Whitecloaks as

their companions crashed into them, and in that moment of distraction, Ana barreled past them.

With a leap, she was on the scaffold.

The lead Inquisitor's yell cut off as Ana seized him with her Affinity and lifted him into the air. The world was alight in flames and blood, the air rippling with heat. Her hair had come undone, and as she turned to face the Imperial Patrol head-on, her long red cloak swept out from beneath her in a sudden gust of wind.

Shouts of confusion melded with gasps all around them as the crowd began to see what was happening.

The kapitan dangled in the air before Ana. When he looked closer at her, shock registered on his face, followed by recognition.

A cry went up somewhere in the crowd. "It's the Blood Witch of Salskoff!"

And then another. "It's the *Crown Princess*! She's alive!"

And a third. "The Little Tigress of Cyrilia has come to save us!"

Somewhere between her getting from the crowd to onstage, her hood had slipped from her face. The night air, swirling between the fire's heat and the winter's cold, gusted against her cheeks.

Ana's first instinct was to hide. Fear, drilled into her from her childhood, froze her in place; the stares of thousands of pairs of eyes weighed on her chest until she could barely draw breath. Her mind blanked; nausea roiled in her stomach.

But then, through the ringing in her ears, filtered another sound. A far-off, high-pitched noise. Something that reminded her of the Salskoff Palace, of her father standing before his court, his hands raised, his eyes bright.

Cheering.

It was faint at first, but as her eyes roved through the crowd, she saw it, here and there: People's hands were raised toward her, and they were clapping.

The people had spoken. For *her.*

Heat sparked inside her, spreading to her fingertips and thawing the ice in her veins. The world crashed back in a tangle of smoke and fire and blood. In her panic, she'd let go of the kapitan. He now lay in a crumpled heap at the edge of the stage.

In the corner of her eye, she could see other Whitecloaks approaching, their outfits flashing in the swirling flames and smoke.

Ana ran for the civilians tied at the flagpole, picking up a Whitecloak's discarded sword along the way. Clumsily, she lifted it and slashed at the ropes of the prisoners. They fell forward with cries of relief. Several were only children, the youngest barely up to Ana's waist.

There was a possibility that the children's parents were associated with Affinite traffickers, or that they had engaged in the indenturement of an Affinite through an illegal contract. But the way Morganya's Imperial Inquisition was being conducted gave no distinction between the crimes. And children, barely old enough to understand the concept of Affinite indenturement, had been caught in the bloodshed.

If there was a way to rebalance the Empire, this was far from it.

Ana turned, her Affinity flaring again. In between the formation of his subordinates, the lead Inquisitor had pushed himself to his knees. Blood dripped from his temple, staining the pale metal of his helmet, as he raised his gaze to her.

Ana didn't wait. She lashed out with her Affinity at the Inquisitors—the soldiers with powers that she would have the hardest time fending off—and tore.

The world blanched around her, fading to a darkness splattered with searing spots so bright they burned.

When she came to, she was drenched in sweat. Blood steamed all around, coating the air and pulsing in waves beneath her fading Affinity. She looked up and saw the procession of Whitecloaks closing in on her beyond the scaffolding. They advanced slowly, their swords raised, expressions of horror twisting their faces, firelight lancing off the unmistakable gray glitter of blackstone on their armor.

Where she might once have felt disgust at her own actions, now Ana only felt a sense of weary necessity. In war, she was beginning to learn, there was only kill or be killed.

The cheering had stopped by now, replaced by the sound of shouts and screams as the crowds around her realized the Imperial Inquisition was closing ranks around them. The town square was awash in commotion as civilians began to flee.

Ana tried to focus on the Whitecloaks, grasping for their blood, but her Affinity had hollowed out. Sweat trickled down her lip. She tasted salt and smoke as the flames from upended torches ringed higher around the platform.

She wouldn't get out of this. Not without help.

In the chaos, something drew her attention: an echo of her Affinity, catching on to blood threaded through with darkness.

Ana lifted her gaze.

Seyin stood at the edge of the square, his black eyes

unflinching as he watched her. Yet it wasn't pride, or approval, or camaraderie that burned in his eyes.

It was cold fury.

They looked at each other for what seemed like an eternity: he, still as stone beneath the shadows of a dacha; she, drenched in blood and firelight, swaying where she stood.

Against her wishes, against her pride, a single thought gathered itself from the edges of her consciousness. *Help me,* Ana thought.

Seyin looked at her a moment longer. And then he turned away, leaving her with a hollow echo of his voice as he disappeared into the crowd.

The monarchy must die, Anastacya.

Something whizzed through the air, arcing past the wall of flames and bouncing on the wooden platform. Ana had only a brief glimpse of it—a glass vial of some sort—before it exploded.

Blue smoke filled the air, along with a charred smell that carried with it the faint scent of incense. The world became shadows and noise and fog.

Through the flickering haze of her Affinity, Ana could make out two bodies—horse and rider—fast approaching. There was a tint to the rider's blood that was familiar: bright, sharp, rimmed with icefire blue, the calm of rosewater.

A figure emerged from the smoke, shawl and patterned pants fluttering in the breeze.

"Ana," said Shamaïra, her eyes fierce. She swung her horse to the edge of the platform. "Take my hand!"

Exhaustion stole whatever questions might have been at the tip of her tongue. Ana barely had the strength to hobble over. Shamaïra was surprisingly strong for someone so small, her callused fingers gripping Ana's hand. Shamaïra pulled her onto the back of the saddle, and she wrapped her arms around the Unseer's waist.

The blue smoke Shamaïra had conjured blended with the bitter black plumes from the torches and the burning scaffolding. Ana clung tightly to her friend as they charged forward, galloping past people blundering their way through the confusion, shadows staggering past fallen torches, still burning to the end of their wicks.

Gradually, the firelight receded, churning into ash that coated Ana's tongue. Darkness closed in upon them. The scenes of the Imperial Inquisition swirled in her head like smoke, along with a final, damning whisper.

The path to becoming a ruler is painted in blood.

6

In the span of one moon, everything and nothing about Shamaïra's dacha had changed. There was something muted about the house now, once alive with colored lamps and scents of roses and tea. Only a single lamp flickered in the hallway, washing the walls a dim yellow. Ana padded quietly after Shamaïra, their shoes left at the door.

The brocade curtain partitioning the parlor from the hallway hung limp, and Ana hesitated before it. It felt like only yesterday she had trailed in with a group of Affinites, carrying the weight of a small body in her arms.

"Make yourself comfortable, child." Shamaïra's voice was its usual steel, but there was something softer, kinder about it tonight. "I'm going to make tea."

Ana ducked past the curtain into the parlor. The fire and blood and screams from the Imperial Inquisition were still fresh in her mind, and the sudden silence was jarring, as was the homey scene before her. It felt as though she had stepped into another world. A crackling fire blazed in the hearth still, the one that Shamaïra kept alight throughout the day and night, filling the room with a musky warmth. Bookcases lined the far wall, creaking beneath the weight of tomes labeled in the curving letters of the Nandjian language. A Nandjian rug filled the center of the room, upon which stood a round oak table strewn with tattered tea-stained maps and cheap goatskin scrolls, scribbled through with elegant handwriting.

Ana sank into one of the settees, closing her eyes and letting the events of the night stream through her mind.

Patrols, their white capes drenched crimson from their own blood.

Her face, unhooded. Facing the crowd for the world to see the red of her eyes, the truth of what she was.

Who she was.

Footsteps interrupted her thoughts. Ana opened a bleary eye to see Shamaïra ducking through the brocade curtain, tray in hand. "Tea," the Unseer said matter-of-factly as she settled on the divan across from Ana and began to pour steaming liquid from a silver samovar into a glass cup. "Drink up."

Ana gratefully accepted the cup. The tea was dark, strong, with the faint taste of cardamom and roses. She hadn't realized how utterly drained she was until now, her Affinity nothing but a faint flicker at the back of her mind, barely registering Shamaïra's presence in the room. The tea settled in her stomach, somehow filling her with warmth, from her nose to the tips of her fingers. "Shamaira," Ana said, lowering her glass. "Thank you."

Shamaïra poured her own cup and huffed a sigh as she leaned back and took a long gulp. The silk of her shawl shone in the candlelight: a plum purple today that beautifully complemented her olive skin. There were dark bags beneath her eyes, which were the same blue of ice that Ana remembered.

"You're going to ask me how I knew you were here,"

Shamaïra said, stealing the words from Ana's lips. "I've waited for your return, Little Tigress." She paused, then frowned. "And you can close your mouth and wipe off that stupid expression of surprise now. You forget who I am."

Shamaïra was an Unseer, a practitioner of a Nandjian magic that gave her the ability to see fleeting glimpses of Time: past, present, and future. Her faith consisted of two halves of a whole: Brother and Sister, light and dark, physical and metaphysical.

Ana had first met her through Yuri one moon ago, when Shamaïra had provided shelter for the Redcloaks and the Affinites they had rescued from Kerlan's Playpen.

The thought gave her a jolt of unease now. "I met with the Redcloaks earlier, Shamaïra," Ana said. "I thought I was meant to ally with them and we would bring down Morganya, together. But . . ."

"You find differences in your paths," Shamaïra said softly. "I believe you've met Seyin, then."

"You're still involved with the Redcloaks?" Ana asked.

"I do what I can. Most are so young, still children. Even the leaders are merely the age my son would be today." Shamaïra's tone turned hard. "But you'd best stay away from Seyin. That boy sees only his goal, and nothing else."

"What he said, about the monarchy . . ." Ana frowned into her tea, the liquid swirling like her thoughts. "I couldn't think of how to answer him. He only thinks of our differences, but we must remember that we face a common enemy."

Shamaïra's expression was soft, her eyes filled with understanding and wisdom of a life beyond what Ana could imagine. "Little Tigress, let me ask you this first." The gold glow of the fire burnished the Unseer's face. "What would you sacrifice for your empire? For your people?"

Something drew Ana's attention to the window. In the darkness, she could just make out the silver of a trellis of winterbells, beneath which someone very precious to her lay buried in the gentle earth. A child, with ocean-eyes. The thought still cut, and the wound was fresh, but day by day, it had been getting better.

Ana swallowed, and the answer came out in a whisper. "Everything."

Shamaïra's eyes were sad. "I suppose that is something you will not know until the time comes," she murmured, almost as though to herself. "Your wish to protect this empire will come at a cost. You will need to choose between two paths, for there are two Anastacyas now, my love: the girl you once were, and the ruler you will become. A day will arrive when you will be asked to sacrifice that which you hold dearest for the good of your empire. *That* is the choice you must make: which of the Anastacyas you shall be."

The words churned in her head, but their meaning remained as elusive as smoke. How could she separate the ruler she was to become from the girl she was now? Both were an intrinsic part of who she was, one bleeding into the other. "I will always choose what is best for Cyrilia," Ana replied. "I was there at the Imperial Inquisition, Shamaïra. I saw what Morganya is doing to my empire. I heard my people cheering for me when I took a stand against the atrocities the Whitecloaks are committing. They support me."

Shamaïra watched her very carefully. She took another sip

of tea. "Then why is it that it still seems you are trying to find your path, Little Tigress?"

"I just . . ." Ana gripped her teacup, thinking of Seyin, of her throne, of the way he had shifted her entire world with just a few words. "I need to speak to Yuri. We have our differences, but we need to work together to bring down Morganya first." She let out a long breath and met the Unseer's eyes. "I need to know if this is the right path, Shamaïra."

Shamaïra swirled her tea and took another long drink before setting it down on the saucer. Her eyes pierced. "You will remember what I told you of my ability to see the future," she said. "That it is equivalent to dipping a single finger in the great river of Time. The future is ever-shifting, depending on the choices that *you* make, and those of others that inevitably shift the course of your life. I can only catch glimpses of certain events along certain paths." She tilted her head back, her gaze growing distant. "For your path, Little Tigress, I see an ocean."

Ana looked up. "An ocean?" It wasn't what she had expected, in the tangled web of allies and enemies, monarchs and revolutions. "What do you mean?"

"The visions the Sister permits me to see are not always singular in purpose," Shamaïra said. "But there must be a strong reason behind it all. The ocean represents the direction you must take in all aspects of your path. Think, Little Tigress. What might it signify?"

There were many aspects in her path that could be tied to the ocean, now that she paused to consider it. The ocean had brought her May; it had, in some ways, brought her Linn, whom Ramson was still trying to track down with his snowhawk.

Ramson. Like the ocean, he wasn't someone she could

harness or control. There was a wild freedom to his spirit that was as open as the sea.

With a start, she remembered that she was meant to meet him at the Broken Arrow—and that she was about two hours late. *He'll wait,* Ana thought more aggressively than needed, determined to push him from her head and focus on the task at hand.

The ocean. There was something else. "Goldwater Port," Ana said quietly. "That's where I was headed." She paused, and her voice grew soft. "Where Yuri is."

Shamaïra watched her through heavy-lidded eyes. "There is much more to be discussed between the two of you. The path of the Empire lies in your hands."

A shadow of doubt stole over Ana. "Seyin didn't leave much room for negotiation when I spoke to him," she said quietly. "I don't know what I'll do if I cannot convince Yuri."

In the light of the fire, Shamaïra suddenly looked tired; the lines of her face seemed more pronounced than they had ever been. "Seyin wants a revolution, and you want the throne. All I want is a life in what's left of the world after all this—a life with my son, without war or bloodshed or pain. Without waking up in the middle of the night, calling his name only to find him gone." She closed her eyes briefly, and when she opened them again, they glistened with unshed tears. "I know that you'll find, in your heart, what is best for your people. What they—what *we*—want."

Ana gazed at Shamaïra, taking in the sight of the extraordinary woman who had crossed the Dzhyvekha Mountains and survived the Syvern Taiga, all in search of her son. She'd been fighting alongside Ana and alongside the Redcloaks all along, and yet the ordinary people did not care for the power struggles of kings and queens. When monarchs played at war, it was the people who suffered. And sooner or later, Ana thought, her gaze tightening on Shamaïra with newfound fear, it was those she loved who would bear the cost.

Abruptly, she stood. "You shouldn't have done this," she said quietly. "You shouldn't have saved me, shouldn't have brought me here. . . . What if they come after you next?"

Shamaïra lifted her chin. "Let them try."

Ana closed her eyes for a brief moment. Yet again someone had saved her life, offered her food and shelter; yet again she had incurred a blood debt, one that she had no means to pay at the moment.

Ana stood and knelt by Shamaïra's side. She took the woman's hand, callused and wrinkled with time. Gently, she kissed it. "I mustn't stay long," she said. "If the Whitecloaks are hunting me, it isn't safe for you if they track me here." She hesitated. "But if you'll permit, I'd like to say hello to an old friend."

Shamaïra's smile was tender. "She is out in the back garden, where the flowers grow."

"I'll be right back," Ana said, and made for Shamaïra's garden.

The cold air filled her lungs with the scent of snow and conifers. Out here in the garden Shamaïra kept behind her dacha, the snow remained untouched, a blanket of white over the sleeping earth. Farther back, the tall, jagged outline of the Syvern Taiga cut into the night sky.

A lovely trellis stood a little ways from the dacha, and the sight took Ana's breath away: the wood, pale and completely uncovered even after the thickest of snowfalls, and the small winterbells that clung to it, white and lovely, the moon dusting them so that they seemed to glow in the night.

Ana knelt beneath the trellis, resting a hand on the untouched snow. The structure arched over her and the winterbells cocooned her, their soft leaves and velvet petals curling against her neck. For a brief moment, she let herself believe that magic had made this garden of vines and flowers that grew from the spirit of a little girl.

"Hello, May," she whispered.

A small wind picked up, and all around her, the little winterbells seemed to stir, drawing the soft scent of snow.

It was when she returned here, Ana thought, leaning her head against the trellis and closing her eyes, that she always found herself and her purpose.

May had died to free dozens of other Affinites. She had only been ten years of age—and she'd spent most of her life indentured to her employer, working to clear the debt she'd accumulated from a contract she hadn't even been able to read when she'd signed it.

Promise me, Ana, she'd whispered even as her ocean-eyes turned still, *you'll make it better.*

Ana dipped her head. She knew, in her heart of hearts, that *this* would always be the reason she chose to fight. That she'd meant what she said when she told Shamaïra she would sacrifice everything to protect her empire, to protect her people, to protect the most vulnerable of her citizens.

She fought so that not another Affinite would become exploited in this empire that had trusted her and another long line of monarchs to watch over their well-being.

She fought so that sometime, somewhere, another little girl could sit on snow-frosted ground and bring a flower to life with her bare hands.

It wouldn't do if there no longer existed a world for her to rebuild after everything.

Ana drew a deep breath and touched a hand to the ground. "Wait for me," she murmured. "I made you a promise, and I'm going to see it through." She paused, and her breath misted in the cold before her as she added, "No matter what it takes."

When she returned to the parlor, Shamaïra stood at the open window. The wind was as cold and sharp as knives; the fire in the hearth flickered as the Unseer turned to Ana. She held something in her hands. On the windowsill, a snowhawk spread its wings and took off into the night. "Little Tigress," she whispered, and held out a scroll.

The parchment was damp with snow and soft between her fingers when Ana took it and unfurled it. Surprise bloomed in her stomach.

It was a portrait of her, in a scene that was all too fresh in her mind, and all too familiar.

The artist had painted her in the moment she'd stepped onto the wooden scaffold at Novo Mynsk and seized the Imperial Patrol with her Affinity. Her face was twisted with fury, her eyes crimson, her scarlet cloak sweeping behind her in a magnificent arc. In the background, a fire raged.

Red Tigress Rising, the gold-emblazoned title blared triumphantly. *The Crown Princess lives. The rebellion begins.*

Ana looked up. "Who made this?" she asked.

Shamaïra's eyes were bright. "The people, Ana," she said. "Your people."

Ana closed her eyes and pressed the poster to her breast, letting this moment sink in.

She had fought for her people.

And now, her people were rallying behind her.

Seyin had tried to convince her that she wasn't what the people needed, but here, clutched between her fingers, was the very proof that they were supporting her.

She'd ride for Goldwater Port. She'd speak with Yuri, show him this poster, recount to him how the people had supported her. How they would follow her. And she'd reassure him that their goals *were* one and the same—that Ana's ultimate goal was based on nothing more than a promise she'd made to a small girl, a friend. To make it all better.

"I'm going to Goldwater Port," she said and clasped her hands over Shamaïra's. "From the bottom of my heart, Shamaïra, thank you. Do not think that I have forgotten all the help you gave me. I owe you my life, and I'll repay that with a life. When I return, when I am Empress, I promise you I will find your son."

Shamaïra squeezed her hands. "Remember my words. Most of all, remember who you are. Who the people need you to be." Her eyes grew hard as steel. "Take the valkryf, my child. The beast spends half its days stamping around in my stables; an old lady like me can hardly keep it entertained. You'll need it more where you're going."

Ana fastened her cloak and slung her rucksack over her shoulders. It held everything she had left in this world—two bronze cop'stones, several globefires, a map, a pouch of coins, and a compass. That, and the silver Deys'krug she wore around her neck, to remember the promise of an old friend. Yuri had promised they would meet again.

"Sweep the tracks leading to your dacha," she told Shamaïra. "Once I get back to town, I'll have the Whitecloaks glimpse me so they won't think to look for me here. If they hunt me there, you'll be safe."

Shamaïra waved a hand. "You underestimate me. I can take care of myself."

Despite herself, Ana felt a smile linger at her lips. "Oh, I've no doubt," she said, turning to open the front door. Night air rushed in, sharp with cold and smoke.

Ana breathed in deeply.

She would need to find Ramson first and offer an apology for being so late. She huffed a sigh. She could already imagine his smug look, the lopsided grin he would give her.

They would make for Goldwater Port together, for a sturdy ship and steady sails that would take them to Bregon.

Behind her, she heard Shamaïra call softly: "Deys blesya ty, Red Tigress." With a sweep of her hand, she drew her hood up and stepped into the dark.

7

In the early morning, Novo Mynsk lay in ruin and darkness. The snow was streaked with ashes, the smell of smoke and war churning in the air. Ana kept her Affinity flared as she hurried her valkryf through deserted streets, keeping to the side alleyways, the snow muffling their steps. A hollow wind had picked up, whistling through cracked doorways and dragging on the glass of broken windows.

Once or twice, Ana passed the flare of a distant torch and the corresponding tug of blood on her Affinity.

The Broken Arrow was several streets from the outskirts of town, near the Dams, a district once known for criminal activity. The area now lay silent and still, the small river flowing through it frozen thick with ice.

Ana turned the corner and paused before a building with broken-in windows. It took her several moments to make out the name on a wooden sign creaking slowly in the early-morning draft, the shaft of an arrow protruding from one end and the tip protruding at another, at odd angles.

The Broken Arrow.

She wrinkled her nose in disgust. She'd expected Ramson

to make slightly different—*better*—accommodations in Novo Mynsk, the city he'd boasted to hold in the palm of his hands. Of course she shouldn't have trusted his word.

She settled her valkryf in the empty stables and entered the inn. The parlor was empty, ransacked and looted so that all that remained were a few upturned chairs and tables. Overhead, a broken chandelier dangled from its chain, its shadows reaching like crooked fingers across the parlor.

"Ramson," she called softly. When there came no response, she called on her Affinity. It came slowly, reluctantly, faint as a memory and half-alive, like the ghost of a dream. She'd expended too much of it earlier in the night, there was little left to use. Gritting her teeth, she swept it around the place, once.

Blood lit up in her senses, up the stairs, beyond a wall. It was cold and still, and she could make out two distinct pools.

Her heart began to beat fast. If anything had happened to Ramson—

Ana hurtled up the stairs, two at a time. The door to the first chamber was open. Moonlight spilled through a cracked window, illuminating the two bodies on the floor.

She scrambled to them, checking their faces, and then sighed in relief. She had no idea who they were, but the important thing was that Ramson was nowhere to be found. And that meant he was alive.

If anything had happened to him, she would never forgive herself.

In the maelstrom of her thoughts, she didn't catch the pulse of blood flickering to life in her Affinity until it was close.

Ana had half turned when pain exploded in her back. Her mouth filled with blood, warm and metallic.

The intruder yanked the dagger from her. Her body screamed, her Affinity exploding in a way that drowned all her other senses. She fought to stay conscious. Her fingers had become sticky, wet. Her head rang with a strange, high-pitched whine. Ana grasped at the blood, anything to stop it, to slow it, but her head was light, her power weaving in and out of focus. The pain was electric.

She was aware that she'd slumped against the wall, feeling only a numbing fatigue spread through her body. Her vision was beginning to blur, dark spots filling the world.

Out of that darkness stepped a figure.

"I'm sorry it had to come to this, Anastacya," a familiar voice said. The Second-in-Command of the Redcloaks stood over her, wiping his dagger on a pale handkerchief. "It's really nothing personal."

Ana tried to speak, but blood was all that bubbled from her lips. The world was fading fast.

Seyin sheathed his dagger. There wasn't a spot of blood on his white shirt. "As I said, the monarchy must die. Now that I'm done with you, I have only Morganya to take care of." The shadows began to thicken around him until he was swallowed by darkness. The last Ana heard was his voice, fading into the night.

"Good-bye, 'Red Tigress.'"

8

Gods be damned, where *was* she?

Ramson leaned against the cold stone wall of a darkened alleyway in Novo Mynsk, clutching at the cramp in his side. He could still hear the panicked crowds, taste the smoke and ash on his tongue.

He'd tried the Playpen, and when that had yielded nothing, he'd followed the steady thrust of people that had been trickling toward the town square, fearing the worst. Yet when he'd arrived to a scene of dachas burning and people screaming and blood—so much blood—spilling from the bodies of Imperial Patrols, he'd known all too well whose handiwork he was staring at.

"A little *subtlety,* Ana?" he gritted out at the cold night air. But, of course, subtlety was likely not a concept she had absorbed into that stubborn head of hers.

He'd taken advantage of the chaos in the square to look for her among the living and the dead, and then he'd followed the stream of people, slipping out and melting into the shadows of the city that he knew better than the back of his own hand.

Ramson ran a hand through his hair. He was going to kill her. Hells, he was going to *find her* so he could kill her.

Gods be damned.

There was only one other place in this town where she might go.

His steps were quick, sure, as he made his way down the cobblestone streets, his breaths unfurling before him in sharp, measured beats. The glow of fire from the town square reflected on the clouds overhead, casting an unnatural, hellish light around him. The streets were even emptier now, the civilians having either barricaded themselves indoors or fled town or been arrested by the Imperial Inquisition.

The night was cold; the Cyrilian Empire had settled into a true northern winter, the temperatures plummeting to below freezing. Gradually, the streets turned to dust roads covered by snow that was relatively undisturbed. The dachas thinned out, and the shadow of the Syvern Taiga loomed against the night. Shamaïra's dacha sat at the edge of the boreal forest.

Only, someone else had gotten there first.

A black wagon was out front, its shadows thrown long by the torches that flared bright around the outside of the dacha.

A sense of foreboding crept over Ramson. He stole through the conifers of the Syvern Taiga toward Shamaïra's dacha. When he was close enough, he knelt in the shadow of a tree and peered out.

The wagon came into clearer view, and Ramson's heart sank. It was another blackstone wagon, the sight of which had become synonymous with the Imperial Patrols.

Two Whitecloaks stood guard, the shimmer of their cloaks reflecting a cruel red in the night. Two more waited at the front door.

Ramson immediately noticed a slight difference between

their outfits. One of the Whitecloaks—the one holding the torch—had on a uniform of a slightly paler shade of gray than the others.

It was then that Ramson realized the Whitecloak wasn't holding a torch.

He was *conjuring* the fire with his bare hands.

It took a moment for the image to click. This was one of Morganya's new Affinite Inquisitors—ones who, until now, Ramson had only read about in ominous newspaper articles. Watching the man juggle fire in his palms, Ramson felt his own misericord would hold up about as well as a twig if it came to a fight.

There was movement at the back of the house. Three more Whitecloaks came into view, striding from Shamaïra's garden. Ramson's hand tightened on the hilt of his weapon, the plans he'd been spinning now shifting as he took in this new information. There was no way that he could get to Shamaïra without being detected, but then, a new thought grasped him with urgency.

Was Ana inside?

In an instant, he was up and moving, his senses pricked and his misericord gripped tight in his fist as he jogged closer to the dacha. He could now make out some words from snatches of the Whitecloaks' conversation. A few more steps, and—

The front door banged open. Light spilled sharply over snow.

Even from about twenty yards out, Ramson recognized the stout, strong figure standing in the doorway, haloed by the light.

"Spirit curse you, do you have any idea what time it is?" Shamaïra snapped.

Ramson's grin faded when one of the Whitecloaks began to speak. "You are hereby accused of treason and sin against the Kolst—"

Shamaïra's sharp cackle cut across his words. "Oh, it's sin now, is it? Your Empress fancies herself a god now, too?"

"—the Kolst Imperatorya," the Whitecloak pressed on, "by harboring rebels and traitors of the Crown. We therefore place you under arrest and command the right to search your property for evidence of these accusations."

Shamaïra's laugh rang out again. "You'll arrest me *before* you search for evidence?" she snorted.

"Shut up, Shamaïra," Ramson gritted under his breath.

"I'll give you all the evidence you need," Shamaïra continued, and her voice settled, turning deep. "*I* declare myself a traitor to the Crown, and a rebel against the Kolst Imperatorya. *Don't* touch me," she snarled, so viciously that the Whitecloak approaching her hesitated. "I'll go myself." She swept a glance around, and for a moment, Ramson swore she looked directly at him. "But if anybody still wishes to search my property, they are welcome to do so. You'll *certainly* find overwhelming evidence in what an old lady paints before bedtime!"

Two Whitecloaks signaled at each other, then stepped forward and disappeared into Shamaïra's dacha.

Ramson was frozen in place, his mind playing out all scenarios, possibilities, and strategies to get ahead of the impossible scene before him. Trying to find *some* way out of all this.

Help her, a voice urged. Ana's voice. She would never have hesitated.

But he was one man to the Whitecloaks' seven, including an Affinite Inquisitor. If there was one thing he was good at, it was calculating the odds. Ramson Quicktongue could recognize when not to enter a losing battle.

He watched Shamaïra walk to the wagon, head held high and shoulders thrown back as though she held command. He watched them lock the doors, mount their sleek, pale valkryfs. Watched as the unit set off at a brisk trot, their powerful steeds moving at almost twice the speed of any ordinary horse.

He could go after her. Follow them, find a time when their security was loose and rescue Shamaïra.

But Ramson remained where he was, his senses wound tighter than a spring, his eyes scanning the periphery. Waiting.

As though on cue, an orange flicker appeared at one of the windows, and voices wound through the night. One of the Whitecloaks who had gone in to search Shamaïra's dacha appeared. He seemed to be speaking to someone behind him. "Mad old fortune-teller." His voice was faint, but just audible from where Ramson crouched. "Why does the Kolst Imperatorya want her? She doesn't *actually* believe the old woman can see the future, does she?"

A chill went down Ramson's spine. Morganya was looking for Shamaïra?

A deeper voice answered. "Mind your own business. We were given orders; it is our job to execute them." From inside the dacha, the Inquisitor emerged. Flames licked up the skin of his bare hands, and for a moment, they washed over the twisted look on his face. "Stand back."

The night lit up in a brief flash of light. Fire shot from the Affinite's hands, swirling over the wooden walls and the thatched roof of Shamaïra's house. It caught ablaze easily, flames snaking up the sides in rivulets, spreading faster than ink on parchment.

Ramson hid in the shadows of the trees, watching as the two Whitecloaks mounted their steeds and galloped after their unit, the fire throwing long, crooked shadows behind them.

Coward, a voice whispered.

But Ramson knew, with certainty, that had he been given the choice again, he would have chosen to save himself, over and over and over. Just as he had at another time, another place, almost a lifetime ago, with the sleek shine of the arrow in torchlight, the soft black of Jonah's hair as he lay on the floor, eyes as still as the surface of a glass lake.

Ramson fisted his hands against his face. Shamaïra—in the last moments, she'd been brave. He thought of her piercing blue gaze, sweeping the periphery of her dacha, almost as if . . .

. . . she'd been looking directly at him.

Ramson shot to his feet. Before he knew it, he was running, sprinting as fast as he could toward the burning dacha.

But if anybody still wishes to search my property, they are welcome to do so.

It hadn't been an accident. Shamaïra *had* been talking to him.

You'll certainly *find overwhelming evidence in what an old lady paints before bedtime!*

Heat gusted in his face as he drew closer, the light of the fire searing his eyes. The entire front wall was ablaze.

Ramson drew his scarf over his face, sucked in a deep breath, and barreled through the open front door. Immediately, his eyes watered; smoke filled his lungs.

It took him a few moments to reach the parlor; he could see the glow of flames working through the wood of the roof.

Ramson made a desperate scan of the room. Books had been pulled from their shelves on the wall, precious texts from Nandji strewn carelessly across the floor. They'd slit blades through Shamaïra's divans; the insides spilled out like guts, red in the firelight. Her table was upturned, the center of her beautiful Nandjian rug slashed through, revealing rough wooden floorboards beneath.

Through all the wreckage, a painting easel lay knocked askance at the corner of the room. Paint had spilled from shattered pots, but when Ramson retrieved the canvas, he knew in his gut that this was what he sought.

Shamaïra had painted a blue swath of an ocean, and then swirls and swirls of white atop. And, at the very edge, the canvas had been burned through, the dull sheen of molten metal clinging to the edges.

Ramson would recognize gold anywhere.

Gold. Ocean. White. And in the midst of it all, a streak of red that blazed across the page like fire, like blood, like . . . a scarlet cloak.

He might have grinned at Shamaïra's brilliance. She'd depicted Goldwater Port and the Whitewaves, both in the painting and symbolically. And right in the middle, she'd painted Ana.

It couldn't be an accident. She must have known he would come searching for her, and this was the message she'd left him: that Ana was safe, and that he would find her in Goldwater Port.

Ramson left the painting in the parlor, flames crawling closer and closer to the center of the room until there would be nothing left but ash.

The back garden was surprisingly peaceful: a world of snow and ice and stars. It almost felt as though it had a spirit of its own, waiting for him quietly as he stumbled out and inhaled lungfuls of cold, clean air.

Ramson paused by a wooden trellis. Winterbells had grown on it, delicate vines winding steadfastly to the pale wood. If he believed in the gods, he might also have believed that a small soul rested beneath.

Still, he couldn't help but bend down and touch a hand to the ground, to the quiet earth slumbering beneath it all. "Take care of the old woman, all right? Leave the rest to me."

As Ramson straightened, a small wind stirred. The winter-bells nodded; drifts of snow brushed against him.

It was good he didn't believe in the afterlife, Ramson thought as he turned to leave, or he might have believed that there, behind the scene of so much violence and sacrilege, a small soul protected the sanctity of the garden and had just spoken to him.

9

Linn was going to die.

That was what the prison guards said, anyway—the ones who rotated shifts before her blackstone-enforced cell. The mineral, she knew, was mined from the Krazyast Triangle of the north, prized by the men who conducted trade in their caravans across the frozen tundras of this empire. The men who had traded her.

She remembered the sensation of sitting in those caravans for weeks on end: that slight, swaying motion, the uncertainty of day and night, the knowledge that she could be beaten at any point in time, and the darkness—the type that smothered your sight more fully than a blindfold and seemed to swallow you whole until you doubted your very existence.

That was what this prison felt like—as though she'd taken a step back and fallen right into the fabric of her nightmares.

But the Wind Masters had always taught her to hone her weaknesses into her strengths. The darkness had become her training ground, forcing her to sharpen her other senses. The chains had become her friends; she'd learned to fight without her hands within a confined radius, and to adjust to a different center of balance. And the beatings had taught her to numb her mind to pain and made her body more resilient.

No, it wasn't any of these that made her hate this place. It was the space she feared.

The space—or lack thereof—in her tiny, cramped cell, in which she could barely stretch out her legs without touching the other end. The space that pressed against her in the silence and the darkness until it seemed to become a living thing, breathing against her face and neck and threatening to devour her.

She'd spent the first few days curled against the wall, thinking of the high mountains of Kemeira that rose into the skies, mist weaving between them like a Moon Dancer's sash. She'd known those mountains since her connection to wind had manifested at the age of five. There had been a time when she'd jumped off those cliffs and flown as easily as a bird, soaring with the wind in her ears and the sky at her back.

When her brother disappeared, it had felt as though her entire life had shattered.

She'd stopped flying after that.

A wingless bird, her Wind Masters whispered. *What warrior cannot master her affinity to her own element?*

Yes, she had been a wingless bird—and a caged one, now.

She'd broken her wrist and twisted her ankle in that jump off the Salskoff Palace. The river—and her winds—had saved her from a swift death, and she'd crawled out half-frozen, half-conscious. She had worked her way down the Empire village to village, until she'd run into a group of Imperial Patrols, freshly dispatched by the new Empress herself. Half-feverish and still injured, she'd barely put up a fight before they'd taken her down.

Now, here she was, in a prison they called the Wailing Cliffs, far from freedom and even farther from Goldwater Port. To be tried for treason and executed as a Kemeiran spy.

They had tried to beat some confessions out of her, and she had told them what they wanted to hear. Because the petty crimes she'd admitted—of spying on Cyrilia and attempting to sabotage the Empire—were nothing compared to the truth.

That she was a friend and ally of the refugee Crown Princess Anastacya, and that she was plotting to find her way back to her.

A muffled clanging sound filtered through the blackstone door. The guards were coming for her. It was time for her daily interrogation.

The thought sent a wave of nausea through her stomach, but Linn brushed off the fear that tugged at the back of her mind. Silently, without even a single clink of her chains, she slipped from her straight-backed meditating position into a fetal position on the floor.

A rattle of keys at her door, and then it slid open.

Torchlight blinded her. She dragged a heavy hand across her face to cover her eyes. A jangle of metal as keys were pocketed again. Footsteps rang sharply against the floor, and someone knelt by her side.

"She still alive?" She recognized this as the voice of her guard, Isyas. Twice a day, he slipped a tray into her cell in a small, rectangular opening in her door, splashing the contents of her cold porridge and hard rye bread onto the floor. They'd laced her food through with Deys'voshk, the poison that inhibited Affinities. That was how they kept their Affinites in check—a lazy yet horribly effective method. Nobody could survive without water or food. And the dosage of Deys'voshk they added lasted at least two days.

There was a snort of laughter from a second voice. "If you kill her, you don't get to play with her anymore." Her interrogation officer—Vasyl—was bred for cruelty. Her first day here, he'd hurled her into the cell and dumped a bucket of cold water on her. She'd spent the rest of the night shivering from the cold; she'd been sick the next week.

But that had been a petty act of malice he'd inflicted on her to teach her the rules. It was during her interrogation sessions that the true monster he was really came out.

Linn's back ached with echoes of the wounds he'd inflicted. But that didn't matter. Flesh wounds were just that: physical. It was the mental wounds one had to watch out for.

Still, she couldn't stop a sharp cry from escaping her lips as Vasyl's foot slammed into her ribs.

"There we go." He grinned as she doubled over, winded and gasping for air. "Ignoring us, you slit-eyed deimhov?" He suddenly grasped her neck and shoved her against the wall so hard that her skull cracked against the rough blackstone. Linn gritted her teeth against the stars that burst before her vision, forcing herself to remain motionless.

She needed to have them believe she was weak. She'd struck back in the beginning, landing blows and jabs at her guards and Vasyl—and she'd been punished for that. Strapped to the wall without an inch of moving space for days. Deprived of water and food until her lips bled and she passed out.

Day by day, her struggles had weakened, her blows landed softer and softer, until one day, they'd found her curled up in a corner of her cell, head bowed, arms clasped. They'd sneered, and she'd tolerated their dominating touches and lingering fingers as though they owned her.

Little did they know that it was all part of a coordinated act.

She kept silent as they dragged her up, her cuffs chafing against her wrists, cracking open flesh that had already rubbed raw. Linn allowed her head to loll slightly and let her legs trail limply against the floor.

"Deities-damned useless Kemeiran," Isyas growled as he lugged her after him. "Get the hell up, won't you?"

She ignored them.

"We're executing her in a week," Vasyl said to Isyas, and despite everything, Linn shivered at the callousness of his words. He spoke of her death with less emotion than he'd speak of livestock. "We're not to touch her after today; they want her healthy and alive for the axes."

They hauled her past cell after cell and then up a flight of spiraling stairs, during which the air grew steadily less rank and the darkness began to turn into flickering light. Fresh, snow-scented breezes brushed her cheeks, feather-faint, yet she found her senses awakening as a flower would to sunlight. The Deys'voshk that ran through her blood blocked any response from her Affinity—yet still, despite all of that, the cool winds stirred in her chest, breathing life into her. Life, and hope.

It was when they continued up the stone steps that she realized something was different. Normally, they crossed through the first set of blackstone doors to a corridor of interrogation rooms. Today, they continued: up, up.

As though sensing her trepidation, Vasyl smirked at her over his shoulder. "There's something special waiting for you," he said, and the pure glee in his voice made her shudder. "We'll see if you don't spill all your filthy secrets today, Kemeiran."

She stumbled on one of the steps, her ankles chafing against the rough stone. Isyas let out a frustrated groan, and together, he and Vasyl hauled her up the last few steps—through a different set of blackstone doors, followed by a second set of iron doors.

Her bare feet hit clean, cold marble. Tapestries appeared on pristine white walls, depicting white tigers, the Deities, and the usual Cyrilian fanfare.

Her escorts led her down several forks and turns, and she noticed the elegance of the polished oakwood doors, the tiger's-head brass handles, the alertness of the guards. This had to be a place for highly ranked guests frequenting this prison. Linn knew little about Cyrilian prisons, and less about the Wailing Cliffs other than the possible fact that it was on a set of high cliffs. The entire prison was a tower with no windows and a single, highly guarded entrance that promised a swift death if one were to try to escape—even for someone like her.

It was a risk she would have to end up taking.

Isyas unlocked one of the heavy oakwood doors. Linn followed his hands as he looped the key back onto his belt and fastened the metal buckle with a secure click. The door swung open, and before she'd even had a glimpse of the room, Vasyl shoved her inside with a vitriolic push.

"Enjoy your last interrogation, deimhov," he sneered, and the door slammed shut.

She was lying in a crumpled heap on the floor. Yet slowly, her senses stirred as she realized that her face was warm with a familiar, delightful sensation, like a mother's kiss.

Sunlight.

In an instant, Linn was on her feet, the chains on her wrists and ankles lighter than air as she crossed the room in two, three steps. The window was shut tightly, sealed on the outside by thick iron bars that broke the sunlight into blocks.

Linn pressed a hand against the cool glass, her breath fogging so that the snow-covered landscape beyond was a hazy, glittering stretch of white. The Syvern Taiga spanned out beneath her, specks of dark green peeking out from the crusted snow. Above, the sky unfolded in a brilliant, eternal blue.

She was so mesmerized by the view that she almost—*almost*—missed the silent opening of the door, and the footsteps that fell like shadows.

Linn spun around as the door clicked shut.

She wasn't sure what—or whom—she had been expecting, but in the midst of her shock, there was also the realization, like a tightening of tangled strings, that this was fate. *Action, and counteraction.*

"You," she whispered.

He was even more vibrant and alive than she remembered in her memories of the moonlit tower. As he stepped into the sunlight, each line of his muscles looked to be sculpted, his every edge sharpened to the lethal precision of a warrior.

The yaeger's boots clipped on the floor as he paced forward, his movements as deliberate as those of a tiger circling its prey. He was still dressed in armor—but she noticed that it was no longer the glittering gray livery he'd worn back in Salskoff. His new outfit was a smoother, silver-white metal that glinted in the sunlight, and the snowy cloak that he'd worn so proudly was gone.

Somehow, it made him look incomplete.

"I didn't think we'd meet again so soon." There was the slightest hint of amusement to his words.

Linn bristled. He was insulting her, even before he began whatever cruel methods of interrogation he had planned.

Keep silent, she thought, eyeing him warily. *Find out why he's here.*

But she couldn't stop herself from quipping back, "You would think I gave a strong hint, after I threw myself from that tower to get away from you."

"And, now, here you are. It seems they've clipped your wings, little bird."

Her breath caught. *Little bird. A wingless bird.*

She kept her face as placid as his, but his words had set off a drumroll of a heartbeat inside her chest. It was the same thought he'd triggered in her that night atop the Salskoff watchtower, before she'd jumped.

He knows, she remembered in a sudden, wild bout of panic. The yaeger was the only person who had seen her in close proximity that night at the Palace. The only person who knew of her alliance with Ana.

What do you want? Linn thought again. His eyes bore into hers, and she had the strangest feeling that he could see into her past, her very soul.

"I'm surprised you haven't tried to break out yet," he said instead. "The guards reported you as unruly and combative in the first few days—and now, docile, submissive, and *weak.*" He paused, as though waiting for her to speak.

Linn kept her lips sealed. She could feel his eyes roaming over her, taking in the slight lean to her stance, favoring the ankle that wasn't twisted, and the way her shoulders hunched and her head bowed. She must look pitiful, her hair disheveled, her clothes torn, covered in dirt and grime and excrement from the past two weeks.

Good, she thought, dipping her head even more. *Let him think that.*

The yaeger continued, "That sounds nothing like the warrior I met in Salskoff. Which means . . ." He stopped pacing suddenly and turned to her, his eyes pinning her like two daggers. "You're planning something."

Linn fought to keep her expression blank, but high-pitched bells pealed in her head with increasing desperation. *Say something,* she thought, and at the same time: *Keep silent.*

"Help me," she said instead, and the break in her voice was half-real. It was against Kemeiran honor to lie and to beg, but years of forced servitude had taught Linn that to survive was equally important. And it didn't matter how others perceived her, so long as *she* knew that at her heart, she was still as strong and as proud as the young Kemeiran windsailer who had stood at the edge of cliffs and flown.

But am I? a small voice whispered inside her.

"Look at me."

She could sense that he'd stopped pacing, and when she finally raised her eyes to meet his, he stood outlined against the brightness of the only window in the room, his face swathed in shadow.

His voice was a low breath. "I need your help, too."

His eyes were the mesmerizing, inscrutable blue of glaciers in the north of Cyrilia, the ones she'd seen from between the cracks of the hull of her trader's ship. And Linn felt a cold sensation in her chest as well, as though the ice of his gaze were creeping up the fissures of her heart and twisting its grip around her, seeing exactly what she was thinking and who she was.

She looked away. “I do not know what you mean.”

“You’re not a very good liar.”

She hated the way he watched her—as though she were clear as glass, and he could break her with just a tap.

Be brave, she thought, but without her winds at her back, she could not hear the voice that had guided her through her darkest moments.

The yaeger’s expression flickered like the tip of a snake’s tongue: a shift so subtle that it raised Linn’s guard. “I was a soldier in the new Empress’s army,” he said quietly. “For the past moon, I rode with her throughout the Empire, following her as she established her reign.

“She’s *murdering* people, Kemeiran. That may not mean much to you, but I came to Cyrilia as a child and a part of me is bound to this empire, no matter what. And I cannot stand by watching as the new Empress burns down this world.” His words crackled in the air, lightning before a storm. “I resisted, and she had me sent here. I am as much a prisoner as you are. Stripped of my honor and my ranking.” His hand flicked slightly by his side, almost as though he were brushing the ghost of a cape that was no longer there.

“You say you are a prisoner, yet I do not see you in chains and a locked cell,” Linn said. “I do not know what you want with me, but if it is to beat your anger into me, then go ahead.” She bowed her head, quelling the tremor that threatened to start inside her when she thought of the whip and the slashes of pain that seared like fire across her back.

A few seconds passed in utter stillness. And then she heard the *schick* of his dagger. Linn closed her eyes, burrowing herself into the darkness and spinning a cocoon of her own flesh around her consciousness. She would do this back in the days when the traffickers had beat her, because that was the only way she made life bearable: by telling herself that flesh wounds healed, and that it was the strength of her heart and spirit that she needed to protect.

But the touch of his thumb, warm and coarse on her chin, jerked her back out. Her eyes sprang open. Even in the silence, he had closed the gap between them without so much as a stir in the air.

Who was this man? This silent warrior who stood before her, inscrutable and cold as ice, fierce as fire?

"I want to join the ranks of the Princess Anastacya," the yaeger said.

Linn forced her face to be a mask, a mirror, reflecting his.

He continued, "In two days' time, when I've had enough time to make the necessary preparations, I will come for you, at the midnight shift. And we will leave this place, together."

Two days. Her thoughts whirled.

The yaeger raised his dagger, and this time, Linn couldn't help but shrink back. "Are you going to hurt me?"

Something shifted in his eyes—the faintest melting of ice. "I am a soldier, Kemeiran, trained on the Cyrilian values of honor and dignity. I imagine you have similar values in Kemeira. Should we duel again, it will not be when you are chained and starved and reeling from your guard's last beatings."

The yaeger brought the blade down on his own finger with striking accuracy.

Blood welled at his cut, dripping onto the floor. Linn stood very still as the yaeger touched his bloodied hand to her cheek, her neck, her grimy clothes.

He knew. He knew that Vasyl would beat her if he saw no traces of blood on her.

Gratitude stirred briefly in her heart before she stomped it down. This man was dangerous—this man was the enemy, a threat to Ana if she believed him. He was trying to buy her favor with some preplanned acts of kindness.

In two days, at midnight, he would come for her.

And he would find her cell empty, her long gone.

The yaeger's hands were infinitely gentle as he dabbed her in his blood. But Linn's thoughts were already elsewhere, a plan beginning to form in her mind. Ana had told her that the Redcloaks' base was in Goldwater Port; it was the only place Linn could think of that she might find some clues to Ana's whereabouts. She would make her way down south, to the territories not yet fallen under Morganya's influence.

Her eyes darted to the window in the back of the room.

It didn't matter that there were two thick panes of blackstone glass, and iron bars stood sentry, solid and unbreakable. It didn't matter that they were so high up that the Syvern Taiga looked like an unending ocean of distant trees.

Where there was a window, there was a way out. Because no matter how many chains they wrapped around her, no matter how many locks they threw her behind, no matter how much her body was battered and bruised and broken, she would never forget who she was in her heart.

I am shadows and wind. I am the invisible girl.

I will fly.

10

Darkness. Pain. Then, gradually, the tiniest flickers of light. A sharp coldness on her face.

Ana cracked her eyes open. It was still dark, the world before her spinning as she tried to focus on the faintest dustings of light from the moon outside. She was lying in the same spot at the bottom of the staircase in the parlor of the Broken Arrow, where Seyin had left her.

Had stabbed her.

Had thought he'd killed her.

She had no idea how much time had passed. But even with her Affinity weaving in and out of focus she could tell she had lost a significant amount of blood. It was so cold that she could barely feel her fingers. Her breath misted in the air.

Ana tried to shift into a sitting position, but the pain in her back nearly made her pass out again. She could still sense blood seeping from her wound, slowed by the cold. If she stayed here, she would die. And no one was coming to save her this time.

Ana gritted her teeth and homed in her Affinity to the knife wound. It was long, slipping through her ribs in a cunning and malicious cut. She could sense her blood trying to coagulate at the spot.

With all the energy she had left, she focused her Affinity on hardening the blood where flesh and organ had sliced open like fruit. She had to stop every few seconds to catch her breath, and once or twice she relapsed into bouts of dizziness so strong that she thought she would faint.

After what felt like an agonizing amount of time, she managed to clot the blood at her wound enough that the bleeding was stanched. She let herself lie on the floor for several moments, focusing on steadying her breathing. Her Affinity flickered softly in the back of her consciousness. There were no signs of blood besides her own and that of the two bodies in the room. The inn was so silent, she could hear the whistle of the wind outside. It was still night, impossible to tell how much time had passed.

She needed to move.

Ana took two, three deep breaths, clamped down her teeth, and eased herself up.

Blood rushed from her head. She drew a sharp breath as her temple collided with the wall, her hands scrabbling against torn wallpaper for purchase.

The world swayed, then stilled.

She waited for her sight to clear. She'd left her valkryf in the stables; she would need to make her way there. Ramson had gone, and in her current state, she couldn't search for him. She would need to find a healer of sorts outside town, where she couldn't be easily recognized.

And then . . .

Her head spun with the impossibility of it all, the way her plan had completely fractured.

There were still pieces to be picked up.

That started at Goldwater Port.

Ana put one foot before the other. Step by agonizing step she began to walk, pausing every few feet to catch her breath, to anchor herself against the pain thrumming in her midriff.

Somehow, she made it to the front desk. Then to the inn door.

The night was cold, the air bitter with the stench of smoke. Ana stumbled to the stables and was relieved to see her valkryf still there.

She managed to hoist herself onto the saddle, biting back a cry as her wound broke open again.

It took her several tries to ignite her Affinity, and then many more long minutes before she could wrap it over the blood leaking from her wound, hold it in place, and wait for it to coagulate.

With her other hand, she gripped the reins of her valkryf.

The world reeled around her when she emerged from the stables, slumping forward in the saddle, her head pounding, her blood dripping down the length of her hand and dotting the snow. Fighting, with her every last breath, to live.

11

Linn counted down the seconds on the second day from her conversation with the yaeger. She sat, stone-still as her masters had taught her to, and thought of time passing as the slow *drip, drip, drip* of water wearing through rock. It was the Kemeiran way, of balance and harmony and staying attuned to the elements around you, aligning the ones inside you.

Drip, drip, drip.

For with patience, even water would carve through rock.

It was difficult, though, to think of water now when she'd barely had any in almost three days. Her mouth was excruciatingly dry, her tongue sandpaper against her throat, and she found herself thinking of the flat, wide rivers that cleaved the jagged mountains of Kemeira, how the waters turned the color of mandarins during sunsets, splashing against her skin in golden drops, cold and sweet against her tongue.

Someday—perhaps even someday soon—she'd see it all again.

With difficulty, she wrangled her thoughts back to the present. It had been two days since she'd had any food, and the minimal amounts of water she'd had were just to keep her from exhibiting any further symptoms of dehydration. Slowly, second by painful second, the Deys'voshk she had been consuming from her food was being weaned from her bloodstream. And it was working.

Her Affinity was returning.

Even as she sat against the wall, slightly dizzy and lips chapped from thirst, she felt it: the stir of her powers, attuned to the movement of wind between the cracks of the rough-hewn stone walls, the slightest whorls in the air with every breath in and out.

She was ready. Any moment now, her plan would be set in motion.

She heard it then, the faraway clack of footsteps that sent hollow echoes through the corridors and vibrations up the stone walls, dragging her from her stupor. In seconds, the small rectangular chute would open and her tray of food would tumble to the floor. They meant for her to slurp the kashya from the ground like a dog.

Except she wouldn't. And she never would again.

The approaching footsteps belonged to Isyas: that slightly uneven, sloppy edge to each step that was so different from Vasyl's cruel, calculated clicks.

When the food flap opened, she was ready.

Linn sprang from her position like a viper. Her arm shot through the chute, her fingers clattering past the tray of food and latching on to Isyas's wrist. She yanked him against her cell door, and before he could let out a sound, her other arm was through, hand clapping against his mouth.

Linn needed only one hand to kill a man.

She twisted.

Isyas's body went limp. Linn heard the jangle of his keys cut short as they scraped against her cell door, tucked awkwardly in that position at his hips. Leaning against the cold blackstone door, she tugged him against the opening at the chute, fingers creeping along his uniform until she found the cold metal and sharp-cut edges of the keys.

With a few deft twists of her fingers, the keys were in her palm, and she couldn't still her trembling as she fit them into the keyhole.

The door swung open with a cringingly slow creak.

She hauled Isyas's body into her cell, swiping two daggers from his uniform and strapping them to her wrists. She had to throw her entire body weight against the door to press it shut. It closed with a grating sound that echoed throughout the corridors.

It took all of her willpower to shove the upturned tray and bread through the chute and to ignore the watery kashya porridge already seeping into the cracks on the floor. It should have turned her stomach, but she swallowed against the urge to drop to her knees and lap it all up.

Her head spun as she started down the dimly lit dungeon corridor, dehydration sending nausea pulsing through her stomach. The daggers were heavy in her hands, and once or twice, she leaned against the wall, certain she was going to pass out.

It had felt all right sitting there in the darkness, yet standing outside, she realized how weak she really was. She'd overestimated herself.

As another bout of dizziness crashed into her, one thing kept her grounded. A pair of fire-ice eyes. A deep, steady voice.

I will come for you, at the midnight shift.

No, she had to be far from this place by then. She'd planned this precisely so that she would escape during her mealtime, hours before the midnight shift. Hours before that yaeger would come for her. She didn't trust him, and there was even less of a chance that she would lead him to Ana.

She was breathing hard as she navigated the corridors, tracing the familiar paths she had taken twice each day to the stairs. The shadows around her seemed to shift, and once or twice, she thought she caught movement at the corners of her vision that turned out to be nothing.

A small draft stirred her Affinity. She latched on to that. She was close, so close.

Linn slowed before the last turn. Taking care not to make noise, she pressed herself against the wall. Two guards always stood sentry before the spiraling staircases; she caught the tremors in the air from their breaths, pulsing warnings against her senses.

She'd have to fight them to get past them.

Gods, she thought, drawing deep, silent breaths, as though that would replenish her strength. She palmed the daggers she had stolen from Isyas. Her hands shook as she lifted the blades before her face in a silent prayer.

Footsteps clattered in the corridor beyond. Before she'd had a chance to react, the dungeon doors burst open, and Vasyl's snarl echoed in the corridors. ". . . don't care that that Nandjian bastard's ordered us to lay off. I'm the Deputy Warden, and I'll get a confession out of that Kemeiran if it's the las—"

Linn sprang the moment Vasyl and his guards rounded the corner. Her daggers cut two wicked red lines across their throats. Their bodies thumped as they fell to the floor, blood gushing down the gray of their armor.

Vasyl was backing away and screaming at the remaining two guards at the entrance to *get her, get her.*

Linn's head pounded; her hands shook as she refocused her blurring sight on the two guards charging her.

The Wind Masters had taught her that the most successful warriors borrowed from each of the elements, their bodies attuned to whichever suited the moment best. Fire. Water. Air. Earth. Always adapting, always fluid.

In that moment, Linn became water.

She slid beneath the outstretched sword of the first guard, curving around the twist of his body like water around a rock. And then she was fire: her arm shot out, dagger plunging into his back. Crimson splattered her as she slashed.

A sharp pain pierced her side. Linn clamped down on the urge to scream as her senses blanched into a mass of white-hot pain.

She stumbled.

Her knees gave out.

"I've got her!" the fourth and final guard crowed, like a child who had ensnared a small animal by accident. "Lieutenant!"

Boots clacked against the cold stone floor, and Vasyl slammed his knee into her stomach.

Linn coughed blood. The dungeon ceilings swam in and out of focus, and under the flickering torchlight, Vasyl's face cracked in a terrifying smile. "Some things just don't change, Kemeiran," he whispered, his breath cold and rotten against her face. "You slit-eyed deimhovs aren't meant for this world, and I would gladly enforce that for you."

Linn screamed when he twisted the knife in her. It scraped against bone. She fought against the darkness blotting her vision.

Was this how it all ended? Memories, images, or dreams—she could no longer tell—flashed before her eyes, of Kemeira, her home, a past she'd forsaken and a future she'd lost. Kemeira, an endless maze of mountains and mist, set afire by the blazing sunrises that she longed to chase to the ends of the world. Kemeira, haunted by the brightness in her brother's eyes, a scattering of stars against a midnight sky, as he took after her on makeshift wings he'd been born to fly. A brightness that had disappeared the day the traffickers took him, a streak of a comet against the night, too quickly gone.

No, she thought, and a sob choked her throat. No, she wasn't ready.

Through the darkness that threatened to drag her down and the pain that numbed her mind, she found a sliver of wind, whispering at the back of her mind. Her companion, her shield, her sword.

Linn latched on to it. And pulled.

Her Affinity roared to life. Vasyl's weight lifted from her and she heard him shriek as he slammed into the opposite wall. The gale howled; the torches in the dungeon went dark.

Somehow, Linn dragged herself to her feet.

Somehow, she picked up the discarded dagger by the dead guard's side. Limped toward Vasyl, the winds screaming at her back, the knife in her midriff slicing with every shift of her body.

"We slit-eyed deimhovs have our rights to this world every bit as much as you do," she managed, and the words, instead of becoming lost, seemed magnified by the wind, echoing down the lightless corridor. "And I will show you what I can do."

She brought her dagger to his chest and pushed.

The hatred, the animosity, and the terror faded in Vasyl's eyes. Within moments, Linn was staring into the blank gaze of a corpse.

She crumpled a second after he did. Her winds had gone; the corridor was eerily silent. The torches were out. Her prison garb was sticky, she realized, from a mix of her and Vasyl's blood. Lying there, alone in the darkness, slowly bleeding out, she held a hand before her.

Was this it? Had she endured and survived years beneath the hands of her traffickers and exploiters, only to die without anyone even knowing? She thought of her mother, who would never know what had happened to her that day she went to the ocean and never returned.

Her thoughts blurred; she was slipping. Her brother's face came to her first, radiating joy, forever frozen in childhood. A memory . . . a dream, of him alighting at the edges of the cliff, his footsteps echoing as he approached her, laughing. *No fair, ane-ka, you cheated!*

Enn, she tried to say, but her arms were heavy as she reached for him, and the shadows were closing in.

His face morphed then, eyes gleaming strangely silver in the darkness, his skin a deeper hue as he drew closer. The world rocked gently. She fought for consciousness, her limbs dragging against her urge to move, *move, move,* or she would be—

"Calm down," a deep voice said, "unless you want to die."

It grew lighter. Warmer. The face swam in and out of focus,

and her wearied brain struggled to make sense of it. She was on a flat surface, the world anchored around her.

Something cold touched her lips, trickling down her tongue and sloshing over her chin.

Water.

She drank greedily, half-aware that she clung to a rough hand that held the waterskin before her. She drank until she paused to gasp for air.

Her head still pounded, and her body ached as her consciousness rose to clarity. The first thing she noticed was the draft, subtle but cold and pine-scented. It slipped through the cracks in the window to her left, carrying over the oakwood desk where she lay, and stirring the flames of the candle.

Window, she thought, and everything came rushing back.

"No," Linn gasped, sitting up—which was a terrible mistake. Her head threatened to split into two, and a sharp pain sliced through her abdomen.

"For one so stubbornly alive, you seem quite intent on dying."

Her head whirled. "You," she choked out.

The yaeger watched her, leaning against the marble wall of his study, arms crossed. The flickering candlelight sketched the sharp ridges of his outline, the cords of muscle that showed even through his uniform. His eyes were narrowed, his head tilted just slightly, as though she were a particularly difficult puzzle he was trying to figure out. "Please relax. You were unconscious for nearly twenty-five minutes, and I've given you all the healing draft I have. I'd rather not have you pass out on me again."

Linn suddenly realized the ache in her head was fading. Even the pain in her side dulled as she sat still, watching him watching her. Her wound was cleaned and bandaged, and an oversized cloak was draped over her.

Her hands sat on her lap, disturbingly empty. Her knives. Where were her knives?

"In case you're looking for these." A sweep of his fingers, and Linn's daggers—the ones she'd stolen from Isyas—appeared in the yaeger's hands.

Linn tilted her head down slightly, watching him approach, her body coiled like a spring. Injured and barely revived, she couldn't do much against him even if she wanted.

The boots stopped clicking. The yaeger was an arm's length from her, dagger held lazily in his hand. A dull red wound marked his palm. She thought of the way his hands had touched her cheeks, her shoulders, her clothes, his blood—which had passed for hers—slick against her skin.

"I told you I would come for you, and we'd leave this place together." His voice was deep, cold, with an undercurrent of command. "You would rather risk death than trust me?"

"Death, thirst, and starvation," Linn corrected, but her voice was small and shaky.

"I told you, I am not your enemy."

She was silent, the cogs in her brain working faster now. He'd told her he wanted to join ranks with Ana, but she didn't trust him.

She couldn't escape him, either. Not now, when she'd lost all her strength. "You wish to defect," she said, stalling for the moment. "You would throw away everything—your rank, your honor, your badges—to join a rebel group?"

He didn't move, but there was the slightest shift in his eyes, like a cloud passing overhead. He turned away, brows creasing.

"I told you. I cannot stand under the leadership of this empire, watching innocents—*children*—die."

A memory rose, unbidden: men seizing her from her bed aboard the trader's ship, rough fingers on her shoulders and back hauling her out, piercing sunlight, and then a view of a cold, frozen land. Soldiers at the docks, in uniforms of pure white, silver insignias flashing at their chests.

She'd recognized the silver-tiger emblems of the Cyrilian Empire.

Help, she'd screamed in the Kemeiran tongue. *Please, help!*

They had looked at her, and they had laughed.

Linn said nothing.

The yaeger watched her a moment more, then crossed the room. He fumbled in some drawers, and moments later plonked a set of folded clothes and leather boots beside her. "Get dressed. We move soon."

Move? He was asking her to move already, when it hadn't even been an hour since she'd been stabbed? Linn frowned at him, then gathered what was left of her dignity and straightened. "What is your plan?"

He drew a set of keys from his belt and unlocked the window at the corner of the study. The metal-latticed shutters banged against the walls. A cold wind swept in, scattering papers on the oakwood desk and stirring Linn's thin linen shirt.

The candle extinguished, plunging them into darkness.

By the windowsill and draped in night, the yaeger looked as though he had been cast in liquid silver and shadows. "My plan," he said, "is to throw us out this window, seeing as you're so good at jumping from tall places."

It took her a few moments to realize he wasn't joking. Linn

gaped. "You are an *Imperial Patrol,*" she emphasized. "Surely you have other methods of escape?" She waved a palm. "The front gates, perhaps?"

"I am as much a prisoner here as you are," he replied. "The Empress and my kapitan sent me here in lieu of exile. Disobeying the Empress's direct orders is punishable by death. I'm worse off than I would be should I defect." His head snapped up, and his gaze sharpened. "That's why I'm here with you."

Linn watched him carefully. She didn't trust him nearly enough to lead him to Ana, but she did need him to escape this wretched prison.

It helped that he was exceptionally skilled at fighting. And that he might have some knowledge of Morganya's troop movements and plans.

She slipped from his desk, testing her balance. Her wound warned her with subtle pulses of pain, but she ignored those and limped toward the open window.

A wintry breeze rushed toward her, the cold stinging her cheeks and bringing with it the scent of snow and darkness. Linn shivered but leaned forward. Embracing it. *My element,* she thought, and when she opened her eyes again, the world became the movement of air, the subtle shift in currents and drafts as they circled each other in a never-ending dance.

I am the girl of wind and shadows.

"We go," she said.

The night swallowed them as they climbed out onto the sill, stars unfurling above Linn's head in a kaleidoscope of silver. She breathed in deeply, entranced for a moment by their quiet magic and ever-present glow, the light of other worlds glimmering through that vast stretch of fabric of the sky.

A story flitted through her mind—one her mother had told her, of how the stars were formed by the tears of two lovers separated. *Their love now lights the night sky,* Ama-ka had said, before she brought her eyes to meet Linn's, *just as mine will light yours and Enn's, wherever you are.*

Linn pushed the memory away, and it dissipated as easily as snow in the wind. "This is going to be—" she began, but the word *hard* dissolved on her tongue as the yaeger cinched something around her waist.

Smooth, transparent fabric, shimmering just slightly to give it existence, draped over her shoulders. She would know this fabric anywhere—just as she would know this contraption around her waist and shoulders. By her side, the yaeger had stepped out onto the stone ledge and strapped himself to her.

Linn's heart tumbled as she touched the fabric between her shoulders. "Chi," she said, in her native tongue, the word tasting bittersweet. *Wing.* "A Kemeiran chi. Where . . . where did you get this?"

"I'm an Imperial Patrol," the yaeger replied, looking faintly amused. "Surely I'd have *some* better method of escape than jumping off the edge of a cliff."

A strange knot formed in her throat—a tangle of hope and happiness followed by such insurmountable grief that she thought she'd crack open. Her fists clenched tightly around the chi.

The last time she'd flown with one of these, Enn had been taken.

"I don't know if I can do this." She tried to keep her voice strong. It came out small.

She felt the yaeger shifting beside her. When she glanced at him, his eyes were trained on her, his gaze as steady as his hold on a silver knife. "It's all right," he said, and somehow, the deep tone of his voice grounded her. "I'm what they call a yaeger, after all. I control the flow of your Affinity—I can suppress it, or in this case, I can channel it." A wry smile came to his lips. "I much prefer the latter."

Linn stood, and the world dipped, expanding into a stretch of a cliff that sloped down sharply, alternating between shadows and ghost-white snow. Beneath, the pines were only a mass of darkness, as small as grains of rice she could hold in her palms. Her head spun, and the familiar nausea, combined with that cold touch of fear, gripped her. The image came back to her, jarring in all the ways it was wrong: Enn's body, crumpled, his chi folded in on itself, plunging from the skies.

She sensed movement next to her, and the next thing she knew, strong hands—strong, but gentle—clasped around her shoulders, their warmth shielding her temporarily from the cold of the night. "Look at me," the yaeger said. She met his gaze; it anchored her. "I won't let you fall. All right? I won't. Just focus on me and focus on your Affinity."

Linn forced herself to nod. He'd been a lieutenant before his expulsion—and she knew from the Wind Masters that power came not only from physical strength but from mental fortitude as well. The best commanders had high sensitivity to their subordinates' thoughts and knew how to manage their troops' emotions when needed.

Perhaps she was being managed.

But if she died, then he would die, too. That was cold comfort.

Linn drew a deep breath and closed the gap between her and the yaeger in a single step. He went stone-still as she clasped her hands around his waist, her head barely at his neck.

"Hold tight, and listen for my signal," she said, hoping she sounded commanding.

Her Affinity leapt to her call and her winds roared to life: triumphant and strong and free. Her heart ballooned with the fabric of her chi, the transparent silk blooming over their heads, buoyed by the draft.

"Now!" Linn cried.

The ledge fell away from beneath them—and then they were falling.

At first, that was what it felt like—free-falling, tumbling in a messy tangle of limbs and hair and fabric. Linn tugged on her winds, and she felt another presence descend upon her Affinity in her mind, warm and strong as a guiding hand, pulling with her. Her chi spread like two stretches of gossamer wings above her shoulders, pulling them back, back.

And then they were flying. Soaring, in an infinite sky of stars and snow, the wind whipping their faces and howling past their ears. The ground beneath felt so far away—because she was *flying*—and the world had stretched into a boundless realm of possibility and hope and . . . magic.

Something rose in her chest, buoyed by the winds that lifted her, and suddenly she was laughing, shrieking with glee as they soared over the summit of a mountain, its jagged peaks and snow-topped caps reaching for them from far below. The moon was a scythe in the midnight sky, and for the first time in many, many long years, Linn thought she could reach the stars.

Hope unfurled in her chest: tiny, broken wings.

Would she find her way home, after all? Was she still worthy of acceptance from her family, her Wind Masters, and her empire?

They were descending now, and her winds seemed to have taken a mind of their own. They cradled her like giant, invisible arms that extended from the night sky, gently lowering her and the yaeger on the chi that flapped lightly overhead.

The shadows below parted into the tops of individual pine trees, snow glittering silver between them beneath the moonlight. Linn tugged on her Affinity, deftly weaving her winds like pulling strings at a Kemeiran shadow puppet show. They spiraled down, landing in the snow.

The world stilled.

Linn pushed herself to a sitting position. The elation of her flight gone, she was suddenly shivering. Using her Affinity so soon after an injury had hollowed her bones and swept away her energy, leaving her an empty husk.

Something warm was draped over her shoulders. Fur tickled her chin.

"Take my coat," the yaeger said, his deep voice melding with the night. "You've earned it."

Linn didn't even have the strength to reply. As she drew the coat around her, she heard the sound of rummaging behind her. A moment later, the yaeger appeared with a cold bliny pancake.

A sharp pang of hunger tore through her, insistent now that

her adrenaline had faded. It was all she could do not to snatch it from him. Linn finished it in three bites, the faint taste of fish and cream lingering on her lips.

She glanced around them for the first time. They'd landed in the middle of the Syvern Taiga, with nothing but trees surrounding them for miles and miles.

"We camp here for the night." The yaeger was already spreading the chi around them, the fabric shimmering just slightly as it unfurled over the snow. This was why chi was the ideal material for Kemeiran windsailer scouts and warriors: It was light as air, thinner than silk, yet possessed tremendous heat preservation properties.

A small ounce of gratitude sparked within her as she watched him spread another blanket over the ground. She didn't think she could have walked a single step more, and she was glad he didn't suggest it.

The yaeger sat himself on the thicker blanket, laced with bright colors and intricate patterns that did not resemble anything Cyrilian that Linn had ever seen. He nodded at the makeshift chi pallet. "I'll take first watch. Get some rest."

Linn dredged up every last ounce of strength left in her and stumbled over to the chi. It was older, stiffer from lack of use, but if she clutched it in her fists and closed her eyes, she could pretend it was the one Ama-ka and her Wind Masters had gifted her after her Affinity had manifested; the same one she'd taken with her when she'd flown with Enn, and they had lain beneath a star-strewn sky and whispered about their futures.

The light of the stars was cold, the night sky as black as her grief. Her fists shook as she wrapped the chi around her, wishing it could cocoon her from the reality of a world in which she might never see her family and her home again.

"Kemeiran girl." She heard the yaeger's voice as though from a distance. "I never learned your name. We . . . started off on the wrong foot."

The last thing she wanted to do was to answer him. After all, she didn't plan to go far with him. In the next few days, once she had healed adequately to journey by herself, Linn would leave him.

Still, he had saved her life. She owed him this.

Linn pushed past the ache in her throat. "My name," she said, "is Linn."

Sleep came to her, its edges jagged with the promise of uneasy dreams. Dimly, in the twilight between wakefulness and dreams, she thought she heard his response.

"My name is Kaïs."

12

Snow fell, dusting the world in an eternal gray.

Ana brought her valkryf to a stop, her breath curling in a misty puff, the pain in her back muted in the cold. Up here on the mountains the air was thinner, the conifers frozen beneath a coat of white that offered little shelter against Cyrilia's unforgiving winter storms.

On the other side, though, was the start of Southern Cyrilia—and her destination, Goldwater Port.

The regular route to Goldwater Port was around these mountains, on the main road that merchants and trade wagons frequented. It would also be crawling with Imperial Patrols. Injured and alone, Ana had made for the quicker and far more dangerous path: the notoriously difficult Ossenitsva Cross.

Overhead, the sky had turned a shade of dark gray that promised snowfall.

She pressed a hand to the small of her back. She'd found a flesh Affinite healer who'd closed her wound in a remote village, asking no questions about the scarf Ana kept wrapped tightly over the lower half of her face. But the flesh was still raw and puffy as it settled into a puckered scar, and she'd been instructed to clean it each night. The constant ache still drained her, slowing her pace considerably.

The Ossenitsva Cross should have taken her less than a day's time to pass. But night was falling, and still the maze of conifers stretched beyond her sight, icicles clinking erratically in the wind.

She should stop and make shelter before true night fell and the temperature plummeted.

And yet . . .

She had heard stories of the Ossenitsva Cross, where the Deities' Lights pressed low against the mountaintop and, in the darkness, turned to a magic more vicious and haunting. Hunters and traders and excursion scholars had disappeared up the frozen roads, never to return.

Ana squinted at the distant horizon, where the last light of the sun drained a cold, ice blue from the sky, yielding to night. She was so close to the bottom of the mountains. Another hour or two and she should be there.

Ana clicked her tongue and dug her heels into her valkryf. The steed huffed and began to steadily plow ahead, its clawed hooves finding grip through the snow more easily than any other horse, its milk-pale gaze cutting easily through the dark. Ice had frozen to its thick white mane; snowflakes clung to its long lashes.

By now, Ana had thoroughly given up on brushing or shaking the snow off herself. Her fur cloak, varyshki boots, and leather gloves were iced over, the scarf she'd wrapped over the lower half of her face frozen from the humidity of her breath. It scratched her cheeks as she swayed astride her valkryf, the world blurring into a mass of darkness and pale gray.

Her valkryf snorted.

Ana blinked, unsure of when she'd fallen into a stupor. It was easy to become drowsy in the cold, and in the days when she'd traveled with May or Ramson, they had kept each other awake and talking.

Phantom laughter flitted through the trees.

The hair on her arms rose. All around, a strange silence had fallen to replace the howl of the winds. Snow fell, in agitated flurries. The air thickened.

Her valkryf gave a shrill whinny. The sound raised gooseflesh on Ana's skin. Her steed had slowed and begun tossing its head, the whites of its eyes rolling. Ana tightened her grip on its reins and flared her Affinity, searching for traces of blood in the storm.

Nothing.

It was then that her valkryf screamed, and Ana heard it: a high-pitched howl, threading through the vast, empty mountains.

Beyond the blinding curtain of snow, something moved.

Her horse shrieked again, and Ana reached for her dagger. "Steady," she murmured. She spoke as much to herself as she did to her valkryf, gripping the reins tightly to stop her hands from shaking.

Two pinpricks of light appeared ahead—a sickly, pale blue, the color of the dead. They moved too steadily to be torches or anything human.

Wind gusted past her in a howl, and the childhood stories and rumors of creatures that haunted the distant mountains of her empire swept through her mind. Too late, Ana realized what it was—and that her dagger held not even a modicum of use against this type of creature.

An icewolf stepped through the snow.

It towered over her valkryf, carved wholly of ice, its weathered body veined through with frost, fangs of icicles longer than her forearms. Most terrible were its eyes: corpse white and dotted with a tiny blue pupil.

Her valkryf was thrashing desperately against her reins as it retreated. Yet Ana was shaking so hard that she couldn't move, the muscles in her legs gone soft.

They'd encountered ice spirits before, she and May: harmless syvint'sya that took the form of wild animals and small snow flurries. But there were other places in the world where the gentle magic of the Deities' Lights turned into malignant spirits that prowled deep within the Syvern Taiga and frozen tundras of Cyrilia. The icewolf was one of them.

The myths said that the only way to defeat an icewolf was to kill the syvint'sya at its core: the pinpricks of glowing blue light in its eyes. The easiest way was by fire.

Ana's fingers were cold as she rummaged around her pack. She'd run out of globefires; she'd rationed them out over the past few days, and she'd calculated for today to be her final travel day.

No fire. Blade it was, then.

The dagger felt heavy in her hands. Her grip was unsteady even as she raised her hand, the wind pounding at her. In this weather, chances of her aim sticking were slim to none. And her Affinity was useless against a spirit of ice and snow.

But, Ana thought suddenly, there *was* a way for her to combine blood and dagger.

She angled her knife toward her own thumb and slashed. Blood began to run; she ran the tip of her finger over the blade, leaving a trail of red that immediately froze over the metal. Her Affinity stirred, the crimson seeming to glow brighter as her power latched on.

A snarl distracted her; she snapped her gaze up. The icewolf watched her with eyes that emitted an untamed and utterly wild light.

Without warning, it sprang.

Ana lobbed her dagger and flung out her Affinity. She closed her Affinity's grip over the blood on the blade. Focusing on the icewolf's eerie blue eyes, she pushed.

Her dagger hurtled forward. Its aim was true.

The icewolf twisted in midair and uttered an unearthly scream. When it turned its gaze to Ana again, the hilt of the dagger protruded from one of its eyes. The light had flickered out. Blood dripped from the socket.

Its other eye, though, still blazed blue.

Ana swore as the ice spirit's growl blasted through the trees around them. Blood—she needed blood—

Her valkryf screamed, and Ana's world tipped sharply off-balance as her horse bucked her off.

She slammed into the snow and lay there for a moment, stunned and winded. She felt the thumping of paws on the ground as the icewolf broke into a run toward her; heard its snarls, growing closer. The forest around her grew blindingly white. Snow and ice lashed at her from all directions. Frost pressed up her clothes, her shoulders, her neck.

Ana lifted a hand. Her vision blurred; her Affinity wove in and out of her focus as she grappled at the blood that clung to her thumb and wrist in frozen spirals. There wouldn't be enough for her to make it into any semblance of a weapon to fight with. And she had run out of time.

The icewolf pounced.

Ana screamed.

And the night exploded in fire.

Flames, bright red and searing orange, swept through the snows, arcing triumphantly against the shadows of the frozen pines all around. Ana closed her eyes against the piercing brightness, pressing her face to the ground as powerful waves of heat tided over her. The mountains shook from the impact.

Through the roar of flames, she heard an eerie screaming sound, half-animal and half-phantasmal, followed by the hissing of water tossed into fire.

Ana twisted to look.

Against the night sky, flames coiled serpentine around what was left of the icewolf. The vapor around it was so thick that Ana could only see a shadow of the beast, its howls fading into ghostly moans and, finally, nothing at all.

In the silence, the only sound was that of water vapor rising from the gently steaming ground where the icewolf had stood.

The fire had sputtered out, shrinking and outlining a dark silhouette behind.

"You weren't easy to find," Yuri said, blowing at his smoking fingers. "Hello, Ana."

13

Linn dreamt a familiar dream.

At first, she was flying. Soaring, over an endless ocean of Kemeiran fir trees and mountaintops jagged against the horizon, the wind in her face and the wings of her chi buoyed like sails. The golden sun, threading through a fabric of mist over the shimmering sea, and the sky open and the earth endless, stretching all around her in infinite possibilities. Her brother, Enn, dipped ahead of her like a black-tailed sparrow, his laughter trailing in the breeze.

The dream always ended the same way.

She awoke with a gasp and sat up straight, her senses sharp as blades, her hands on the daggers at her hips. For a moment, there was only the darkness and the lingering taste of salt water and fear, fading fast as sleep gave way to wakefulness. And for a terrifying few seconds, she was once again sitting in the traffickers' caravan, drugged with Deys'voshk.

A soft wind stirred, bringing with it the sharp scent of snow and pines—and a presence that was at once familiar and not.

Linn turned and met a pair of eyes silvered by the snow.

"Bad dream?" From the shadows of a nearby pine, the yaeger—Kaïs—stepped forward with the grace and lethal poise of a Kemeiran snow leopard.

Linn tensed. "Yes and no," she murmured. What did you call a dream that was also your reality? She closed her eyes, trying to wash out the images of Enn's body, folding and bending in all the wrong ways, falling toward that foreign ship with the flower-emblem sails and sailors whose hair looked to be spun of gold. Only later, once she'd boarded a similar one in search of Enn, had she understood what the ships were.

She could sense his gaze, still on her. Those piercing eyes had a way of making her feel as though he saw everything in her head. Her soul. "What was it?"

"My brother." The words left her before she had a chance to stop them. Not that he could use that information to hurt her, anyway. That was one good thing about the dead. "He is the reason I came here." She paused. "Was."

She had learned not long after her arrival in Cyrilia, from a broker's log she had stolen that had earned her twenty vicious lashes, that her brother had died in an accident at a factory in a remote Cyrilian town.

Kaïs lowered his eyes. "I am sorry."

Linn stood. The chi fell to her feet, exposing her to the cold of a predawn morning in the grand Northern Empire. Her head had cleared, her hunger and thirst were bearable, and whatever balms Kaïs had given her had reduced the pain of her wound to a dull ache.

Kaïs watched her test her body and balance. "We should keep moving."

They were two days out from the Wailing Cliffs, but one could never be too cautious about whether guards were on their trail.

Her wound still throbbed beneath the salves and bandages she had applied, but she was glad Kaïs insisted on moving. It was a soldier's approach—and it assumed nothing less of her.

"We go," Linn said. She bound the chi and strapped it to her back, her fingers lingering on its shimmering, translucent fabric.

Kaïs shouldered their pack and turned to her. "Where are we going?"

Linn froze, small bells pealing in alarm in her head. *Goldwater Port,* she thought. She knew, only tangentially, that the Redcloaks' base was there, and if there was anywhere she might get closer to Ana, it would be there.

Besides, Linn had studied the map in Kaïs's office last time she was there, and it was the only town large enough in their vicinity where she could lose this yaeger, if she needed to. Cloak or not, he was still an Imperial Patrol, and her distrust of them had started eight years ago on the moonlit shores of the Cyrilian Empire.

"Perhaps it is better that I lead," she said instead. "Do you have a compass?"

Kaïs looked at her for a long moment. And then he held up his hand and tossed her something.

Linn's fingers closed around the cold glass surface of a compass. She didn't look at him as she looked down and found southwest, to Goldwater Port, and began walking. She suspected he already knew she didn't trust him.

In which case, this was a gesture of faith. A step back, letting her lead.

He followed her, his boots making almost no sound in the freshly fallen snow. He didn't say another word, never pressed her. Perhaps that was why she started talking.

"I boarded a trader's ship to Cyrilia," she said quietly, her voice barely carrying, "when I was ten years old. When I arrived, the first thing I saw were Imperial Patrols, standing guard at the harbor checkpoint. I remember their silver armor and the crest of the Cyrilian tiger on their chests. I saw their white cloaks.

"I cried out to them. I pleaded that I was here against my will. I begged them to take me back home." Her voice was steady, but she felt less steady than she'd been in years. Her knees threatened to buckle beneath her with each agonizing breath she took. "They laughed at me."

It was all she could do to keep plowing forward, the snow at her ankles, her breath hitching as she fought against the pain of those memories she'd kept locked away.

"I'm sorry."

She reminded herself that his words meant nothing.

"I know you don't trust me," he continued. "But trust me when I say that I will change all of this. That I will help you get back home."

Home.

What would be left of her home? The thought inevitably drew the last memory she had of Kemeira, watching the misty coastlines and jagged mountains grow farther and farther away from the trader's ship. The image of Enn's body plummeting toward the ship, seared indelibly into her mind. The thought of Ama-ka, sitting by their wooden hut stirring rice and salting fish, gazing out at the setting sun from between the fir trees for a glimpse of her two children who had vanished into the fog.

She'd long ago stopped believing in anything. Promises were made to be broken and lies were easier than the hard truth. But something in this soldier's voice gave her pause.

"I know it's hard to believe," Kaïs continued in that steady bass of his, "but I was like you, once. I was born in Nandji and taken to this empire at a young age by a trader's caravan." His voice was calm, as though he were reciting facts instead of his life story. "When they discovered my ability as what they call a 'yaeger,' they took me away from my mother to train as an Imperial Patrol."

Linn clutched the compass to her chest. It had been years, almost a decade, since she'd opened herself up to someone like this. Since someone had confided in her in turn. "You told me you were searching for her still."

A pause. "Yes," Kaïs said, softly and heavily at once. "I want to find her. And when this all ends, I want to take her back home. Across the Dzhyvekha Mountains and the Aramabi Desert."

His tone stirred something in her. Linn looked at him, his face clear in the light of day that had broken across sleepy blue skies. "Do you still remember her?" she asked. She did not mention that the memory of her own mother faded a little every day, and that there was so little to cling to that Linn didn't know if she still had enough of Ama-ka and Enn to love.

"I do," Kaïs said at last, and this time Linn let herself look back at him, allowing herself to drink in the quiet loveliness of it all. It was one of the few moments of truth between them that she would remember. Perhaps, in another life, they might have been friends. "I remember the scent of her. The feel of her. She always told me I had her eyes."

Her gaze lingered on his eyes for a moment longer than she

had intended. They were striking: the pale blue of clear springs that first broke through winter's ice. "What is her name?" she asked.

Nearby, a hawk cried out, sending showers of snow tumbling from a nearby conifer as it took off into the misty gray skies.

Kaïs's reply was a long time coming. "Shamaïra," he said softly. "Her name is Shamaïra."

The name meant nothing to Linn, but she understood, all too well, the way he spoke it, with a gentle tenderness that belied an ocean of longing and love. Perhaps, she thought as she picked up her stride again, there was something she shared with this yaeger after all.

They continued onward, the sky giving way to violets and then corals and then the gray-blue of a Cyrilian winter morning. The sun hid behind clouds that promised snow. At some point, Linn sensed it: a thrumming in the air around them, an urgency to the breezes that whispered to her.

By her side, Kaïs tensed. "Patrols," he said, his eyes narrowed as he scanned the area around them. He nodded at a large cluster of pines. "They're on horseback. We'll hide there and let them pass. Can you sweep our tracks?"

Linn drew a deep breath and summoned her winds. She held out a hand and guided them over the footprints they had left in the snow until there was nothing left but a smooth, glittering surface.

Together, they crouched behind a thicket and waited.

Gradually, they heard the rhythmic squeak of wagon wheels and nicker of horses. A procession of Imperial Patrols emerged into view, sitting tall on their valkryfs. The first, presumably the kapitan, bore an unfamiliar emblem on his breastplate.

"That's an Inquisitor," Kaïs said, his voice low. "Affinites handpicked by Morganya to run the Imperial Inquisition."

Several Whitecloaks rode behind the Inquisitor, followed by a tall black wagon that emanated cold and made Linn think of her prison back at the Wailing Cliffs. "Blackstone," she whispered.

Kaïs shifted his head in an almost imperceptible nod. He then paused, and pointed, his eyebrows creasing.

The wagon was followed by another lineup of Imperial Patrols. Linn had never seen so many accompanying a single blackstone wagon. She remembered, so vividly, the feeling of coldness and emptiness seeping into her very veins, robbing her of her power and her breath. The view, through the bars, of a shifting landscape of ice and snow, crystalline trees and gray skies, and the ever-present flash of a white cloak, a pale-eyed valkryf.

By instinct, she shrank back, her pulse quickening, her palms sweating.

A firm hand on her shoulder. "It's all right," Kaïs whispered. "They won't find us."

She swallowed, counting. Twenty Whitecloaks, accompanying a single wagon. "I have never seen so many."

"Me neither."

A scream cut through the silence, an animal sound so raw that Linn felt it scrape against her insides. It tapered into a moaning sound, eerie as the whistling of the wind between empty peaks, and Linn found herself digging her nails into her skin, the hairs on her arms standing.

The Inquisitor signaled, and the entire procession drew to a grinding halt. Linn watched as the man disembarked, along with several of his patrols. They drew their swords as they rounded to the back of the wagon. One Whitecloak stepped forward and slammed a fist against the door, shouting something at the prisoner inside.

For a moment, the keening stopped. And then another fit of strangled yells exploded, the wagon visibly rocking on its wheels as whatever was inside pounded against the walls.

The Inquisitor made a motion, and a patrol stepped forward with the keys. As soon as the doors were unlocked, flames exploded from within. The shouts from the men nearest were cut off as they were engulfed in the searing fire.

There were cries of alarm, and the Inquisitor moved to dash forward—but stopped. Snow and ice had wrapped around his feet to his thighs, freezing him in place. Linn watched in half fascination, half horror, as snow rose from the ground, condensing into ice as it snaked up patrols' boots, freezing them in place.

"Affinites?" she said sharply.

Kaïs hesitated. Slowly, he shook his head. *"Affinite,"* he corrected. "There is only one inside the wagon."

Before Linn could ask him what he meant, a man stumbled out from the wagon doors. His eyes were aglow in light blue, as though covered by a sheen of ice. Yet his arms and hands were charred black. One of his handcuffs was a peculiar green color, so tight that it seemed to have melded with his skin. With every staggering step he took, ice trailed behind him as flames crackled from his fingers.

"It's not possible." Kaïs's voice was hollow. "He has two Affinities."

Linn's mouth went dry. The man had fallen to the ground, twitching. Flurries of snow began to swirl around him, intermingling with bright flares of fire. "Get it out of me," he screamed. Blue light had bled out from his eyes and was slowly spreading down his cheeks and his neck. The flames swirled up his arms, turning them red, and then black.

Wrong, something screamed inside Linn. *Wrong wrong wrong wrong wrong—*

Behind the Affinite, the Inquisitor had managed to break out of the ice. Unsheathing his sword, he turned to the fallen prisoner.

"Kaïs." Linn's teeth chattered. "We need to help him."

By her side, Kaïs held absolutely still. His gaze locked on the scene before them. The Inquisitor, approaching the Affinite. The man, spasming on the ground, a whirlwind of ice and fire growing fiercer and larger around him.

Linn's hands found her daggers. She crouched.

Without warning, Kaïs pounced—not toward the Affinite, but toward *her.* His hands locked around her wrists as he pushed her back behind the trees that hid them from view. She sensed the iron grip of his Affinity clamping down on hers, and the world grew still as her connection to the winds broke.

She twisted, preparing for a move to throw him off, but he'd anticipated it; with a grunt, he pushed her into the snow. "We cannot help him." His voice was a low growl. "We cannot sacrifice our mission for one person."

Linn turned back to the scene before them. Through the low-hanging branches partially obscuring her view, she saw the glint of the Inquisitor's sword. Heard the neat slice of metal through flesh, a sound like cutting fruit. And then felt the heavy silence.

Low murmurs of discussion, the sound of a body being

dragged through snow, the clang of wagon doors shutting, and, eventually, the squeak of wheels as it continued its journey.

Kaïs released her and drew back, breathing hard. "I apologize."

Her breaths were shallow; her head felt light. "Do not touch me again. Ever." Her voice was barely a croak.

He looked away, his outline silvered by the dust of a distant sun. When he turned back to her, his eyes were flat, cold. "You were about to give away our position and jeopardize our journey. There would have been no use in trying to save him. That man's Affinities were consuming him."

Linn closed her eyes briefly, steadying her breath. "What was wrong with him?"

"I don't know."

Sparks of anger ignited in her from a wrath old and bitter. "I do not believe you. Those were Imperial Patrols. You were one of them."

"I did what I had to do to survive." His gaze seared like fire. "You want to find out what that was? You want to bring down this regime? We find Anastacya, and we do it together."

He was right, Linn thought, tension unfurling from her in a sigh. She'd started off wanting to find her way back to Ana because that was the only thing she still knew. Now, the mission took on new urgency.

The image of the Affinite haunted her, the way the blue veins of the ice and the black of the fire—tells from both his Affinities, she assumed—had swirled on his skin. *Get it out of me.*

Why had a squad of Imperial Patrols been transporting an Affinite in a blackstone wagon, if Morganya's prerogative was to protect them? And not just any Affinite—one with *two* types of Affinities.

It was unheard of. Unnatural. Back in Kemeira, they'd had wielders and givers—people with connections to the world around them, and people without. They had existed in harmony, each doing their own part to contribute to a greater whole.

In all her trainings with her Wind Masters, in studying the principles of alchemy that built the foundation of their world, she had never heard of a wielder with *two* connections. What were the chances that Morganya's Imperial Patrols had found such a person?

There was something bigger going on here, and she needed to find Ana to deliver this information. *We find Anastacya, and we do it together.*

Linn looked at Kaïs. He sat in his disheveled uniform, hair loose and slick as black ink, looking further and further from the image of the terrifying Whitecloak she'd conjured in her mind for so long. His expression was troubled, his gaze dark, and for several moments he resembled a boy who was just as lost as she was.

They should have been enemies—and they once *were*—but he'd helped her. He'd broken her out of that prison and saved her life. He'd used strategy and militaristic logic to steer her in the right direction just now.

Linn found that her head was telling her one thing and her heart another. Perhaps . . . perhaps there was something redeemable within him, after all.

Linn pushed herself to her feet. The compass he'd given her spun in her palms as she turned. "We go."

14

Ramson was on a boat sipping wine, and all seemed right with life again.

He leaned back, watching the last dredges of night fade into the dirty, washed-out color of dawn. The infamous Black Barge, a ship converted into a floating pub at the unsavory end of Goldwater Port, had cleared of customers from earlier in the night. Ramson had sat watching as transactions took place beneath the tables of rotting wood. The excited babble and roar of drunkards had subdued into a handful of murmured conversations, and now the Barge was almost empty.

He'd arrived two nights ago, and immediately started checking in on his old haunts, careful to keep his face hidden. He'd been to the underground markets, the shadiest of inns, eavesdropping and striking up conversations with strangers. There were no bounds to a man's tongue once you offered him a goblet of whiskey or five.

The most reputable crooks, it seemed, *had* caught wind of a trade ongoing between Cyrilia and Bregon. None could name what, exactly, was being traded but claimed to have seen midnight ships leaving docks on silent waters. And word was, they sailed for Bregon.

The contact Olyusha had given him, it seemed, frequented the Black Barge. Apparently, she only showed herself at dawn.

Daya, he thought, turning the name over in his head, and annoyed that Olyusha hadn't been able to give him anything more. The name could belong to anyone, from any demographic—Northern or Southern Cyrilian.

"Can I bring you anything else?" the bartender offered, catching sight of his near-empty cup. "We're closing soon."

Ramson swirled what was left of his drink in the brass cup and set it down. "Not today," he said, tapping his fingers on the chipped wooden surface of the bar top before turning away.

His contact would have to show soon, if the bar was closing.

The morning breeze was just beginning to pull in from the ocean, carrying with it a cool, briny tang that almost transported him back to another time, another place. Here, in the south of Cyrilia, the air was warmer, the days stretched longer, and Ramson leaned back in his seat as the sun seemed to break through the surface of the ocean, gilding it with glittering shards of gold.

His gaze swept past the mast, where posters had been pinned. Swept past, then back again.

And stopped.

Ramson stood abruptly, nearly knocking over his chair. In three strides he was at the mast.

Flapping gently in the breeze, nailed amid a number of other solicitations and signs, was a poster with an image of a girl. Her crimson cloak swept in an impressive arc behind her, and her hands were raised in a striking pose that he knew all too well.

Ramson peeled back the other notices to look at the full poster. *Red Tigress Rising,* gold letters declared. *The Crown Princess lives. The rebellion begins.*

It couldn't be.

He'd spent entire days stalking the streets of Goldwater Port, hitting up all the shady inns where coin was exchanged for information on missing persons, but he'd found no sign of her.

Seeing a poster of her now, the scarlet of her cape curving just like it had in Shamaïra's painting, felt nothing short of a miracle.

Ramson sensed someone brush up behind him a moment before the knife sank into the wood of the post with a *thud,* right between two of his fingers.

"I don't believe you've paid yet."

It was the bartender, her lips curled in a grin. Delicately, Ramson extricated his fingers from near the blade. He turned and easily swiped back the three cop'stones she'd stolen from his pocket. He recognized a good thief when he met one, and this one had almost gotten past him. Though he supposed not having paid for his drink yet made *him* the thief. "Lesson number one, love," he crooned. "Wise men never keep all their coins in one place." With a flick of his hand, the cop'stones vanished. "Is this how you get your tips?"

The girl laughed. "Only for those who come a-lookin'," she said, and something clicked in Ramson's head.

"You're Daya," he said.

She flashed him a grin of acknowledgment and tapped

two fingers to her forehead in a mock salute. Ramson chanced a glance at the ocean, the sky streaked with brilliant tints of corals and reds, the sun warming his face. Dawn at the Black Barge.

Of course. He should've caught it.

Easily, he switched his demeanor, a wry grin springing to his face. Ramson plucked the knife from the post and flipped it so the blade pointed at his new companion. "Well, Daya," Ramson said, "you'll find that politeness pays." Another flick of his fingers and the knife switched sides, handle sticking out toward the bartender.

She raised an eyebrow. "Oh, I find that dead men pay even better." She snatched her weapon from him and slipped it into a chain hanging loosely from her hips. Turning, she crooked a finger at him.

Ramson slipped the poster of the Red Tigress into the folds of his shirt and followed. Daya sashayed to an empty booth and plonked herself down. She took a swig from a bottle she'd swiped at the bar and surveyed him through heavy-lidded eyes. "So, word is there's something you want from me."

A quick twirl of his fingers, and a bag of coins appeared in his palm. Ramson jingled the fat leather pouch at her. "I'd prefer to think of it as a Trade," he replied. "I'm a businessman. I don't take without giving." The bag vanished with another twist of his hand.

Daya let out a loud, long snort. "That's the stupidest lie I've ever heard."

"Truth, lies—it's all just a matter of perspective," Ramson replied pleasantly.

The girl cackled. "I like you," she said. Her gaze roved to his now-empty hand. "But I like the sound of your money more. So, tell me. What is it that you want?"

Ramson tilted his head. "I never do business without knowing a bit more about my partners."

The girl grinned at him. "Sure, I'm an open book," she said cheerfully. "Daya of Kusutri. Set foot on a boat as a kid and never got off, never looked back. Made my days sailing. Business's been bad here in the great Northern Empire lately, so, I'm sailing where the wind blows and where the goldleaves shine." She raised her bottle of liquor at him before taking a swig.

The Crown of Kusutri was a small coastal kingdom neighboring Nandji, known for its skills in seafaring. Now that Ramson had a closer look at this girl, he noticed her skin was a shade darker than most people in Southern Cyrilia, her hair ink black and braided in the intricate hairstyles of some of the Southern Crowns. He heard, too, the subtlest difference to her intonation of certain vowels, the way someone tried to bury a foreign accent. Like his own.

He watched her carefully, taking in the shift of her linen shirt over her shoulders as she raised her bottle of liquor and took a swig. Peeking over her left collarbone was a tattoo: a woman with the sun haloing her head, rays of it spiking like a crown. Amara, the Kusutrian goddess.

At least this girl was honest.

Ramson leaned forward. "I'm interested in hearing more about your jobs to Bregon," he said.

Daya raised a dark eyebrow. "What about them?"

"Specifically, what types of jobs you did for Alaric Kerlan."

Her face tightened. "I know you," she said softly, her gaze glinting as she traced over his face again. "Last I heard, you'd famously broken out of prison. Ghost Falls, was it?"

Ramson morphed his face into a wolfish smile. "Then you'll know that I'm looking for Alaric Kerlan," he said, "and willing to pay anything for his head." He gave a delicate pause. "Unless you have any lasting loyalties."

"I do have loyalties. My loyalties are to whoever pays me most." Her eyes landed on his hands.

Ramson took the signal. Deftly, he slid the pouch of coin across the table to her.

Daya snatched the pouch, running it through her fingers. A wicked smile crossed her face. In the blink of an eye, the coins vanished. "Well, then, Portmaster," she said. "You wanted to know about my jobs for Alaric Kerlan." Daya cupped her chin with a hand. "My first job for him was well over eight years ago."

"Eight—" Ramson bit down on his words. That would have been shortly after Kerlan was exiled by his father. What kinds of trades had Kerlan carried out back then? Ramson had always thought any jobs overseas had sprung up after his own involvement in establishing Goldwater Port as the hub of foreign commerce. "Never mind. Go on."

"He needed ships that weren't recognizable," Daya continued. "Small and quick. Mine fit the bill perfectly."

"What was he trading?"

"Ah," Daya said. "See, that's the thing. Alaric Kerlan was not trading anything back then. He was shipping people to Bregon."

Ramson's stomach tightened. "Human trafficking?"

"No, not in that sense." Daya scratched her head. "Rather, his *own* people. He had me bring members of his Order to Bregon, all on one-way tickets."

Ramson's mind was already spinning. "Do you know what he was doing with these men?"

Daya scratched her chin. "I think he has unfinished business in Bregon," she said at last. "I've heard rumors of his exile . . . but I think he planted members loyal to him in Bregon. I think he still has men in Sapphire Port, awaiting his return."

The world seemed to shift, like two pieces of a puzzle coming together to form a bigger picture. Ramson had thought that after Morganya's takeover, Alaric Kerlan and his Affinite trafficking business would have been utterly destroyed, the Goldwater Trading Group crippled by this loss.

All this time, though, Ramson's former master had been years ahead of the game, building up a network not only in Cyrilia but across the Whitewaves as well . . . in the largest Bregonian trading port.

"Why?" His words were quick, urgent. "What is he planning in Bregon?"

Daya shook her head. "Beats me. I took care not to eavesdrop or show any interest in his business. Had a feeling Kerlan wasn't the type to leave loose trails. I only did a few jobs for him. Seems like bad luck to associate with this man."

"You aren't wrong," Ramson said.

Daya leaned forward. "Though," she added, "there *has* been word of new activity on his end here in the black markets . . ."

"I'm listening."

"Well." Daya jingled her pouch of coins suggestively. "I could use a little more . . . persuasion."

Ramson put his chin in his hands, mirroring her pose. "How about a job?"

It was an old trick in negotiating, but Ramson found that it always worked: to throw them the bait before offering the fish. The key was to set the other party's expectations lower than what you planned to offer, so that they were more willing to accept once you put forth your actual proposal.

Daya had the look of a fish on a hook. "What type of job?"

Ramson looked to the ocean, which was beginning to sparkle under the morning sun as though it held a thousand tiny, fractured diamonds. The water here was a stunning cobalt blue, and no doubt ruthlessly cold. It was a sight that he'd grown to like, and one that, he found, he wasn't quite ready to part with just yet.

He drew a breath. "You give me the information I need, and I'll hire you for a trip to Bregon." He reached out and plonked the second pouch of coins in the middle of the table. It landed with a considerably heavier *thud.*

Daya licked her lips. "I think we're about to be great friends," she said, and then lowered her voice. "Rumor has it that Alaric Kerlan brokered a new Trade deal—a trafficking scheme to Bregon." She gave him a pointed look. "*Affinite* trafficking."

Ramson considered. Olyusha had said Kerlan's new schemes had something to do with a new development concerning Affinites. This could certainly fit the bill.

"I've been watching the ports," Daya continued, "and I've seen unmarked ships set sail at night. I can confirm I've seen people board those ships after dark . . . and I can confirm that the last of them left several days ago with Kerlan on board. If you want to catch him, we need to move quickly."

Ramson hesitated. Why would Kerlan begin an Affinite

trafficking scheme to Bregon? More important, who on the Bregonian side could be the buyer of such a transaction? The militaristic kingdom of his birth was not one that particularly cared about the magen, its population of Affinites.

He had a feeling that the conspiracy ran deeper, but for now, one thing was clear. If he wanted to find his former master, the answers lay in Bregon.

A weight settled in Ramson's chest. From the folds of his shirt, he drew out the piece of parchment, smoothing it out against the warming wood of the table between them. If he left now, they might never meet again.

But he couldn't afford to wait forever.

He tapped his fingers to the painting. "Any idea what this is?"

Daya raised a dark eyebrow. "You want to be careful who you show that to. They say the exiled princess was spotted at the Imperial Inquisition in Novo Mynsk."

Ramson's grip on the parchment tightened. "Do you know who made this, and where I can find them?"

"Nope. I've only heard rumors that people are rallying to her name. Times are hard, with the new Empress. You've heard that she's persecuting non-Affinites. I fled the north just in time, Amara bless." She shuddered. "Not a bad time to get out of this empire, Portmaster."

Ramson looked to the sea. He thought of Shamaïra's painting, with the gold and the water and the slash of red in the midst of it all. He'd thought that was a sign for him, that he would find Ana again in Goldwater Port, that, by some miracle or twist of fate, their destined paths would continue to intertwine.

He held up the poster of the Red Tigress. Beneath the sun and golden haze of waves, the image of her scarlet cloak on the poster cut a streak of bright red against the scenery, an almost-perfect rendition of Shamaïra's painting.

Perhaps signs were for fortune-tellers or fools after all.

Ramson blinked. And blinked again.

There, outlined against the warm morning light of the sun, was a shadow, fast approaching. Too large to be a gull.

He was on his feet, his boots thudding across the deck of the Black Barge, until he reached the wooden quay. A startled laugh burst from him as he lifted an arm.

The snowhawk landed on his shoulder, talons biting into the thick leather of his coat. It regarded him with intelligent golden eyes, the wind ruffling its snowy feathers.

"Gods be damned," Ramson said softly, and then his gaze latched on to the object in the bird's beak. The lock of black hair glistened like silk in the morning sun, and the entire world seemed to shift.

Linn.

Over a moon ago, when she'd disappeared after the battle at the Salskoff Palace, Ramson had sent out a snowhawk with her scent to track her. He'd thought it a lost cause.

Until now.

"Is that . . . a bird?"

Ramson turned. Daya was gaping at him, her gaze darting to his snowhawk.

Suddenly, it was as though disparate threads were coming together. The snowhawk, bringing him news of Linn. The poster of the Red Tigress.

And he had been looking for just one sign.

"It's not just any bird," Ramson replied, and with a few light steps he was back at their booth. He snatched up the poster, picked up the pouch of coins from the table, and tossed it to her. "Wait for me here. Consider this down payment."

He might have laughed at her bewildered expression. "Wait! Hey! *Hey!*" she shouted as he barreled past her. "Should I ready the ship?"

But Ramson had already leapt onto the dock and was running down the streets of Goldwater Port, his snowhawk soaring in the air above him, his steps surer than he'd felt in a long, long time.

15

Ana rode through the night with Yuri and his companion, a Redcloak girl who had tracked Ana's movements through the mountain with her Affinity to snow. "Follow me" was all Yuri had said to her before turning away and mounting his valkryf. It had been a quiet journey, each of them wrapped thickly in furs, focused on the tread of their steeds.

The sun had just broken from white-capped waves when they arrived at Goldwater Port, and the city was beginning to wake. The squeaking of wagon wheels blended with the screeches of gulls overhead. Here and there, colorful tarpaulins propped up as the morning markets sprang to life, raising calls from vendors hawking fish and seafood and rainbow-hued fabrics.

Ana felt as though she had stepped into a different world. One of the southernmost cities of Cyrilia, Goldwater Port bordered the Dzhyvekha Mountains that separated the Northern Empire from the Southern Crown of Nandji. Long ago, nomadic tribes that wandered the Dzhyvekha Mountains and the Aramabi Desert had settled into Southern Cyrilia, building cities of their own and taking the cultures of the two lands and shaping them into something at once familiar and new.

My mother included, Ana realized. She'd never seen so many people with Mama's complexion—rich fawn skin and umber-dark hair. Mama had been born here, yet raised in the north in Salskoff, the capital of Cyrilia, where the climate and people were colder and the buildings were pale, with drops of color in red rooftops and gilded domes.

Southern Cyrilia was warmer and vibrant, thriving with dozens of colors in the space of a dacha: sun-yellow domes dotted with green circles and sky-blue turrets with gilded edges and poppy-red spindles on rooftops that spiraled in alternating patterns of deep violet and royal blue and lime green. It made Ana think of Shamaïra's brightly colored quilts and settees, the brocade curtains she used as room separators, and everything in her dacha that she had brought with her to the Northern Empire as a reminder of her home.

Mama's ancestors had come from here. And it was half of her legacy that Ana had inherited.

"We're here." Yuri's tone was still closed off, his face unreadable.

They stopped in front of a shop with a cheerful yet faded lemon exterior and a redbrick roof. Large glass windows looked in and the early-morning sun hit a chipped wooden sign hanging on the door. *Dama Kostov's Kafé,* it declared. *Closed.*

Yuri's companion stepped in without pause, but Ana grabbed Yuri's wrist. He froze, and when their eyes met, his were no longer the steady coal gray that she had known her entire life. A fire roared within them.

A distance stretched between them, filling with everything they hadn't said until it gaped into a bleeding abyss. And Ana thought of the shadows, of a knife in her back and a cold voice. *You are the antithesis to our movement.*

"What do you want from me?" Her voice came out hollow from days of neglect.

Something flickered in Yuri's eyes. "I just want to talk."

He stepped into the shop, leaving her looking after the silhouette of a boy she'd once known.

Ana drew a deep breath and entered.

She was standing in a restaurant. The inside was pleasantly warm, the wooden floorboards creaking beneath her boots. Bright yellow tablecloths draped over the tables, spotted with patterns of leaping fish and birds. Farther in the back were several booths, an empty counter, and a door that led to the kitchens. It smelled of bliny and fish.

Yuri gestured at a booth by the window. "Have a seat," he said shortly.

The snow Affinite had disappeared through a set of doors at the back of the restaurant. The entire place seemed empty but for the two of them.

Something tightened in Ana's chest. "Why did you save me?" she demanded. Her wound gave a sharp throb, and the words spilled from her lips before she could help it. "Did you ask Seyin to do it?"

Anger broke on Yuri's face, and Ana found herself relishing it. Anything but that cold, forced calm. "All these years you've known me," he said, and she felt a part of herself crack. "Do you think me a coward, Ana?" He drew a tight breath and looked away. "Seyin acted of his own accord. He has been dismissed from his position."

Before they could say anything else, there came the sound of plates clanking and a thudding noise, and the next moment, a wooden door swung open at the back of the restaurant. A girl emerged, squealing as she charged at Yuri.

Yuri's mouth dropped, and he caught her as she barreled straight into him. "Liliya—"

"You're back, Firebraids!" she cried, reaching up to pull at his ponytail.

The tips of Yuri's ears flamed red. "We agreed you would stop calling me that," he muttered, but tugged back at one of her gold pigtails. "And I told you to stay—"

"Who's that?" The girl—Liliya—now turned to Ana, her eyes wide.

Yuri looked helplessly at Ana. *We'll talk later,* his expression said as he tousled the girl's hair and told her, "Liliya, this is Ana. Ana, this is Liliya, my sister."

The girl grinned toothily at Ana, looking every bit like a smaller version of her brother down to the freckles on her nose. "You're the princess!" she squealed, and sank into an awkward curtsy with her peony-patterned skirts. "Kolst Pryntsessa!"

But the greeting only tightened a string inside Ana's chest. She didn't look at Yuri as she smiled and dipped her head.

More footsteps thudded from the back; moments later, a woman emerged. She had Yuri's solid build and heated gaze, softened by wrinkles around her eyes that made her look as though she were smiling already. Her bright red hair was swept back in a bun, and she held a wooden ladle in her sturdy hands.

"Liliya," she was shouting, "I told you to never leave the butter by the cooking stove or—"

The woman broke off as her gaze fell on Ana. Her eyes widened.

"Ma, this is Ana," Yuri said. "Ana, this is my mother."

"Please," Yuri's mother said, turning as red as her hair as she sank into a curtsy. "Call me Raisa, Kolst Pryntsessa."

"Please, call me Ana." A sudden surge of guilt clutched at Ana's chest as she dipped her head and bid the woman to rise.

Back at the Palace, Yuri had always mentioned a mother and a sister in a village down south. She had never given a second thought to them, but now they were here, in the flesh. For most of her life, she'd thought of Yuri only as her friend, and a servant at the Palace. Never the fact that he had a whole family, a whole life, outside of bringing her hot ptychy'moloko and keeping her company. That he'd lived away from it all when he'd been with her.

Ana looked at Raisa's linen kirtle, a faded red covered with splotches of various oils and sauces, at the woman's swollen wrists and ankles, her hair spilling from her bun. She looked at the modest furnishings in the restaurant, the air smelling like grease and batter. At Liliya, whose sleeves were rolled up and whose hands were covered in soap water.

Up until now, the livelihoods of ordinary citizens of her empire had never seemed real, never seemed more than a sentence in a dusty tome or a letter of law penned in expensive black ink.

It all felt like a dream as Raisa ordered Yuri into the kitchens to set up some breakfast, and then led Ana up the rickety stairs to the wash closet. They passed a second-floor landing spaced with many rooms. "This used to be a boardinghouse," Raisa explained, "but now Yuri's children live here, and I provide room and board."

"You mean the Redcloaks?" Ana asked as they squeezed between a plain clay tub, a gently steaming bucket of hot water, and a number of neatly organized drawers.

Raisa exhaled sharply. "A fancy title they give themselves. Most of them are young, with nowhere to go, believing in a cause too big for them to bite. I do what I can for them." She rummaged in a cabinet. "Here—a medical kit. I can tell you have a wound from the way you move. Sit down, child; let me help you."

Raisa's hands were gentle as she peeled back Ana's shirt and the bandages she had applied herself. "When Yuri got the post at the Palace, it was the best day of our lives," she murmured, lathering warm water from the bucket and cleansing the wound. "We had moved down south because we heard it was safer down here for Affinites compared to the north. The Empire's policies against Affinites are looser down here because it's so far from Salskoff. Not," she added quickly, glancing up, "that there was anything wrong with them."

Ana caught Raisa's gaze. "There was so much wrong with them," she said gently, and Raisa's shoulders loosened.

"He spoke so well of you," Yuri's mother whispered, her fingers nimble as she applied salve from a tin can and began to wrap fresh gauze around Ana's midriff. "He said you are kind, and fair, and just. No matter what, I am glad for your friendship with my son."

Ana's throat tightened. "Thank you."

They continued pleasantly, the clay tub sturdy as Ana leaned against it, Raisa telling Ana stories of her children punctuated by her warm, booming laughs and her chiding commentary.

By the time Ana went downstairs, the clock hanging over the faded cream wallpaper announced it was a little past eight hours, and the sun threaded orange through the winding streets of the Southern Cyrilian town.

Yuri and Liliya had set up a mouthwatering spread of food at one of the booths. Ana sat down, and it was all she could do not to lunge at the steaming pelmeny dumplings and golden pirozhky oozing with potatoes and minced beef. The interrupted conversation with Yuri felt like a distant past, mended with Raisa's gentle hands and tender words.

Liliya had retreated upstairs. Yuri sat across from her, silent, his gaze distant. Ana poured herself a cup of koffee from a worn metal samovar. The hot liquid soothed her stomach. "Your mother has quick hands and a quicker wit," she said into the silence. "And Liliya has stolen my heart. I'm glad I met them."

Yuri's hands tightened around his mug. "Ana," he said, and finally looked up at her. "Things can't be as they were. You understand that."

Just like that, the dreamlike peace of the morning shattered. The soft beige wallpaper, the creaking wooden table, the warmth of her koffee dissolved into a familiar nightmare: cold, shadows, a blade between her ribs, and a familiar whisper. *The monarchy must die.*

"Not as long as you lay claim to the throne," Yuri continued. "I believe Seyin made that clear."

Crack. She'd knocked over her mug. Black koffee spilled across the tablecloth, warm and sticky on her fingers.

"Ana." Yuri pressed down on the tablecloth with his napkin. "I'm sorry. For what happened."

She looked up at him now. The brittle morning light carved his face in sharp planes, and for the first time, she noticed the bags under his eyes, the stubble at his chin. In the course of a moon, Yuri had become a stranger.

"I went to look for you as soon as Seyin sent me a note. He'd gone back to . . . to bury your body." He looked away, his napkin fisted tightly in his hand. Koffee dripped from it, forming a puddle on the floorboards. "If I'd known this would happen . . ." His voice shook, and she caught the glimmer of tears in his eyes.

Drip, drip, drip.

Ana stared at him, the sunlight shrouding them beneath a golden haze in this singular, inevitable moment.

A day will arrive when you will be asked to sacrifice that which you hold dearest for the good of your empire.

Could this be what Shamaïra had foreseen?

"What do you want to happen, Yuri?" It was as though someone else spoke with her voice, pushing the words past her lips. "When we spoke back at Shamaïra's, you said you loved me—"

"And I still do. You're like a sister to me, Ana."

She dragged a long breath before fixing her gaze on him. "Back then, you asked me to stay," she said softly. "You said we'd begin our revolution here, in the south. What changed?"

The sadness in his eyes was a chasm. "The world changed, Ana," Yuri said. "Morganya took the throne, and I saw, with my own eyes, the destruction of my empire at the hands of a vicious monarch." He shook his head, and there, she saw it again, behind the coal gray of his eyes, a spark of fire catching life. "The era for the monarchy has come to an end. A broken system makes villains of even the best people, Ana—surely you must see that."

Ana looked away, at the patterned tablecloth, at the cracks in the wall, at the overturned mug of koffee—anywhere but at the boy who had been by her side since she could remember. There was an ache, deep in her chest, as though a part of her already knew what was to come. "And what is it that you want from me?"

Slowly, Yuri reached into the folds of his tunic and drew out a crumpled sheet of paper. He handed it to her.

Ana felt only a numb shock spread through her veins. It was the same poster that Shamaïra had shown her the night she'd left Novo Mynsk, only this one had been freshly painted and seemed unmarred by snow or storm. And it had reached not only an entirely different city but an entirely different region of her empire.

"If you want to work with us . . . if you want to join our cause to make this an empire ruled by the people for the people . . ." Yuri suddenly sounded very distant. "Then you must abandon the throne and renounce your cause as the Red Tigress." The table creaked as he leaned forward, grasping her hand with his. "Join us, Ana. Together, we can make a better world."

Ana tore her gaze from the poster to look at him. For the first time since they'd crossed paths again, Yuri's eyes were bright, the warmth and hope of a time long past brimming in his gaze. In them, she found the boy who had crept to her chambers at the sound of her weeping, who had knocked softly against her tall mahogany doors. *Why do you cry?*

The one who had sat with her through all those empty days and lonely nights. Who had brought to her hot tea and freshly baked desserts and, most important, the companionship of a friend.

Her silver Deys'krug pressed against her neck. He'd gifted it to her a moon ago, promising they would come full circle again.

"Think about it, Ana," Yuri was saying. "The Redcloaks are growing in numbers—we have over a hundred in forces, and counting, spread between here to the north. This provides us with a constant stream of intelligence on Morganya's movements." He hesitated, his eyes roving to the poster she held between her fingers. "And with the new movement in support of you, if you joined our cause, we could take down Morganya in one fell swoop. Finish the revolution and put the power in the hands of the people."

A dull ringing sound grew louder in the back of her head, drowning out his words.

There are two Anastacyas now, my love: the girl you once were, and the ruler you will become.

Ana looked at him, but she was no longer seeing Yuri, her childhood friend, the one who had stayed by her side all these years.

Yuri was the leader of a revolution.

And she was heir to the throne.

It had been a dead end from the start, an utterly unachievable alliance between two parties with opposing goals.

She looked into his face, seeking out the trace she'd just seen of the boy who had been her friend. He gestured animatedly with his hands as he continued to speak, and she thought of how easy it would be to slip her fingers between his and promise him that they would be friends forever, that they would fight to the death together. She already knew how they would feel: callused and strong and hot. Once upon a time, they had made up her world.

But those memories belonged to Ana, the girl who had been lost and desperately lonely and frightened of herself.

She was no longer that girl.

That *is the choice you must make.* Shamaïra's whispers stirred in her mind. The poster in her hands seemed to glow from the gold of the sun. *Which of the Anastacyas you shall be.*

"And what," Ana said slowly, "would you do if I refused?"

They gazed at each other a moment longer, the inevitable truth hanging between them. Yuri opened his mouth. Before he could speak, a shadow fell across the window at their booth. Ana turned to look.

Standing outside, on the cobblestone street, was a Kemeiran girl, made of shadows and wind.

Linn.

Ana stood so abruptly that she knocked against the table, rattling cups and saucers. But whatever joy she'd felt dried on her tongue when a second figure appeared around the corner.

Sprinting across the street was a tall, dark-haired man. Linn had half turned, shock registering on her face, when he bowled her over, knocking her to the ground. He looked up, and when Ana looked into his eyes—the blue of ice and fire—recognition locked into place.

Ana had just taken two steps toward the door of the restaurant when the windows before her exploded.

16

Everything hurt, gods be damned—and the air smelled of smoke, singed and cloying. Ramson groaned as he picked himself up from the cobblestones, glass clinking as he brushed it aside and climbed to his feet. His ears were ringing, the world was swaying, and when he looked down at his hands, there was blood on them.

As though from a distance, he heard shouting. High-pitched . . . screaming.

He looked up, the world blurring in and out of sight as he struggled to focus. It wasn't until someone crashed into him, screaming and covered in blood, that he realized what was going on.

The dust settled and Ramson saw, advancing down the streets, bulldozing through the crowds, Imperial Patrols, blackstone-infused armor shining, white cloaks billowing behind them, astride their sharp-eyed valkryfs.

Except it wasn't just a squad of them, or even a platoon of them.

No, there were hundreds of them, stretching as far as the

eye could see, a snaking army of silver white slithering through the streets.

Cold ran down Ramson's spine.

The Imperial Inquisition was here.

Ramson squinted, shaking his head to clear it of the ringing. His snowhawk. Where was his snowhawk? He'd been following it through Goldwater Port because it had found Linn—*Linn,* whom he'd thought he would never see again—when the restaurant across the street had exploded.

Amid the columns of black smoke and clouds of dust, the snowhawk was nowhere to be seen.

Ramson looked at the approaching Whitecloaks. The kapitan, leading the charge, was close enough that he could make out Morganya's unmistakable new emblem on his breastplate.

There was no way he would find Linn now, with his snowhawk gone and the Imperial Inquisition wreaking havoc in this town. And Ana . . .

The poster was crumpled in his hands, covered in a layer of soot and dust, the red of the painting barely visible.

Ramson smoothed the parchment over, his fingers lingering on the image of the girl. If he ran now, he could get far enough away to avoid capture. Daya was waiting for him; he could board her boat and leave for Bregon and never look back at the doomed Northern Empire again.

Ramson scanned the frantic crowds one more time. He paused, only for a brief moment, before he slipped into them, disappearing like a fish into water.

17

The world was muted but for a distant ringing, the scent of smoke in her nose and burning in her lungs. Ana squeezed her eyes closed, then open, then closed again, waiting for the world around her to stop spinning. There was blood drenching her breeches and the back of her shirt—she could feel it all, bright spots of light against her Affinity, warm and flowing. But none of it was hers.

She forced her eyes open again. Across from the wrecked booth, Yuri lay facedown on the floor in a pool of crimson.

"*Yuri!*" The cry tore from her throat as she scrambled up, and the world came crashing back in a whirl of smoke and sound. Rubble covered the restaurant floor, interspersed with broken glass and shattered kitchenware. The breakfast they had been enjoying just moments ago—pelmeny and pirozhky and pies—was splattered across the floor.

Ana knelt and wrapped her Affinity around Yuri, trailing the familiar hints of smoke and fire and, at last, faint but fluttering like a dying butterfly, the soft gasps of his pulse. Without her help, he would die.

And if he dies, a very small voice whispered inside her, *your path is clear of political rivals. The resistance movement will rally to you.*

Yet in this moment, she looked down and only saw the familiar edges of his face. She touched her fingers to the bright red of his hair that she'd loved since as far back as she could remember, now dirty with blood and debris.

Ana looked at her friend, and in her heart of hearts, she knew that this was one of the moments Shamaïra had seen for her. The choice that she made now would begin to define which path she walked. Which of the Anastacyas she chose to be.

Ana rested a hand on her friend's chest, closed her eyes, and applied her Affinity. The moments crawled by; the blood pouring from Yuri's wounds slowed to a leak, and then a drip. She sensed someone crouching next to her, and when she opened her eyes, she saw Raisa, medical kit out, already pressing against some of Yuri's wounds with her clean gauze. The woman raised her eyes to Ana's. "You saved his life," she whispered.

Ana touched a finger to Yuri's wrist. It was warm. Beneath the pale, freckled skin she'd known her entire life, something fluttered. A pulse: weak, but fighting.

"You saved mine," she replied.

From somewhere beyond the shop came a faint rumbling: a thrumming sound, like footsteps or hoofbeats. Hundreds of them, marching.

Raisa looked up, her eyes fierce through the shine of her tears. "The Imperial Inquisition," she gritted. "We'd all wondered when they would reach this town. Go, Kolst Pryntsessa."

"And you," Ana said, looking at the torn wreckage of Raisa's shop. Searching for a glimpse of the gold-haired girl who was

Yuri's sister; the snow Affinite who had led them here. "What will you do?"

"We have long prepared for this," Raisa replied. "I have a wagon that will take the children to safety. *Go,* Kolst Pryntsessa. It is you they want."

Ana hesitated. First Shamaïra, now Yuri and his family. She despised this, that she was constantly taking so much without the power to protect. That her very presence put those who were willing to help her in danger. That the only thing she could offer in return was the far-off promise that, once she was Empress, things would be different—by which time thousands of lives might have already been lost.

"I'm sorry," she said, and she wasn't even sure to whom she spoke or what she was sorry for.

A gust of sweet, cold wind swept into the shop, stirring the chimes above the door. Linn stood in what remained of the doorway, her black tunic and hair fluttering in the breeze. In just a moon, the girl's face had thinned, the rings dark beneath her eyes and her chin-length hair ragged. She looked frighteningly frail, but when she moved, Ana recognized the grace and fluid strength of the warrior who was her friend.

"Ana," Linn said. In three light steps, she closed the gap between them.

Ana took her friend's hands in her own. "Linn," she breathed. "How did you find me?"

"The Redcloak base," Linn replied. "You'd mentioned to me before that it was here, in Goldwater Port."

A figure stood several steps from them, still as stone, his double swords strapped to his waist. It was the yaeger from

Kyrov. The sight of his face brought back painful memories—a small girl, standing in the middle of a deserted square. *You will not hurt her.*

"*You.*" Ana's Affinity surged with her anger.

"Ana, I can explain," Linn said quickly. "He is not with them. He saved my life."

The yaeger was silent throughout their exchange. His face remained cold, as though cut of ice. Only those pale eyes of his flickered, like blue fires. "If you want to live, we need to make for the docks right now," he said. "The Imperial Patrols' practice is to seal off all roads by land. Therefore, that leaves us the sea."

Screams rose from the streets outside, followed by the sound of an explosion. They were running out of time.

Ana made a swift decision. "If you're lying, I will hurt you in all the ways I've wanted to since that day." She thought she saw something flicker in the yaeger's eyes, like the smallest wind across a flame. Ana turned to Linn and nodded. "We make for the docks."

They stumbled out into the streets, into chaos. Raisa's restaurant was not the only location to have suffered an explosion. All along the winding streets of Goldwater Port, black columns of smoke plumed into the air, and dust blotted out the sunlight. People stumbled through the streets, some disoriented, others crying out. The crowd was already pushing forward, in the direction of the docks.

Fighting against the tide, Ana turned and looked back.

An entire army of Imperial Patrols marched toward them from down the road. Their cloaks glimmered ghostly amid the smoke, a sea of white that stretched far beyond their street.

Even as Ana watched, the kapitan at the front—an Inquisitor—raised his hand, shouted something, and brought his arm down sharply.

Behind him, two other Inquisitors raised their fists, which started to glow red.

The crowds began shoving forward in a frenzy, scrambling to get away from the incoming army. Somewhere amid the commotion, Ana heard Linn call her name; the throng of people had pulled them apart.

"Linn!" she shouted, but her voice was drowned out by a high-pitched whistling in the air.

She looked up to see streaks of fire falling from the skies.

Ana dove aside as the fireballs smashed into the streets. She landed on her side, debris showering on the ground all around her. Her wound gave a sharp throb as the stitches stretched, and she sensed blood warming her shirt as she pushed herself into a sitting position. She was in a narrow side alley between two dachas, pressed against a wall with nowhere to go. Dust from the explosion filled the air. She could make out the shapes of people streaming by on the main road, hear the metal of swords somewhere near her.

Pain seared in her back; sweat broke out on her forehead as she wrangled her Affinity to concentrate on her reopened wound and force the blood to clot. Her vision swam in and out of focus, and there was a hollow ringing in her ears.

Through the blinding smoke that swirled in the alleyway, a shadow cut into view.

"There you are," came a voice, sounding very distant. A shadow fell over her; a pair of hands hauled her up by her elbows. "I've been looking for you."

The world focused, and it took her a moment to piece together what she was seeing.

"Hello, Witch," said Ramson.

He was panting, sweat slicking his hair, his cheeks scratched. A thin trickle of blood ran down his chin, but it was him, truly him, hazel eyes and long nose and crooked grin and all.

Behind them, the main road had grown quiet but for the sound of hooves and heels, fast approaching.

Ramson's hand tightened around hers. Pressing a finger to his lips, he led her through the settling dust. Ana barely caught a glimpse of riders and their horses before Ramson pulled her into an empty dacha.

Shutting the wooden door as best as he could behind him, Ramson guided her to the closest wall. Ana slumped against it gratefully. In the silence, she could hear their harried breaths rising and falling as one, feel the warmth of Ramson's hand on her hip, the other on her shoulder, holding her in place. It was dim and stark inside, the floor strewn with glass from a shattered window across from them. Sounds drifted in, and Ana could make out flashes of silver armor and white cloaks. They were surrounded; it was only a matter of time before they were discovered.

Ramson's eyes darted around the dacha, looking for ways out—but there was only the window and the door. "How's that Affinity of yours looking?" he whispered.

She tried to steady her breathing. "Even I can't beat an entire army of Whitecloaks, Ramson."

His gaze landed on her face momentarily, and he cocked a grin. "Must we always meet in the direst of situations?" he whispered, and she found her lips curling in a smile. His hand moved to stroke her waist, where her shirt was dark with blood. "What happened here?"

She shivered. He was probably trying to distract her as he came up with a plan, and she hated to admit that she was so exhausted, it was working. "The Redcloak meeting went poorly," she said with a grimace. "It became an assassination attempt."

Ramson's hands tightened around her. "Gods be damned," he swore. "I went looking for you that night."

"And I you." She chuckled, and then winced as her wound throbbed. "I guess we were meant to miss each other."

At that moment, something drew her attention—a sight that sent a deep chill plunging through her heart.

Outside, the procession of Imperial Patrols had come to a stop. At the far end of the street, a figure sat astride a valkryf, almost perfectly framed by the jagged edges of the broken window. Even from afar, her skin glowed an otherworldly golden sheen, her eyes the pale green of the Rushoyt Ice Lakes of the East, her hair glistening bright and black as liquid night.

Morganya, Empress of Cyrilia, looked like a Deity among humans as she faced her army beneath a sky of gathering storm clouds. She raised a hand in command, each gesture almost ethereal. Her lips moved, and an entire army sprang to action.

"They're going to interrogate each house," Ana said, flaring her Affinity.

Ramson drew his misericord. His profile cut sharp against the dimness as he crossed the room to the other side of the door, his muscles tensed as he shifted his stance. "You ready, Witch?"

Outside, there was a flurry of movement, the harsh sound of fists pounding down doors. It wasn't moments until she sensed a figure approaching.

The door creaked open.

Ana lashed out with her Affinity.

And froze.

The man outlined in the smoke and swirling shadows put a finger to his lips. The light from the broken window illuminated his pale prayer robes, and she caught the flash of his bald forehead, the whites of his eyes that bulged from his thin face. She was looking, Ana realized, into the face of the Palace alchemist, Pyetr Tetsyev.

He'd changed since they'd last seen each other over a moon ago, when he'd saved her life by feeding her a paralysis poison and declaring her dead in front of Morganya. His cheekbones were sunken, the dark bags beneath his eyes making them look even larger.

Still, she'd learned to see that face as that of her parents' murderer.

"*You,*" Ana hissed, but Tetsyev slipped inside, blocking the open doorway behind him. He raised his hands.

"Please, Kolst Pryntsessa, I don't have much time." His voice was as thin and breathless as she remembered it, but beneath it was a sense of quiet urgency.

"How did you find us?" Ramson demanded. He remained where he was, weapon half-raised.

"I have been searching for you," Tetsyev said, "but I can assure you that nobody else knows you're here, and I intend to keep it that way. Now, listen carefully. Once Morganya rounds up the non-Affinites in this area, she's going to move on. As soon as she does, you must take to the back alleys. Make for the docks."

Ana narrowed her eyes. "Why are you helping us?"

"Because I need your help in return." Tetsyev brought his hands together, as though in prayer. "I saved your life that night, because I knew the Empire would need you someday." The words sent shivers up Ana's spine. "The time has come. Morganya has purged the Salskoff Palace of dissenting councilmembers; the rest she continues to influence under her Affinity to the mind. Her Imperial Inquisition sweeps across the land."

"I know," Ana said quietly. Her voice rang hollow to her ears.

"Ah, but there is something you don't know. Something that could change the tides of this war, forever. Something that could change this *world*." His gaze focused on her with sharp intent. "You and I both know that Morganya is not interested in making a better, fairer world for Affinites. She uses that to justify her ruthless hunger for more power—always, more power." Tetsyev closed his eyes briefly, and Ana thought of what he'd told her once, that he and Morganya had known each other for a long, long time. "Her quest for power has led her to uncover a powerful artifact in Bregon."

Bregon. Ana froze, Shamaïra's words whispering to her. *For your path, Little Tigress, I see an ocean.*

"What kind of an artifact?" she breathed.

Tetsyev lowered his voice. "I have heard that it can bestow Affinities unto its bearer. In alchemy, we have blackstone, which inhibits Affinities. Yaegers can manipulate existing powers. But this thing . . . this artifact seems to *create* it."

"That's impossible." If what Tetsyev was saying was true, then it was a dangerous weapon—and it would make its user powerful beyond imagination.

Tetsyev shook his head. "It does not make sense, under the laws of alchemy. The source of power in this world is finite. To give an Affinity to someone who does not already possess it . . . to give someone *multiple* Affinities . . . it must come at a terrible cost." He paused, his eyes drifting to the window and then back to Ana. "You know the lengths she is willing to go in order to solidify her power." His eyes glittered, suddenly dark. "She is here to destroy anyone in her way."

From across the room, Ramson spoke. "Well, what is this artifact? Where in Bregon can we find it?"

"It seems to have existed for many years already, hidden away and unbeknownst to the world. But someone made her aware of it when she took the throne, and she has been pursuing it relentlessly since. I do not know it, but I have seen its creations, an experiment sent from Bregon consisting of an Affinite with multiple powers." He shut his eyes briefly, as though trying to block a memory out. "You *must* find a way to warn Bregon. If Morganya acquires it, then she will be unstoppable."

Through the half-open door, footsteps thundered past; voices drifted on the wind. Tetsyev paused to listen. "I must leave you now," he said. "I will inform them there was no one in this dacha."

"Wait." Ana swallowed, hating that she needed to ask anything of him. "If you have news of the Palace . . . are Kapitan Markov and Lieutenant Henryk safe?"

Tetsyev paused, looking over his shoulder. "They are," he said softly. "They await your orders upon your return."

Before she could say anything else, he turned and swept the door shut behind him. The last that Ana saw of him were his eyes, wide and pale, lingering on her.

Ramson crossed the room to her. He was breathing hard, his gaze narrowed as he glanced at the door where the alchemist had stood just seconds ago. "We're about to find out if Tetsyev was lying," he said, his grip tightening on his weapon. "Ready?"

Through the window, Ana watched Tetsyev hurry to Morganya's side in the distance. Their exchange seemed to last forever. The seconds trickled by. Ana held her breath.

At last, Tetsyev bowed and stepped aside.

Her relief was short-lived. Ana watched as Imperial Patrols brought several civilians toward where Morganya stood, lining them up in a row. She had a terrible premonition of what was to happen.

She could stop this. She was the only one who had the power to stop this.

She could try to end it all, right now.

"Ana." Ramson's voice cut through the silence, as though he could hear her thoughts.

"She's right there, Ramson." She clenched her fists as the wound in her back gave another sharp throb. "I could—"

"No." Ramson closed the gap between them. "There are probably a hundred Imperial Patrols here, Ana. I'll fight you if I must, but I'm not risking losing you again."

Her eyes stung—whether from his words, or from the scene outside, or both, she couldn't tell. In the distance, Morganya raised her hands, and the men and women before her fell to their knees. They held still, rigid under the control of Morganya's flesh Affinity. Desperately, Ana scanned their faces, her heart jumping to her throat as she searched for a glimpse of red hair, of gold ponytails. She hated herself for the slightest loosening of her stomach that followed; was it fair that she should feel relief that these were strangers instead of her friends? Was it fair that she was letting them die to save her own life? That promise that things would change once she was Empress had never seemed so distant in this moment, as Ana stood by and watched six lives await their deaths.

Ramson exhaled, a sharp sigh. In a sudden motion, he pulled Ana forward, and his arms closed tightly around her. He was comforting her, but also sending her a message: that if she wanted to get to Morganya, then first she had to go through him.

The civilians' pleas drifted to her through the open window as their empress raised her other hand and brought it down.

Flesh tore. Bodies fell. Blood warmed Ana's senses, growing white-hot against her Affinity as it snaked across the cobblestones. Ana held very still, but she forced herself to watch all of it, to remember this moment.

Morganya lifted her head, and this time, her words were faint but audible. "Let it be known what happens to traitors and oppressors who refuse to bow to me," she said, and swung her horse around. "Forward."

The images of the bodies and the blood seared into Ana's mind, remaining even after the hooves and footsteps of the Imperial Inquisition faded.

Ramson stepped back. His hands were tentative against her shoulders as he searched her face for clues.

Ana met his gaze. "One day, I'm going to kill her," she said quietly.

Ramson nodded. "I know." He held out his hands. "But for now, we need to get out of here."

The streets of Goldwater Port were empty when they emerged. Quietly, they slipped into the deserted back alleys, Ramson's steps quick and sure as he led them forward.

Overhead, the sky had darkened, the peaceful, golden glow of the morning having given way to the smell of a storm. The air grew thick with the stench of smoke. Gradually, there came screams and shouts, drifting to them on briny winds.

The port unfurled around the next corner: a scene of chaos in the impending tempest. Ramson led them to the edge of the water, where waves lashed at the stone quays, threatening to overturn ships and boats of all shapes and sizes. Abandoned fishing nets were strewn about the docks, wooden crates of the morning's catch splayed on the ground. People ran to and fro on the docks, crying and calling out to each other. Fishermen herded their families into their barges while those without boats stood on the jetties, begging for passage.

"Wait for me here," Ramson said, and turned and ran down the length of the jetty to a large black boat anchored at the end.

The sound of a horn rippled through the air. Ana's blood chilled as people streamed out from the streets facing the port, shouting and stumbling in their panic. From behind, herding them like a flock of sheep, emerged the Imperial Patrols.

They made a formidable line: steel-gray helmets and tomb-white cloaks, advancing with machinelike uniformity. And, in the midst of them all, their empress, sitting tall astride her valkryf, her face carved of stone as she watched atrocities unfold before her at the hands of her army.

A father, begging as they hauled away his wife and children, as they forced him to his knees on the dust-covered cobblestones and raised a sword to his neck.

The wife's howls, cut short as they plunged blades through her chest.

Fire, roaring to life at the coaxing of a Whitecloak's hands, licking up the wood-paneled walls of the house and consuming it in a roaring inferno.

"Ana!" A voice cried to her from several jetties down. Linn ran to her, weaving through the masses of people. Behind her, Kaïs followed, his double swords drawn. "Ana, we go!"

But Ana couldn't move. The screams of her people pulled her back, back, begging her to stay, to help. The winds were picking up speed, and the clouds churning across the sky, the air trembling with the promise of violence. She couldn't leave, not now, not when the townspeople of Goldwater Port—*her* people—were being slaughtered like cattle.

This couldn't be the right choice.

"Ana, please." Linn slowed as she approached, reaching out for Ana. Her hands caught Ana's wrists, grounding her. "You cannot win today. Live today, so that you may fight tomorrow."

Ana looked into her friend's face. She thought of Novo Mynsk, of the fire that had raged both outside and within her, of her certainty that fighting for her people's lives had been the right choice, right there, and right then.

Leaving now meant abandoning people who needed her help.

Leaving now meant returning to fight another day, to fight when she was more certain to win. It was the strategic choice. The choice of a leader.

"Ana," came another shout. Ramson stood at the end of the quay, motioning frantically at her. "This way!"

Ana gritted her teeth. Forced her feet to move. Then she was running with Linn and the yaeger at her back, the end of the wharf in sight, and Ramson was ushering them up a gangplank onto a ship.

"What in Amara's name are you doing?" shouted the sailor as they stormed past her. "You bought *one* ticket—"

"I'll pay you the rest later!" Ramson yelled. "Haul anchor and set sail, or we all die!"

Another explosion stained the clouds orange, as though they were swollen with blood. The sailor spewed a few profanities as the ship tilted hard under wind-tossed waves, the sails ballooning. The air filled with the sound of shattering glassware as bottles of liquor slid off the bar table in the center. "All right!" the sailor—presumably the ship's captain—yelled, slapping her hand on the wheel. "Haul anchor! And hang on to your hats!"

Ana threw herself against the wheel of the anchor windlass. Together, she, Ramson, and the yaeger turned it, and bit by bit, with great screeching sounds, the anchor chain rose.

"Anchor's up!" Ramson shouted. He ran to the captain's side, where she struggled against the wheel. With a grunt, he grasped it, and the ship began to move. "Linn, a little help, if you will!"

Linn stood, balancing easily on the rocking ship. A powerful gale rose, pushing against their sails in the direction of the open ocean.

The ship lurched forward like a fish plunging through waves. The ocean battered it, and Ana clung tightly to the mast as the deck tilted beneath her. Several times, the ship groaned so loudly that Ana thought it would splinter right beneath their feet.

And then, slowly, the rocking calmed. The winds began to die down, and soon, Goldwater Port was behind them, shrouded in the shadow of the looming storm.

The ship's captain slumped to the deck. "Amara's flames," she muttered, wiping her brow.

Ramson leaned against the wheel, breathing hard. Linn sat beneath the sails, stonelike but for the winds that stirred her hair and clothes. The yaeger stood by her side.

They all looked behind them at Goldwater Port, the city they had left to die. The docks grew smaller, and the once-colorful houses had drained gray in the storm and soot. Fires raged farther within the city, reflected red upon a sky that seemed to weep blood.

The books Ana had read in her childhood, of the greatest rulers of history and legends, were all tales of warriors and heroines who fought against evil and triumphed.

None of the stories, she realized, sang of empresses who ran from their falling kingdoms. Who chose to leave behind a world of bloodshed to survive.

Some rulers' reigns were forged with steel, some with gold, and some with might.

And mine, Ana thought, closing her eyes. *Mine is forged by blood.*

18

There was a time in her life when she'd never thought she would see the open ocean again. Or at least, Linn thought, not an ocean so beautiful.

The seas had calmed, the storm clouds having given way to a periwinkle twilight that blinked into existence the light of a thousand stars. The moon hung low and round before them, carving a silver streak on the gently lapping waves. The air was cool and fresh, the winds out here salt-tanged.

Ramson and the sailor named Daya spoke at the wheel, arguing over the technicalities of the ship. Their voices tided over Linn.

In front of her, standing at the stern, was Kaïs.

His dark hair billowed lightly in the breeze, sweeping past the dirt and blood and burn marks on his face. He'd gotten those when he'd shielded her from the explosion, back at Goldwater Port.

As though sensing her gaze on him, he shifted to look at her. The silver in his eyes looked like smoke, like ghosts.

And, abruptly, he turned away.

Linn sensed someone come up behind her. Fingers, small but strong, closed over her shoulder.

"I didn't know if I'd be able to find you," Ana said, leaning against the guardrail next to her. She sounded weary, her voice so soft.

Gently, Linn slipped her hand into her friend's and squeezed. "Our paths are irrevocably crossed," she said. "It seems the fates looked upon us favorably."

Ana squeezed back. "Thank you," she whispered, closing her eyes. "For not giving up on me."

It was the first chance Linn had to look at her friend up close. It was as though, in the past moon, Ana had aged a year. Her cheekbones jutted sharper and there were dark smudges beneath her eyes. What Linn wouldn't forget, though, was the haunted look in her gaze.

Those eyes flitted open, and Linn saw that behind the shadows smoldered a fire.

"How did you and . . ." Ana's expression darkened as she glanced at Kaïs.

"Kaïs," Linn said, and told Ana the story of their journey from the prison.

Ana listened to Linn's story with a crease between her brows. When Linn finished, she turned her gaze to Kaïs and said, "He took someone very dear to me." So few words, with so much weight. It was a story for another time. "You trust him?"

Linn hesitated. There was still so much left to untangle between her and that silent warrior, beginning with her own distrust and prejudice against soldiers like him. All this time, though, he had been the one saving her. "I want to" was all that she could offer. She thought of the steadiness to his grip as they'd leapt from the tower on the Wailing Cliffs, of how he'd offered her his cloak on the mountain. The way his face had filled with sadness when he'd spoken of his mother.

"He saved my life," Linn continued. "More than once." Three times. She'd counted. "He tells me he is running from the Empress, too; that he searches for his mother, and that he wishes to join your ranks. Give him a chance. Please."

Ana's eyes narrowed, and Linn saw them flick to Kaïs again, considering. A muscle twitched in her jaw.

And then the flames, the anger went out. Ana exhaled. "All right. He stays with us. But we tell him nothing—not until he proves to us that he is trustworthy. We don't know if he's working with the enemy."

In a low voice, Ana began to tell Linn of the few weeks they'd spent apart, of the pieces of information she and Ramson had come across. Linn listened in part fascination, part horror, as Ana recounted Tetsyev's appearance back at Goldwater Port, of Morganya's plan to create Affinities, and of the rumored weapon in Bregon.

The words brought a memory back, one that she'd wanted to bury. Even thinking about it made her shudder. "During our travels together, we saw something." Linn described the blackstone wagon, the man with the two Affinities, the way the Whitecloaks had lost control of him and murdered him. "Kaïs could help us," she finished. "He knows more about the Imperial Patrols than any of us."

Ana's face had gone pale. "So it's true," she muttered. "This is important. We need to talk with Ramson." She paused, and her voice became gentle. In an instant, it was as though she'd switched from commander to friend—as though there were glimmers of two girls inside her, struggling to find a balance. "I'm sorry, Linn. I haven't yet asked you what you want." There was a vulnerability to her voice that Linn had seldom heard. "Are you still with me in this fight?"

The chaos and destruction at Goldwater Port haunted Linn, the screams and pleas of helpless civilians lingering in her mind. She shivered when she remembered that man with Affinities to ice and fire, his moans cut short by the fall of a sword, the flash of a silver helmet.

Morganya, Linn understood, had promised to bring justice to Affinites, to the oppressed, to those wronged by the system.

Yet what Linn had seen that day, a scene of Imperial Patrols overpowering and hurting an Affinite, was utterly familiar. It held echoes of the memories that had been carved into her bones, of when she'd landed on the Empire's icy shores and begged for help from the soldiers bearing Cyrilia's Imperial insignia—only they had turned away.

Nothing had changed with Morganya's new regime.

Looking into the ever-fierce eyes of her friend, Linn found that she'd known the answer all along. She would fight, for every Affinite and civilian who had felt the helplessness and terror she once had; for every child who had lost their innocence in that shadow war . . . and for every sister who had lost a brother to the traffickers.

Linn leaned forward. "I am with you." Her voice rang steady and clear. "I would not be anywhere else."

Ana exhaled, as though she had been holding a long breath. "And after all this, my friend?" she said gently. "What do you want after all this?"

Linn wasn't sure she could answer that question herself. The ship pulled them west, toward Bregon. Beyond that, she knew, beyond the expanse of sea that made up the Jade Trail, was the Kemeiran Empire.

It suddenly hit her that she could very well be looking at the same sky, the same stars, as Ama-ka. And someday, *someday,* that same sky would no longer be unreachable, and she would watch the sun rise with Ama-ka's hand in hers, the creak of their bamboo hammock stirring in the winds between the Kemeiran cypresses.

Perhaps that was why she was here.

"I want to go home," she found herself saying, the words drifting from her lips as though the winds had stolen them from her breath.

Linn looked at the ocean, and for the first time in a long time, it opened before her, a stretch of possibility.

19

Night had fallen, surprisingly quickly and peacefully. They were far enough out now that there was nothing but ocean on all sides, reflecting the sky like a rippling mirror. Ramson had always loved how the stars were clearer out at sea.

After going through the ship's mechanics, he and Daya had been relieved to find that the Black Barge had sustained no major damage. There were some burn marks along the hull, and pieces of debris had smashed into the deck, but, as Daya had proclaimed, slapping her hand on the bar counter, there wasn't much eight crates of alcohol couldn't fix.

Ramson had left her to count stock and supplies in the hold of the ship.

The Black Barge was a generously sized cutter, double-masted and installed with makeshift booths from its now-bygone days as a floating bar. Ramson swiped an aluminum tankard—the glassware was all broken—from the counter, selected a remaining bottle of whiskey, and leaned against the guardrail.

He drew a deep breath, and it hit him suddenly—the rocking boat, the star-strewn sky, and the whispering waters—it was something he hadn't known since he'd been twelve years old and had turned his back on Bregon for what he'd thought was forever.

He'd been running all these years, and now he was *still* chasing after the ghosts of his past—for what? He took a swig from his tankard, the liquor searing down his throat. He couldn't look to the future when his past was still a part of him, haunting him every day.

Once he ended this saga with Alaric Kerlan, he would be free to live as he wished. Go after whatever he wanted.

He wanted . . . he wanted—

"I've been looking for you."

Ramson spun, the liquor in his cup splashing. Ana stood before him. He was struck by how she managed to look imperious even with her clothes disheveled and soot streaked across her face. She held one hand near her back, where a dark stain blotted her shirt. Daya had found bandages for her on board the ship, and she'd managed to wrap up her wound. Gingerly, she leaned herself against the railing next to him.

It was the first time he'd gotten a close look at her since the night they'd parted ways in Novo Mynsk. The silver of the moon softened the new sharpness to her features, coating the fall of her hair, the curve of her lashes.

Ramson knew the look in her eyes. He knew it so well, in the form of a pale-skinned boy with crow-black hair.

It was guilt. Earlier, she'd slumped against the guardrail as they sailed away, looking blankly at the burning city until the sea swallowed it.

He leaned toward her, aware of every subtle shift of her muscles. "Well, I'm here."

They were silent for a few moments, the air between them heavy with words unspoken.

At last, Ana said quietly, "Shamaïra warned me about this, in a way." She pressed a hand to her chest. "My heart tells me I should be back there, fighting with my people—yet my mind tells me this is where I must be."

Ramson wanted to hold her and tell her that everything was going to be fine. That might have been kinder, but it would also be a lie—and he had told too many of those in his lifetime. Instead, he raked a hand through his hair and broke the news to her. "They took her. The Whitecloaks—they took Shamaïra. I went to her dacha to find you, but you weren't there."

Her knuckles turned white against the railing. "Those bastards."

"I overheard them talking," he continued. "Morganya wants Shamaïra—which is a good thing. It means she'll keep her alive."

Ana shut her eyes. Slowly, she nodded. "We're going to get her out of there. As soon as I'm in Bregon, I'll write to Yuri. He loves Shamaïra as much as I." She hesitated, and then her expression crumbled. "It's all my fault, Ramson. Shamaïra saved me the night of the Inquisition in Novo Mynsk. The Whitecloaks must have tracked me to her house, and . . ." Her voice broke into a whisper. "If something happens to her . . . I don't know if I could ever forgive myself."

Standing by her side against the railing, Ramson might have understood a little of how she felt: the guilt of putting the ones you loved in harm's way, and being powerless to do anything about it. "Shamaïra seemed . . . prepared," he said slowly, the words tasting callous on his tongue. "I found a painting in her dacha—a painting of the ocean. It led me back to you."

"She seemed prepared?" Ana repeated. She looked pensive, that crease appearing between her eyebrows as it did whenever she was deep in thought. "Shamaïra told me something. She said that for my path, she saw an ocean."

"Very precise of her." His tone was light, the joke quiet.

"I'm starting to think . . ." Ana hesitated. "I'm starting to think there's a reason behind it. The weapon Tetsyev mentioned—the one he said could replicate Affinities . . . I think he was telling the truth. Linn told me she *saw* a prisoner with the Imperial Inquisition—a man with *two* Affinities." She paused. "But why would the weapon be in Bregon?"

Bregon.

Hope sparked a small flame in him, and suddenly, his future unfolded like the pages of a storybook. A future in which his path and hers might lead to the same destination.

"There is something else," he said, and he told her everything he had found out about Alaric Kerlan and his new trafficking scheme with Bregon. She listened to him with a frown, chewing on her lip. "I'm going to find him and put an end to all this," Ramson finished.

"But you don't know who the buying party in Bregon is?" Ana prompted.

"That's what I'm going to find out," Ramson replied. "The Bregonian Kingdom has never shown interest toward the magen—our term for Affinites. It must be a black market activity."

Ana turned to him. "We should work with the Bregonian government."

"No." He spoke too fast, the word tumbling from him in panic.

"Why not? I've been thinking about it. With the Redcloaks'"—she hesitated for a brief moment—"withdrawal, I need to think of other possible alliances. Bregon would be a good place to start. If I extend the offer of an alliance with their leadership—"

"No," Ramson repeated. His tankard clanked loudly against the guardrail.

Ana raised her eyebrows. "No?"

He fumbled, his heartbeat quickening in his chest. "The Bregonian leadership will never agree to negotiate with you." His voice sounded hollow, even to his own ears.

She swept her eyes to the distant skyline, and for a moment, her pupils flashed red. "I'll ask to speak to the King." A thoughtful expression crossed her face. "I'll warn the Bregonian government about Morganya's pursuit of this artifact and propose a strategic alliance with them to protect it. They might even agree to a counterattack against her. They have the most powerful Navy in the world, after all."

Ramson put a hand on her shoulder, turning her to face him. "Ana, I can see you're trying to strategize, but this isn't going to work."

He regretted the words as soon as he said them. Ana met his gaze, and he noted the jut to her chin, the spark of challenge in her eyes. "Why not?"

A flash of alder trees, a cold shoulder, a shadowed face.

Tell her the truth, pressed a voice. *Tell her whose son you are.*

But the thought of her knowing who he was—who he *really* was, down to the core of his childhood and those whispers of *packsaddle son* and *bastard*—sent a wild bout of panic through him.

At his hesitation, she narrowed her eyes. "Ramson," she said, "you have to promise me you won't hide anything from me anymore. We're in this together."

He balked. He knew, from experience, that expectations of honor from him would only lead to disappointment. "I don't make promises, Ana," he replied. "That way I don't have to break them."

She fixed him with an imperious glare. "Fine."

"Look, you do whatever you want with whoever you want," Ramson found himself saying. "I'm going to track down Alaric Kerlan and find out what he's doing trafficking Affinites to Bregon."

"I've always done whatever I want," she replied. The wind swept her hair back, and her expression shifted, her smile turning dagger-sharp. Ramson began to draw back, but her hand darted out, fingers coiling around the fabric of his shirt, rooting him in place. "But while I have you here on this ship, you're going to help me with *whatever* I need." She tilted her head. "Did you think I forgot where you were from, Ramson 'Quicktongue'? Or should I say . . . Bregonian Navy defector?"

Ramson's thoughts scattered like leaves in the wind.

"You're going to tell me everything you know about Bregon," Ana said. "When we get there, you go after Alaric Kerlan, and I'll make for the Blue Fort." She released him and held out her hand. "Well? Do we have a Trade, con man?"

It was a good solution, Ramson had to admit as he considered. He would help her get as close to the Blue Fort as he could, and then he would split off to take care of his business with Kerlan. This way, he would never have to return to the place he had run from all those years ago, and she would never learn the truth of who he was.

He nodded. "All right. Trade up."

Her palm was warm in his as they shook, and he realized that this would be the first deal he made with her in good conscience, one that he would hold true to his word. No false promises, no broken expectations. And when he finished what he was after in Bregon, he would be free to live his life far, far away. He would turn his back, once and for all, on this strange chapter of a story he'd never meant to play in, and a princess he'd never meant to fall for.

20

By the time Ana and Ramson returned to the main section of the deck, lamps were lit and a meal of tinned food had been laid out across the bar counter. The captain of the ship, Ana learned, was a sailor from the Crown of Kusutri: a girl several years older than Ramson, quick of smiles and even quicker of wit. Her eyes widened slightly when Ramson introduced Ana.

"So you're the one they claim will save that empire," Daya said, unchaining a small knife from her belt. She stuck it into a can of tinned sardines and gave a woeful sigh. "The Red Tigress. I'll have to apologize for the food on this ship—I wasn't told we were having more guests." She shot a nasty look at Ramson, who was digging into a chunk of hard bread slathered over with beet puree.

Ana was about to accept the sardine sandwich when she sensed two bodies approaching.

Linn sat down at the counter; following closely behind was the yaeger. He stopped when Ana stood.

Linn gave Ana a panicked look. "Ana," she said softly.

Ana gestured at the bar top before them. "You can have a seat."

The yaeger hesitated, then stepped into the warm circle of lamplight.

He looked exactly as she remembered: tall and dark-haired and chiseled. Now, however, his skin bore a crisscross of new scars and blooming bruises; his left cheek had turned an ugly red from a burn. Dressed in a plain gray tunic and breeches and without the adornment of his bright white cloak, he was still as lethal as he had been back in Kyrov.

She couldn't look at him without memories and a familiar anger stirring inside her. He was a part of the reason May had been captured, forced into an indentured contract, then killed. Ana had had to bury her friend deep in the earth, shutting the bright turquoise eyes of a girl who had seen yet so little of the world and was owed so much. And now May was still gone, and he was still here, standing right before her.

Ana stepped forward. Facing him, addressing him, went against every instinct in her body.

It was the yaeger, though, who spoke first. "I understand if you want to kill me." His voice was a quiet bass, barely audible over the splash of waves and the creak of the ship's hull. "But I have my reasons for everything."

"I'd kill you if it could bring May back," Ana retorted without missing a beat. Her voice was rough, harsher than she'd intended, if only to cover the ache of tears at the back of her throat. "You're only alive because of the mercy my friend showed you." She sensed Linn flinch. "You'll have to earn it, with me."

The yaeger's face was smooth, unreadable. "After Morganya's coup, I stayed with the Imperial Patrols because I thought they would protect Affinites," he said. "But the

Empress—Morganya—she's slaughtering those who choose to leave her side. Even Affinites who simply wish to live in peace. You saw her troops back there.

"I was trapped as a soldier, with no way out. I wanted to reach the rebellion, and you were the only way for me to do that."

His words struck Ana as true, ringing echoes of something else he had told her, moons ago.

In this empire, if I am not the hunter, then I become the hunted.

"Let me help you," the yaeger continued, his eyes now fixed intently on Linn. "I can give you information on Morganya's plans." He shifted his gaze back to Ana. "I can train you to wield your Affinity better. I can fight with you. All I ask is that you give me a chance."

She knew it was the more strategic move to give him a chance and take whatever information she could from him, but all her instincts screamed against it. She couldn't even look at him without seeing the glare of the sun reflecting off his cloak in the Vyntr'makt that day. Without remembering May, standing in the middle of the square, holding up her small hand. *You will not hurt her.*

It wasn't fair. It wasn't fair that he was here, alive and well, when May was not. She didn't want to give him a chance, when he hadn't given one to May.

There was the scrape of a chair, and Ramson stood. His eyes flicked to hers and he gave her a nod, almost imperceptible. She could almost hear his voice in her head, whispering for her to calm down, to think logically.

Ramson prowled forward to face the yaeger. They were almost the same height, but Ramson's gait, the small smile on his face, the insouciant tilt to his head, revealed who was in control.

"We'll give you a chance," Ramson said, folding his arms in front of his chest. "You can start by telling us everything you know."

They spoke long into the night, Kaïs recounting everything Morganya had done since she'd taken the throne. Most of it was information Ana already knew; some revelations twisted her stomach.

"She murdered children." The yaeger's voice had grown quiet. "She extorts the weak and the helpless. She separates families, holding them hostage in order to get what she wants." The cool front Kaïs had put up fell away, leaving behind something so raw, so desperate.

"And what about the Affinites the Imperial Inquisition is kidnapping?" Ramson leaned against the bar, drink in hand. Behind him, Daya held a bottle of amber-colored liquor, listening intently. "Heard anything about that?"

Confusion crossed Kaïs's features. "Do you mean the Affinites she has conscripted into her army?"

"And the man with the two Affinities," Ana cut in, her irritation growing. "What do you know about that?"

He shook his head. "I only saw what Linn saw. I don't know anything else about it. I *felt* it, though—that he had two Affinities, warring inside him."

Frustration pinched at Ana. The yaeger seemed to know nothing more than what they already knew.

Ramson caught her eye. He tilted his head, and Ana followed, gesturing at Linn to do the same. They left Kaïs with Daya, who was rearranging the supplies beneath the counter.

"Nothing new that we didn't know," Ramson said when they were out of earshot. He ran a hand through his hair.

"Do you think he's hiding something?" Ana asked.

To her surprise, it was Linn who spoke. "I think he is telling the truth," she said quietly. "When we saw that blackstone wagon, he looked . . . scared." She swallowed. "Whatever they did to that Affinite, I think he is as afraid of it as we are."

"We tell him nothing more," Ramson said. "Especially not about how that Affinite you saw could relate to Morganya's artifact."

They slept that night in the cabins belowdecks, curled up on cold pallets dusty from disuse and tucked under moth-eaten blankets. Ana dreamt of fire, of shapes and shadows in smoke.

She awoke to patches of sunlight warming her face. The air was warm when she emerged on the deck, the sea stretching turquoise and flecked with caps of white everywhere she looked. Voices drifted to her on the wind, from the bar.

She found Ramson and Daya hunched over a yellowing map at the counter, plates of bliny and cheese and various other tins of food set out. A bit farther away, Linn was balanced impeccably on the bowsprit, her face tilted to the sun, her hair billowing in the breeze. A few white-tipped blueswallows were circling the air around her, and she was sending little puffs of wind into their midst. The blueswallows would spin up like tiny feathered balls before diving down again, their chirps mixing with Linn's quiet laughter. Ana watched for a few moments, her lips curving in a smile. Moments like these were moments when she remembered what a better world might look like, what kind of an after she fought for.

"One fortnight to Bregon," Ramson announced when she joined them. "That means you have one fortnight to learn everything you can from me."

Ana took a piece of bliny. It was cold, but delicious. "And two weeks to come up with a plan. Is that caviar?"

"Good thing we had some left over from when this was still a pub," Daya said cheerfully. "Figured everyone could use a treat to celebrate our first day here."

Ramson leaned into Ana. "I just paid her," he muttered.

"And for good reason, you lying son of a pig," Daya snapped, her sunny disposition vanishing instantly. "You never mentioned guests in our original deal, not to mention—" She began to gesture at Ana, but her eyes flicked up and the playfulness vanished from her gaze.

When footsteps sounded behind them and a shadow fell over them, Ana saw why.

Kaïs had appeared. He stood between the steps to the cabins in the hold and the bar. Without his two swords, he suddenly looked much younger than the imposing Patrol figure that had been seared into her mind since they'd met. The sun warmed his face, lending a shine to his oil-black hair, and there was more of a spring to his step.

He surveyed them awkwardly for several moments. Then he stepped forward and cleared his throat. "Let me help you," he said, and his gaze landed on Ana. "Let me train your Affinity with you."

Ana was about to snap back a retort—*I don't need your*

help—when she felt a hand touch her wrist. Ramson leaned over the bar top and gave her a meaningful look.

Use your enemies.

"You have a crude control over your Affinity," Kaïs continued, and she knew they both thought of the incident at Kyrov's Vyntr'makt, when she'd seized his blood in fury and almost killed him. "There is much that you can do, with an Affinity like yours. Power is a double-edged sword. In the right hands, it is a shield of valor and honor, used for saving lives and for mercy. In the wrong hands, it is a weapon of destruction, used for suffering and killing."

Ana thought of Morganya, of how eerily similar their Affinities were. One, an Affinity to flesh and mind; the other, an Affinity to blood. They held power over the very makeup of human bodies.

Kaïs's eyes bore into hers. "I can teach you to use it *for* people," he said. "I can teach you to heal. I can teach you to draw away pain. I can teach you to fight for those you seek to protect."

It was as though he'd reached into her and drawn out her deepest desires, or heard her most fervent prayers over many long nights. Papa's convulsing body, May's blank eyes, Luka's fading smile—all those deaths she'd blamed on herself, for not being able to save them when she alone had control over their blood. How many times had she wished to heal instead of hurt, to save instead of kill?

Luka's words stirred in her mind. *Your Affinity does not define you. What defines you is how you choose to wield it.*

The decision lay there, before her.

"All right," she said. "Teach me."

21

The winters in Southern Cyrilia had always been milder than those up north. Yet this year, snow fell like ashes.

Or perhaps they *were* ashes, Shamaïra thought as she canted her head to skies swollen with gray clouds.

They had blindfolded her and locked her in the back of a blackstone wagon for days. The soldiers had slipped bowls of cold borscht and hardened bread through the barred window of her moving prison. She'd counted six, seven days, before the wagon had stopped.

The doors were flung open.

The light was blinding at first, the grip of hands hard against her bones as she was escorted out. She was dizzy from the weight of blackstone binding her wrists and ankles, but Shamaïra stood straight and proud.

They were in a Southern Cyrilian town, marked by the colors of the houses and winding streets, messy compared to the straight, wide roads of northern towns. The air tasted of sea.

Yet what had once been a vibrant, thriving city had turned to a smoldering ruin of a town. The wind carried an acrid smell and the bitterness of death. The dachas around them had burned black. As far as the eye could see, smoke snaked toward the sky in jagged coils.

A long procession of Imperial Patrols lined the street before her. They seemed to be waiting. Shamaïra didn't even bother trying to reach her Affinity, her connection to the Brother and the Sister and the flow of Time. The blackstone manacles chafed unbearably cold against her skin.

And then, an eerie stillness seemed to fall upon the world around them. Far down the line of Whitecloaks, between the swirls of gray dotting the sky, emerged a shadow. She was outlined in a colorless shade of white, her hair as black as liquid night against ruby-red lips. The wind held its breath and the falling snow seemed to part for her as she rode her horse, seeming to cleave through the two lines of her army as though she were parting waves.

The Whitecloak escorting Shamaïra shoved her roughly to her knees. "Pay your respects, old Nandjian fortune-teller," he barked.

Shamaïra held her head high. Yet as the figure approached, fear stretched its long claws into her heart.

The Glorious Empress of Cyrilia reined her horse and descended with a sweep of her cloak. By Shamaïra's side, all Whitecloaks had sunk to their knees, their heads bowed low, their hands clasped in fists over their chests.

Morganya's eyes swept over them—and locked on Shamaïra. She smiled.

Up close, she seemed to be carved in monochrome like a statue, her beauty even more terrible. And her eyes—Shamaïra had never seen such cold eyes. She thought of the paintings of the cold, deathly still Silent Sea of the North.

Morganya turned and walked into the dacha closest to them. The two Whitecloaks escorting Shamaïra sprang to their feet and hauled her forward. They stepped through a shattered storefront.

The inside looked like a ravaged restaurant. Debris was strewn across wooden floorboards, along with remnants of food. Booths stood silent and empty, tablecloths fluttering in a ghostly wind, faded yellow patterns layered thick with dust.

There was movement from the back of the restaurant. A man emerged. He wore a silvery fur cloak, his black hair parted over a long, pale face. Most disturbing were his hands: long-fingered and limp, like a monstrous, colorless creature. "Kolst Imperatorya," he murmured, his voice soft and slippery, slithering around Shamaïra like a serpent.

Shamaïra's fists clenched tighter. The winds that twined around her seemed to whisper danger. *Deities give me strength,* she thought, steeling herself.

The Empress turned, her gaze hooking into Shamaïra like claws. "Unlock her," she commanded, her voice cutting like steel.

With a few clicks of keys, the manacles fell away, and it felt as though she were breathing again for the first time. Sound, color, light rushed through her in an endless river of Time, the whispers of the Brother and Sister filling the well of her soul again. She saw ghosts of the past flitting through the dacha: among them, a boy with sleek red hair that caught the burnish of lamplight.

She knew that boy.

Shamaïra's knees almost buckled. This was Yuri's home.

"Do you know why you are here, fortune-teller?" The Empress's voice caressed her like a terrible lullaby, rooting her to the present.

"It does not particularly matter to me," Shamaïra rasped, her voice gravelly from days of abandon. "I shall give you nothing."

The Empress gave her a lovely smile. She was impossibly beautiful, as they all said, and Shamaïra wondered sadly what part of her journey had gone wrong. Glimpses of her past swirled like shadows behind her; whispers and shouts of abuse. She had been born into darkness, into hatred and fear, and she had chosen that path.

A second face came to Shamaïra: fierce brown eyes beneath the shadow of a hood. She knew another, she thought, who'd been born into the same circumstances.

And that girl had chosen light.

"This was the home of a leader of the rebels," Morganya said. "Two days ago, they caught wind of my Imperial Inquisition and fled. I want you, fortune-teller, to find out where they went. Trace them, with your Affinity." She gave a delicate pause and stretched out a hand. A poster dangled between her fingers: wet and smudged from snow and soot. But Shamaïra instantly recognized the figure painted on it, the curve of her crimson cloak. "I want you," Morganya continued, her voice soft and dangerous, "to find *her*."

Hope lit a fierce fire in Shamaïra's heart. Ana had gotten away.

"I cannot track down a person without their possessions," she replied, her words cut-and-dried. "More importantly, I simply won't."

Morganya's eyes bore into hers. "Bring the mother," she said.

Movement from the Whitecloaks stationed at the door and all around the restaurant; the sound of something being dragged, and a thump.

Shamaïra looked down and felt her face drain of color.

A body lay in front of her, but it wasn't the corpse that she saw. It was the past: a woman, folding a young girl into her arms, her face crinkled with laughter, her fire-red hair tucked in a bun. The same woman, cooking in the kitchen, splotches of soups and sauces dotting her faded linen kirtle.

The scene shifted, and the woman was carrying Yuri in her arms and tucking him gently in the back of a small wagon, beneath bags of beets and potatoes. She was crying as she kissed her daughter over and over again, and then the wagon was pulling away and she was running after them, following for as long as she could until her old legs gave out.

Another scene, and she stood amid rubble, broom clutched in hand, frozen as her door creaked open and two men entered her house. One wore a pale white outfit and bore a tear mark on his cheek; the other was made of shadows and long, white hands.

Shamaïra cut off the visions. She didn't need to continue to know how this story ended. "You sicken me," she growled.

Morganya had been watching her closely, her eyes narrowed in cunning. She let out a laugh. "Oh, we're just getting started." She spun, spreading her arms. "Now that Goldwater Port belongs to me, I'm going to root out the rest of these rebels and stamp out the rebellion once and for all. The streets will flow crimson with their blood." She smiled at Shamaïra. "Are you not proud to have a chance to serve your empire? To establish the foundation of a new regime?"

Shamaïra looked the Empress in the eyes. "I would rather die," she said calmly.

Morganya's smile stretched. Shamaïra suddenly felt her body seize, as though an invisible force had gripped her and frozen her in place. She couldn't move, couldn't turn away, as Morganya stepped before her and gripped her chin with a hand. Her fingers were ice-cold.

"Such lovely eyes," she murmured. "A very rare color. Blue, like the coldest of glaciers. Like the hottest of flames." She leaned in. "Do you have any family members, meya dama?"

Shamaïra stopped breathing.

"A . . . son, perhaps? Taken to Cyrilia at a very young age?" Twisted pleasure sparked in Morganya's eyes. "We keep extremely thorough records of all our recruits in the Imperial Patrol, meya dama, and I happened to come across some very interesting information recently on a young man who defected. Our records indicate that he is a Nandjian migrant, and he had a mother at the time of his conscription. He has the most beautiful blue eyes . . . quite like yours."

Shamaïra was a woman of flames, her words rapid-fire, her spirit like gunpowder. But this time, when she opened her mouth, no words would come. All that existed was a sickening feeling of cold, of ice, slipping down her throat and spreading through her veins.

"In fact, we've received reports that he was spotted here, several days ago. I've asked my forces to keep an eye out for him." She leaned forward, bending her face close to Shamaïra's. "Surely," Morganya whispered, "we wouldn't want something to happen to him."

"You lie." Despite everything, Shamaïra found that she was trembling.

Morganya looked at her a moment longer before straightening. "The Deities have looked upon you today, dama Shamaïra," she said, clasping her hands behind her back. "I have grand plans for a rare Affinity like yours, which means I shall need you alive for a while longer. But I have other methods of persuasion. Vladimir?"

The black-haired man stepped forward, his smile stretching, and Shamaïra suddenly realized why he looked so familiar. She'd seen that face on a dozen different posters, disseminated throughout Cyrilia.

Konsultant Imperator, she thought, and her head spun.

"One more chance, meya dama." The Imperial Consultant held up a finger, his expression mocking. "Tell us where the rebels are, and where the Red Tigress hides."

Shamaïra had always considered herself brave. She'd traversed the Aramabi Desert by herself with Kaïs almost full-grown in her belly. She'd crossed the Dzhyvekha Mountains with nothing but a globefire and a dagger in search of her son. She'd survived, a lone woman without her husband in a world where that was almost sure to mean doom.

But she could not stop her voice from shaking as she whispered, "You'll never find them."

The Imperial Consultant sighed. "Do you know what my Affinity is to, dama Shamaïra? No, you wouldn't be able to guess—it's quite a special one." He stepped forward, so close that she could see the darkness in his pupils, yawning wide as an abyss. "My Affinity . . . is to fear."

And then he reached out with those long, pale hands of his and clasped them over her cheeks, the shadows in his eyes morphing into monsters, growing and stretching until they turned into nightmares that swallowed her whole, and Shamaïra could do nothing but scream and scream.

22

Ana set about trying to learn everything she could about the Kingdom of Bregon, from its government structure to its society, people, and culture.

And with Ramson as the teacher, this made for some very lively learning sessions.

"If you're going to approach the Bregonian government, the first thing you have to know is who's in charge," Ramson began. He spread a piece of worn parchment before him. "On paper, we are a monarchy."

"It's more complicated than that," Ana pointed out.

Ramson gave her a flat look. "I've literally spoken two sentences, and you're already interrupting."

Sitting between them, Linn hid a smile behind her hands. Ana glared back at him. "I was just trying to clarify some nuances," she said. "I've studied Bregonian government and history."

Ramson shoved the parchment toward her. "Then why don't you teach?"

"I will." Ana took the charcoal pencil from him and began to draw out a diagram, filling in blanks as she spoke. "Nearly ten years ago, King Garan Rennaron died, leaving his young son to rule under the direct guidance of the Queen Regent Arsholla Rennaron. King Darias Rennaron should be about fourteen years old now, making him a young but capable ruler." She looked up.

Ramson raised an eyebrow. "Is that all?"

"Well, yes, if you're speaking of the leadership and decision makers."

Ramson gave her a smug look. "There's a lot more to the picture. Allow me." He leaned forward and plucked the charcoal pencil from her fingers, then crossed out the box with the name of the King that Ana had written. "The Bregonian monarchy works on a supposed system of checks and balances. The King—and in our case, Queen Regent—is at the head of the government, but his policies and deals must pass the government's approval. This was a law implemented by the government itself, to limit the power of the Queen Regent at the time and distribute it among the different courts."

"Checks and balances," Ana said quietly, thinking for some reason of Yuri and Aleksey and their skepticism toward the monarchy.

"Precisely." Ramson began to draw out a diagram with his pencil, his strokes swift and precise. "This brings me to my point: You'll want to focus your efforts on the government of Bregon as well. King Darias and the Queen Regent Arsholla can't pass any laws by themselves; Bregonian law now states that any new decision must come to a vote." He tapped the parchment. "So: the Three Courts. As you probably know, we have the Sky"—he drew a box with a figure of an eagle—"the Earth"—a stallion—"and the Sea"—a seadragon. "These represent our Three Gods and are meant to uphold a system of checks and balances to prevent any one Court from becoming too powerful." Ramson looked up. "That's all a lie."

Ana frowned. "Your faith in your government is inspiring."

"Oh, look—she can make jokes," Ramson retorted, and Linn ducked her head to hide her laughter. He tapped the parchment, which had blossomed into a full-blown chart. "The Sky Court oversees Bregon's spiritual needs: education and religion, governance structure. The Earth Court is responsible for agriculture and infrastructure and the like. And the Sea Court directs the Navy and trade.

"Bregon relies heavily on its military and its seafaring prowess to establish its strength. That means the Navy holds huge sway in politics and government. Which brings me to . . . the Admiral of the Navy, who also heads the Sea Court." Ramson's expression had grown carefully blank. He drew a figurehead on top of the Sea Court's box. "With the Sea Court's overwhelming power in Bregon's government and a monarch heavily restricted by a system of checks and balances, that makes the Admiral the most powerful man in Bregon after the King."

The charcoal pencil dropped from his hand; he shoved the diagram to Ana and stood. "You'll need to win him over, too, if you want any form of an alliance."

Ana studied the sketch of the figurehead. "What do you know about him?"

"Nothing," Ramson replied. "I've been away from Bregon for seven years, Ana. What I'm telling you is from what I learned as a Navy recruit."

"From back in the days, then," she prompted. "You must have crossed paths with him, or heard things about him?"

Ramson's face was inscrutable. "I didn't know him back then," he said, and moved on to the structure of the Blue Fort.

Ana paid particular attention to Ramson's lessons on Affinites in Bregon. The magen existed in Bregon, but on a very different level from Cyrilia. They were treated no differently than regular civilians, living in harmony with their communities and towns and often contributing more due to the unique magek they wielded.

Ana felt her stomach tighten at this, and she thought of her own empire, of how corrupt its treatment of Affinites had become. "How is it possible," she mused, "to create a society of equality between Affinites and non-Affinites?"

Ramson frowned, considering. "I *suppose,*" he said carefully, examining his sketches of Bregonian geography and the diagram of the Three Courts, "the Three Courts do have some form of use, after all. For example, a part of the Sky Court's mission is to protect the balance of our Three Gods. And that means respecting the magen, and treating them as regular people." He looked up, a sardonic smile playing about his lips. "You know, representation of different people and their rights, all those principles of governance. I guess it's done something good for Bregon after all."

"In Kemeira," Linn piped up, "we have a similar principle. Affinites and non-Affinites live in harmony, relying on each other's strengths to build a stronger society." She clasped her hands together, and Ana remembered Linn teaching her this principle. "Yin and yang. Action and counteraction."

"I haven't come across these in the foreign policy books I studied," Ana admitted.

Ramson stretched his arms and leaned back. "That's because the winners write history," he said. "Whoever wrote your books probably didn't want anyone realizing it was possible for people of different kinds to get along."

This lesson, in particular, burned deep in Ana's mind long after the lamps of their ship had fizzled out in the night.

Her skills with her Affinity also improved under Kaïs's tutelage each day. At first, it was strange, sitting across from Kaïs and looking into his face, trying to reconcile the image of the boy before her and the cold-blooded killer she knew he was. And yet, beneath the quiet skies, the billowing sails, and the lapping of waves all around them, Kaïs's voice was low and steady and patient.

They started off slowly, by learning to consciously recognize *signatures.* Each person's blood had a signature, like their scent, and Ana realized that a part of her had already begun distinguishing between them. The shifting sea-salt and sword-metal scent to Ramson's blood, the fierceness of fire and rose-water to Shamaïra's, the calming wind and shadows to Linn's. She'd picked up on them by accident, in glimpses, but now, she learned to attribute them to every person she came across.

Ana left their first few lessons exhausted both mentally and physically—but she could feel her control over her Affinity improving. In particular, her understanding of the nuances to her power had deepened, as though she were gaining deft control over a limb she had only used clumsily her entire life.

She learned to observe the flow of blood through bodies, to memorize the rhythm, and to merge her Affinity into each and every stream of blood. He then taught her to heal. Not in the awkward way she'd been trying to do it, by clotting blood at the opening of the wound—but truly, completely, to heal from the inside out, like guiding the wayward streams of a river.

And, finally, he taught her to fight. To coalesce blood and harden it, to mold it into blades as sharp as steel.

Something else was improving, too: her relationship with Kaïs. Each lesson consisted of him reaching into her mind and senses with his Affinity, guiding her power. At first, they'd worked together stiffly, she subconsciously fighting against him for control.

But one day, as they ended their lesson and she stood to leave, Ana caught herself doing something she'd never done before.

She smiled at Kaïs.

And he smiled back.

As they drew steadily closer to Bregon, their plans began to come together. They would dock at the city of Sapphire Port, the largest port of Bregon, with the easiest entry rules due to the sheer number of trade ships and tourists. Ramson would see Ana and Linn safely to the Blue Fort before returning to Sapphire Port, where he planned to scour the black markets for news on Kerlan.

On the fourteenth day of travel, they spotted land.

The cry came from the crow's nest in the morning. Linn had taken to perching there; the winds and open skies seemed to buoy her spirits. "Land!" she called, and it was as though an invisible string had pulled taut on the ship. Daya straightened at the wheel; Kaïs paused in whetting his swords and stood; Ramson sat up from where he lay on the deck.

Ana scrambled to the prow, leaning as far forward as she could, her heart thudding in her chest.

And . . . *there.*

The sun had just risen and the clouds straight ahead at the horizon were burnished gold at the rims. And, right beneath, drenched in light, was the faint outline of a landmass, rising from the sea. As they drew closer, Ana saw shapes—gray stone cliffs jutting into the sky, haloed by the light of the sun.

Beneath the cliffs was a scattering of ships out at sea—a wide assortment, some of which Ana had never set eyes on—and even more lined up at the docks, a gleaming mass of metal and polished wood.

By her side, Ramson gripped the railing of the ship. His expression had steeled, his eyes taking on a hard glint. "Welcome to Bregon," he said, and there was no joy in his voice.

23

Navigating the port seemed an impossible job with the number of ships waiting to dock, but Daya managed it with effortless skill. A clerk greeted them as soon as they docked, asking their order of business and diligently jotting down all of the words Ramson spewed.

"Land ahoy!" Daya hollered when the paperwork was finished. She leaned against the wheel and tapped her forehead in a salute. "Pleasure doing business with you." She winked at Ramson. "And you can expect to hear from me soon."

"Hear what?" Ana asked as Ramson ushered her off the gangplank.

"Just a little reconnaissance," he said vaguely.

When Ana stepped onto the docks, Kaïs was waiting for her. She approached him warily. Their exchanges had been mostly through his lessons on her Affinity use, but over the past two weeks, something between them had thawed.

Ana was surprised when he sank to one knee. "Kolst Imperatorya, please allow me to accompany you. My swords are yours to command."

Out of the corners of her eyes, she saw a lithe figure step

off the gangplank. Linn approached them from beneath the shadows of the boat.

Ana turned to follow Ramson away from the ship. "You'd better pray those swords of yours are sharper than our enemies'," she called over her shoulder.

They wound through docks crowded with merchants and crew unloading their goods, the air filled with soaring gulls. Ramson pointed out seadoves, the Bregonian messenger bird, their bodies flashing gray and the signature teal of their iridescent wings as they dipped through the crowd to deliver letters.

They passed rows upon rows of ships flying flags from all over the world. Ana spotted several from the Crown of Nandji, bearing multicolored sails arching over their hulls covered in gold decorative patterns. A few others, she noticed, had narrower hulls with sharper prows and sails that resembled fans.

She sensed Linn stiffen by her side.

"Are those . . ." Ana hesitated at Linn's expression.

Linn nodded. Her eyes were black pools. "Kemeiran," she whispered, "and other Aseatic kingdoms. Zeishin Ko, Chi'gon, Chomingguk . . ."

Chi'gon. A thread tightened in Ana's chest as she looked at the ships, wondering whether they carried people from the kingdom that had been May's birth home. She looked to Linn. Despite her firm muscles and the daggers tucked in her belt, Linn looked utterly lost beneath the shadows of the ships.

Ana threaded her arm through Linn's and squeezed.

"Cyrilian ships," Ramson said, his voice low. He put a hand over her shoulder and pointed. "That's where I'm starting my search."

A chill ran through Ana. Sure enough, she spotted several

ship's emblazoned with the distinct script of her homeland and the tiger insignia.

The crowds had thickened, converging at the end of the wooden docks. Beneath the hulls of great ships carrying goods and products from around the world, the ocean tapered into a river.

No, not a river, a canal.

Slim wooden gondolas glided up and down, turning to deposit travelers and immediately picking up more.

Ramson gave the group a mock bow. "Meya damas, mesyr," he said, "on our schedule is a short gondola ride, where we'll see the famous winding canals of Sapphire Port. We disembark at the Crown's Port, an inland trading post"—he lowered his voice, leaning toward Ana—"that'll take you directly to the Blue Fort."

With that, he flung out a hand, and it wasn't long before a gondola steered by a man in a ruffled white shirt and navy-blue breeches pulled up. The man exchanged some rapid-fire Bregonian with Ramson, some of which Ana caught from her childhood tutoring. The Bregonian language was sharper and cut harder than Cyrilian, its vowels short and brusque whereas Cyrilians drew their words out in lilting tones.

Ramson turned around and gestured to them, which they took as their cue to board. And then they were off, their gondola gliding smoothly through the waters, away from the hubbub of the port.

They turned into a narrow alleyway and passed beneath a stone bridge. For a few moments it grew dark, and when they emerged, Sapphire Port opened up to them like pages of a storybook.

Ana had only seen Bregon—and most of the world, she supposed—in the pages of her books. She'd read about the kingdom of stone and metal, surrounded on all sides by vast stretches of ocean and perilous cliffs that made foreign invasion near-impossible.

Compared to the vibrantly colored architecture of Southern Cyrilia, Sapphire Port was a city of muted colors. Buildings carved of gray stone rose on either side of them, tall and angular, windows narrow and evenly spaced. Here and there were drops of brass and edges of bronze, burnishing the sign of a pub or the frames of houses.

Yet the city was alive; it opened up before them, pulsing with crisscrossing canals that ran through it like veins. The waters here were colored a deep, striking shade of sapphire, and glittered like jewels where the sunlight hit it. The stone buildings reflected the light so that it looked as though their stern façades were undulating to the rhythm of the water.

Their gondola followed canals that wound through the entire city, cleaving through stone castles and slipping under bridges, sometimes opening to large expanses of water wide enough to fit an entire Vyntr'makt in the center, at other times turning through alleyways so narrow that only one gondola could squeeze through at a time.

"It's beautiful," Ana breathed.

Ramson turned from his seat to look at her. Something in his expression had changed, his hazel eyes dimmed and his carefree laughter gone. "I'm not sure I'd call it that" was all he said.

Clouds clotted the sky, the sun weaving in and out. The city was bustling with daytime activity, the sound of clanging metal echoing from a blacksmith's shop, the flutter of laundry drying in the breeze, and once or twice, the sound of song threading through the narrow alleyways toward the sky.

At last, the gondola pulled up by the side of a wide street lined with tall, multistory houses.

Ramson tossed a few copperstones to the gondolier and they filed off. By now, the skies had turned gray, and Ana pulled her worn fur cloak around herself as wind rattled the empty streets. A mist had begun to seep between the walls.

Linn shivered. "It's quiet," she remarked.

"We've left the commercial district of Sapphire Port," Ramson explained. "We're on the outskirts, between the city and the Blue Fort." He jerked his chin at the cobblestone streets ahead. "We're about to reach the Crown's Port, which directly serves the Blue Fort. There, you'll take a road named the Crown's Cut; I'll find you a wagon heading for the Blue Fort." He motioned to them. "Follow me."

Their steps echoed between the stones of the buildings on either side of them. Within a few turns, the gently lapping waters of the canals had grown distant, and then fallen silent. When they looked back, fog shrouded the path behind. Overhead, a bird screamed. Ana jumped.

"Bone gulls," Ramson said. He walked several steps ahead of the group, leading them through the narrow alleyway. "They only eat rotting meat."

Another scream, and this time, Ana's Affinity pricked.

She whirled, and at the same time, Linn's knives flashed as she crouched, eyes narrowed, scanning the empty streets and buildings all around them.

"Ramson," Ana called. Her voice bounced between the buildings. In a lower tone, she said, "There's someone here." She closed her eyes and the world darkened into blood. And then shadows began to burn crimson into awareness, high overhead, winking into existence like candles. There were over a dozen, crouched as still as stone on the rooftops all around them. They were surrounded.

Ramson stopped. He slid his misericord from its scabbard. The metal hissed softly in the silence. Linn clenched her knives, the air growing eerily still all around them.

And then, in the dead quiet that had fallen between the hollowed windows and empty doorways and drapes that fluttered in the phantom breeze, came the steady tapping of footsteps.

They reverberated in the alleyways, flat, rhythmic, and strangely cheerful.

Out of the swirling gray mist came a shadow that became a person. He walked quickly, his outline cutting through the fog with the sharpness of a blade. He wore a long hooded cloak, sleek and navy blue. His leather boots were tipped in steel, wicked and sharp.

He came to a stop over a dozen paces away.

On the rooftops and behind corners, out of sight, the watchers watched.

Ana's palms were slick with sweat. She hadn't even sensed the person until she'd heard his footsteps. Even now, as the newcomer stood before them, his face obscured by his hood, Ana found it difficult to grasp his signature. There was something strange about his blood. It smelled of absence, of . . . nothingness.

Ramson stepped forward. His shoulders were rigid, his weapon held tightly in his fingers. "Ane koman?" he demanded in Bregonian. *Who comes?*

Moments lapsed. A draft rippled the figure's cloak.

Beneath his hood, the stranger's mouth tugged upward in a phantom grin. It was a female voice that spoke, the Bregonian words sounding guttural. "Ene maden dar vanden koman." *Just a girl taking a walk.*

Ramson's eyes narrowed. "Show your face," he continued in Bregonian.

The hood canted slightly. Beneath its shadows, Ana sensed clever eyes watching them. "You don't trust me?" the stranger asked, her voice lilting mockingly.

"Sweetheart, the word *trust* doesn't exist in my vocabulary. Nothing personal." Ramson gave a small flick of his misericord. "Reveal yourself, and we can settle this in a civil fashion."

A peal of laughter. "Depends," the stranger said, "on how you define *civil*."

Ana stepped forward. Immediately, the stranger's hood swiveled to her. "I've located your scouts," Ana said in Cyrilian, raising her voice to the commanding tone she had learned from Papa and from Luka. "Tell us who you are and what you want, and we can speak."

The stranger's mouth stretched, morphing into a grin. She gave a low chuckle, and, in an unprecedented move, slid off her hood.

A slim, tanned face framed by a crop of messy auburn hair. Long nose with a snub tip, bowed lips that curved in a mischievous grin. And eyes—quick, calculating eyes the color of black steel.

Ana blinked. The stranger was only a girl, perhaps a few years younger than Ana herself.

Ramson had been shifting his balance between his feet; he now went completely still.

The girl cocked her head, her grin cutting her face in half. "'Just a girl taking a walk,'" she repeated in near-perfect singsong Cyrilian, looking between Ana and Ramson. She spread her arms slightly, and her eyes took on a hard-edged glint. "Do you *trust* me now?"

Linn spoke, her voice quiet and low. "You have fifteen scouts surrounding us. I have found them all. What is the purpose of this?"

The girl's mouth opened wide in glee; she gave a scream of laughter. "Oh, I like this, I *like* this!" she yelled, and moved forward so suddenly that Ana took a startled step back. But she hadn't missed the way the girl's hood fluttered, revealing heavy bronze hilts of swords saddling her hips. "You really don't *recognize* me?"

"You're with the Navy," Ramson said.

"Yes, no, maybe so!" the girl sang, giggling, still advancing. "Oh, but here's a clue: I certainly do *not* know who *you* are!"

There was the slightest pause, and then the slice of metal as Ramson raised his blade.

The girl's teeth glinted like fangs as she unsheathed one of her swords. Slowly, deliberately, she brought it to her lips and trailed her tongue down the length of the blade.

"Liar, liar," Ramson crooned.

"Burn by fire," the girl quipped, and sprang.

24

Ramson danced out of the way as his opponent lunged at him, sword flashing, the whites of her eyes rolling. She barreled past him with a growl, and he allowed himself a smirk.

Bregonians valued honor and courage—and their sword-fighting style showed it. A Bregonian Navy–trained soldier would have parried that blow head-on.

So Ramson dodged.

He'd spent the last seven years of his life training with Kerlan, sparring with criminals and cutthroats of all backgrounds and styles. When it came to swordplay, his versatility was his greatest strength.

But he never expected the girl to match his move.

With a deft twirl, she was attacking again, cloak slashing, the metal tips of her boots stabbing into the ground. She leapt and this time Ramson barely had time to raise his misericord.

The impact jarred his bones, steel screeching in his ears as he met her blow head-on. Ramson twisted, and with a second dagger pinned her blades between his.

The girl shot him a wicked grin over their crossed swords. Spittle dribbled down her chin, and her eyes had a wild look.

"Who knew that seven years abroad would have turned you so weak," she hissed, "brother of mine?"

With a scream, she shoved him back. Ramson stumbled, caught off-balance.

He'd known. A part of him had, at least, as soon as she'd dropped her hood. That long face, hawklike nose, and cunning eyes that cut like the darkest of ocean waters.

It was, without a doubt, *her.* Her face, stretched slimmer and crueler now, brought back memories—whispering alder trees, maroon walls, locked doors, the cold shoulder of a familiar figure. He'd only seen her face in portraits, those auburn curls and that quick grin now turned vicious, standing in the spots where *he* should have been.

That face had a name: Sorsha.

Sorsha Farrald.

Ramson repositioned himself, yet something in him had become unhinged, like an unmoored ship. The hilt of his weapon felt slick in his palm, the ground uneven beneath his feet. What was she doing here? The possibilities left him cold as they reeled through his mind. Had his—*their*—father somehow gotten wind of his arrival? The thought made him sick. No, that was impossible . . . unless someone at the docks had somehow recognized him, chances of which were slim.

Sorsha giggled. "By the look on your face, you're probably wondering how I found you," she said happily. "My Royal Guards patrol the port, but security is especially tight around Crown's Port. When I saw you, I couldn't believe my eyes—I thought I'd made a mistake at first—but then that whore of yours called your name."

Anger surged in him. "You—"

Before he could move, Ana stepped into his field of vision. Her hands were clenched. "What do you want?" she demanded, looking at Sorsha. Linn and Kaïs flanked her, their weapons drawn. "Stop right now." She paused. "Or I'll make you."

Sorsha licked her lips and tilted her head. "Get the hells out of my way." She pointed a sword at Ana. "This is a *family* affair. You or any of your little friends interfere, and my scouts'll shoot those arrows faster than you can blink."

"Who the hell are you?" Ana snarled, and Ramson imagined she was assessing the other girl's blood, fighting the urge to hurl her across the street.

If that happened, they'd all be dead within seconds. Ramson darted a glance at the rooftops above, at the hidden guards and archers waiting to strike.

He spoke before Sorsha could. "Ana, meet Sorsha Farrald."

"Why so formal?" Sorsha shrieked. "Why don't you introduce me as . . . your *sister*?"

Panic shot through him like lightning. Ramson threw a glance at Ana. Her face was creased in confusion.

"Oh." Sorsha looked between them and gasped with delight. "*Oh!* Don't tell me she doesn't *know*! My dearest guests," she said, her voice dripping with mockery as she gestured to the rest of the group, "meet my *dearest* brother . . . Ramson Farrald."

And then she was charging again, landing one, two blows that he parried with grunts. Ramson ducked as her sword sliced the air where his neck should have been. He danced back, back, focusing on leading her away from Ana and the others as she bore down on him, his arms rising to meet her challenge with each slash of her blades.

She was *good.* No, not good—she was *extraordinary.* She fought with all the skill of a well-trained swordsman, each move vicious and each blow immaculately placed. She would have outranked even Jonah back at the Naval Academy, Ramson thought, in skill—but she struck with a wild vengeance that Jonah had lacked.

She struck to kill.

He twisted, slamming both of their swords down so that the tips plunged into the cracks between the cobblestones. Dirt flew in their faces. "Did the Admiral send you as part of a welcome committee?" he gritted.

"Oh, Daddy Dearest doesn't know yet." Sorsha's voice was saccharine, coated with venom. "I'm extending you my own welcome, as Lieutenant of the Royal Guard!" And then her blades were out and she slashed up—

Ramson spun. Sorsha was still caught in the momentum of her blow, her sword tracing an arc through the air.

He curved forward and drove his misericord toward her waist.

He didn't see the metal tips of her shoes swinging toward him until it was too late.

Something sharp and hard slit open his flesh and slid into his side. Pain, bright and burning, slashing through him. Warmth blooming through his tunic and trickling down his side.

Behind him, Ana cried out.

Blood, Ramson thought, and dared a look down.

Sorsha's boot had connected with his ribs—but the metal tip had slid out and turned into a small, sharp dagger, buried inside him.

Sorsha wriggled her foot.

Pain shot through him. Ramson grunted and sank onto one knee.

There was the sound of a *click,* and then the blade disengaged from her boot. With crude casualty, Sorsha yanked the blade from his flesh. Ramson's vision blurred. Blood—his blood—speckled the air like rain and painted the cobblestones crimson.

"I don't think . . . Daddy Dearest . . . would want you to murder me before he met me," he managed, wiping the spittle from his chin.

Sorsha was laughing, dangling the hilt of the small blade like some prize, blood coating it and drip, drip, dripping onto the ground. "You *really* think Father wants the world to know his *bastard son* is alive, after all these years?" she yelled. "He'd thank me on bended knees if I brought your head to him on a golden plate!"

Ramson pressed a hand to his side. His breaths came fast, shallow, and as warmth seeped from him, so did images—images of that arrow turning, curving, through the air, and the crimson that drenched Jonah's shirt. Of the image of his father's turned shoulder and cold gaze that had been carved indelibly into his bones.

He'd never planned to see that man again.

There was the sound of metal scraping stone, punctured by a rhythmic *tap, tap, tap.* And then Sorsha stood before him, face shadowed against the dark storm clouds overhead.

"You little half-breed runt," she whispered. "You've been running all these years. It's time that I put a stop to that." Slowly, lovingly, she lifted the blade that was slick with Ramson's blood to her face and ran her tongue down the length. Her cheeks came away stained crimson. "As I suspected. Gods, it tastes filthy, like the scum from the whoring districts of Sapphire Port." Her sword flashed. "Good-bye, Brother Dearest."

Two things happened at once.

Sorsha swung her blade down.

The arc cut short—and she soared back through the air and slammed into the opposite wall.

"Enough," Ana snarled, stepping in front of Ramson. His vision blurred in and out of focus, but he thought that he'd never seen Ana that furious before. Her lips were curled in disgust, her gloved hands clenched into fists. In the gray light, her eyes were red.

On the opposite wall, Sorsha struggled, splayed like a butterfly.

A flash of movement over their heads. On the rooftop of a building, a marksman appeared. Metal sliced gray in his hands.

Ramson lunged forward, a cry of warning at his throat—but someone leapt over them, light as a shadow, flitting through the air. There were several *plinks,* and then blades clattered to the ground as Linn landed like a slip of wind. Kaïs stepped to Ana's side, his double swords in a defensive position.

Ana's gaze flicked to the roofs, then cut back to Sorsha. "Call off your soldiers."

Sorsha thrashed, and when it was of no use, she let out a screaming cackle. "Or what, you red-eyed bitch?"

Ana's smile was wicked as she tilted her head, her irises swirling a familiar shade of crimson as they caught the light. For a few moments, nothing happened. The wind threaded through their alleyway, rattling empty bottles on the cobblestones.

And then Sorsha gave a shout. She staggered, clutching her chest. For the first time since Ramson had seen her, that smirk slid from her face, and she looked . . . angry. "What are you doing?" she hissed, her eyes narrowed at Ana.

"Teaching you some manners," Ana replied, and stepped closer. "That was just a taste. Call off your soldiers, or I won't hold back next time."

Sorsha spat blood. Slowly, her lips curled, and her eyes brightened like a child looking at a delectable tart. Bloodied spittle dribbled down her chin. "Magen," she gasped. "Blot magen!" *Blood Affinite.*

Ana pulled off her gloves and lifted her hands. Dark veins twisted over her flesh, rising from each of her fingers and stretching to the skin of her arms. Ramson had seen her do this on occasion—had seen a shadow cross her face, morphing her features into something cruel.

"Fascinating," whispered Sorsha, and then her voice rose into a shriek. "This is *fascinating*! I want to see—I want to see you bleed my soldiers dry! Can you do it? Will you do it for me?"

A flicker of uncertainty crossed Ana's face. "I came to negotiate with the Bregonian government, not with you," Ana snapped, and for a moment, her eyes flicked to Ramson. "I demand an audience with King Darias Rennaron and the Three Courts of Bregon."

Sorsha blinked. "And who the hells are you?" she snapped.

Ana lifted her chin. "My name is Anastacya Kateryanna Mikhailov," she said, "and I am the rightful Empress of Cyrilia."

Silence fell across the streets. The shadows lurking over rooftops and hidden in alleyways seemed to still. But Ramson kept his gaze pinned on the only important player in this scene.

Sorsha's face was frozen, caught between a snarl and surprise. She stared at Ana, her thin lips slightly parted. And then she collapsed in a peal of laughter. "The *Empress,*" she shrieked, her voice rising to a hysterical scream, "*of Cyrilia*!"

Ana looked unsettled; she took a slight step back.

For once, Ramson was at a loss for what to do.

"Gods!" Sorsha screamed, tilting her head to the skies, clutching her stomach. "The *Empress* of Cyrilia is here, dressed in tattered rags like a common whore—"

Ramson's mind blanked to a searing white heat. *A common whore.* He'd heard those words his entire life, whispered in the stone hallways of the Naval Academy or in the dank dormitories at the Blue Fort, seen it in the smiles of his peers and in the shadow of his father's turned back. *The son of a whore.*

Something in him snapped then, and before he knew it, he'd sprung forward, his hands closing around Sorsha's throat.

He slammed her against the brick wall of the alleyway, hard enough to rattle the breath from her and shake the laughter from her face.

"Have some respect," Ramson hissed, his face inches from hers, "for the common whores."

Sorsha's lips curled into a cruel sneer. "You'd like that, wouldn't you, my filthy half brother?"

Ramson knew that about a dozen invisible arrows were pointed at him right now, but he didn't care. His plan was shattered, the ugly truth torn out and strewn on the street like blood. There was no point in hiding it now; he needed to focus on turning the situation around.

If he did, indeed, share a father with this girl, then that was something he could exploit. After all, Ramson knew the tactics of his father better than anybody in this world. "The Admiral," he said, his tongue twisting around the word as it had for his entire life, "has an agreement to see her. And I don't think he shared his plans with *you.* Not with a worthless *daughter.*"

It had been a lie, a gamble, but he saw it in her eyes. The mad glint turning to sudden fear, and then cold anger.

Ramson recognized it. The years and years of subtle, cutting remarks that slowly but surely burrowed into your heart like a thorn, and bled you little by little. A turned shoulder, a cool glance, the knowledge that you were never good enough.

Perhaps Sorsha was more his sister than she realized.

They were both, after all, their father's children.

One illegitimate son, barred from power for his birthright, and one angry daughter, barred from inheritance for her sex.

There was only one way to save this situation: by convincing Sorsha that Ramson had planned this with their father, all along.

So Ramson seized that thorn their father had buried in Sorsha's heart throughout all these years, and he twisted it. "He has a grand plan, little sister, that doesn't involve you," Ramson whispered. "Do you really think it a coincidence that his long-lost *son* would show up on his doorstep with the rightful *Empress* of the largest empire in the world?"

There it was again, that uncertainty that writhed like a shadow across her face.

Ramson pushed deeper. "What do you think he would do to you if he found out you'd interfered in his great plans to gain a stronghold over the Cyrilian Empire?"

"You're lying," said Sorsha, but her breathing came too quickly, and her eyes were too wide.

You have much more to learn, little sister, Ramson thought. Out loud, he only said, "Do you really want to find out?"

Their gazes clashed, hers the bitter black of their father's, and Ramson's the sharp hazel of his mother's.

Sorsha's eyes narrowed in cunning, and Ramson found an exact mirror of himself reflected in his half sister's face. "Guards!" she shouted. "Surround them! We'll take them to the Blue Fort." And then, in a lower voice so that only Ramson could hear, she hissed: "*I* found you. If I take you and your whore empress to Daddy Dearest, I get the credit."

The soldiers hidden on rooftops and behind houses and alleyways now came into view. They stepped out of the coiling mist, wrapped in leathers and decked in metals. Ramson caught the flashes of the Bregonian insignia—a roaring seadragon—on their chests.

Sorsha whipped her cloak around her, metal boots and swords clinking as she stalked past them. "Follow me," she said brusquely, and the Royal Guards turned on their heels and swept after her like a wave.

In the silence, the reality of his situation sank in. He'd just bartered his way back to the place to which he'd sworn never to return. To see the man he'd left behind in another life.

The sound of boots drew farther from him, and it occurred to Ramson that this was his last chance to run. He'd come to Bregon to see an end to Alaric Kerlan and to take Goldwater Port and the rest of what Ramson had built over the years.

This wasn't part of the deal.

Ramson turned and met Ana's gaze as she strode over and pressed a hand to his bleeding wound. Her touch both unmoored him and anchored him.

"Farrald," she said quietly, looking up at him. Her hands, still bare, became ribbed with black veins as she applied her Affinity to his wound. "Admiral Roran Farrald." Her gaze snapped to his, crimson, a question burning in them.

He looked away, his breathing going shallow with her so close, her fingers curling against his skin.

He could tell she was gathering her thoughts, trying to parse her emotions into logic. "I read in the books the Bregonian Admiral had a daughter. I didn't know . . . You didn't tell me . . ." She trailed off, and he would have preferred her anger to the mixed sympathy on her face.

"They wouldn't have written me into history books," Ramson said shortly. "I'm his bastard son."

She fell silent for several moments, her forehead creased. Her hand was still warm on his wound, his blood crusted all over her skin. The bleeding had stopped. "And you were going to keep this from me forever?" Her words were as sharp as blades.

His laugh was bitter. Ramson flung her hand from him and turned to follow the Royal Guard. "Ana, you're the heiress to the world's most powerful empire," he said. "There was never going to be a forever."

25

Ramson followed close on Sorsha's heels. Even when she walked, his half sister had an erratic sort of stagger that made her appear almost drunk. She wove in front of him like a phantom, mist clinging to her.

Behind, Ana, Linn, and Kais followed quietly.

As they passed through the narrow alleyways and curving streets, the city came alive in the shadows of Ramson's memories, and it was as though he had been plunged back in time. The rough-hewn stone gilded with touches of brass and bronze, the multistoried buildings stacked high, the smell of ale and steel in humid air.

Another thought came to him then, one that sharpened his gaze and honed his senses.

Kerlan was somewhere in this kingdom.

He had never planned, so long as he lived, to ever return to the Blue Fort, or to see the monster that was his father again. But it seemed the gods had thrown them on a collision course. There was no escaping the reckoning that had been due seven years ago.

The thought—the inevitability of it all—steadied him like

steel. He would play along for now, return to the Blue Fort and help Ana with her plan. As soon as he had a chance, he would leave to do what he'd come here for in the first place.

They turned, and the alleyway ended sharply, cobblestones giving way to the lap of waves from another branch of the canal.

Sorsha stopped, and her procession of guards halted behind her. Ramson watched them carefully. This wasn't the way to the Blue Fort as he knew it.

A foghorn sounded, and a boat cut through the veiled gray mist. Not a gondola, but a steel-plated barge, masts reaching to the sky like daggers. The sails billowed midnight blue, a gold Bregonian seadragon roaring proudly like a phantom from the mists.

Sorsha barked rapid-fire orders and a small gangplank was lowered. She threw them a glance. "You stay in the back with that beggar empress of yours," she sneered, and boarded with her escorts.

The barge was small enough to navigate the winding canals of Sapphire Port, yet large enough to fit over two dozen people. Ramson swept his gaze over the Royal Guards as he boarded, noting the dark blue uniforms and the bronze seadragon badges glinting on their chests, indicating their affiliation to the Navy. There were three, however, dressed in livery of a blue so pale that it appeared white. Their pins bore a seadragon, a stallion, and an eagle, all enclosed in a circle.

That was new, and Ramson had no indication of their meaning other than rankings to the Navy that had been added after his departure. He kept his eye on them as he settled in the back, leaning against one of the masts. Linn perched against the edge of the ship and gazed out, seemingly oblivious to Kaïs as he stopped by her side. Ana stood rod-straight, her knuckles white as she gripped the railing of the ship.

With a slow-grinding creak, they began to move. The barge glided forward in silence but for the lap of waves against its sides. The alleyways faded into tall stone walls that loomed into the sky on either side. The waters undulated black beneath them, and when Ramson looked hard enough, he could make out shapes skimming through the darkness of the depths.

Linn leaned over the railing, watching them with quiet interest.

"Wassengost," Ramson offered. When both she and Ana looked at him, he jerked his chin to the shapes in the water. "Water spirits."

Linn's mouth formed a soft O. "Like ice spirits?"

"I suppose. Ours are quite harmless." He pitched his tone toward skepticism. "Legends say they're the last remnants of magic that the gods left in this world."

As Linn turned back to play with the wassengost, sending small gusts of wind toward the surface of the water, Ana turned to Ramson. Her gaze was hard and piercing. "Can you tell me more about your father?"

He could see other questions in her eyes, words unspoken lingering in the air between them; this question was clinical, cold, and carefully chosen. Not for the first time, he wondered what it would take for the trust between them to be broken beyond repair.

"My father?" he repeated, turning to look at the water. Cold glances and cruel smiles. Smashed mugs, red blood, the shadow of someone whom he'd spent his lifetime chasing. "He's an asshole."

She focused a glare on him.

"I'm sure you'll have no trouble with him," Ramson continued. Already, he could feel his voice tightening almost as a bodily reaction, coldness clamping on his chest, and his face shuttering by instinct. "You've spent several moons dealing with *me,* after all."

He could sense her anger rising like a tide, but to his surprise, she only folded her arms and reined in her expression. "Tell me something that will help me win him over." Her tone was cool, controlled.

He'd been baiting her, and a part of him even wished for her fury at this moment. He would rather have her anger than nothing at all.

He turned away, mulling the question over. How would one negotiate with his father?

The answer was right in front of him. He simply hadn't wanted to see it.

"He's just like me," Ramson said quietly. The words tasted like ash in his mouth. "He won't give anything for nothing. Everything is a negotiation to him, a game of politics. And he doesn't waste his time with people who he thinks have nothing to offer him." *Like my mother,* he thought. "To win, you have to make him an offer he can't resist. Something he wouldn't find anywhere else."

Ana opened her mouth, but they were interrupted by a gasp from Linn. "Look!"

The fog was beginning to clear, and Ramson saw what Linn was so excited about. The waterway had turned into a river, flowing between high cliffs that knifed to the sky on either side of them. Ahead, it pooled into a lagoon, extending in a wide circle as far as the eye could see. Estuaries and streams flowed into the main waterway from all directions before plunging into the sea from the cliffs at the end of the river. And in the center, the live, beating heart of it all, was the Blue Fort.

Tucked into an outcrop of rock at the base of where the cliffs met the sea, its sharp towers rose almost as high as those of the Salskoff Palace, made of a glistening sea-blue material that wove and wended like waves, winking in the sudden sunlight.

"It looks as if it is made of water," Linn breathed.

"That's searock," Ramson said. "Ranks among the strongest materials in the world. Our myths say it has magical properties." It was also one of the few resources that Bregon refused to trade.

His attention caught on something else. Beyond the searock structure of the fortress itself stood a new, second ring of crenellated walls. This set loomed tall enough that ships docked at the quays beyond it were cast in its shadow; it was made of a dark gray material that looked to be part stone, part metal.

Ironore—the heaviest and most expensive alloy, supposedly created by magen for defensive weapons.

Ramson could only imagine what an entire wall made of ironore would have cost.

There was silence but for the sound of their ship sluicing through the water. As they sailed beneath the shadows of the walls, Ramson saw that they approached a massive set of gates, shimmering in the gray-metallic hue of ironore. In the center of each gate was a massive metal branding, almost as large as their entire barge. On the left gate, an eagle, its talons outstretched as it soared in the skies. On the right, a stallion, mane flowing as it reared on its hind legs.

And, in the center, the head of a roaring seadragon, connected to the other two carvings through a triangular marking that adjoined all three.

In his years spent in Bregon, he had never seen anything like this.

On either side of the boat, the water seemed to rush by faster, swirls forming in their depths. A cry came from the head of the barge. "Helmesgatten!"

The three light-cloaked guards took positions at the prow. In perfect synchrony, they swept their hands up, and as a strange, humming energy filled the air, Ramson realized what they were.

Magen. Affinites.

Wind roared. Fire exploded. And water rose in a massive wave.

A gale howled through the statue of the eagle, blasting through its open beak in a shriek, tunneling through the triangular marking. Fire lit up the stallion's stone figure, its eyes glowing as bright as suns, swirling up the second leg of the triangle.

And, finally, water swept through the maw of the seadragon, its whiskers and gills rippling as though it were *alive*—

And the three elements met in an inferno in the triangle.

Ramson felt as though he were gazing upon magic, upon a foreign sorcery. When he'd left, there had been few, if any, magen serving in the Navy. Most had been regular civilians, perhaps with slight advantages to their everyday lives.

This, though . . . was something utterly different. As the

roar of the three elements sweeping into the gates compounded to a crescendo, Ramson felt his own emotions awaken, part awe, part fear. This gate was something three magen should not have had the power to move. It was something that had not existed in his time at Bregon.

In seven years, the government had utterly revolutionized Bregon's relationship with the magen. And his father had undoubtedly had a hand in it all.

There was a rush of air that set their sails billowing—almost like a celestial sigh—before the ironore gates glided open.

Ramson felt as though he had stepped back in time, into an impossible memory, as the Blue Fort revealed itself to him. Before him rose the section of buildings that made up the Naval Academy, its courtyards made of solid stone, a wide set of steps leading to the quays where he'd spent many an afternoon as a child.

Ships dotted the waters beneath the vast sprawl of courtyards and searock buildings that clung to the cliffs as though they had been formed by melding stone and sea. Their barge passed rows upon rows of gleaming Navy warships, anchored beneath the Blue Fort. It would only take a signal to launch them.

At last, they rounded to the main section of the fort. Before them, searock pillars rose ten, twenty times the length of their barge, supporting square domes overhead. Sunlight filtered through the top, and the waters flowed lapis blue, carrying them forward.

Ramson felt his chest tighten and something lodged in his throat, before he unstuck it and said in the coolest tone he could muster, "Welcome to the Blue Fort."

A memory flashed in his mind. The last time he'd come this way, he'd been barely tall enough to see over the side of the barge, afraid to hold the hand of the man who had become his father and ashamed of his yearning for the mother he'd left behind.

Thirteen years, and he still felt like that boy, lost as a brig in a storm. If Ramson could turn back to tell him the truth of what would become of him—

He wouldn't even know where to begin.

The waterway ended at a set of wide marble steps the length of four or five of their barges. Royal Guards lined the steps, dressed in the same navy-blue, bronze-buttoned uniforms; upon seeing Sorsha's flag, they saluted. This, Ramson recognized. It was the waterway for kings and admirals; one that he'd never been allowed to use.

The water magen held out a hand and the barge drew neatly to the steps, rocking gently.

Ramson's heart thudded heavily against his chest as they disembarked and followed Sorsha and her procession of guards up the high marble steps. He was suddenly aware of how he appeared: dirty and disheveled, his clothes the same tunic and breeches he'd worn since Cyrilia. Of all the times he'd thought of returning to the place that had both made him and broken him, this wasn't what he'd imagined.

By his side, Ana's dark eyes were steady, her chin set in that stubborn look he'd grown to know. Her hair was drawn in a tight bun, her tunic muddied and torn in places—but Ramson thought that despite it all, he'd never seen anyone more regal.

Yet the Bregonian Courts, Ramson thought darkly, were a different matter altogether. The age-old Bregonian stories told that women bore ill omens. The highest positions in the kingdom were held by men, and a combination of superstition and tradition kept it so.

Judging by Sorsha's reactions to his taunts, nothing had changed in the last seven years.

Ahead, the sound of boots stopped. Sorsha stood at the top of the steps, her petite outline framed against a set of searock doors. Her easy demeanor and wicked smile had vanished, leaving cold-cut cruelty on her face.

She smirked at them. "I would welcome you to Godhallem," she said, "but I don't wish to give off the wrong impression. Guards!" She gestured with a hand, clipped her heels together, and grew stone-still.

The doors swung open, and Ramson entered the place that had once made up his most desperate of dreams and his worst nightmares. With each step, he felt as though he were traveling back to his past, the blur of cold faces and cruel smiles and whispers behind his back accompanying his every move.

But his gaze roved through the gathered crowd, the knowledge of that person standing in the same room as him pulling at every fiber in his body.

And . . . there.

Ramson went cold as he found himself looking into the merciless black eyes of Admiral Roran Farrald.

26

Ana had never seen paintings of the inside of the Blue Fort, but the sight that met her eyes was even more regal than she could have imagined. Whereas the Salskoff Palace was all white marble and curved domes and gilded statues, the governing hall of the Bregonian Naval Headquarters was a collection of sharply cut pillars and polished searock walls, stone furnished with brass and bronze. The hall they stood in was square, with only two walls on either side of them. Directly ahead, the turquoise searock tapered off into sharp cliffs and open air. A breeze blew in, blue gossamer curtains billowing gently and open to the ocean hundreds of feet below.

Godhallem. It meant "hall of gods."

Overhead hung a line of giant bronze bells. The wind brushed gently against the insides of their domes—large enough to fit an entire person within—and they seemed to tremble with an invisible force, filling the hall with their low, steady hum. Ramson had told her of these famous bells—the War Bells, which the Earth Court presided over. The lever hung below the carving of a stallion on the far left wall, as a tribute to the Bregonian ground soldier who had once single-handedly saved the kingdom and established this tradition.

On the other end of the hall was the Sky Court, its wall bearing the symbol of an eagle. And beneath both symbols were rows of seats. Officials—*men,* Ana noticed—lounged beneath.

Yet it was the center of Godhallem that drew her attention as they approached. Water flowed in from the open-air balcony, cutting a square around the center of the court before flowing back out. It rushed into a pool at the open end of the hall, which spilled over the edge and then disappeared, plunging into the ocean below.

And on the small island at the center, like a little fortress in itself, was a raised dais that bore a throne. It seemed to be molded from a combination of ironore and searock, the blue and black intertwined like oil and water. Its arms were bronze, and upon it sat a boy.

He looked to be several years younger than Ana. Hair so dark it appeared black spilled to his shoulders, framing his delicate face, a shade paler than the tanned complexions of most Bregonians Ana had met. He wore a navy-blue Bregonian doublet threaded through with gold, and atop his head sat a crown.

This was the King, Ana realized with a sharp pang of surprise. King Darias Rennaron was smaller and frailer than she'd imagined. He was fourteen years of age now, but he still resembled a child. Above all, she was struck by the emptiness of his expression as his gaze met hers.

For a moment, she thought he would react, thought she saw a spark in those eyes, the shifting gray of storm clouds, of rain.

But just as quickly, the moment passed, and the King's eyes

flicked back to an empty spot on the back wall. He gave no other reaction.

Beside the throne, a figure stepped forward, and immediately, the entire hall's attention shifted to him.

Ana recognized him instantly for who he was. That long, slender face, hawklike nose, cunning eyes and sandy hair—she could see traces of Ramson in the Admiral's face, in every feature.

Ahead of them, Sorsha seemed to straighten, the erratic stagger to her steps falling into neat, rhythmic clacks. She came to a standstill and lifted her hand in salute. "To His Royal Majesty the King and the Three Courts of Bregon, may the Gods of Old defend," she recited in Bregonian. "I bring to you guests from Cyrilia."

The Admiral's gaze swept over Ana, and she had the impression that she was being pulled under black, moonless waters. Whereas Ramson's were a playful hazel, the Admiral's were cold cut steel.

"Guests," the Admiral repeated from his place by the throne, his voice low and deep as a starless night. "Very well, Lieutenant, you may step aside."

Just like that, Sorsha was dismissed. The girl gave a sharp bow and melted into the shadows.

On the throne, the boy king continued to gaze at them serenely, his lightless gray eyes as vacant as smoke. Ana felt a chill run through her. There was something about this arrangement that struck her as so . . . wrong. Where was the Queen Regent?

Her stomach twisted as she turned her gaze back to the Admiral. Though he stood beneath the throne, the attention of the room focused on him. His expression held amusement whetted by cruelty. "Well then, nameless guests. I bid you introduce yourselves."

The balmy Bregonian air was suddenly cold against Ana's skin. She knew her hair had come partially undone from its bun, and the plain tunic and breeches she wore felt like rags compared to the sharp gilded livery of the Three Courts. On either side, the highest-ranked men of Bregon watched and waited.

Ana threw her shoulders back and stepped forward. "Your Royal Majesty," she said, addressing the King. "Three Courts of Bregon. My name is Anastacya Kateryanna Mikhailov, rightful Empress of Cyrilia. These are my allies."

King Darias only blinked. It was the Admiral who spoke. "Rightful Empress," he repeated, and his eyes trailed her body once, up and down. A few laughs broke out from either side of the court, and Ana wanted to wrap her arms around herself.

Instead, she lifted her chin a notch. "Yes," she said. "Rightful Empress. And I seek an audience with your Courts today."

Roran Farrald swept a hand over the gilded throne. He wore a large gold ring on his left hand, which glimmered as it caught the light. "This, my dear girl, is the Blue Fort," he said. "We entertain foreign ambassadors and the most powerful men from around the world in these halls. Not little girls in beggar's clothes dreaming up fantasies of being empress." He lifted his shoulders in a slow, mocking shrug. The badges on his silk uniform gleamed gold and silver and bronze, their lights flashing against the thin tunic and worn felt boots she had on.

Words evaporated from Ana's lips. A familiar fear curled itself around her stomach, squeezing until she could barely breathe. Throughout her childhood, she'd come to fear public events. All those eyes on her, the voices whispering, wrapping stories and lies around her. She wanted nothing more than to disappear, to run out those doors and never look back.

But, Ana thought, that had never been an option. Fail, or try—the choice had always been hers.

She swallowed, straightened, and held the Admiral's gaze. "You must be mistaken, Admiral," she said, her voice carrying across the hall, loud and clear. "For I am a girl, and I am standing in your halls. I only ask for an audience with the Bregonian government." She turned, and this time spoke only to the King. "Your Royal Majesty. Please hear me out. I come seeking an alliance with you."

"I think not," the Admiral said, and stepped in front of the throne. His hand went to the hilt of the great sword at his hip. "You come into these halls requesting an audience—an *alliance*—yet you bring in unwelcome guests." He turned suddenly, and that was when his gaze slid to Ramson for the first time. "A traitor and deserter kneels among us. Guards, arrest Ramson Farrald."

It felt as though the ground were tilting beneath Ana.

The slice of metal sounded all throughout the hall as the Royal Guards lining Godhallem drew their swords in unison. By her side, Linn reached for her daggers.

Bewildered, Ana held up a hand. "Admiral—"

A hand closed over her shoulder, warm and steady. "Trust me," Ramson murmured. He stepped forward, positioning himself between the dais and her, misericord drawn. "I didn't expect this warm a welcome," he said, his voice growing sharp, "Admiral."

A shadow peeled off from the walls at the side of the hall. Sorsha drew her sword from its scabbard, flashing silver in the sunlight. "He's mine," she called out.

"Kolst Imperatorya." Kaïs's voice was low, urgent, his hands on his two swords.

"Ana," whispered Linn. "We must fight."

Ana's mind raced. Fighting could mean the end of a potential alliance before she even asked. In none of her negotiation classes back at the Salskoff Palace, the trials she had studied with Luka, had the requesting party ever shown force—on the foreign party's soil, no less.

And yet . . . Ana's gaze darted to Ramson, standing before her, misericord raised. He'd barely gotten away from his last fight with Sorsha, and Ana doubted the Admiral would play fair.

He's just like me, Ramson had said to her on the boat when she'd asked how she could win over his father. *To win, you have to make him an offer he can't resist.*

The Ramson Quicktongue she'd met back at Ghost Falls, back when all of this had started, had seemed so different from the one she'd come to know. She thought back to their first meeting in that dacha, when she'd made her first Trade with him. What had he wanted, back then?

Revenge. And . . .

Something he wouldn't find anywhere else.

The answer came to her, so painfully obvious. It would be a risky move, and it could jeopardize their entire mission—or save them.

Besides, if the Admiral wasn't going to play by the rules, then why should she?

"Bring the traitor to me," the Admiral said, and Ana's decision clicked into place.

Sorsha's sword flashed.

Ana flung her Affinity out.

Sorsha's scream echoed in the hall as her body whipped back, slamming against several seats with court officials sitting in them. Her blade clattered to the ground, amid cries of panic and screeching metal as the officials overturned chairs to scramble out of the way.

Ana pulled Sorsha back as easily as though she were a doll, dragging her across the polished searock floor until she was at Ana's feet. With a flick in her mind, Sorsha was in the air, limbs splayed like those of a martyr, head tilted back so that the flesh of her neck was exposed.

Red crept into the corners of Ana's vision, and the familiar urge to hurt flickered beneath it all.

She turned her focus to the Admiral. He held up a hand. Instantly, the shouts and sounds of swords being drawn died down as all of Godhallem turned to watch him.

The Admiral was smiling. He looked at Ana, trailing his gaze up her body slowly, drinking her in as though she were a prized possession, an object in which he'd discovered renewed interest.

Before, she might have felt disgust, even anger, at the way he looked at her. But now, Ana felt only triumph. Her ploy had worked; the Admiral had caught on to her Affinity, his hunger for her power almost palpable.

Ana spread her palms. "Admiral, this man is a part of my court," she said. Out of the corner of her eye, she saw Ramson's head turn to her in surprise. "An attack on any of my allies is an insult to me. I will not accept that." She leveled her gaze to King Darias. "Your Majesty, my apologies if I startled you. I mean no offense. Call off your guards. Negotiate with me. There must be something I can offer you and the Kingdom of Bregon."

The King looked at her blankly for a few moments, and then began to smile. It was a distorted smile, one so at odds with his pale, peaky face. "Negotiate," he echoed, and the Royal Guards drew back, taking their posts again at the walls, swords sliding into scabbards. In the same breath, Ana let go of Sorsha. The girl gasped and stumbled several steps, massaging her throat.

Several heartbeats passed as the hall watched the King, waiting. Ana stole a glance at Ramson. He stared ahead at the throne, a small crease between his eyebrows. "Your Majesty," he called. "Perhaps it would be best if the Queen Regent Arsholla were present as well. We wish to abide by the rules."

Admiral Farrald moved forward, each step slow and deliberate as he kept his gaze on Ana. She recalled seeing a similar hunger in Ramson's eyes when they had first met. Yet Roran Farrald's was different: older, crueler, more wicked.

"There is no need. Our Majesty has spoken," he said, and Ana wondered whether she was imagining the contempt in his words. "We will entertain your request to negotiate. But first, on behalf of the Sea Court and the Royal Navy, I must punish those who fail at their duties."

The Admiral stopped next to his daughter. In a single, sudden motion, he drew a blade from his belt and slashed it across her throat.

Blood sprayed into the air.

Ana shouted.

Sorsha slumped to the floor as blood gushed from her gaping wound, hot and slick. It poured down the skin of her neck like wine from an uncorked bottle, soaking the gold thread of her collar and darkening her navy-blue tunic.

Nausea coiled through Ana's stomach. Somehow, Kaïs's voice found her. *Power is a double-edged sword.*

Ana looked down at the girl bleeding out in front of her, who had called her a beggar empress and tried to hurt Ramson. Instead of hatred, she felt only an overwhelming pity.

She drew a deep breath and forced the maelstrom from her head to clear. Her mind settled on her Affinity, drawing it out long and sharp. She narrowed her view until there was only the blood pouring from Sorsha's neck, bright as molten metal.

Ana burrowed, deeper and deeper, until she found the source of the opening, the severed skin and the blood that spilled from within.

Carefully, she wove her Affinity into the flow of blood, and began to direct it back, back, into skin and flesh and veins.

Sorsha's slashed collar gave a glimpse of her skin, tanned from her days in the sun—yet crisscrossed with white scars around her collarbone. She wore a black necklace at the base of her throat, and Ana caught a glance as she focused her Affinity on the girl's neck, applying the healing techniques Kaïs had taught her.

Gradually, the bleeding stopped. Ana exhaled and leaned

back, letting her Affinity recede. The world slowly swam back into view: Sorsha's body on the floor before her, chest rising and falling gently. The light streaming in from across the hall. The carvings of the eagle, stallion, and seadragon on either side, the Bregonian officials half standing, half gawking beneath them.

And finally, the Admiral, standing with his hands clasped behind his back, delight dancing in his eyes.

Fury rose in her, white-hot, threatening to spill over. He'd done it on purpose, to test her. There was nothing more she wanted to do than to shake some sense into this man, who'd drawn his own daughter's blood for naught but a *game*. A *negotiation.*

Ana straightened. This was a show, she was beginning to realize, a demonstration of power. And she would give them one.

With a sweep of her hands, she gathered the blood spilled on the polished searock floor, the droplets that had splattered on her boots. She spread her hands and the blood snaked over her palms, twirling into ribbons that glittered like rubies in the light. She was aware of the entire hall's eyes on her, watching in fascination.

Ana smoothed her voice, sharpened her words. "King Darias, Three Courts of Bregon, I thank you for your attention. We face a common enemy, one that grows in power day by day. One that sits on the throne of Cyrilia, murdering my people. And now, she has turned her attention to the Kingdom of Bregon—to an artifact that would make her powerful beyond our imagination. One that would destroy both your world and mine."

Her words reverberated across the hall, echoing in the utter silence of Godhallem. The officials of the Three Courts held their breaths.

Ana brought her hands closer together, the twisting strands of blood arching to close the gap between them. She drove her point home. "I stand before you, as the rightful Empress of Cyrilia, to negotiate an alliance with the Kingdom of Bregon."

The Three Courts burst into an uproar as courtiers began to talk over each other, their voices rising into a crescendo. Amid it all, movement at the side of the hall caught Ana's eye. A young, dark-haired man in white robes and a set of spectacles had risen from his seat at the end of the hall, parchment in hand, taking notes. His outfit was collared with teal edges that rippled with each step he took. He paused at the back of Godhallem and, as though sensing Ana's eyes on him, looked up.

For a moment, their gazes met. Then, he blinked and disappeared through a set of doors leading out through the back.

Admiral Roran Farrald held up a single hand. Almost immediately, silence fell across the Courts. Finally, Ana felt their eyes on her, their gazes alert not in skepticism or mockery but in interest, and in fear.

Yes, she thought, lifting her chin a notch so that the sunlight caught the fading crimson of her eyes. Power was, indeed, a double-edged sword.

Roran Farrald tilted his head, his eyes narrowed. "I think, Blood Empress," he said slowly, "that we have something to negotiate after all."

27

Ramson stood at the open-air doorway to his chambers. It was almost evening, and even in the southern kingdom of Bregon, the sun hung over the unsteady sea, twilight unfurling overhead.

He had been placed in a guest suite in the Ambassador's wing of the Blue Fort several courtyards away from Godhallem, with Ana and Linn being shown to their respective chambers. Ramson's was a large room with pillars of searock and a balcony that overlooked the Whitewaves to the east, finer than any of the dormitories he'd known at the Naval Academy.

A set of steps led down from his balcony to a veranda below. This was the courtyard that stretched between the various towers in the fort. Winding streams of water flowed where crevasses had been carved into the ground, like veins that held the lifeblood of the structure. And interspersing the winding streams were the alder trees of his childhood.

The sound of wind and water and trees filled the air with a susurrus that washed over him like an old lullaby, dragging him back to a place of memories.

Bregon. *Home.* Seven years he'd been away from this place,

yet it felt like a lifetime ago that he'd hidden on the back of a supply wagon, heartbroken and drowning in his grief.

He shut his eyes and shook his head to clear the memories. He was no longer the boy of seven years past.

He'd washed and dressed in the crisp white shirt and pants that had been laid out for him on his bed. As he fastened brass buttons and straightened his ironed cuffs, Ramson felt more like his old self than he had in a while.

Yes, he thought as he caught his reflection in the window glass, sharp-cut and sleek-haired, *this* was the man he'd been made to be. The type of person he'd been trying to become: smooth and polished with a heart carved of stone and secrets.

When the door to his room slid soundlessly open, he turned and realized that a lifetime of preparation could not have readied him for this moment.

His father had aged in the years Ramson had been gone. Yet time wore well on Roran Farrald in the way it did with leather or fine wine. His jawline had broadened, his entire frame thickened so that he looked even larger and more powerful than he had when Ramson had been a boy. He was still clean-shaven, his hair short and now threaded with silver that gleamed in the torchlight.

They stood, staring at each other for several moments, and Ramson realized that he'd grown to be the same height as his father.

The Admiral's face broke into a smile. That unsettled Ramson more than any dagger or poison. "Well," Roran Farrald said, spreading his arms and swaggering in. "I have been waiting for this moment for seven years."

"You've a funny way of showing it," Ramson replied drily.

He felt shaken in a way he'd never felt when he'd made Trades for the Order of the Lily. Dealing with his father felt akin to trying to understand the motives of a wild animal. "Were you truly going to arrest me?"

"Oh, that was merely a test." The Admiral's teeth shone bone white. "I wanted to see what I could push that girl of yours to do."

Something hot and loose uncoiled in Ramson. He held very still, reminding himself that he had been through this many times before; that his father possessed the unique ability to hide threats in the most innocuous words to undo his enemies.

"I always knew you'd be back," Admiral Farrald continued, moving to the cherrywood cabinet by the wall. "You've always loved yourself too much and been too cowardly to die, I reasoned, and whatever you've been through in the past seven years can't be worse than the scars from here—that boy Jonah, your mother, what-have-you." His father flashed him a smile from across the room and held up a bottle of Bregonian liquor, the large gold ring on his finger scraping against the glass. "Brandy?"

To hear his father talk of his past so casually—each word felt like a cold knife against his skin. Ramson's voice sounded distant to his own ears when he said, "No, thanks."

"Shame. It's very good brandy."

The smell of liquor wafted across the room, and memories came flooding back: the slip of an arrow, the sigh of a lost life, the explosion of crimson against a wall. It had been hot chocolate mixed with brandy, Ramson suddenly remembered, in the cup the Admiral had handed him after Jonah had been murdered. His father had attempted to buy him off with a cup of hot chocolate and brandy.

He would not fall into the same trap again.

Ramson narrowed his eyes. The hot, molten anger flowing inside him just moments ago cooled. "I imagine you've had your fill of it since I've been gone," he said. "The Kingdom of Bregon is quite different from the version I left seven years back."

There was the clink of glass, the sound of liquid pouring, and then the thud of a bottle. Slowly, deliberately, the Admiral turned. "I couldn't have Bregon sit still and watch as Cyrilia grew powerful beyond our control."

Ramson thought of the new searock walls, the ironore doors, the trained magen in the Royal Guard. So his father *had* been behind it all.

What else had he done?

"You judge me," the Admiral said softly. "But someday, when I am gone, look from the sky to the shining sea, across the magnificence of this kingdom our ancestors have built from the ground. And perhaps, then, you will know a little of how it feels."

Ramson looked at the man who was his father, twilight shadows cutting his face into sharp edges. For a moment, he tried to imagine Roran Farrald as not the cruel father he had known but a man who helmed a great kingdom and had to make difficult decisions.

But the raven-black eyes of Jonah Fisher came back to him. The soft hazel ones of his mother. All gone now, not out of necessity but out of *greed*. Out of a lust for power.

Ramson swore to himself to never become like him. "Why are you here?" he replied tonelessly.

The Admiral raised his tumbler to Ramson. "I have a proposal for you. It's about that girl of yours."

Cold spread through his veins. "She's not my girl," Ramson said quietly.

"I see the way you look at her. The way you communicate with just a touch, or a glance. I have, after all, experienced it myself."

Something drew taut in Ramson. "Don't speak as if you've ever loved anybody in your life."

The Admiral's smile was indecipherable. "You can hide nothing from me. As much as I despise it, you are, after all, my son. My creation. And you seem to have forgotten the most important lesson I've taught you." He swirled the brandy in his glass. "Love makes us *weak,* boy."

Ramson forced his face into the cold, cruel mask he'd worn so often that he wondered whether it had become a part of him. "Fitting, then, that I've never loved anyone but myself," he said. "It seems I am your son, after all."

"Oh, good. Then perhaps you'll do what's logical for our kingdom." The Admiral's gaze sharpened. "It seems this Blood Empress has quite a talent. A rare magek."

Ramson kept silent.

The Admiral set down his glass. His next words surprised Ramson. "I am prepared to accept her offer of alliance. Undoubtedly, she will make a bid for Cyrilia's throne, and I am prepared to negotiate. The Cyrilian Empire has shown itself to be a threat of increasing magnitude. Even more so, with the latest events and the current Empress, I want to hedge against that threat. The enemy of my enemy is my friend, as the trite saying goes."

Ramson's mind spun. His father was not one to give without

taking, and most often, his offers came with a steep price. "And what do you get from this alliance?"

The Admiral paced to the open-air doorway. The evening light struck his lined face, his eyes distant like cold black waters. "The magen, Ramson, are the true lodestar to our developments and defenses. You'll have noticed their addition to the Navy, to the Royal Guard. I aim to create a generation of magen more powerful than any. I aim to harness their power as the world has never before seen.

"In return for our alliance, I will ask the Blood Empress to let us study her magek." He turned to Ramson, and at last, the full meaning of it all blossomed on his face in a smile. "I want you to speak to her about it, before the official negotiation. Persuade her, if you will. My alliance—for her power."

Ramson studied his father, considering. Roran Farrald wanted something from him—and Ramson had learned to never give without taking. Perhaps there was a way for him to get information for both his and Ana's missions. Two fish with one hook.

"So you'll work with her to protect the artifact she spoke of today?" he asked. "She won't agree to any deal without that. And don't even try denying it," he added as his father opened his mouth to respond. "We have good information on its existence. I've heard of the magen with multiple powers."

It had been a gamble—they didn't even know whether the artifact Tetsyev had spoken of was in the Blue Fort, or whether the Bregonian government was aware of it. Yet as the Admiral's eyes narrowed, Ramson felt a spark of delight deep inside. He'd hit gold.

"You, of all people, should know that we guard our secrets

closely," his father said coldly. "It is why Bregon has remained one of the strongest military powers in the world. If we gave our weapons away to everyone—"

"And she has no interest in taking it," Ramson interjected. His mind was already spinning a narrative, layering it within the murky web of motivation he'd glimpsed from his father. "Think about it—her people are dying, her empire is burning. She came all this way to ask for an alliance. The last thing she wants is to turn Bregon against her, too."

His father watched him, clutching his glass of brandy. "You mean to say that she will not cede without information on the artifact?"

Ramson shrugged. "I'm just laying the groundwork for the deal. I'm not interested in your politics, but if you want me to persuade her, this is the only way. To me, it sounds like two fish with one hook for you. She lets you study her blot magek, you work with her to protect your artifact from the Cyrilian Empress. She has good information on the Kolst Imperatorya Morganya's plans to seize it."

It sounded as though he were backing down, but really, Ramson had gotten precisely what he wanted. Roran Farrald had all but directly confirmed that the artifact with the ability to bestow multiple Affinities to its bearer lay right here, within the walls of the Blue Fort . . . in possession of the Bregonian government.

Admiral Farrald took a sip of his drink. "Very well," he purred. "You can advise her that, on behalf of the King and the Three Courts of Bregon, I am prepared to make such a deal with her."

Any ordinary person might have stepped away from this

conversation with their gains, but Ramson Quicktongue had been Deputy of the most notorious Cyrilian criminal network for a reason. "My . . . loyalty doesn't come without cost," he said. "If you want me to whisper in the Blood Empress's ear, then I want something in return."

A glint of caution mixed with amusement in his father's eyes. "You've learned well," he said. "What is it that you want in return?"

"Information."

Admiral Farrald waved his tumbler at Ramson. "Go on."

Ramson parsed the facts that he had, which bits to reveal to his father and which to keep to himself. "As I said, I didn't return to Bregon to play politics. I came back to kill Alaric Kerlan."

It was satisfying to see his father's face tighten. Roran Farrald had exiled Alaric Kerlan from Bregon many years ago; it seemed that Kerlan had built his criminal empire in Cyrilia, biding his time, waiting for the day he could take down Roran Farrald.

Ramson pushed forward. "I have it on multiple sources that Kerlan is back, and that he is running a magen trafficking scheme, kidnapping them from Cyrilia and bringing them here."

"Impossible." Roran Farrald's voice had grown cold. "The trading ports are tightly guarded. Sorsha is in charge of them, as Lieutenant of the Royal Guard. We would never have accepted any trade agreement with him."

With him. Ramson watched his father carefully. "Are you denying that Kerlan could be back, or that Bregon could have trafficking activity?"

A pause, and then there was the *thud-thud-thud* of boots against searock as his father crossed the room to him. Ramson knew he had pushed too hard, too far, but he stood his ground as Roran Farrald drew within a hand's reach of him. He could hear the rumble of his father's breathing, the smell of brandy bringing him back into memories that strung him taut with terror.

The Admiral clasped a hand over Ramson's shoulder and squeezed, digging his fingers into Ramson's collarbone. Pain bloomed. "Don't mistake my hospitability for generosity, *boy*," his father gritted, and Ramson finally saw a flash of the man who had killed a child in cold blood, who had let his lover die out of convenience. "Who do you think you are, wandering back here after seven years living as a lowlife, demanding answers to topics you can't even begin to fathom?"

Ramson couldn't breathe; he clenched his teeth to stop himself from making noise. It was all that he could do to keep upright when his father let him go. Ramson massaged his throat, aware that the Admiral had moved away. There was the sound of another drink being poured; heavy footsteps, the clink of two glasses against the coffee table. Admiral Farrald stood before him and bent close. The pungent scent of liquor hit Ramson. "I should remind you that your beggar of an empress doesn't seem to have many choices," he said, his voice growing dangerously soft. "If I refuse this alliance, then where will she go?"

Ramson kept silent. This was the danger of playing both sides: your opponent could use the information you'd given them against you.

"Counsel your Blood Empress to accept my conditions, and I'll continue our negotiation with whatever else you wish to have," the Admiral said as he handed the other glass of brandy to Ramson. His gaze was gripping, and Ramson remembered the sensation of plunging into an abyss whenever his father looked at him like that. "What is it that you want? Gold? Power? An army, to help you on your quest for vengeance?"

After all these years, his father still thought him unchanged from the desperate, lost boy who had run from this place. Thought that, with a simple offer and a cup of brandy, he could buy Ramson once again.

Ramson leveled his gaze to the Admiral's. He had absolutely no desire to have anything to do with the Bregonian government.

But for now, he had to let Roran Farrald believe that he'd won. That Ramson had been bought. "Actually, that doesn't sound half-bad," he said, swirling the liquor in his tumbler. "But if I convince the Blood Empress to agree to your conditions, then I don't want just an army. I want to be captain."

Slowly, the Admiral smiled. "Now, there's the son I know," he murmured. "If the deal goes through, Ramson, I'll have you reinstated in the Royal Navy as a captain." He raised his glass. "Drink . . . my son."

Ramson looked at the man before him, tan-skinned and brown-haired and cold-eyed, and saw traces of himself, of what he might have become, in that face. But he said nothing, only curled his lips in a semblance of a smile, as he raised his glass and pressed it to his lips.

The brandy was sickly sweet with a tinge of spice, and it burned his mouth, his throat, his chest, every part of his body down to its core. Ramson clutched the cup, and he drank it all.

 28

Early evening in the Kingdom of Bregon was beautiful, Ana had to admit as she made her way to the courtyards. The terrain of the Blue Fort was peppered with verandas that were connected with steps that adjusted to the shifting elevation of the cliffs. The wind was warm, and from beyond the Blue Fort's high walls came the constant crash of waves, faint but clear.

The sky was a forget-me-not blue, the silver disc of the moon beginning to rise. Lamps were lit among the alder trees and hung on walls, lending pockets of yellow light. Here and there, figures strolled in the gentle lull of night, their murmured conversations carried by the breeze.

Ana sat on the edge of a stone fountain. The Admiral had set them up as guests in the Ambassador's Suites, several courtyards away from Godhallem, where they'd settled down and changed. Ana had chosen the least complicated outfit in her wardrobe: a slim white gown that glittered, spilling down the length of her legs like a sheath, and a matching pair of elbow-length gloves.

The first thing she'd done upon her arrival was to pen a letter to Yuri, informing him of Shamaïra's capture. Still, even as Ana had stood by the windows of the Bregonian courier room and watched the seadove fly into the distance, she couldn't help but feel that this wasn't enough. Shamaïra had saved her life. And she, Ana, was in a foreign kingdom an ocean away from returning the favor.

Her hands fisted. She needed to secure an alliance with Bregon, fast; she needed to return home, to Cyrilia.

A familiar voice cut through her thoughts. She looked up sharply. On a path between two rows of trees stood Sorsha Farrald, in conversation with someone else. The thick foliage and semidarkness hid Ana from view as she crept closer to see who it was.

With a jolt, she realized that she recognized the other figure. Dressed in the same elegant white robes and carrying a set of scrolls, the young scholarly man from Godhallem spoke softly, his words punctuated by Sorsha's rapid-fire speech.

Who was he? Why had he been the only noncourtier—at least, she'd surmised—to appear at Godhallem earlier, and more important, why was he speaking to Sorsha?

As Ana watched, her Affinity sensed two familiar signatures approaching behind her. Ana turned.

Linn and Kaïs appeared from the doors of the Ambassador's Suites, nearly unrecognizable in their new attire. Linn wore a dress of deep blue threaded with green that rippled like ocean waves when light struck it. They brought out the hues of dark blue in her hair and eyes, the colors playing off each other like ocean waters beneath a midnight sky. And Kaïs had donned a navy-blue shirt with black breeches.

Ana pressed a finger to her lips and nodded to the alder trees. When she turned back, however, Sorsha was gone; only the young scholar remained, looking deep in thought.

Linn crouched next to Ana. "Him," she breathed.

Kaïs frowned. "He was at Godhallem."

Ana nodded. "I just saw him talking to Sorsha Farrald." It would be good to meet someone else in the Blue Fort, perhaps someone whose inclinations were less clear than the Farralds'. She had more questions, anyway, starting with the newest version of the Bregonian government's personnel. Ramson had clearly left a few things out.

Speaking of . . . "Where's Ramson?" she whispered.

"He did not answer his door," Linn said.

Ana glanced back to the young scholar, who had begun to walk away. No matter—she would find Ramson later.

She motioned at Linn and Kaïs, and they hurried after the scholar.

The young scholar led them to an open courtyard; Ana watched him enter a large domed building—the only one of its kind in the Blue Fort's array of stern, square structures with crenellated walls. As they neared, Ana saw that this building's doors were made of ironore, woven through with searock that seemed to undulate in the light of the moon.

Ana lifted a hand to the bronze knockers—the Three Gods of Bregon curving around a single scroll—and pushed the doors open.

The interior was cool, dimly lit with low-burning lamps. There were no windows here—the sun's rays were damaging to books—and it took a few moments for Ana's eyes to adjust.

The first thing she saw were books. Thousands upon thousands of them, stacked on gilded shelves that lined the walls and the crescents of alcoves, giving the impression of endless waves of leather tomes. A single hallway cut through the center of the space, and overhead was a giant mural that stretched from this entrance to the very end of the library.

"Oh," Linn whispered. "Ramson told us about this. The Livren Skolaren."

Ramson had introduced the Livren Skolaren to them as the Great Scholars' Library of Bregon, said to house the most complete records of the kingdom's history. Its use was restricted to courtiers of the Blue Fort and recruits at the Naval Academy.

Ana looked around. The center of the library was lined with oakwood desks. Scholars sat scattered throughout, their white robes dotting the otherwise dark décor. The air was filled with the quiet rustle of their pages, the scratches of pen, the occasional murmur.

There were others here, too: regular officials of the Blue Fort in the standard royal-blue Bregonian uniforms, perusing volumes or taking notes from thick tomes. Several glanced Ana's way, their gazes trailing her, but clearly the Admiral's word had gotten out, for they were left alone.

At the back of the library, studying the tomes on a shelf, was the scholar they had been following.

Linn and Kaïs took their positions to stand guard by the entrance while Ana made straight for where the young scholar stood, his hand hovering over gilded spines. "Excuse me," she said in Bregonian.

He turned to face her. Surprise bloomed on his face, which quickly turned to recognition from behind his spectacles. "Can I help you, meindame?" His voice was soft, like the trickle of water.

"I thought I saw you earlier, in Godhallem, and wondered if you might be able to help me," Ana said.

He looked at her a moment longer, then inclined his head. "Head Scholar Tarschon, meindame. I run the public and private records of the Livren Skolaren and oversee educational research."

The man was at most five, six years older than her. To have been made Head Scholar at such a young age—Ana was familiar enough with court politics that she knew someone had to have placed him in that position for a reason other than knowledge.

That aside, it made him an extremely valuable resource. Ana put on a smile. "Well met, Scholar Tarschon," she said. "I'm unfamiliar with navigating the Livren Skolaren, and was wondering whether you'd be kind enough to direct me."

"And what is it that you are searching for?"

"I'm trying to learn about ancient artifacts of Bregon."

"All of our recorded artifacts are merely historical and have either been relocated to museums or been destroyed." He watched her politely, as though waiting to be dismissed, but it was a signal: He wasn't going to help her.

Still, he wouldn't outright reject her, either, which left a little room for her to try again. "Is there any artifact that fits the description of the object I spoke about earlier today?"

His expression didn't change. "I'm afraid I can't help you, meindame."

A clear signal—he wasn't going to yield much more. "Is there anyone else I can speak to about this matter?" Ana pressed. "The Queen Regent, perhaps—it seems she was not at Godhallem earlier."

Something shifted in Scholar Tarschon's face; he looked guarded. "I cannot advise. Admiral Farrald would be your best contact." He paused, and inclined his head again. "I must excuse myself, meindame—I do have other matters to get to."

Ana couldn't think of how else to persuade someone who was reluctant to help, to say the least. She watched him leave, feeling as though she'd just lost a good lead.

She felt the smallest stir of winds, like a breath against her cheeks, as Linn appeared beside her.

"Did you find anything?" Linn asked, gazing after Tarschon.

Ana shook her head. "I felt like I was talking to a wall," she muttered, but then a new idea struck. If she couldn't coax anything out of Scholar Tarschon directly, perhaps she could gather information indirectly, instead. "Linn, can you follow that man?"

A shadow of a smile curled her friend's lips. "It would be sad not to test out how well my new clothes blend into the shadows."

Ana found herself grinning back. "I'm going to stay here and see what else I can find. I need more information on the Bregonian courtiers and officials of the Blue Fort."

Linn nodded. "I will report back tonight," she replied, and turned and made for the doors where Tarschon had exited. She stopped to murmur a few words to Kaïs, who nodded and remained where he was. His eyes, though, trailed her with what Ana thought were glimmers of concern.

Ana spent the rest of the evening in the Livren Skolaren poring over anything and everything she could find about Bregonian defense strategy and weapons. Her search for artifacts had led her to read lengthy chapters on searock and ironore, the two materials found only in the Corshan Gulf in the south of Bregon. The newer sections on those records included details on how the Bregonian government had discovered new properties that could strengthen their defenses and had begun excavating it en masse.

As time passed and the night deepened, the patrons of the Livren Skolaren began to wrap up. Books were shut, lamps were doused, and the doors opened and closed incessantly as scholars trickled out. Ana had just started reading about the ability of searock to absorb the properties of other precious stones and metals when a shadow fell over her.

"Oh," Sorsha said, smirking. "What a change a bath and some new clothes can make." She leaned against the other end of the table, color returned to her cheeks, looking for all the world like her own father hadn't slashed his sword across her neck earlier in the day. She'd changed outfits into a standard Bregonian blue doublet and breeches, cinched by a gold-studded belt at her waist. Daggers glinted like ornaments at her hips, unsheathed. The tips of her boots sloped into metal sharper than knives' points, designed to cut. She'd undone the top part of her previously tightly buttoned collar; resting at the base of her throat was the glittering black necklace that Ana had noticed earlier. The color matched her eyes.

Below it was a pale white scar, the only indication of her father's earlier assault on her.

Sorsha traced Ana's gaze and brought her fingers to her neck, stroking it lovingly. "The healers in Bregon work wonders," she crooned. "Don't look so shocked; this is far from the worst my father's done to me."

Ana's stomach turned. "What are you doing here?" she snapped. There was no one else around; the library had completely emptied out. Only Kaïs stood in the same spot he had since they'd arrived. He stood straighter now, his eyes glinting as they caught the lamplight.

Sorsha's lips curled. "Why, as Lieutenant of the Royal Guard, I thought I'd check in on you."

Ana reined in her anger. There was nothing to be achieved from antagonizing this girl, who saw no rhyme or reason. "You can report back to your father that I'm doing quite well," she said curtly.

"I see that." Sorsha giggled. "You even have your own bodyguard now." She gestured at Kaïs.

Ana bristled. "He's not my bodyguard."

"Oh?" Sorsha smiled coyly in Kaïs's direction and crooked a finger at him. "Then am I free to persuade him to work for me? I could make a *very* convincing argument."

Ana stood, her chair scraping loudly in the silence. "Leave him alone," she growled. "And the rest of my court, too." A fierce defensiveness surged in her as she thought of Ramson, the look on his face when his father called for his arrest. "You try to touch any one of them and I'll finish what we started back at the Crown's Port."

Sorsha Farrald tipped her head back in a sharp laugh. It echoed down the hallway. "I see the way you look at me," she said. "Like you're afraid." She lowered her voice, giggling. "You have *no* idea."

Faster than a blink, she danced past Ana's side, her arm darting out. It was only when the coppery tang of blood snaked into the air that Ana realized Sorsha had sliced her cheek with a blade.

"What—" Without thinking, Ana lashed out with her

Affinity, slamming Sorsha against the searock floor. At the sudden movement, Kaïs drew his double swords, but Ana held up a hand.

Sorsha was panting, her eyes wide in ecstasy, a fleck of Ana's blood dotting her lip. Ana watched in disbelief as the girl's tongue snaked out and she licked the blood away. "Mm," Sorsha murmured. "Such a *delicious* magek."

"You're sick," Ana said.

Sorsha gave a high-pitched laugh. "Oh, go on!" she shrieked. "Throw me against the floor, *harder*! What?" she added, pouting as Ana loosened her grasp on the girl. "Are you *afraid*?"

Wordlessly, Ana dropped her Affinity from the girl and took a step back. Something about Sorsha unsettled her down to her core.

Sorsha clambered to her feet. Her hair was disheveled; strands stuck to her face, but she seemed not to notice. "How disappointing," she said, and for a moment, she sounded like an echo of her father, their tones dulcet and cold. "Such a powerful magek, wasted on a spineless little girl like you."

"Killing you wouldn't do me any favors for my meeting with your father tomorrow," Ana replied.

Sorsha's face darkened. The transformation was so stark that Ana felt as though she were looking at a completely different person. "Don't," Sorsha snarled, "assume you know *anything* about my father. He'd never give a second thought to killing me if it weren't for the fact that he could *use* me."

"What do you mean, 'use you'?"

Sorsha cackled. "Nothing much." She leered at Ana. "I'd like to think we're not so different after all, you and I. Monsters make the most powerful weapon in the arsenal."

The words chilled Ana. She averted her gaze from the girl's scars. "If you won't leave, then I will."

She left Sorsha standing in the midst of the great library, a wild smile stretching from ear to ear.

"Are you all right?" Kaïs's voice was deep and low as they descended the steps to cross the courtyards back to the Ambassador's wing. The trees on either side of their walkway danced as wind brushed through them. High above, stars shimmered in the heat haze.

"Fine," Ana replied. "If she bothers you, come to me. I told her to leave us alone."

"I will."

It had never occurred to her that she might defend this yaeger, or that she might even feel a rush of gratitude toward him. "Thank you for staying with me," Ana added.

He inclined his head. They spoke no more as they traversed the courtyards, yet this time, the silence between them had shifted to something less hostile, even companionlike. At the steps of the Ambassador's Suites, Ana bid him good night. The weather was beautiful, the air warm, and she wanted to walk a bit more to clear her head and mull over the information she had learned today.

Yet even as she strolled around the veranda behind the Ambassador's wing, she couldn't stop thinking of Sorsha's bone-chilling laughter, the wildness to her eyes, the way she dismissed her father's abuse without batting an eyelash.

Monsters make the most powerful weapon in the arsenal.

29

Darkness had fallen and moonlight cut bright through his open balcony doors when Ramson finally got back to his feet. He'd been stretched out on his silk divan, staring up at the ceiling, the overlapping carvings of sea and sky and earth blurring and swirling into one with his thoughts.

His head was still aching, but he'd managed to wade through the voices eddying in his mind to begin to string together a coherent set of actions.

Which all started with getting off his chaise.

The room swayed as he stumbled to the balcony. The sea glimmered as far as the eye could see. The Bregonians thought it symbolic that they could see all three major oceans from the Blue Fort. To the east, the foam-flecked waters of the Whitewaves that led to Cyrilia and the Southern Crowns. To the west, the swirling turquoise of the Jade Trail, their trade route to the Aseatic kingdoms. And to the north, the unknown Silent Sea that held glaciers as deep as the bottom of the ocean itself, waters colder than ice, it was rumored.

Ramson leaned against the balustrade. Night had sucked the moisture and warmth from the air, and the breeze that greeted him was cool and refreshing. It cleared his head immediately, snatching the alcohol from his breath. Gods be damned, he'd forgotten how strong pure Bregonian brandy could be. The rest of the evening had been a blur—he could only recall the silhouette of his father's back turning on him, the door shutting with a click.

Gathering his thoughts felt like trying to hold broken glass: the fragments of information were sharp and refused to fit together. His father hadn't been able to—hadn't *wanted* to—give Ramson a clear answer on the Affinite trafficking in Bregon. He'd vehemently denied that Alaric Kerlan could be let back into this kingdom. And he'd easily given away a high-ranking position in the Navy to study Ana's Affinity.

Most important, though, he'd confirmed that the artifact with the ability to bestow multiple Affinities upon its bearer lay within the walls of the Blue Fort. *That* was the most important piece of information he had to get to Ana . . . before he left the Blue Fort.

By whatever twisted sense of humor the gods had, he watched her stride into his sight at that very moment.

Ana approached on the path that cut through the alder trees, her hair and gown spilling behind her and silvered by the moonlight. She was walking quickly, and he noted her stiff posture, the way she shifted her head every now and then, as though trying to glimpse behind her.

It took him no time at all to spot the two guards trailing her, ducking between the trees.

With a light leap, Ramson flipped over the railing of his balcony. It was a low drop to the ground, and the sound of wind and water masked his footsteps as he took a path that would cut directly into the walkway she was on.

Ramson slipped behind an alder tree, counting down the even beat to her footfalls. *Five, three, two steps—*

An invisible force wrapped around him and slammed him against the tree trunk.

Ramson coughed as a familiar figure stepped in his path. "Ana—it's me—"

"Deities, Ramson," she hissed, and he felt her Affinity loosen from him.

He straightened. "You're being followed."

"I *know,*" she scoffed, and in the dim moonlight, he saw her eyes flash crimson as she rolled them toward where he'd last seen the guards.

"I need to talk to you," he whispered. "Without . . . *them.*"

She frowned. "Where?"

The alcohol swirled in his head, emboldening him. He reached out and grabbed Ana's hand, giving her a light tug toward him. Gently, he spun her and pressed her against the alder tree, shifting so that they were in a clear patch of moonlight.

She stiffened as he closed the gap between them. "What are you—"

He lowered his lips next to her ear. "Old trick, remember?" he said, and he knew they were both thinking of Kerlan's mansion, of the way they'd dodged the yaeger back then. "Can you sense the guards' movements?" She nodded, her hair tickling his chin. "Let me know when they turn around."

Her chest brushed against his as she inhaled. Wedged between him and the tree, she was tense, her breaths coming quickly. Ramson drew back slightly to give her space, and in that moment, she looked up, her features bright and clear beneath the moonlight. He couldn't help but notice the soft curve of her lips, the flutter of her lashes as her eyes, too, roved his face.

Her fingers slipped into his, cold but firm. And then she was leaning toward him, her lips parting and his thoughts were scrambling—

"The guards," she whispered. "They've turned away."

Then, with a light tug, she drew him behind the alder tree, and into the shadows of the courtyard.

30

It wasn't difficult to lose the guards. Ana followed Ramson through the trees, past winding paths and across streams, his hands tight against hers. The flickers of blood around them grew sparse and the trees thicker as they headed toward what Ana thought might be an older section of the Blue Fort.

They stopped when they reached a section of the walls that were made of stone, close to the cliffs. Beyond, Ana could hear the crashing of the waves. Vines climbed up the wall, thick and dotted with small red flowers. They filled the air with a sharp, spicy fragrance.

"Ramson," she panted. "Where are we—"

Ramson reached out and swept back the curtain of vines to reveal a set of stairs, leading into the wall. He gave a small bow. "Meya dama, up these stairs you'll find the best ocean views this kingdom can offer."

The steps were narrow and weather-worn, severely needing repair. There were no balustrades, but Ramson kept a tight grip on her wrist. It was pitch-black but for slits in the wall, where moonlight dusted the darkness and small breezes stirred the stale air around them.

Finally, it began to grow light, with the distant sound of waves. They emerged to open air.

A small *oh* escaped Ana's lips as she surveyed the scene around them.

They stood on the walkway of a wall that had been built into the cliffs. Sections of it were crumbling, and the stone was so weather-beaten that it seemed to have melded with the cliff. Beyond them was nothing but the dark expanse of ocean, moonlight glinting like shards of glass on its waves.

"It's beautiful," Ana breathed.

"It's an old guard tower," Ramson said. A smile softened his mouth, and his eyes sparkled with a joy that she had almost never seen in him. The wind stirred his locks, and for a moment, he looked like a boy, standing at the edge of sea and sky. "I used to come up here with a friend."

There was something raw to his voice, a tender honesty in the way he spoke. Ana realized that he'd kept his fingers twined around hers, and the touch sent shivers through her belly.

"Wait till you see the pool," Ramson said, and pulled her forward.

The walkway tapered off into a flat stretch of cliffs. Water gushed from a crevice higher up in the cliff wall, collecting in a natural basin before spilling over the edge and plunging out of view into the sea below.

Ana thought of the waterfall they'd jumped down at Ghost Falls, of the roaring white currents of the Tiger's Tail river. She shrank back. "It looks dangerous."

Ramson's smile was wicked. "It probably is," he said. "It has a rather gruesome origin myth. Want to hear it?"

Ana raised an eyebrow. "This had better not be what you brought me here for."

"Legend has it," Ramson began, "that the first King of Bregon fell in love with a siren. He possessed the magek to water—that is, he was a water Affinite—so he manipulated the current of ocean water so that it flowed uphill at nighttime. That was when they would reunite, with only the stars and the moon as their witnesses."

Ana thought of the statue of the man and the siren in the Livren Skolaren.

"In his old age, the King simply vanished one day. Bregonians think that he dove into the ocean to be united forever with his lover. By drowning," Ramson added, as though to clarify. "As a kid, I'd always thought—if there was any truth to such a preposterous tale—that this might be where he dove off and died."

She frowned at him. "That's a horrible love story."

Ramson grinned. "It's a very Bregonian love story."

"Well, remind me not to fall in love in Bregon," she replied. He caught her gaze, and the teasing smile on his face softened as something flickered in his eyes. Heat crept up her neck, but before she could say anything, Ramson strode past her, kicked off his shoes, and dove into the pool.

Ana rushed to the edge of the water, her heart thrumming as she searched for him. There it was, that age-old fear, pumping adrenaline into her veins, heightening her panic.

For several moments, Ramson was submerged, darkness clouding him. And then, from beneath the surface of the pool, the water began to glow. It was as though the moon were blooming from *beneath* him, dusting light from the depths that fractaled up all around Ramson as he swam the length of the pool.

"It's glowing," she exclaimed when he surfaced.

Ramson laughed and straightened, his hair dripping water, his shirt wet and clinging to the ridges of his body. He pushed aside a lock of hair, looking up at her through half-lidded eyes. It took her a moment to realize that *he* was glowing, silver trickling like liquid mercury down his cheeks, his jawline, his neck, glistening on his shirt and pooling at his chest.

Ramson held up a hand, silver droplets threading down his wrist. Ana could just make out the faint outline of his tattoo, a curled stalk with three stems. "Seadust," he said. "They're actually infinitely small creatures that glow when they come into contact with heat, but Bregonians believe they're the souls of the ones we've lost, come to greet us in the oceans." He dropped his hand into the water again, making a small splash. "It's why our oceans glow during the hottest days in the summers, and why our Moon Lagoon in the south shines the brightest. Whereas you Cyrilians celebrate the First Snows, we celebrate Sommesreven, the Night of Souls." His smile dropped slightly, and his eyes had a distant look. "We commemorate those we've lost on Sommesreven, when the oceans are brightest and the souls of our dead linger in between, held by our Three Gods."

She'd never learned this in her studies, which had always been focused on politics and economics. "It's beautiful."

His gaze snapped up, and he held out a hand. "Try it. Seadust is good luck. Go on."

She hesitated, but he waded to her and took her hand in his. His eyes flicked to hers and he paused, one finger hooked under the edge of her glove, as though asking for permission. When she didn't protest, he gently peeled back her glove.

She shivered at the combination of cool night air, the rough calluses of his fingers trailing feather-light against her skin. As though he held an infinitely precious object, Ramson set her glove at the edge of the pool and clasped her hand in his. Slowly, he lowered it into the water.

"There," he said. Was it her imagination, or did his voice sound huskier than normal? "Now you're blessed by our Sea God."

She chuckled, wriggling her bare fingers and marveling at how the water lit up. "Well," she said, lifting her gaze to look at him from beneath her lashes. "Please extend my thanks to your Sea God."

A far-off sound interrupted them. At first, Ana thought it was the whistle of the wind between rocks, but the noise grew louder: a haunting keening sound that echoed off the rocks surrounding them, cresting.

Ramson straightened, gazing out at the expanse of night, stock-still. "Gossenwal," he murmured. "Ghostwales."

Beneath the surface of the ocean far below, Ana could see glimmers of light weaving through the water. They grew brighter and brighter until one burst through the surface, emitting a call that sent shivers down her spine. Even from this high up, she could make out their fins, the sleek twist of their bodies and the curve to their tails as they arced out of the water before diving in again.

"They're beautiful," she whispered.

"The Sea God," Ramson said quietly, "had a disciple named

Jonah. The myths say that after he died, he was reincarnated as a ghostwale. That his soul still wanders the oceans every night."

Ana had never heard this story, but she was surprised at the way his voice caught.

Ramson looked as though he were in a dream, his face bright with reflections from the water. Ana could have stayed here and listened to him talk about his kingdom and his gods forever. The sky, strewn with stars like a canvas smudged with the dust of pearls, the whisper of the water and the wind, and the glow of seadust draping them both in light—it *felt* like a dream, like another world.

And perhaps it was the surreality of it all that held her still as Ramson turned to her and reached out a hand to brush aside a strand of hair that had fallen into her eyes, his touch blazing heat down her cheek.

"Do you believe in Sommesreven?" she asked, her voice barely a breath.

Ramson's eyes were half-shut as he trailed his fingers down a lock of her hair. "No. What's dead is dead, and there is nothing in this world or the next that can bring them back."

She shivered at his words, the faces of her dead swirling in her mind. Mama. Papa. May. Luka. All those who had died by her hand.

And all those who would die, if she didn't find the artifact before Morganya.

"Ramson," she said, pulling her attention from the tips of his fingers on her hair to her words. "Tell me about your father."

Ramson turned his gaze away. Drops of silver liquid clung to his lashes. "Don't trust him, Ana," he said. "There are things he's not telling us regarding the artifact. It's here. He knows about it."

Her stomach tightened. "What did he say to you? When did you see him?"

"He came to see me earlier. I bluffed; he fell for it, and let it slip." He ran a hand through his hair. "It's very likely that the Bregonian government won't want to tell us more about this artifact for defensive purposes, but I have the feeling my father is hiding far more than that. I asked him about the Bregonian Affinite trafficking scheme, and he wouldn't give me a direct answer, either." Ramson narrowed his eyes. "I keep thinking there's a bigger picture we're not seeing."

"Affinite trafficking—as in, Alaric Kerlan's scheme?" She frowned. "Why would your father make a deal with him?"

Ramson shook his head. "I don't know," he replied quietly. "I don't think he would, either—but the Sea Court controls the ports, which means no ships enter without their knowledge. Unless someone else is approving Kerlan's entry." He met her gaze. "I'm going to get to the bottom of all this."

"You're leaving?" Ana suddenly felt cold. "In the midst of all this?"

"Ana, listen to me carefully." His voice was low, his words coming fast, urgent. "The Admiral is going to make you an offer: an alliance, in exchange for the chance to study your Affinity."

An alliance. Her heart leapt. Yet . . . "To study my Affinity?" she repeated. "Why?" She'd expected the Admiral would be interested in her and her Affinity—perhaps as a valuable addition to their forces, certainly, to fight with . . . but to be *studied.* That invoked memories of her childhood, of dungeons and Sadov's pale white fingers prodding at her in the dark. Ana suppressed a shudder.

"I know as much about it as you do," Ramson said. "But in the event that he does . . ." He blew through his mouth. "I just don't feel good about it, Ana."

"An alliance, though," she said quietly. It was all so tantalizingly close, just within her grasp. Everything she had been working toward—an army, a rebellion, challenging Morganya—suddenly seemed possible . . . if she just gave a bit of herself away in exchange. "I know we don't trust your father, but if I work with the Bregonian government—the King, the Queen Regent, and the Three Courts—then it should be fine."

Ramson sighed and combed his fingers through his hair again—a sign, she had learned, that meant he was stressed. "Look, I don't want to let my personal biases get in the way. It's your decision."

"Are you leaving tonight?" she asked instead.

He averted his gaze and gave a nod. For some reason, disappointment surged through her. She'd expected this, she'd known that he wasn't in Bregon purely to help her, and in their original plans, he'd never meant to end up at the Blue Fort. But with everything they had just learned, she'd thought he would change his mind.

She'd come to rely on him too much. This time, she had plans of her own. It started with gathering all the information she could . . . and tracking down a certain scholar again. For if Admiral Farrald was aware of the artifact Morganya was after, then Tarschon had most certainly lied about it.

She also had the Admiral's offer to consider.

Ana stood. The air had grown cold, the crash of waves on the cliffs below rising to a roar. Ramson still stood in the pool, but the seadust had dimmed, and only a faint glow remained in the waters around him. She thought of the levity to their conversation earlier, the way his fingers had sparked heat on her skin. It had seemed too good to be true, and now she realized that it had been. Their paths had always led to different destinations.

"Good luck, Ramson," she said, and left him standing there, still as a statue in the pool that tumbled over the edge into the ocean below, the seadust shimmering faint around him like remnants of a dying dream.

31

By the time Ramson went back to his chambers and put on a fresh change of clothing, the clock on his mantelpiece showed that it was past midnight. He made sure to be noisy, banging around the cabinets and splashing water in his bathroom. He extinguished his candle, waited several minutes, and then snuck out through his veranda. The guards stationed outside his chambers didn't suspect a thing.

The Bregonian court outfit he'd changed into was a deep royal blue, almost black. It wasn't difficult to blend into the shadows, to slip through the courtyards into the section of buildings that made up the Naval Academy.

Here, the buildings were older and made of solid stone, with none of the new searock and ironore enhancements Ramson had seen in the Naval Headquarters. Ramson passed by a training hall and looked inside. A feeling, both tender and painful, rose in his throat as he took in the empty stone hall, inevitably filled with memories of Jonah Fisher.

It wasn't long after that he began to make out the faint torchlight of the keep at the Crown's Cut, which inspected supply wagons coming in and out of the Blue Fort, usually leading to connecting towns. When he'd left Bregon as a boy, he'd learned that the inspection was much more stringent on incoming wagons than outgoing ones. This was the only way out of the Blue Fort without boarding one of those gondolas at Helmesgatten and attracting his father's attention.

At this hour, the courtyard was relatively empty, but there were several supply wagons still parked in line, waiting to leave. Ramson drew a breath and, with a prayer to the gods, he darted forward and leapt onto the back of a wagon. A flick of his wrist, and a pin appeared; within seconds, the wagon door was open, and Ramson slipped in, latching the door behind him.

He had a sense of déjà vu as he crouched in the back of the wagon, watching as the lights of the Blue Fort winked smaller and smaller until the night swallowed them.

Sapphire Port was deserted when the wagon pulled up at the stables. Ramson hopped out and ducked into the shadows of the streets. He retraced his steps to the docks. The Black Barge was a silhouette against the night.

He whistled and a head appeared over the railing. "Finally," said a familiar voice, and the next moment, a rope was thrown over the side of the ship. With enviable agility, Daya swung herself overboard and slid down the length of the rope. "Where in the name of Amara have you been?"

Ramson tapped two fingers to his forehead in a mock salute. "Sorry. Ran into a slight delay."

Daya rolled her eyes. "Well, the party's over now."

His senses perked; his hand tightened on the hilt of his misericord sheathed at his hip. "What do you mean? You found something?"

He had asked Daya—for no small price—to keep an eye on

the port for him while he escorted Ana, Linn, and Kaïs to the Blue Fort. He'd reasoned the investment was one worth making, since she was familiar with the way Kerlan did his business in this kingdom.

And, Ramson thought with grim pleasure, it seemed he'd been right.

Daya stuck her tongue out. "Duh. Told you that you were paying for some high-quality *reconnaissance.*"

"Show me."

She huffed a breath and crooked two fingers. Their boots stole soft against the wooden quays, the night filled with the rush of the ocean and the whisper of the wind. They were headed, Ramson guessed, to the very end of the port.

As they walked, the ships grew scarcer and became a more ragged assortment of smaller brigs and fishing boats—until a massive galleon loomed before them. From the dim moonlight filtering through the clouds, Ramson could see that it flew no flags.

"No sigil," Daya whispered, "no particular design. Most ships are painted over with symbols like a pirate's got tattoos, but this one is trying not to stand out. It's been here since we arrived this afternoon, but no one was around it until earlier tonight. The port's closed by six bells, and it was long after that when I caught a line of people disembarking. And Amara look upon me, I *recognized* several of those bastards." She looked smug. "They'd been on my ship before."

"Kerlan's men?" Ramson muttered.

"Kerlan's men," Daya confirmed. "Sneaking around like they didn't want anybody seeing them. Tsk, tsk. Definitely up to no good. Oh, but here's where it gets creepy . . ."

Ramson threw her a skeptical look.

"What?" she snapped, shooting him a glare. "You'd be scared, too, if you'd been here." She swallowed and touched a hand to her collarbone, where her tattoo of the goddess Amara was. "I thought I heard screaming coming from it."

Ramson looked around. This part of Sapphire Port was remote enough that no one would come looking. "Screaming?" he repeated.

Daya nodded, her eyes wide. "At first I thought it was just the wind, but when I listened more closely—hey, where are you going?"

"Only one way to find out," Ramson called over his shoulder. He heard her hissing curses at him, which turned to whisper-shouts threatening that he was on his own if anything happened to him.

Before him, the ship Daya had pointed out was a silhouette looming against the night. When he reached the end of the jetty and glanced back, Daya had disappeared into the shadows; he caught a flash of her eyes as she watched him.

Ramson paused to listen. There was nothing but the sound of the ship creaking as it bobbed up and down, the sound of water gurgling beneath its hull.

With a light leap, he swung himself onto the anchor line. It clinked gently as he began to haul himself up, his feet scampering easily over the chain links, his hands steady. When at last he reached the top, he peered over the hull and, seeing no one, he hauled himself over the railing and onto the deck.

The ship was a midsized vessel, with a large hull for storing goods. Ramson searched the captain's cabin first, which was predictably empty, and then turned his attention to the hatch—the door that led to the hold belowdecks. It was locked, which wasn't a surprise, and it took him a few moments' work with his pick before the trapdoor clicked open.

Quietly as he could, he descended the rungs of the ladder. The air here was musty, and it took some time for his eyes to adjust to the dimness. Slowly, shapes began to emerge—piles and piles of crates.

Ramson stole over to one of them. It took him longer than usual to work the lock in the darkness. At last, the lid popped with a satisfying click.

He peered inside.

The crate was filled to the brim with searock. Under the faint moonlight that filtered through the opening above, he recognized the rippling patterns across the material's surface. One piece caught a blue-green hue as he held it higher and turned it over in his hand.

Why would Alaric Kerlan be hoarding searock? More important, *how* had he gotten his hands on so much of it? Searock was a precious mineral available only in the south Bregonian seas, its mining tightly controlled by the Bregonian government.

Had Kerlan somehow stolen it?

He investigated several other crates, which all yielded the same result. Finding nothing else, he made sure each crate was shut tight before he left.

Daya looked immensely relieved when he rejoined her. "Well?" When he gave a slight shake of his head, she continued, "Try again tomorrow."

But Ramson remained deep in thought as they stole back to the Black Barge to settle down for the night. Olyusha had said

Kerlan's trade with Bregon was related to a new development with Affinites. How was searock connected to this?

He drifted into uneasy sleep, plagued by dreams of searock prisons and shadow ships, and monsters in the dark that lay in wait.

32

Bregon was a kingdom of water and sea, but there was wind here, too. Linn had hitched her dress into the breeches she'd worn under it, her own leather boots silent to the steel-tipped toes of the Bregonian Navy uniform, and she felt like herself once again.

Most important, her knives hung at her waist, strapped tightly and yielding to her body's bend and flex as though they were a part of her.

She'd been following the scholar for a good portion of the evening, tailing him through the whispering alder trees and flitting between the gray-shingled roofs of the Blue Fort like a shadow. So far, he'd stopped by to meet with several officials before returning to what Linn assumed were his own chambers.

She leaned against the wall of his balcony, one leg dangling over the railing, watching as the lamplight in his room flickered. Before long, it went out; she heard the creak of his bed, and then silence.

Linn sighed. She waited. Minutes passed; she counted. When he didn't stir again, she stood and stretched. She considered returning to her chambers to tell Ana that the scholar had been up to nothing and that she had no useful findings to share—but inspiration struck her as she looked around the courtyards, utterly empty at this hour.

If she were to explore more of the Blue Fort, it was best done under the cloak of night. There was no telling what she might find.

Linn heaved herself onto the balustrade and began to climb.

Her thoughts wandered to what Ramson had taught them of the magic that people possessed in Bregon. Linn knew that in Cyrilia, Affinites were born to nothing but the rawest forms of their Affinities. Most were left uncultivated, like a seed without sunlight.

In Kemeira, wielders learned harmony: to extend their minds and their souls so that they were one with their element. Every aspect of life, Kemeirans believed, was a circle of some sort: a giant cycle in which they all took part, in which there was give-and-take from every person and every life. Wielders depended on givers—those without magic—to harvest food, to build shelter, and in return, they gave back safety and protection. Action, and counteraction. Yin, and yang.

There was something to the artifact that could create new wielders, new Affinites, that seemed off to Linn. She had always been taught that the amount of power and energy in this universe was finite, and that there was no give without take. How was it possible, then, that power could be created?

Her musings were interrupted when a curl of wind brushed against her shoulder. It carried to her a sound.

Someone was weeping.

It was a soft, high, keening sound, so mournful that it wrapped around her heart and squeezed. She cocked an ear toward it. It was more than she'd seen or heard that night, and unknowingly, she found herself pulling at her winds to guide her toward it. It was coming from a set of balcony doors three floors down.

Carefully, Linn dropped down to the next balcony and peered over. It was a far leap from here to the balcony doors. She watched them for several moments, taking in the way the gossamer curtains ballooned out in the breeze, and how the inside of the room appeared dark.

Then, taking a deep breath, she jumped.

The searock was slippery, and her foot plunged forward. Linn gasped as she lost her balance, tipped over, and crashed against the far wall. She scrambled, squeezing herself against the wall and out of sight from the open-air windows.

In the room beyond, the crying had stopped.

Linn froze. Had they heard her? She couldn't risk discovery—she shouldn't even be here.

Drawing another breath, she grasped the balustrade and was about to fling herself over when a thin, high-pitched voice spoke.

"Hello."

Linn spun around. Between the billowing curtains and half-ensconced in the darkness of the room stood King Darias. His hair was tousled, his cheeks flushed, and his eyes bright as he looked at her.

Panic closed Linn's throat, choking her words. Options—not very good ones—flitted through her mind.

"Please don't be afraid," the boy king continued in slow, singsong Cyrilian. "I just want to tell you about the monsters beneath my floors."

Linn swallowed. He made no sense. Could she even convince him to keep quiet?

She opened her mouth to speak—and then something very peculiar happened. The boy pressed a finger to his lips and gave a small shake of his head.

"Yes," he continued loudly, and suddenly, Linn wondered whether there was more to the King's nonsensical babblings. "Yes, the stars are beautiful tonight. I will come out to look."

He stepped out, his feet bare and his nightshirt thin in the wind. He moved closer to her and paused, and that was when she caught it: the barest tip of his head, a flick of his eyes back to the room. He took two more steps toward her and then fell still, remaining just in sight of his windows.

They were so close now that she could see the flush to his cheeks, the unnatural dilation to his pupils. He held a cup in his hands; the liquid inside sloshed as he moved to the balcony. In a single motion, so swift that she might have missed it if she blinked, he dumped the liquid over the balustrade into the bushes below.

King Darias caught her gaze. "Poison," he said, and this time, he spoke matter-of-factly, his voice low. "There is a guard stationed in my room, and many more outside the parlor. If I do not finish my daily dosage, they will force it down my throat."

There was no strange, slow lilt to his words now, no odd vacancy in his eyes. His gaze was suddenly sharp, focused solely on her.

A chill ran through Linn. Ana had told her the story of her father and brother being poisoned by those who sought power. "How can they do this to you?" she whispered. "Why would the Queen allow it?"

"My mother is long dead," the King replied, a flicker of sadness crossing his face. "The Sea Court has suppressed all information of her passing, and Admiral Farrald began to administer this poison to me in order to take control of my government."

Her head was spinning, but the King continued to speak.

"I am glad you came," he said. "The answers the Cyrilian princess seeks lie beneath our floors, in our research dungeons."

Linn's heart began to beat a fast, erratic rhythm. "The artifact?" she whispered. "It exists?"

King Darias's eyes were wide. He gave a single nod. "The research wing is at the back of the Naval Headquarters, behind a walled courtyard. Look for a set of ironore doors with a scroll carved on top. It will be heavily guarded."

"What is there?" Linn asked. "Is it the artifact?"

Before he had a chance to respond, another voice called out from inside the chambers. "Your Majesty?"

King Darias pressed a finger to his lips. Slowly, he began to retreat, his expression returning to the blank vacancy of earlier. A placid smile curled on his lips, and by the time the King turned back to his chambers, Linn might have believed every part of the act of the puppet king he was putting on.

Her mind was abuzz with the information she had learned, and she needed to get back to Ana to discuss. Linn slipped over the balustrade. Before she left, she took a last glance into the King's chambers. A soft golden light emanated from inside; the billowing white curtains had swallowed everything but the boy's voice.

"The moon is bright and beautiful tonight," sang King Darias. "And there are monsters on it."

33

The Kingdom of Bregon and its Three Courts duly request the presence of Anastacya Mikhailov at Godhallem at eight bells of the evening.

Yours,
Darias Rennaron
King of Bregon

The note lay on the oakwood surface of her parlor table, where Ana and Linn's breakfast was splayed out with an extravagant assortment of rolls stuffed with caviar, cured meats, plates of tiny salted fish drenched in sweet sauce, and platters of tropical berries. Ana had just finished listening to Linn recount the extraordinary events of the previous night, including her conversation with King Darias.

"I knew they were hiding things," she murmured. "And they expect me to negotiate tonight."

The Queen Regent dead, a government cover-up, and a possible new lead. Ana chewed on a slice of buttered bread, considering it all. It seemed she'd stumbled into more than she'd bargained for. With a hostile foreign government, her task had just grown insurmountably harder.

Not to mention, the person she needed most, the only one of them who could help her navigate this tangle of lies and deception, was gone. Ramson had kept true to his word: He had left. Ana had passed Ramson's door on her way to her room last night, and a quick sweep of her Affinity told her the room was empty.

Linn leaned closer, ignoring her cup of steaming black tea. "We must get to the bottom of this, before you agree to an alliance tonight. What is an ally hiding secrets but a potential snake in the nest?"

It was an apt Kemeiran proverb to describe their situation. Head Scholar Tarschon had lied to her face about the Queen, and about the whereabouts of the artifact. "I'm going to request to speak with King Darias," Ana said. If the Bregonian government was asking for a meeting tonight, she needed to cut straight to the source.

"What about the research wing that King Darias told me about?" Linn asked.

Ana hesitated. Linn had said the wing would be heavily guarded; there was no use risking a break-in the day of her negotiation. "Can you take watch there for the day, and meet me at the Livren Skolaren at six bells?"

Linn nodded. "I go now," she said, finishing the rest of her food in several quick bites. "Kaïs stays with you." She narrowed her eyes. "I do not trust anyone in this kingdom."

Ana smiled at her friend's concern. "I can take care of myself."

After Linn left, Ana changed into a crisp ocean-blue dress. Kaïs wasn't in his room, to her surprise, and after a quick search of the Ambassador's Suites yielded nothing, Ana decided to set out alone.

She headed for King Darias's chambers, two of the Royal Guards stationed outside her door trailing her. She'd studied a map of the Blue Fort; the King's chambers were located in the building directly behind Godhallem. The air was balmy, warmer even than that of Southern Cyrilia. The sky was overcast today, and a wind had picked up, rattling the grasses and slamming doors and window shutters.

Ana ascended the steps to the King's residency and found herself blocked by an entire squad of Royal Guards. Their livery, navy blue with emblems of the Sea Court emblazoned on silver plates, reminded her of Sorsha's.

One stepped forward, the badge of a silver shield on his chest marking his higher rank. He saluted. "Can I help you?"

Caution tightened inside her. These were Sorsha Farrald's men, and if Ana guessed right, they were the ones poisoning the King.

Ana schooled her features into careful blankness. "I'd like to request a meeting with King Darias Rennaron."

"My apologies, meindame. King Darias is not taking guests at the moment."

"Would you convey my request to him?" she asked, but at that moment, footsteps sounded from inside and a man pushed through the doors.

His uniform was different from those of the Royal Guard: lighter blue, with brown shoulder pads and stripes, bronze buttons dotting the sleeves. As he descended the steps to her, one hand on the hilt of the sword strapped to his hips, Ana saw that the badge on his chest was the rearing stallion of the Earth Court.

He stopped sharply before her and saluted. "Captain Ronnoc of the King's Guard," he said. "Can I help, meindame?"

The Royal Guards fell back with a noticeable ripple of tension. It seemed the King's Guard was a separate branch from the Royal Guard, dedicated to the protection of the King himself.

Ana inclined her head. "My name is Anastacya Mikhailov of Cyrilia," she said. "I'd like to request a meeting with King Darias."

"My apologies, meindame, but the King is currently not taking guests." Captain Ronnoc paused. "Per my briefing on his schedule today, he is to meet with you at eight hours of the evening at Godhallem."

"There is something important I must discuss with him beforehand," Ana pressed. "Would you relay my message? I can wait here."

The captain hesitated, but the Royal Guard spoke. "We have our orders, meindame," he said sharply. "No visitors."

Frustrated, Ana made her way to the Livren Skolaren. It was the only place she could think of where she could find information, even if it was all tangential to what she was truly after. She spent her day reading about Bregonian history and trade policies. She found a number of details that she hadn't come across in Cyrilian textbooks. There was particular emphasis on searock, a stone that Bregon coveted and refused to trade with foreign nations. She recalled her previous day's readings on the uncanny way searock absorbed the properties of other precious stones and metals, which made it extremely valuable. It was probably why, she thought, leaning back against her chair and staring at the mural over the high ceiling of the Livren Skolaren, most of the buildings in Bregon had been built out of a combination of searock and other construction material.

It was halfway through a section on blackstone that something gave her pause. She'd been making slow progress, arduously translating the terms from the Bregonian language and learning about how Bregonian scholars had imported blackstone from Cyrilia not to control its magen population but to study the alchemy of it.

> *From studies of the properties of Bregonian searock and Cyrilian blackstone on Bregonian magen, it was concluded that the source of energy in matter is limited.*

Ana blinked, and reread the phrase. No, she had interpreted it correctly—studies of searock and blackstone on Bregonian magen. On Affinites.

She flipped back through the pages, scouring the text. Nowhere had it ever mentioned that searock had been used on Affinites before—there were only copious notes on its use as construction material.

She turned back to the section. It ended abruptly, but at the bottom, a scholar had carefully inked in the reference to the studies. Ana read it over, and her blood went cold.

> ** Studies conducted by the A. E. Kerlan Trading Company.*

She stared at the words until they seemed to blur together. Her breaths were coming fast, and her mind felt frozen.

It wasn't possible. This had to be another A. E. Kerlan—perhaps it was a common surname in the Kingdom of Bregon. Ramson had told her that Kerlan had been banished from his home kingdom and driven to establish himself in a foreign empire, but—

Ramson.

She stood, gripping the tome so tightly that her knuckles went white. Ramson had left to investigate allegations of trafficking by Alaric Kerlan. He'd been so adamant that they were somehow missing something of the bigger picture, and she hadn't had the patience to listen.

Footsteps sounded behind her, loud in the utter silence of the hall. It was getting late, and the Livren Skolaren had emptied; a shadow fell over the flickering lamplight of her table.

Ana whipped around and found herself face to face with the man she had been hoping to glimpse all day.

The surprise on Scholar Tarschon's face quickly shifted into caution. "Meindame," he greeted.

Ana swallowed, trying to steady the thumping of her heart. "Head Scholar," she said. Her throat felt dry; she was still struggling to wrap her head around what she had just read.

The scholar inclined his head and made to move past her, but Ana held up a hand. They were near the back of the great library; the aisles around them were deserted.

"You lied to me," she said. The time had passed for holding up appearances. "About several things."

His expression grew tight. "I'm not sure I understand."

She held his gaze. "Queen Arsholla is dead. You neglected to tell me that yesterday."

He opened his mouth, then closed it and looked down. "It is not my decision as to what information is classified and what is released to the public."

"You run the records of the Livren Skolaren, the most important source of information in Bregon. You have a duty to the public." Ana took a step closer to him. "Scholar Tarschon, what exactly is going on in your kingdom?"

Scholar Tarschon flinched almost imperceptibly, but to his credit, he remained where he stood. "Meindame, I am but a scholar. My job is to document information at the government's direction."

The words stirred an old anger within her. *The winners write history,* Ramson had said—but that wasn't fair, and it shouldn't be that way. "Your job," Ana said coldly, "is to write the *truth.*"

Tarschon fell silent at that.

"You also refused to answer my questions about the artifact I described, or even tell me if such a thing existed." She watched his face carefully, searching for clues. "But I've been told it does, and that it's right here, in the Blue Fort."

He looked away. "I cannot help you with that."

Ana held up the book, open to the page she'd stopped at earlier. "Then tell me, Scholar, how is it possible to create an Affinity and bestow it upon someone else? One fundamental law of alchemy is that the source of power in the world is finite." She thought of Tetsyev's pale face, his fear and urgency almost palpable. "If this artifact exists as I understand it, then there must be a cost to what it does." She stepped closer, lowering her voice. "Scholar Tarschon, a mad empress is searching for this artifact—the same empress that would slaughter thousands of innocents. I don't need to know where the artifact is, or what it is. But I need to understand what could happen if this thing falls into her hands."

Tarschon was quiet for a long time. The lamp between them burned, casting flickering shapes onto the ceiling. The figures on the mural seemed to ripple, as though the Bregonian gods themselves were watching their conversation.

And then Scholar Tarschon said, "The artifact that you seek does not exist."

Ana looked at him a moment longer, feeling only flat disappointment. She'd tried her best. If he would not yield, then she would bring this to Godhallem tonight.

Without a word, she turned and began to walk away.

She was halfway through the Livren Skolaren when she heard the scholar speak again, his voice so quiet that she almost missed it. "We do not have such a weapon because it is impossible to create power."

Ana spun around. The scholar's face was swathed in shadows; he stood as still as if he had been carved from rock.

"To create, you must also take." His words reverberated in the space between them. His eyes were dark, distant pools. "This weapon you seek does not bestow magen upon its bearer by creating them. This weapon bestows magen by stealing them."

34

"Two queens of steel, and a knave of coins!" Daya slapped her cards down and clapped her hands in delight. "Victory is mine, Amara bless! Hand over the coins, Quicktongue."

Ramson rubbed a hand over his face. How was he losing at Crib the King? "Gods be damned," he muttered.

It was evening on the second day of his arrival in Bregon. The sun had set and a wind had picked up, ushering clouds over the scattered light of the stars. The air had grown cold over rippling ocean waters, but the lamp in Daya's captain's cabin provided warmth.

Ramson fished out one silverflake from his pocket and flipped it to her. Daya caught it but raised an eyebrow at him. "Two more cop'stones," she said, holding out her palm. "Don't be petty."

Ramson handed her the remaining sum, watching as his money vanished through a twirl of her fingers. "I need a break," he said, glancing out the smudged glass window. The port had almost emptied; it was time.

He left Daya in her captain's cabin, ducking out the door and taking care to shut it behind him. It was imperative that nobody knew they were here, camping out. He walked to the mast and easily swung himself up, the ropes stretching taut beneath his boots as he climbed. With a hop, he was on the crow's nest, one leg dangling over as he balanced precariously, the thrill of the fall shooting adrenaline through his veins. From here, he could see most of Sapphire Port, smudges of shadows in the night sprinkled through with the light of candles inside windows. The docks, though, were completely dark.

The sound of the ocean and gentle rock of the Black Barge lulled him into a stupor. He didn't know how much time had passed when suddenly, he jerked up.

Silhouettes, darting through the docks. It was too dim to make out their faces, but they were headed for the far end of the port.

Ramson followed, sliding down the mast and stealing across the docks, from the shadow of one ship to another.

True to his suspicions, they stopped at the very end of the quay, in front of the ship Ramson had inspected the day before. Ramson stood in the shadows of another large galley. He counted about a dozen of them.

A long whistle sounded in the night, followed by two short ones, raising the hairs on the back of his neck. It was a code that the members of the Order had used.

Daya had told him, back when they'd first met, that she suspected Alaric Kerlan still had men waiting for him in Sapphire Port. Now, watching as the gangplank was lowered and the men stole onto the ship, Ramson began to have an inkling of just how deep his former master's secrets ran.

Ramson waited a while more, counting the seconds to

himself. It was well over five minutes by the time he heard footsteps again. As the men began to make their way back down the gangplank, Ramson listened to their low conversation, wondering if he would recognize their voices. Bogdan had to be here, somewhere.

The sound of the Order members' quiet murmurs drew farther away, and silence fell again. It was now, or never.

The ship was bobbing up and down more violently as he approached it, the waves stirred up by the wind and approaching storm. Ramson shinnied up the anchor line, his hand slipping several times as the ship tossed about. He paused at the railing, peering over.

The deck appeared to be completely deserted. Still, he took caution as he hauled himself on board, scanning the blur of shapes to catch for any movement.

When he found nothing, he made for the hatch. This time, it had been left unlocked. Anyone else might have assumed it was out of carelessness, but Ramson had learned to never make assumptions when it came to Alaric Kerlan.

He pressed his ear against the trapdoor and listened.

And then he heard it. At first he thought it was the wind, but as he listened, the sound registered as human: a faint keening, like a high-pitched moan, coming from belowdecks.

Daya had said she'd heard screaming.

Ramson lifted the hatch a crack, and then all the way. From his hips, he drew his smallest knife—an oyster shuck he'd stolen from the Blue Fort—and slipped in.

The air was still dank, and from the shapes of the crates, it seemed as though nothing had moved. Ramson frowned as he looked around again, slowly. The moaning sounds had stopped, but as he cocked his head to listen, he couldn't hear the sound of anyone alive in this space.

His eyes caught on something—a slight shift to the outline of shadows he'd seen just yesterday. *There.* One crate of searock had been pushed aside. And as Ramson stood, trying to figure out what it was about this place that looked so wrong to him, a realization hit him.

The space from floor to ceiling of this hold was far too narrow for the hull of the ship. He could have smacked himself for not seeing it sooner; back at the Naval Academy, he'd studied plans of ships that had secret second layers to their holds, often to carry illegal goods.

He'd just taken two steps forward when he heard the faint rattle of chains, the creak of wood as the gangplank was lowered again outside. The thud of wood, and then footsteps.

Shit. He hadn't expected them to return so quickly.

Ramson scurried to a corner, where the crates were piled high on top of each other. With several light steps, he scrambled up and flipped himself behind the boxes. He crouched there, listening intently.

Footsteps on the deck, muffled voices—and then the hatch swung open.

". . . arriving later tonight?" an unfamiliar woman's voice was saying in Cyrilian.

"Oh, yes," came a second, lilting voice, and Ramson's insides froze—one that he would recognize anywhere, that haunted his nightmares. "The plan is in motion. The siphons are ready for export. They're expecting another wagon of Affinites tonight."

Ramson knew his old master's mannerisms so well that he

could *hear* the smile in Alaric Kerlan's voice. The clack of heels on the ladder rungs, and then they were belowdecks, so close that he could hear the rustle of their clothes. The sound of a match being struck, and a moment later, lamplight blazed to life. Ramson looked at the shadows cast on the wall behind him. He counted five people.

"Some of the test subjects are not doing so well," the female voice said.

A pause steeped in displeasure. "Well," Kerlan said, "let's see. Our Bregonian ally seems to have used it quite successfully." He switched to Bregonian. "Scholar Ardonn, would you do us the favor?"

Ramson's heart thudded in his chest. Not only was Alaric Kerlan working with a Bregonian ally, he was also working with someone within the Blue Fort. A scholar, no less.

"Yes, meinsire," came a third voice. Ramson watched as the shadows on the wall moved to the center of the hold. A click of a lock, and the sound of a door opening. Ramson suppressed a groan. He could kill himself for not having thought of a trick compartment in this ship last night. Now, the chance was gone.

There were footsteps; one by one, the shadows of Kerlan and his companions disappeared as they descended through the trapdoor. Ramson waited, counting to three, before he turned and peered out.

The landing was empty, the lamplight flickering out from the trick opening in the center of the hold.

He steeled himself, drew a silent breath, and stood. And that was when he heard the moans—clearly, this time. It sounded like someone pleading from behind a gag. Something about the voice struck him as strangely familiar—but then again, Ramson thought as he slid over the pile of crates, he'd stood by for so many of Kerlan's torture sessions, they'd all started to blend together.

When he drew close enough to the trapdoor, he dropped to his hands and knees. Sending a prayer to the gods, Ramson pressed himself flat against the floor and peered over the opening.

It looked like the inside of a laboratory, built in the hull of the ship. Metal tables had been nailed to the floor, and makeshift shelves were strapped to the walls, holding jars and scalpels and scrolls. Two figures clad in long white robes sat at the table, scribbling notes on parchment beneath the glow of the lamp.

"Well? Is it working?" Alaric Kerlan stood almost directly beneath the hatch. He had changed from his Cyrilian-style purple suit to a sharp-cut Bregonian vest and breeches, studded through with gold. By his side was a woman that Ramson recognized by the blue-black sheen of her hair: Nita, his Deputy, the Affinite who specialized in manipulating strength. There were two others behind them, cronies that Ramson recognized from his days at the Order.

"The siphon works. But the subject is in frail condition." The scholar who spoke was barely visible from Ramson's vantage point; all he saw was a flash of white robes.

"Show me," Kerlan commanded, and the scholar turned, his robes vanishing from sight. Ramson heard the click of locks, and a low groan. When the scholar returned, he was dragging someone by a set of chains. Roughly, he shoved the prisoner to the floor.

The scholar held out a hand. In his palm was an ingot of

gold. "Lift this with your new magek," he crooned in Cyrilian, the words sounding harsh and clumsy. "Like we practiced."

The man let out a moan. His hair was matted and hung over his face; his shoulder blades protruded from thin, tattered clothes. It was odd, Ramson thought, peering closer, that the prisoner's jacket looked to be made of velvet, in the fashion of a Cyrilian nobleman's outfit. He could swear those were gold stitches at the collar.

It was when the prisoner lifted his head that Ramson realized why. He nearly dropped the hatch door in shock.

Looking up was the once-handsome face of Bogdan Ivanov, the Penmaster of Novo Mynsk, and Olyusha's missing husband.

35

It had taken Linn little time to find the walled-off courtyard that King Darias had mentioned. The ironore doors indeed bore the carving of a scroll, but they were guarded by an entire squad of Bregonian guards surrounding the courtyard. Linn had sought out a vantage point to observe and found that within the walls was a second set of doors that looked to lead into the back section of the Naval Headquarters itself.

There was no way she would get inside with the guards watching in broad daylight, so she had settled onto a nearby veranda directly overlooking the courtyard, watching and waiting.

The day had gone by unremarkably; though courtiers and other members of the Blue Fort passed by the Naval Headquarters frequently, no one had neared the courtyard. The sun crawled across the sky, falling into the sea; the winds turned urgent, carrying with them the distant scent of rain.

The bells chimed six hours of the evening, and Linn had just gotten to her feet, ready to head for the Livren Skolaren to meet with Ana, when something caught her attention.

From far off, threading through the other sounds of the

night, came the clacking of heels against stone. For some reason, all of Linn's hairs stood on end. Her muscles tightened as she peered out.

A familiar figure emerged from beneath the canopy of the trees. Linn would have recognized that erratic gait anywhere.

Sorsha wore her regular Sea Court livery, but even in the semidarkness, Linn could see that there was something different to her posture. She cut through the stone paths of the courtyards with a brisk efficiency that Linn had only seen her display in Godhallem.

And she was making straight for the walled courtyard.

The guards saluted her as she approached. Sorsha held a hand up and barked a few orders at them in Bregonian. They leapt to her command, pulling open the doors into the courtyard and bowing her through.

Linn watched as Sorsha stopped before the second set of ironore doors inside, retrieving something from her waist. Keys, by the sound of their clinking. With a series of complicated clicks she unlocked the doors and dragged them open. She stepped inside and vanished, the doors slamming shut behind her.

Linn hesitated. It was long past dusk, and Ana would be waiting for her. Two more bells, and she'd be at her negotiation.

The doors yawned wide open, beckoning to her. It wouldn't take two bells for Linn to quickly look inside.

She stood from where she crouched, assessing. Walls and guards might keep out everyone else, but they weren't a problem for her.

She backed to the end of her veranda and took off at a run, summoning her Affinity as she did so. With a kick, she launched herself off the edge, the breeze at her feet rising into a sudden gale, propelling her forward.

She landed on the crenellated wall as silently as a cat, and the breeze fell. Voices of the Royal Guards drifted up from beneath her, probably commenting about the weather. To them, she would have been nothing but a shadow in the night.

Linn dropped into the empty courtyard. In five steps, she was at the ironore doors. She wrapped her fingers around the bronze knockers, sent a quick prayer to her gods, and tugged.

They opened with a resounding creak that set her heart stuttering. Linn quickly lifted a gust of wind that rattled the alder trees, but even as she did, she heard the guards speaking, the grating of the ironore doors outside.

Linn pushed more wind against the door, so that it clanged open against the opposite wall. She had to hope that the guards would think Sorsha hadn't closed the door properly, and that it had blown open in the strong wind. Blades in hands, she darted inside and pressed herself against the wall, holding still.

Outside, she heard a guard calling to his companions, the grind of metal as he heaved the heavy door shut, trapping her inside.

It took a few moments for her eyes to adjust. She was in a corridor of the Naval Headquarters that appeared to be quite deserted. The walls were made of actual stone, and the entire place felt older than the polished halls of the Livren Skolaren or Godhallem that gleamed with ironore or searock enhancements.

There were doors on either side of the hallway, which stretched so far, it seemed to swallow itself into an expanse of darkness. There was no one here, but Linn sensed a shift in the air as the currents settled back into the space a body had just moved through, almost like the wake of a ship. Sorsha had come through here.

Linn followed the trail to a door that looked the same as the others she had passed. Cautiously, she opened it.

Stone steps descended into a yawning stretch of darkness below. The air here was cold, but as Linn pressed her Affinity to it, she found a swirling trail leading forward.

Sorsha had gone down here.

All of her senses rang in warning against the dark, the stillness, the silence, the enclosed space behind the door. Her mind leapt to memories she'd tried to keep buried—the chafe of chains against her wrists, the taste of sedatives on her tongue, the bouts of consciousness and the blurred in-betweens.

Linn shook her head. *You are overreacting,* she thought sternly. Bregon was not Cyrilia, and she was here of her own free will, supporting a cause that would fight against inequality and oppression, that would ensure that no other young girl from a foreign kingdom went through what Linn had gone through.

This was her way of fighting. She would need to be stronger than her fear.

Linn palmed a dagger. She drew a breath, as though to steel herself, and then entered, drawing the door shut behind her.

It was pitch-black inside, and she kept a hand on the wall next to her as she began to descend. Here, there was only the sound of her own breathing, the slight swirl of air currents before her as the trail Sorsha had left began to close. Several times, she could swear she saw shapes moving—but, she reasoned with herself, it was merely the effect of fear and darkness on her imagination. She kept one hand on the wall as she counted her steps, her Affinity sorting through the heavy tangle of air before her, searching for any disturbances.

Gradually, she thought she began to see enough to be able to distinguish shadows around her, blurred shapes. And then she began to make out the outlines of walls and steps before her, and at last, flickers of torchlight.

She was close.

The stairs ended abruptly, before another set of doors. Light emanated from the cracks beneath them, but when Linn grasped the handles, she let go immediately, as though she'd been burned.

Blackstone. These doors were made of blackstone. It was unmistakable—the unnatural coldness, the way her Affinity seemed to fade beneath a pounding pressure in her head when she touched it.

She swallowed. She hadn't expected to find blackstone in a highly guarded section of the Naval Headquarters.

Holding her dagger before her like a torch, she reached out, turned the handle, and slid the door open a crack.

At first, she thought she was looking at a healing wing of some sort. Pillars were spaced evenly along the walls. Austere metal tables stretched in the center of the long chamber, neatly stacked with papers and pens and several bottles. The slick black walls curved and wove into shadowed alcoves, the walls between each one lined with shelves that bore medical supplies. Rows of scalpels that glittered like teeth, large and small bottles of liquids, gauze and needles in glass jars.

In one of the alcoves, something moved.

Linn bit down a cry.

There was a girl bound to the walls, long golden hair unkempt. She looked no more than skin and bones, her fingers curling like claws against her manacles. A black collar encircled her neck, dull beneath the shine of light.

More blackstone. There was so much of it here, she was beginning to realize: woven into the material of the walls, the pillars interspersed through the chamber, even the ceiling. Her Affinity had been reduced to the faint flicker of a candle.

Voices drifted to her, echoing in the empty chamber. The first was a male voice. The Bregonian words were rough and unfamiliar to Linn, but his tone was quiet, smooth, if not tense.

A second voice spoke, and Linn instantly recognized its unsteady tones that slipped easily into threatening snarls. Linn pushed the door open a bit wider, her heart hammering.

Sorsha came to a stop before the alcove with the girl. She gestured, and a man in white robes swept forward. He produced a key and unlocked the prisoner's chains, including the blackstone band around her neck.

The girl crumpled to the ground.

Without so much as a flicker in his expression, the scholar grabbed one of her wrists and hauled her forward, disappearing from Linn's field of sight.

She was debating whether she should follow them farther inside when the screaming started.

Fear bloomed. Her every nerve, every sense, whispered at her to run.

Monsters, came King Darias's whisper. *I just want to tell you about the monsters beneath my floors.*

His monsters were right around the corner; she could feel it like the press of destiny at her back. The need to act pushed her forward, the knowledge that she was on the brink of discovering something greater than herself, than her fear. She had to see what lay down there.

Yet that didn't stop her heart from beating like a trapped bird in her chest, her knuckles turning white around her grip of the dagger.

I am afraid, Ama-ka. She'd spoken those words aloud once, at six years old, before her first flight. Linn thought them now, her hands cold around her blades.

Ama-ka's response came to her, the faintest glimmering threads in the shadows all around.

That, my daughter, is when you can choose . . .

The darkness was suffocating. No one would come searching for her down here if she was caught. No one was here to witness her choice. She was but a pawn in this war, where glory was reserved only for the few.

Sometimes, Linn thought, bravery was not loud, or grand, or brilliant as the blaze of a thousand fires.

Sometimes it was quiet. Unremarkable. Unknown. The resilient wend of water through rocks, year after year after year.

. . . to be brave.

Linn drew a breath, lifted her dagger, and slipped through the gap in the door.

36

Bogdan's once-handsome face had hollowed out to the point of becoming skeletal, his cheekbones jutting sharply. His hair, which had before looked to be spun of gold, hung in grime-slicked strands to his chin. But what haunted Ramson most was the look in his eyes—that of a wild animal, of frenzied desperation.

Scholar Ardonn held out a hand. "Perform," he ordered.

Bogdan moaned, and Ramson felt chills down to his bones. It was the sound he had heard earlier—the long, drawn-out keening noise, half-human, half-animal. He raised his arm—now stick-thin—and Ramson caught sight of a band around it. The material undulated in waves, reminding him of the ocean.

Searock, he thought. That looked like searock.

And then it started to glow. Fissures of light spread from the band onto Bogdan's skin, crawling like veins up his arm, his neck, his cheeks, and to his eyes.

The gold rose into the air from Ardonn's palm, gleaming in the light. It spun. The veins on Bogdan's face began to bulge. And Ramson thought of Ana's hands, the way her veins engorged with blood and turned dark when she used her Affinity.

No, this wasn't possible.

Bogdan was not an Affinite.

Yet something was happening to Bogdan. The bar of gold had begun to spin in the air. The glowing fissures that had spread on his skin were growing more rapidly, spreading to his entire body.

Kerlan took a step back in alarm. "What's wrong?" he demanded. "What's happening?"

Scholar Ardonn examined Bogdan's wrist, leaning as close as possible without risk of being hit by the bar of gold. "The siphon seems faulty. It's fracturing."

"Please," Bogdan whimpered. The bar of gold was spinning faster and faster, starting to veer out of control. "Please, Master—"

Kerlan ignored him. "We'll need the other one in the Blue Fort, after all," he snarled at the scholar. "Is the problem with the siphon, or is it with the bearer?"

"Likely both, though I've advised that giving a siphon that has collected multiple mageks to a nonmagen could break the test subject." Scholar Ardonn began to back away, but he shot Kerlan a pointed look. "The siphon you gave him had gold magek, herb magek, and salt magek. He must be overwhelmed."

Indeed, Bogdan was now trembling violently. The threads across his body lit up like currents of lightning, splintering his face as though his skin were peeling from his bones. "Please, get it out of me, please—" His voice rose, cresting into a scream.

"Take cover!" Nita shouted, hauling Alaric Kerlan out of the way.

The searock-like band around his wrist exploded in a burst of light.

The force blew Ramson backward. He grunted as the sharp edge of a crate smashed into his ribs. Pain coursed through his body.

From belowdecks, there was the sound of a sword being drawn, of metal meeting flesh, and then silence. Footsteps.

He'd just pushed himself to his hands and knees when the shout came. "Intruder!" A blow struck his face, sending him reeling.

He heard Kerlan's reply, slightly out of breath. "Tie him up. And someone clean up this gods-damned mess."

Dimly, Ramson sensed cuffs being clipped over his hands and feet. A piece of cloth went over his mouth; he groaned as it tightened. He was lifted by his armpits and dragged through the hatch, then shoved onto the deck.

Throughout the silence came a distinct noise: a rhythmic *click-click-click* of heels striking wood. Something about the noise awoke a primal fear in Ramson; echoes of screams, memories of searing heat and black water.

Two spots of yellow appeared in his vision, flashing. They grew brighter and more solid until they merged into a pair of gold-heeled shoes. They stopped right before Ramson.

"Well, well," came a voice. "Look what the tide washed in. Stand him up."

The world shifted as he was hauled to his feet. A face swam into view.

"Hello again, Ramson," said Alaric Kerlan. "I certainly didn't think I would be running into you here, old friend."

Behind him, figures were emerging on the deck, more than he'd counted, dressed in Cyrilian furs and attire. The worst thing, Ramson realized, was that he recognized some of them.

He'd seen their faces back at the Order of the Lily; he'd even worked with some of them in passing.

Olyusha had been right. Kerlan had brought what was left of his Order to Bregon.

Nita nudged Ramson with a boot. "What shall we do with him?"

"I'm quite enjoying the look of horror on your face, my son." Kerlan bent and cupped a hand under Ramson's chin. His nails dug into Ramson's cheek. "I must say, though, I thought I'd left you for dead the last time we met." His grip tightened. "I won't make the same mistake this time."

The gold buttons of his sleeve brushed against Ramson as he stood and gestured at one of his men. "Bind weights to him."

It dawned, with a slow horror, that Kerlan meant to drown him tonight.

Ramson tensed against his manacles, his fingers feeling along the chains for any weaknesses.

As a crony began to strap weights to him with a second set of chains, Ramson realized, for the first time, that he had no way out. He'd been stripped of pins and blades and any sharp objects that he could use to pick a lock, and his hands and feet were shackled so tightly that he could feel his circulation cutting off.

With a grunt, he kicked his legs up and slammed the man in the chest. He fell back with a snarl, and Ramson managed to sit upright—

And then, in a flash, the strength left his body.

Ramson collapsed onto the deck.

"Marvelous, Nita," Kerlan said. "Now, take the others and load them onto the two wagons for the Blue Fort. Leave some to guard the ship. We must make haste. I shall join you, once I deal with my old friend, over here."

No. A voice in Ramson's head was screaming, but he couldn't move.

Click-click-click. Kerlan's shadow fell over Ramson, and for a moment, he looked down with mild pity.

Then he bent and wrapped his fingers around Ramson's neck hard enough to cut off his air supply. His face morphed into cruel fury.

"Did you really think I'd let you ruin it all?" Kerlan hissed, spittle flying from his mouth. "Nearly fifteen years, I've been waiting for this—did you really think I'd let one pathetic son of a whore interfere?" He thrust Ramson's head back against the wooden deck so hard that Ramson saw stars.

He coughed, sucking in air through his cloth gag, his stomach heaving. Yet his mind latched on to Kerlan's words. *Fifteen years.* Kerlan had been planning this for fifteen years.

He thought of Daya's words, of how she'd told him that her first job for Kerlan had been eight years ago, that Kerlan still had men waiting for him in Sapphire Port. Ramson had grown up listening to his father's stories of Alaric Kerlan and his criminal empire. But, he realized suddenly, with a growing dread, he'd never known the reason why Roran Farrald had exiled Alaric Kerlan in the first place.

A small smile was playing about Kerlan's lips. "I've made many Trades in my lifetime, paid pretty sums for pretty things. But the look in your eyes right now, my son, is simply priceless. The confusion. The anger at my triumph. The helplessness." His smile stretched. "Tell me, did you bid good-bye to your beautiful blood princess?"

Something in Ramson snapped and he twisted, choking against his gag, his chains rattling.

Kerlan laughed. "Imagine my surprise, my utter *delight,* in hearing that the so-called Red Tigress had landed in Bregon, right into the lap of my network of spies. Intending, I heard, to warn Bregon about Empress Morganya's intentions to steal their weapon." He chortled, wiping a tear from the edge of his eye. "Who do you think developed the siphons fifteen years ago? Who do you think *told* Morganya about its existence in the first place?"

Ramson couldn't breathe. His head spun, struggling to process what Kerlan had just revealed. The greater picture that he had been seeking all along, spanning oceans and kingdoms and decades.

"Yes," Kerlan crooned, watching him carefully. "Oh, how lovely it is, watching you connect all the pieces of my lifetime of work. But how could you have known? All along, you've only seen the tail end of my grand plan. All those enhancements to the Blue Fort, the searock that those pitiful little fools in the Naval Headquarters now tread on—who do you think mined those materials in the first place, discovered the properties that made them so powerful?"

It couldn't be. Back at the Naval Academy, they'd learned about the A. E. Kerlan Trading Company, which had excavated precious stone and supplied it to the Kingdom of Bregon. They'd been told that it had been a criminal empire operating under a façade, and that it was Admiral Roran Farrald who had banished its notorious leader forever.

"And then came Roran Farrald, my supposed *friend*"—Kerlan spat the word—"who rose so quickly in the ranks of the Navy, and declared me a criminal once he saw what I had developed with searock. He sent me into exile, and took over everything I had built, all the knowledge I'd discovered." He straightened, his face sliding back into mild serenity. "He'll get his retribution tonight. My forces have already infiltrated the Blue Fort. Within hours, my army arrives, and we strike.

"And," he said, slowly, with relish, "once I take down Bregon and deliver your Red Tigress back to Empress Morganya, I shall be crowned King of Bregon in the new era of our world." His gray eyes bore into Ramson's. "But first, I'm going to savor this moment: seeing you die, knowing just how hard you've failed. Knowing that everything you've ever loved and cared for is about to end." He stood. "I'm afraid I've got to get going, Ramson. The biggest party in all of the Blue Fort awaits me tonight. Good-bye, my son."

Ramson vowed that he would never give Kerlan the satisfaction of hearing him scream. Yet as he was dragged to the edge of the ship, the waves below black and impenetrable, he found his resolve wavering, his entire body beginning to shake against his will. But his frantic, scrabbling fingers met nothing but the smooth metal of his cuffs, and the weights chained to him were hard and unyielding.

In his last moments, images flashed through his mind. His father, eyes flat and black as an abyss, as he waved for the guard to kill Jonah. As he ordered Ramson's arrest. As he slashed his blade through Sorsha.

Kerlan, jamming the hot brand to his chest, taking the broken, jagged pieces of him and sculpting them into something cruel and ugly.

And Ana. The way she had looked under the moonlight

that night, seadust shimmering over her skin, lovely and bright. How she made him feel like a boy again, wretched and inadequate and fumbling and awkward.

How desperately, desperately he had wanted to kiss her.

A splash as the weights were hauled over the edge. Ramson barely had time to draw breath before Kerlan's foot slammed into his stomach and the ground fell away from him.

The sky and the sea wheeled overhead as he hit the surface of the water. For a moment, he floated, and a wild, irrational part of him thought that if he kicked hard enough, he would stay afloat, he would escape.

But then he felt a sharp yank and the next thing he knew water, cold and black, closed in over his head, and he was being dragged down, down. And then he could only watch, his lungs on fire and his head spinning, as the surface drew farther and farther away and the light of the moon became a faint sliver, and then nothing at all.

37

Pressed against a pillar in a room of blackstone and chains, Linn felt as though she had been thrown back into a nightmare. The chamber had the septic smell of drugs mixed, Linn could tell now, with a rotten metallic stench that sent nausea spiking through her.

Linn edged forward until she could see the white robe of the scholar, the leather heels of Sorsha's boots. The blond girl was slumped in between them.

Sorsha was facing a shelf; when she turned back, she held something in her hands. It resembled a bracelet made of a material that looked like jade and lapis lazuli interwoven. Like . . . searock.

Sorsha spoke some words, low and crooning, to the scholar before her. His head snapped up sharply, his eyes widening in fear. "Nen," he said, raising a hand and backing away a few steps, gabbling some other words that Linn couldn't understand. "Nen, nen—"

Sorsha lunged at him, teeth bared, dagger drawn. The scholar might have been physically bigger than her, but he was no match for Sorsha's violence. He shouted as she knocked him against the wall.

Click.

The bracelet closed over his wrist, the sound echoing across the chamber in the sudden stillness. The energy around them seemed to shift for a second.

The band shrank, tightening around the scholar's wrist until it seemed to meld with his flesh. It shimmered with what Linn might have believed was the ancient magic or sorcery that her elders had spoken of. It looked as though an entire ocean had come alive in that band.

The scholar had collapsed against the wall. He'd covered his face with his hands, and his shoulders shook with sobs.

Sorsha knelt by him. In a motion that could almost be described as tender, she lifted her blade to his throat and murmured words in his ear. Linn could only hear the man's sobs of *nen, nen, nen*—the Bregonian word for *no,* she had learned—pounding a desperate fear into her chest.

Sorsha grasped his wrist and turned to the girl. With the casualness of slitting an envelope, she drew a gash across the girl's neck. The girl gave a muffled moan as blood pooled and began to seep crimson.

Sorsha pressed the scholar's searock band to the girl's blood.

The effect was instant. The girl jerked as though every nerve in her body had been drawn taut. Her eyes widened and veins bulged from her forehead as she opened her mouth in a scream.

The scholar tilted his head back, lips parted in what resembled equal parts ecstasy and equal parts pain. The girl's blood, Linn noticed with horror, had stopped dripping; instead, it seemed to be flowing *into* the searock band. The veins in the scholar's wrist began to turn black, spreading up his arms and to his neck, bleeding into the whites of his eyes like ink to parchment.

It was over in a moment. The gold-haired girl sprawled on the ground, her skin pale like wax paper. It was her eyes, though, that would come back to haunt Linn: utterly empty, as though her soul had gone.

Monsters, King Darias had said. *There are monsters beneath my floors.*

The scholar was slumped against the wall, trembling violently. And as he did so, the glass bottles and containers on the shelves began to shake, too, filling the entire chamber with an ominous thrumming that grew louder and louder.

Sorsha's face cracked into a smile. She crooned something into the scholar's ear. In response, he covered his face with a hand and raised the other.

Glassware exploded all around them, splintering into thousands of fragments that arced through the air. For a moment, everything seemed frozen in time: the glittering shards, Sorsha's mouth parted in wonder, the scholar's face slack with terror.

And then it all came crashing down.

Amid the shower of glass, Sorsha took the scholar's hand, gently stroking the searock band.

And then she slit his throat.

The scholar's arm dropped to the floor, the searock band clanging as it fell off and rolled to a stop. Slivers of darkness writhed across its surface.

Sorsha picked up the band. Even her movements were tempered, as careful as though she were holding a newborn infant. "The siphon is ready," she said. She spoke in Cyrilian now.

It was then that Linn saw something stir in the very back of the chambers, outside the glow of the lamps. She'd thought there was no one else in here with them, but the overwhelming amounts of blackstone here had blocked her connection to the air currents in this room.

A figure stepped forward, and Linn felt her knees grow weak.

"Godhallem, then." Kaïs's voice was colder than ice.

Sorsha cackled. Carefully, she looped the searock band—the siphon, as she'd just called it—onto her belt. "Oh, Kaïs, you forget, we have a *dear* friend to find first. A certain little Blood Bitch."

Kaïs's face was emotionless. "Very well."

"What a good soldier you make," Sorsha crooned. She slunk past him, stroking a finger along his chin in an insolent gesture that Linn had never thought he would tolerate. *Do not do this,* she thought, pleading silently for him to move, to lash out. *Fight back.* "Even dogs know to be obedient once they've tasted pain."

Kaïs remained standing, still as a statue carved of stone.

Sorsha slid her bloodied dagger into its sheath and turned. "Come, then," she said as she moved toward the doors, her steps clipping sharply. "We have a *feast* to attend at eight bells."

Linn shrank back as Sorsha swept past the spot where she was hiding. Her heart was pounding so fast in her chest, she thought it would burst. Under any normal circumstances, a yaeger would easily have sniffed her out, and she would have been discovered. But Kaïs must not have sensed her Affinity because of the blackstone in this place. It must have blocked his power as much as it did hers.

For a moment, Kaïs paused right before the doors, his muscles tensed in a way that she'd grown to read. He began to turn his head, as though to turn toward her, but then gave himself a small shake, stepped forward, and disappeared through the doors.

Linn didn't lower her dagger until long after the echoes of their steps faded.

38

Ana felt as though her entire world had shifted. "The artifact *steals* Affinities," she breathed, the words sounding surreal even as she spoke them aloud.

Scholar Tarschon nodded. "The siphon drains a magen of their power and lends it to the bearer." He held out his hands, palms upturned. "The principles of alchemy hold: to give, one must take. The mageks stay within the siphon; the bearer merely channels them."

Ana felt sick. She thought of what Linn had told her of the man with two Affinities they had witnessed in Cyrilia, the way her friend had spoken with such fear.

Scholar Tarschon's gaze drifted to the book in her hands, the page on which it was open. "Long ago," he said softly, his voice echoing beneath the holy paintings, "the gods parted from our world. Yet they left traces of magek in their wake. Gossenwal, wassengost . . . and in us, in the magen. Cyrilia received the gift of blackstone. And Bregon . . . we received searock.

"Nearly two decades ago, a man by the name of A. E. Kerlan discovered searock and began to mine it." Scholar Tarschon nodded to the tome Ana held. "You know the rest of the story.

Kerlan discovered its magical properties of absorption, and he developed that into a potent weapon capable of absorbing magek.

"When Admiral Farrald found out what he was doing, he reported it to the Bregonian government. The former King Rennaron declared this an act of cruelty against the magen in those experiments. He had Kerlan exiled forever, and all of his research and siphons destroyed. All . . . but one."

Ana felt like she'd stepped into a dream—a nightmare. Tarschon's words came to her as though from very far away.

"Unbeknownst to the King, Admiral Farrald preserved a single siphon, and began to experiment with it privately. It took him a long time to catch up to where Alaric Kerlan had been. Once he understood their power, he established a research unit in the Blue Fort . . . to develop the perfect siphon, and to create the next generation of magen."

The information swirled in Ana's head. "Why are you telling me this?" she whispered. "Why haven't you tried to stop it?"

Sadness crossed his features. "My father was the first scholar who worked with Admiral Farrald on these experiments. He was killed in an accident with a siphon, and so Admiral Farrald appointed me as his successor."

It made sense, then, that Tarschon had been appointed Head Scholar at such a young age.

"He threatened to reveal everything to the government should I not comply," Tarschon continued, bowing his head. "I never had a choice."

His words reminded her of Kaïs, when she'd confronted him in the town square back at Novo Mynsk. She thought of him, of Yuri working at the Palace as an apprentice to feed his mother and sister down south, of the countless others who'd suffered under a greater power.

Ana realized then that choices were a luxury. "You made a choice just now, Head Scholar Tarschon," she said softly. "And that choice will come to define you."

He looked at her for a long moment from behind the panes of his spectacles. The great library had gone quiet, the murals of the gods above watching.

And in that silence came another sound: the unsteady *click-click-click* of heels tapping against stone.

The double doors at the end of the hall swung open and Ana and Tarschon spun around.

"*There* you are." Sorsha's smile was sharp as she stalked toward them. There was something different about her, almost as though she were filled with a new energy.

Ana bristled, turning to face the girl. As she did so, she caught the unmistakable presence of blood staining Sorsha's navy-blue uniform. "What do you want?" she snapped.

"Oh, I was looking for you." Sorsha feigned innocence, pouting. "Isn't it time that I escorted you to your meeting in Godhallem? All of the Three Courts are gathered for this party!"

Ana was about to respond when a second figure appeared at the doors. "Kaïs," she called, relief sinking into her as she hurried forward.

"But first, let me deal with our Head Scholar," Sorsha said, and something in her tone gave Ana pause. "Dear Tarschon, ever the noble fool. I was beginning to wonder when you'd start spilling our state secrets."

Ana whipped around just as Sorsha plunged her blade into the scholar's chest.

He gave a soft cry and stumbled back, crashing into the shelves on the wall. Blood bloomed across Ana's senses, blossoming red over Tarschon's robes. "No," she gasped, watching as the man who held the answers to saving this world began to bleed out before her.

Ana lashed out at Sorsha with her Affinity—

—and then it was gone. A familiar presence had entered the back of her mind, clamping down on her power like cold metal. Ana gritted her teeth, the sudden disappearance of her power disorienting her.

She turned to see Kaïs watching her calmly.

The realization clicked. "*You.*" A snarl tore from Ana's lips. "I should have known."

Sorsha cackled in delight. "There's nothing I love more than a little shift in alliances!" she shrieked, and slunk up to Kaïs, cupping his cheek. He held perfectly still, his expression unreadable. Her voice was a low, mocking croon as she caressed his face. "Tragic, how our love and loyalty make servants of us."

A flash of emotion across Kaïs's face, so brief that Ana thought she'd imagined it. "What are you talking about?" she growled. "What do you want?"

"What do I want?" Sorsha whispered, and then screamed, "*What do I want?*"

Ana flinched as the girl tore open the collar of her shirt. With a movement that could almost be described as tender, she touched a finger to the smooth band of her black collar. "My father handed me to the scholars on my eighth birthday," she said. "He hated me, you see; he wanted to kill me, for I was evidence of his impotence. A daughter, instead of a male heir, was evidence that the gods were mocking him."

Sorsha pushed up her sleeve, flipped her wrist, and Ana saw something for the first time: a band resembling searock, undulating in the light in ripples of blue, green, and teal. "But there was one thing I had that he didn't: a magen. A powerful one, to iron," Sorsha continued. "You see, he'd begun experimenting on a rare material in Bregon. And he began to test it on me.

"I alone survived, out of thousands of his subjects. I was the sole bearer strong enough to endure the siphon's power. Killing me was the only way to remove the siphon from me, but my dearest father didn't want to risk that. You see, he'd begun to think of me not as his greatest failure but as his greatest weapon." Sorsha's face stretched into an ugly smile. "When you deem someone nonexpendable to you, you become *weak*—and that was where Daddy Dearest erred. He wanted to keep me, but he also wanted to control me. So he put this lovely collar on me." She dug her nails into the scars stretching from beneath the blackstone collar. "Little does he realize that power cannot be fettered forever. I will show him what I can do. I will finish what he has taught me my entire life. To *destroy*." Crimson dripped down her neck, wetting her collar, staining her nails. She let out a crazed laugh. "And he will watch as I bring down his kingdom."

Sorsha spread her arms. Above her, in the last scene of the mural, the stallion, the eagle, and the seadragon seemed to encircle her in a perfect imitation of the painted mage, as though she were part of the scene, one with the great Bregonian gods.

Then she turned her obsidian gaze to Ana. "You came to warn us about Morganya coming after our siphons. It's too late, Blood Bitch." She spread her arms. "Behold."

"Don't do this," Ana whispered.

Sorsha straightened and sheathed her blade. "As much as I'd love to play a while more, Blood Empress, I have other things to do. A grand plan is in motion. The fun will come later." She winked. "In the meantime, I'll leave you to our friend here. Don't be late to the party."

She raised a hand in farewell and flounced down the hall. As she reached the entrance, Ana heard her call back to Kaïs: "Escort her to Godhallem. I'll be joining shortly for the main event."

The front doors shut with a clang. Ana turned to Kaïs. The pressure in her mind held steady, her Affinity still unreachable. "Just tell me." Her voice cracked. "Just tell me why you're doing this."

A muscle twitched in his jaw. "I have no choice."

In a corner, Tarschon had pressed a hand over his chest. Crimson seeped between his fingers, and he grasped the bookshelf to stop his swaying.

"We always have a choice," Ana said quietly.

Kaïs hesitated. "No," he said. "I'm sorry. If I fail, then—" A flash of emotion across those pale blue eyes. He composed himself and steadied his voice. "I must escort you to Godhallem."

A new voice rang out. "Then you will have to go through me."

A wind stirred throughout the hall of the Livren Skolaren, sending the lamplight flickering. In the darkness outside the Livren Skolaren, a shadow appeared, cutting through the night like a knife.

Linn stepped into the halls of the great library, her blades drawn. "I have long waited to fight you on equal footing," she said, and raised her knives. "Be ready, for this time, I will not surrender so easily."

39

In the darkness, there came light. And with light, there came pain. A burning, fiery kind of pain that ached somewhere deep inside.

The next thing Ramson knew, he was leaning over and throwing up on the ground. His body spasmed as he gasped in lungfuls of air. His head spun. His arms ached from just holding up his own weight.

"Take it easy. Breathe, breathe." The voice was familiar. A hand rubbed his back.

Still wheezing, Ramson turned. A figure sat before him. The faint moonlight silvered her braids, her bright eyes and strong brows that were, at the moment, creased in worry. "Daya?" he choked.

"Thank Amara," she breathed. "You're alive."

The world had settled around him. It was still night, and he was splayed against a wooden jetty beneath a familiar-looking ship. The Black Barge bobbed in the waves next to him as a cold wind swept clouds over the moon.

And Kerlan had just tried to drown him.

The thought of the bottomless waters closing over him

made him weak all over again, and he was glad he hadn't tried to stand up yet. "I thought you left," he croaked.

Daya batted a hand. "I told you, Pretty Boy, my loyalties are where my goldleaves lie," she quipped.

Ramson felt giddy as the realization hit him. He was alive. He was, somehow, miraculously, *alive.* "Daya," he croaked. "Thank you."

She snorted. "I didn't do this for free. It'll cost you double your fare." When he didn't respond, she grinned and elbowed him. "Sorry, sorry, I'm kidding. Too soon?"

Ramson summoned a weak smile. "A bit."

"Who were those bastards?"

Strength was slowly returning to his body. Sitting upright was getting easier by the second. Soon, he'd be able to stand. "That," Ramson said, "was Alaric Kerlan. I caught him in the middle of . . . a much larger scheme than we'd anticipated." His head hurt; the facts he'd learned sloshed around his head like water. "Which, I think, if he succeeds, will destroy the world as it is."

He was still working to process what he had seen earlier in the night—the makeshift lab in the hull of the ship, the Bregonian scholar. Bogdan's look, the way he'd pleaded to *get it out of him, get it out of him* even as he'd performed his Affinity to gold.

Kerlan had been the one to inform Morganya of this weapon he'd called a siphon. It made so much sense—that he would cut off the parts of his Order that posed a threat to him under Morganya's new regime and find a way to gain her favor while plotting his vengeance.

And the things Kerlan had said about Roran Farrald . . . no, Ramson couldn't wrap his head around them just yet, no matter how much he thought they sounded exactly like something his father would do.

He needed to get going. What was it that Kerlan had said? That the biggest party of all awaited him in the Blue Fort.

"Goddess Amara. I'm *extra* glad I saved your life, then." Daya tapped the knives looped through the metal hoops of her belt. "Good thing I have a way with locks."

Ramson pushed himself to his feet. The world swayed unsteadily for several moments before settling down. Blood rushed to his legs. He couldn't have been out for long.

Which meant Kerlan couldn't be too far ahead. *My forces have already infiltrated the Blue Fort. Within hours, my army arrives, and we strike.*

The impossibility of the task almost crushed the air from his lungs. Kerlan was going to invade the Blue Fort, *tonight.* He was going to crown himself king and trade Ana back to Morganya.

He'd left for the Blue Fort already with two wagons full of his most loyal ex-Order members. Just how many were left, roaming about Bregon? Were some of them already hiding in the Blue Fort?

Ramson shook the dizziness from his head. He needed to warn someone. He needed to—he needed to get to his father.

A gust of wind slammed into him, cold and sharp and biting. Beyond the quays, the waves grew violent, rearing and smashing against the wooden jetties. The moon slid behind storm clouds.

Ramson tilted his face to the air. It smelled of rain.

A storm was coming.

"Daya," he said. "Where are the nearest stables?"

Daya put her hands on her hips. "You owe me a *lot* of goldleaves." She winked. "It's right over there, next to the first pub."

Ramson looked to where the cliffs met the sea and the Blue Fort loomed. "Something very bad is about to happen. If I don't come back, will you promise me to find the princess and get away from here?"

The playful expression on Daya's face slipped at the urgency in his tone. "Fine," she groused. "I'll have you know that I've never done anything for anyone as a *favor.* Don't disappoint me, Pretty Boy."

The previous version of him would have cringed at a promise to pay back a debt. Now, Ramson couldn't think of anything he wanted more, after it was all over.

If there was an after.

Ramson tapped two fingers to his forehead in mock salute before he turned away. "I hope to the gods I won't," he replied as he set off at a sprint.

 40

Linn splayed her feet and stood on her toes. There were some who preferred to fight like earth or like fire. Linn fought like her element, the wind. She had never been the strongest or the biggest in her classes with the Wind Masters, but she learned the flow of her opponents' energy and then used it against them.

"I do not want to fight you." Kaïs's voice was steady yet low with regret as he reached for his double swords. The sound of metal sliced through the air. "Do not make this hard, Linn."

"I did not," she replied. "You did."

Something in her heart had broken when she'd seen him in the dungeons, shattered by the depth of his betrayal. After so many years of being alone, seeing the silver armor and white cloaks as signs of a ubiquitous enemy, she'd thought him different. She'd begun to trust him.

It had been a mistake.

She felt his Affinity in her mind, yawning over her winds like an unrelenting hand. Her Affinity snuffed out.

Linn stood her ground. She had trained to fight without sight and without sound. In Cyrilia, she had been forced to endure without her winds under the traffickers' blackstone or Deys'voshk too many times.

She wouldn't need them to win, now.

Kaïs watched her with those inscrutable eyes, and she held his gaze. A current of energy seemed to crackle in the air between them, as though they were two moving parts of a whole. A yin and a yang.

He sprang first, and Linn tucked herself into a roll beneath him. The clash of their blades rang out under the paintings of the Bregonian gods, reverberating in the silence.

Linn sprang back to her feet. Out of the corner of her eyes, she saw Ana rush over to the Bregonian scholar. He was leaning against the bookshelves, his mouth opening and closing like a fish as he gripped his chest, trying impossibly to stem the flow of blood down his front.

Linn pivoted, putting them behind her as she faced Kaïs.

She attacked first this time, taking off at a sprint and lashing out. He dodged, but she had feinted; she whipped out her other arm and aimed at his chest. He leapt back just in time; the tip of her dagger grazed the collar of his shirt. A thin gash exposed his skin.

Kaïs looked up. "I'm sorry, Linn. I never meant to hurt you."

Linn raised her hands. "Tell it to my blades."

She charged again, but he moved, surprisingly fast, and then his sword was arcing down at her. Linn sprang out of the way, but his other blade came swinging low, aiming at her feet. She caught herself just in time, twisting and delaying her fall for a moment longer. Her foot hit the flat part of his sword and she launched herself into the air, landing several feet away.

He turned to face her again.

"Do not hold back," Linn said, pointing her dagger at him. "I can always tell when one's heart is not in the fight."

He raised his weapon. "I wish you didn't have to be involved in this."

"This is my fight, as much as it is Ana's." Her tone softened. "And, until now, I thought it was yours."

Torchlight and shadows flickered on his face. "I do it to survive."

Linn allowed herself to taste a small sliver of frustration at last. "Survive?" she repeated. "That is all I have been trying to do these past years, Kaïs. Yet I would never hesitate to give my life to do the right thing."

His expression turned stony. Linn was running out of time. There was something in him worth saving, something worth redeeming. She could almost see it, reach it.

"You are a good person, Linn," he said quietly. "I am a selfish one."

"Then choose to *be* a good person!" The words exploded from her in a shout. Linn charged. In her moment of fury, she forgot her winds; she became fire, surging forward in a storm of blades.

He countered; their weapons clashed. Linn twisted, slashed.

Blood sprayed the air.

Kaïs stumbled back. A line of red trailed across his chest, glistening bright as rubies. He looked up and wiped sweat from his brow. "I would gladly give my life for yours," he said, "but it is not mine I am trying to save."

Linn blinked away the hot tears in her eyes. "Then whose?" she demanded. "Whose life is so important that you would choose the side of a murderer, that you would watch her burn down the world?"

There it was, a glimpse of sadness so profound, it was like trying to look into the depths of the Silent Sea. "My mother's."

Everything seemed to stop then. Linn drew a sharp breath. They'd spoken of his mother, back in the cold, ice-tipped forests of the Syvern Taiga. He'd mentioned it to her, and she'd *felt* the emotion in his words, a gripping ache that mirrored her own feelings toward Kemeira, toward her family.

Kaïs was panting, his double swords lowered. "Morganya and Kerlan have my mother. If I do not do as they say . . . if I do not succeed in this mission . . . they will kill her."

She wanted to drop her weapons right there, for in that moment she saw that they were reflections of each other. There was nothing she wouldn't do to save her family. She'd boarded a strange ship, journeyed to a foreign empire, and spent years of her life in search of her brother.

I cannot do this, Linn thought. *I have lost.*

Beneath an alcove a little way from where they fought, the scholar lay very still on the searock floor of the Livren Skolaren, his blood pooled around him. Ana had straightened and was gazing directly at them.

"Shamaïra," she said quietly.

Kaïs froze. Linn could see the tension in his broad shoulders.

Slowly, he turned to Ana. "What did you just say?"

"Your mother." Ana spoke as though she were gazing at a ghost. "Your mother is Shamaïra of Nandji, is she not?"

Kaïs stared at her. Emotions shifted in his eyes, as though they bore a storm. He gave a single nod.

"I know your mother," Ana said. "She saved my life. She sent me, Kaïs. She sent me here. To save the world. To save you."

Linn had the sensation of fate rushing by her, of the meeting of two threads of life, piecing together jagged fragments of the same story. "You know Shamaïra," Linn breathed, a part question, part statement in wonder.

Ana's gaze never left Kaïs's. "She was an ally to me and to the Redcloaks, a figure of the rebellion. She told me she lost her son to the Affinite trade many years ago, and she's been searching for him since." Her voice cracked. "She crossed the Aramabi Desert for you. She survived for years in the Cyrilian Empire, because she has been looking for you, Kaïs."

Kaïs dropped to his knees, his swords clanging on the floor. He pressed the heels of his hands to his eyes, slowly shaking his head. "No," he moaned. "I can't. I don't have a choice."

Linn lowered her daggers. "You do," she said, taking a step toward him. "I know how it feels, to be trapped. But if there is anything I have learned, it is that you can always make a choice."

"I think," Ana continued, "that if your mother were here, she would tell you that we will not find fairness in this world. But it is up to us to take what we are given and to fight like hell to make it better."

Kaïs buried his face in his hands. When he looked back up, a sheen of tears glistened in his eyes.

Linn knelt. Gently, she placed her knives on the floor between them. Met his gaze. Slowly, she brought her hands together, cupping one over the other.

Action, counteraction.

"Please," she whispered, and the word trembled in the silence between them. "The choice is yours."

41

The wind had whipped into a screaming gale by the time Ramson reached the top of the Crown's Cut. He pounded at the heavy ironore gates, and every excruciating second it took for the guards to emerge from the keep felt like agony.

"Ramson Farrald," he panted. The Royal Guard held his torch to Ramson's face. Satisfied, he waved it once, twice, three times—a signal to open the gates. "Tell me, have two wagons gone through this evening?"

The guard gave him a disinterested look. "Yes, over a bell ago."

Shit. *Shit.*

The first drops of rain hit his face as he sprinted through the courtyards. The buildings and trees of the Naval Academy flew by in blurred shadows, and at last, *at last,* the steps leading to the Naval Headquarters appeared.

Ramson vaulted up the steps three at a time. The corridors were strangely empty—the absence of guards worrying him more. When he reached his father's chambers, though, he was relieved to find a squad of Royal Guards standing sentry.

"Announce me," he gasped. "And do not let *anyone* else in."

One of the Royal Guards opened the door to step inside. With a violent step forward, Ramson shoved his way past the guard and burst into his father's chambers.

Admiral Farrald was sitting at his desk, penning something onto parchment. Relief flooded through Ramson. "Admiral—"

"I hope you've persuaded your Blood Empress." His father spoke without looking up from his writing. "It would be highly inconvenient for the deal to fall through tonight."

Ramson paused, the torrent of thoughts in his mind coming to a standstill. "What?"

"The Three Courts are gathering at Godhallem as we speak." The Admiral's gaze flicked up momentarily. "We meet with the Blood Empress at eight bells."

Cold slipped through his veins. *The biggest party of all in the Blue Fort,* Kerlan had said. "No," Ramson said, stepping forward. "You need to call off the meeting—"

"I thought this would happen," the Admiral interrupted. He set down his pen and stood, the scrape of his chair rattling against Ramson's skull. "So I've already sent Sorsha to escort her to Godhallem. They should be on their way. It is all simply a show, to convince the insipid little King and the Three Courts that I'm adhering to the proper procedures. I'll have your little Blood Empress's magek whether she agrees to it or not."

The nonchalance in his father's voice unleashed something hot and wild within him. Suddenly, they were back on that night seven years ago, pieces of his shattered cup strewn across the floor, hot chocolate dripping down the walls like blood. Jonah's body limp and helpless on the cold searock floor.

For a moment, he considered letting the attack on Bregon happen. He owed nothing to his father, to this wretched kingdom run by a wretched government. Perhaps, then, his father would finally know how it tasted to have all that you had loved and cared for destroyed before your very eyes.

But he thought of Jonah. Of his mother, standing in that cottage by the sea. They had believed in the good part of him. They had loved him and, in return, told him that he was capable of loving and being loved.

And that was what made him different from Roran Farrald.

So Ramson forged his fury into something cool, sharp, and harder than steel. He crossed the room to his father's desk and spread his hands across it. "Tell you what," he said. "Let's make a Trade. You take me to where she is, and I tell you why I'm here. About information I learned of an imminent attack on Bregon." He bared his teeth in a smile. "How does that sound, *Father*?"

The Admiral's eyes bore through him. Father and son gazed at each other in a deadlock, and in that moment, an entire lifetime might have passed.

When Admiral Farrald finally drew back, it wasn't anger or fury on his face.

It was disappointment.

"I loved your mother, too, you know."

Of all the things Ramson might have expected his father to say, it wasn't this. The words hung in the air. Froze him. Turned his plan around and threw it back in his face. "This has nothing to do with my mother."

"I had them bury her, right outside Elmford. On a hill of white heather, by the sea."

"You lie."

"It wasn't fair of me to love something more than I loved

my kingdom, you see. Love made me weak. Love made me a fool. Love *destroys* us." The Admiral circled to the window and looked out. And there, on the windowsill, sat a small pot of white flowers, leaning against the glass.

Ramson's knees went weak. His mind fractured; his world shrank, until there was nothing left in it but his father and that pot of white heather.

Roran Farrald reached out, absentmindedly stroking a petal. "So I made sure to destroy it first." He turned around, circling the table to close the distance between them. "And now, I see that love has made claim on my own son. Would you trade our kingdom, Ramson, for the life of one girl?"

No, he wanted to yell. *Don't you dare put this on me.*

Instead, Ramson lifted his shoulder in the most infuriatingly insouciant shrug he could muster. "It's not my kingdom," he said. "It's yours. And it just so happens that I have information of an attack by Cyrilia."

Roran Farrald's face was serene as he waved a hand. "It doesn't interest me," he replied, returning to peruse his papers. "You see, your beloved Blood Empress was one step behind in the game all along." He lifted his gaze. "I already have an agreement in place with the Kolst Imperatorya Morganya."

The world shifted sharply off-balance.

"Oh, yes," the Admiral continued tonelessly, seeing Ramson's expression. "I have been developing something that requires the help of magen to, ah, test. The new Empress agreed to sell Cyrilian Affinites to me, under the condition that I share our results with her. Much more convenient than having to kidnap our own magen, which ruffled a few feathers in our government when it came to light."

Ramson grasped wildly for words. "The siphons."

His father regarded him with mild surprise. "Yes. It seems you do have some ability, after all. You can see why I took the deal, my son—the Empress never stipulated whether the results I shared had to be *successful.* The siphon I shipped recently to Cyrilia broke en route, with its weak-minded bearer driven mad." Admiral Farrald looked thoughtful for a moment. "I imagine it to be quite overwhelming, to be a siphon bearer exposed to multiple magek at once. It requires an individual strong of will and strong of mind."

With a chill, Ramson thought of Linn's encounter with the blackstone wagon, the Affinite with two Affinities. "Why would you give Morganya a siphon?" he asked.

"I didn't," the Admiral replied with a shrug. "I would never. The entire point of the siphon experiments was to bolster Bregon's defenses against the growing threat of Cyrilia." He paused. "Nor would I be able to give her a siphon, even if I wanted to. Currently, we have only one perfected version, and it rests with my own lifeblood."

Something didn't fit in this picture—something was missing. His father had been purchasing—*trafficking*—Affinites from Cyrilia, under an agreement he'd struck with Morganya. Kerlan had been working with Morganya to provide the shipments and sneak his forces in . . . yet Admiral Farrald had vehemently denied any involvement in this scheme with his old enemy, Alaric Kerlan.

Which meant . . .

There was a third person involved in this picture, a traitor in their midst. Ramson's mind hurtled forward, but it felt as though he was coming to the realization too late.

Crisp footsteps sounded outside, and the next moment, the doors to the study opened.

"Oh, how *interesting.*"

He would have recognized that sharp, lilting voice anywhere.

Ramson turned as Sorsha sashayed into the room. "Did I miss the summons for our little family gathering?"

Admiral Farrald stood. "What are you doing here so soon?" His lips curled, his tone turning dismissive at the appearance of his daughter. "Do you have the Blood Empress?"

Sorsha sank into a bow. Somehow, she made it look mocking. "I certainly do, Daddy Dearest." She stalked up to him, and that was when Ramson caught it: a flash of a band around her wrist, the color of ocean, of searock—the same that Bogdan had worn.

Everything around him seemed to slow.

"Well, Daddy Dearest," he heard Sorsha tease, "do I get my reward now?"

The Admiral had just opened his mouth to reply when Sorsha lifted a blade and plunged it into their father's heart.

42

Scholar Tarschon was dying.

As Kaïs released Ana's Affinity, the sense of blood came flooding back into her awareness. She dropped to the scholar's side, sweeping her Affinity against the blood seeping from his chest. Even as she did, she could sense that there was too much of it, and she was too late.

The man's face was drained of color. His lips were pale, and it took Ana a moment to notice that they were moving. She leaned her face close to him.

He was speaking to her. "The siphons must be . . . destroyed." His voice was a whisper. "Our subjects . . . fell sick. Those whose mageks were taken from them died . . . within several moons." His eyes clouded with desperation, memories of horrors. "Those who bore the siphons' mageks . . . their bodies . . . rejected the change. All died. All . . . but one."

Ana felt sick. "Sorsha Farrald," she whispered, and the scholar closed his eyes in resigned acknowledgment.

"Who else was involved?" Ana demanded, but a large shudder convulsed the scholar's body. Blood bubbled from his mouth, too much of it flooding her senses. He was slipping away. "No, Scholar Tarschon, stay with me—"

"The siphons . . . can be . . . destroyed." Tarschon's voice was fainter than the wind now, and the words sent chills down Ana's spine. "Restore . . . the natural . . . order . . ." His eyes widened as he drew a large, shuddering breath, and then fell still.

For a moment, it felt as though all their hopes had vanished with the scholar. Ana stayed by his side, looking at his face, at his empty eyes, wondering what other horrible secrets the man had carried with him to the grave.

Behind her, Kaïs had wrapped an arm around Linn's waist and stood, gently lifting her to her feet. "I'm sorry." His words echoed around the empty hall. "Forgive me."

Ana closed her eyes, willing herself to remain calm. She thought of striking him, of shaking him with her Affinity, of screaming at him. But she also thought of Shamaïra, of the desperation in Kaïs's eyes as he'd spoken of his mother. *I do it to survive.*

"There is nothing to forgive," Linn said flatly. "We must work together to put a stop to Kerlan and Morganya's plan." She held Kaïs's gaze. "If you truly wish to make amends, you'll tell us everything you know."

Kaïs bowed his head. He drew a deep breath, and when he looked up again, something in his face had set—something that reminded Ana of the fierce resolve she'd seen on Shamaïra's face. "Then there is no time to waste," he said. "Alaric Kerlan has been working with Sorsha to infiltrate the Blue Fort. His and Morganya's joint forces arrive soon to conduct an invasion and take the siphons. They plan to leverage your meeting tonight to assassinate King Darias and have Kerlan crowned as

King." His face tightened. "I was meant to escort King Darias to Godhallem tonight."

Ana thought of the boy king, helplessly surrounded by Sorsha's guards. "Is he safe?"

"For now, yes. He is under guard by Captain Ronnoc of the King's Guard."

If they kept Kerlan's forces concentrated in Godhallem and put up a good enough fight, then the King should remain untouched. "How many forces did Kerlan bring with him?" she demanded.

"He has at least twenty of his men stationed around the Blue Fort," Kaïs said, "half of which are Affinites. His plan is to take control of Godhallem with them."

Even with Ana's blood Affinity, they would be outnumbered. Ana shook her head. "We'll need reinforcements, if we want to have a chance at a fair fight."

Kaïs looked thoughtful. "Kerlan has been trafficking Cyrilian Affinites to Bregon," he said. "Some are still locked in the dungeons of the research wing, waiting to be tested on. If we can free them, there is a chance they'll want to fight on our side."

Ana recalled her encounter with the imprisoned Affinites back at the Playpen in Novo Mynsk. The image of May's eyes, fierce with resolve, would remain indelibly carved into her memories. *I want the whole Empire, every single Affinite, to know how it feels to have hope.*

An ache bloomed deep in her chest. She'd made a promise to her friend; May had been the beginning of the reason why Ana fought. "We'll free them, whether they wish to join our fight or not," she found herself saying.

Linn nodded, taking a step forward. "I will go," she said.

"Ana, you must stop Sorsha. She has a second siphon that she plans to take to Morganya tonight."

Ana looked to Scholar Tarschon's body. "Sorsha is the first successful bearer of a siphon," she said. "Admiral Farrald repressed her power with a blackstone collar."

"She plans to seize the key," Kaïs said suddenly. He looked to Ana, his gaze sharpening with urgency. "You must stop her before she unlocks her collar."

Linn paled. "I saw Sorsha and a scholar unlock an Affinite's collar in the research wing," she said. "Is the key there?"

But Kaïs shook his head. "She would have taken it already," he said. "It must be somewhere she cannot easily reach."

A sense of dread spread through Ana's veins, along with the inevitable answer. *Power cannot be fettered forever,* Sorsha had said as she spoke of her father—the man who had put that collar on her in the first place. The one person who had control over her, the one person against whom Sorsha could not raise a hand, no matter how much he mistreated her and no matter how much she resented him.

"Admiral Farrald," she croaked. "He must know where it is."

"Go," Linn said. Resolve shaped her face. "We will ensure that the King and his guard receive warning." She hesitated. "And we will free the Affinites kept in the dungeons."

Ana looked to Kaïs. "If anything happens to her, yaeger, I'll kill you myself."

His response was a grim smile. "We will join you at Godhallem. Take caution. Kerlan's forces are here already."

Ana turned and made for the exit of the Livren Skolaren, the grand paintings of the gods of Bregon blurring into a whirl as they silently urged her onward.

43

Roran Farrald blinked. For a moment, he looked stunned to see the hilt protruding from his chest.

Sorsha stepped back and their father slumped over her, head on her shoulders like a newborn. "See, Daddy Dearest," she crooned into his ear, "your greatest invention. You raised me with only the capability to destroy. To ruin. And you never thought that one day, the little girl you made into a monster would come back to destroy *you.*"

Ramson would never forget the look on his father's face. His expression opened, the hard planes softening to pure, raw emotion as he beheld his daughter. Regret. Sadness. And something else that Ramson didn't dare name, a glimmer so brief it might have been sunlight in a storm, a shooting star, an illusion of the greatest kind.

Love makes us weak.

But then the Admiral spoke, and Ramson understood. "I'm sorry," Roran Farrald whispered, and Ramson could have sworn he was speaking to him.

Sorsha tilted her head back and laughed. "I won't fall for that again," she said. "Good-bye, Daddy Dearest."

And with that, she yanked the blade from his chest.

Blood darkened Admiral Farrald's uniform, staining the gold of his badges, the bronze of his buttons. Ramson stumbled back.

Sorsha cast him a sharp glance. "In a minute, Brother Dearest," she snapped, catching their father's body. She fumbled for a moment, then held something up. It was the large gold ring that their father had worn on his left hand. Sorsha lifted the ring to the light, beholding it as though it were a sacred relic. Their father's corpse fell to the floor with a thud.

Blood pooled onto Admiral Farrald's smooth searock floor.

Sorsha pointed the ring at her neck, hesitating only briefly before jamming it against the black collar resting at her throat. She twisted, and with a neat click, the blackstone collar opened, leaving behind a pale band of flesh. The collar clanged against the floor.

Ramson felt it: a tremor rippling through the air, as though the earth itself shook. Sorsha's head was tilted back, her auburn hair and clothes rippling as though in a gale of strong, unrelenting wind. Only, instead of wind, it was an invisible energy, a force, that swept through the chambers, knocking over books and shattering glass.

Sorsha leaned against the wall. For several moments, she was motionless, and Ramson wondered whether whatever she had done had actually killed her—gods, he *hoped* it had killed her—

—and then she drew a single, shuddering breath.

When Ramson's sister sat up, everything and nothing about her had changed. Her features were the same, yet everything about them seemed clearer, sharper, as though before he had been looking at her from behind fogged glass. She stood and crossed the room, and the air around her trembled as it would around a flame, and Ramson himself *felt* it as she swept past him.

She looked to the gold ring in her hand. A laugh bubbled from her as she tossed it to the floor.

Then fire erupted from Sorsha, a wreath of flames so hot they were blue, engulfing the ring. Her eyes were wide with glee; her mouth parted as she watched the ring melt into a puddle of gold at her feet.

She lifted her gaze to Ramson.

He ran for his life.

Her screaming laughter followed him as he sprinted out of his father's chambers. The hallway outside was empty but for the bodies of the four guards Sorsha had slain. It all made sense now—painfully obvious sense—how everything pieced together. Who else would be able to clear the guards across the entire Blue Fort but the Lieutenant of the Royal Guard? Who else possessed the motives for revenge and ruin?

Ramson grabbed a sword from the body of the nearest Royal Guard as Sorsha's steps sounded behind him.

"Your turn, Brother Dearest!" she called in a singsong voice.

Ramson chanced a look back and wished he hadn't. As Sorsha swept her hand, sections of stone tore from the walls. They hovered behind her in midair.

Anticipation filled Sorsha's face. With a laugh, she flung her hand, and the first boulder shot at him.

Ramson dodged. He heard the rock smash against the wall behind him. He'd barely scrambled to his feet when the second piece came at his head. The third one caught him in his stomach, knocking the wind out of him as he fell onto the searock floor. His sword clattered against the ground.

Ramson spat blood. He pushed himself to his knees, snatched the hilt of his sword, and glanced back.

"Do you know what the scholars called me, Brother Dearest?" Sorsha held out a hand, and the swords of the dead guards began to rise into the air. They soared to her, splintering as they did into smaller fragments of metal, like needles. "The Iron Maiden."

Shit. Shit, shit, shit.

The pain in Ramson's stomach throbbed as he pushed himself to his feet. Clenching his teeth, he threw himself forward and turned around the bend of the next hallway. He glanced back to see splinters of sword pelting the wall behind him.

"Oh, come now, Brother Dearest," Sorsha called. "Don't run from me! Though, if you'd like to play a game, I'm *more* than willing to engage in a round of hide-and-seek!"

Panting, Ramson straightened himself as best as he could and began to hobble forward. The end of the hallway looked insurmountably far away, and he could hear the jagged clicks of his half sister's footsteps as she stalked him, a cat hunting a mouse.

Ramson let out a stream of curse words as he wiped blood from his mouth, his other hand gripping the sword—now functionally useless against Sorsha's magek.

"I *see* you!" Sorsha's words echoed down the length of the hall in a mocking lilt.

The walls were crumbling around him beneath Sorsha's magek. A portrait of the Three Gods intertwined smashed against the searock floor, and even as Ramson leapt over it, he knew he'd run out of time. The end of the corridor was too far away.

Gritting his teeth, he flung his sword down the end of the hallway as far from him as possible before turning to face Sorsha. She looked like a creature out of a nightmare. Her eyes bulged from her face in glee, her hands were splayed to either side of her, and dozens of fragments of metal hovered at her back.

Ramson thought back to the magek he'd seen her use. Fire first; then stone. And iron, her specialty.

His eyes caught on the fallen portrait in front of him. *Gold and wood,* he thought.

It would have to do.

With a prayer to the gods, he scrambled forward and heaved the frame from the ground, placing it before his body like a shield.

He heard Sorsha cackle with pleasure. "Oh, *clever,*" she shrieked. "In that case, let's play target practice!"

The iron spikes whistled forward, thudding against the wood of the frame. Some more clacked against the wall at the end of the hallway.

But then the ones embedded in the portrait began to shudder, morphing into thinner, longer projectiles.

Ramson uttered a curse and flung the painting aside just as the spikes wrenched themselves free. They turned to him.

Ramson hauled himself to his feet and began to run, but he heard more whistling through the air, followed by an explosive pain through his shoulder that knocked him to the floor. Warmth pooled on the fabric of his sleeve. He didn't have to look to know the metal had buried itself deep, but just shallow enough to have avoided severing a muscle.

He'd been through worse. Kerlan had forced him to become well acquainted with pain. Even Jonah, Ramson thought, had given him worse beatings during sparring practice back at the Naval Academy.

Ramson gritted his teeth and pushed himself back up. "That all you got?"

Sorsha laughed in delight. "Oh, I *love* the attitude! Unfortunately, that's not going to save you." She lifted her arms, and the remaining iron spikes turned toward him. "Good-bye, Brother Dearest."

Utterly defenseless, Ramson raised his bare hands. After an entire lifetime spent running, he'd never thought he would die fighting on his own two feet. Yet as he adjusted his position, he realized that there was something holding him up that was stronger than fear, stronger than any impulse or desire he'd harbored in his life.

In this moment, he thought of Ana, and waited for the spikes to come.

They didn't.

There was a shriek as Sorsha was lifted into the air and sent hurtling down the hall. She slammed into the wall and rolled, her iron fragments clanging to the floor around her.

"He's mine," came a familiar voice. "And I don't share."

Ramson turned to see Ana striding toward him from the other end of the hall, her arms outstretched, her irises ringed red. Her hair was tangled and wet, the dark blue gown she wore now mud-splattered and torn.

Ramson didn't think he'd seen her look more beautiful.

Down the corridor from them, Sorsha snarled. As she lifted herself from the ground, however, a familiar ringing chimed across the fortress grounds.

The bells were chiming the hours.

Sorsha stilled, her head cocked.

Ramson counted. By his side, Ana froze, their eyes interlocked as they silently counted the beats.

Eight bells. Ramson saw the realization bloom on Ana's face. The Three Courts would have gathered, prepared to begin their negotiation with her.

Kerlan's coup had begun.

Sorsha beheld Ana through narrowed eyes, licking her lips. "The blot magen," she crooned, her voice soft with desire. "The most coveted magek of all." She brushed herself off and straightened. "I'll finish this later, Blood Bitch and Brother Dearest."

Without another word, she turned the corner and disappeared.

Only then did Ramson let himself slump against the wall, panting. He swept a hand to the wound on his shoulder. The iron splinter Sorsha had pierced him with was still there, and his fingers came away sticky. His blood, he realized, had spread all the way down to his elbow.

A rustle of fabric; Ana came to stand next to him. Droplets of rainwater clung to her dark lashes as she pressed a hand below his injured shoulder. "Deities," she murmured. "That's a lot of blood."

Ramson's chuckle was rough. "I thought you enjoyed seeing me bleed."

"Only when I'm the cause of it," she said, deadpan.

"Careful, Witch. You're starting to have a sense of humor."

She threw him a glare and ignored him. Her fingers were cold against his skin as she deftly peeled back his ruined shirt. She smelled of wind and storm and sea, and he was giddy in a way that he couldn't tell whether it was from the blood loss or from her proximity. "This is going to hurt."

Without warning, she pulled the shard of iron from his shoulder. Ramson's head grew light with pain; the floor tilted beneath him. He was aware of her arms around him, catching him as he swayed, gently propping him back against the wall.

"Mmf," he grunted, feeling warmth drench the sleeve of his shirt. There was a tingling in his shoulder, a warmth in his veins as Ana placed a hand over his wound. Blearily, he cracked an eye open to look at her.

Her irises were crimson, her brows furrowed in that look of concentration he'd come to treasure, and she worked on his wound, utterly unaware that he watched her.

He could have stayed like this forever, drinking in the sight of her and knowing that he'd almost lost the chance to ever see her again. *I see the way you look at her,* his father had said. *Love makes us* weak, *boy.*

His thoughts swirled, sluggish. There was a truth buried deep in the most cowardly parts of his heart that he simply didn't want to see yet. For love, as his father had always taught him, was something to be destroyed. There was no room in love for selfishness.

And Ramson had always vowed that he would live only for himself.

As though she'd heard the turbulent mess of his thoughts, Ana looked up at him from beneath her lashes. "I've stopped the flow," she said. She pushed back a strand of hair from her face. "You'll still need a healer, though."

"No time for that." He tested his shoulder gingerly. The pain was fresh but beginning to recede into a dull throb. The world around him steadied. "We have a coup to stop."

He peeled himself from the wall and limped down the corridor. Ana followed, picking her way through the rubble and mess of iron. "She took off her collar," she remarked.

Ramson was about to reply, but the words stuck in his throat. They'd reached his father's chambers.

Ana peered in through the open doors. "There is a lot of blood in there," she said quietly.

From this angle of the hallway, Ramson could see beyond the guards' bodies through the slightly ajar door into his father's study. "Give me a moment," he found himself saying as he straightened. As though in a dream, he crossed over the hall to his father's chambers.

Details he hadn't noticed earlier now flooded his mind as he swept his gaze around the room. The walls were the exact shade of maroon as they had always been. The dark cherrywood desk that he'd sat before so many years ago no longer seemed to loom; it came up to the height of his hip.

It seemed like both a lifetime ago and no time at all that he'd thrown his mug against the wall, looked upon his father as both god and monster and sworn to never become like him.

Ramson knelt by his father's body. There was a pool of blood around him, spreading on the floor, but all that Ramson saw was the strange bend of his arms and legs, the way his eyes stared and his mouth was still open in surprise.

Lying on the floor like this, he looked less like the monster in the shadows. He was simply a man, one who bled and died all the same.

Ramson reached over and closed his father's eyes and mouth. In death, the Admiral's facial muscles had relaxed, and for the first time Ramson could recall, his father looked at peace.

A sudden movement across the room caught his eye. At the windowsill, petals from the small white flowers fell, like snow. They twirled in the air for an ephemeral moment before landing on the floor.

I loved your mother, too, you know.

"You loved her, too," Ramson muttered, the words tasting strange in his mouth. *Too.*

It was a possibility he had never considered—that he could stop thinking about himself for a moment to care for someone else. That he could put someone else's needs before his.

Did monsters and men who made bad choices have the capability to love? And did they deserve love in return?

Ramson stood. "Ine verron tane aust Sommesreven," he said. It was a Bregonian parting phrase for the dead, one murmured at funerals as they lit candles and set loved ones afloat on winding rivers or the great, weaving sea.

I will see you at Sommesreven.

Ramson was about to leave when something on the floor caught his eye. It was the remnants of his father's gold ring, the key that Sorsha had used on her collar. She had completely melted it earlier; the gold clung to the floor, no more than a blob of metal. She'd destroyed the key, the symbol of control that Roran Farrald had held over her.

But Ramson wasn't thinking of keys and symbols. His gaze

traveled back to his father's body, to where the blackstone band lay on the floor, cracked open like a lock.

An idea struck him: insurance should their plan go awry.

Ramson crossed the room and picked up the collar, unscathed from the intensity of Sorsha's fire. It was colder than ice against his skin as he unbuckled his belt and looped it through. It weighed heavy against his hips.

Ramson turned and left the room, shutting the door behind him with a soft click.

Ana was waiting for him outside, her arms folded. She straightened at his appearance.

Ramson nodded. "It's time."

44

Ana kept her Affinity flared as they hurried through the Naval Headquarters, their footsteps echoing unnaturally loud in the otherwise silent halls. The building had emptied. Most courtiers would have gathered in Godhallem, waiting for her negotiation.

Which made them sitting ducks for Kerlan's coup.

As they walked, Ramson filled her in on Admiral Farrald's Affinite trafficking scheme with Morganya, on Sorsha's betrayal of her father and her kingdom.

The impossibility of their task felt like a noose coiling tighter and tighter around their necks. "Linn and Kaïs are freeing the trafficked Affinites as we speak," Ana said as they turned a corner. "But Sorsha has two siphons—one she is wearing, and another that she carries."

Ramson's eyes were narrowed in a way that told Ana he was coming up with a plan. "We need to launch the Bregonian Navy," he said at last.

Ana nodded, their task settling deep into her belly. "We must ring the War Bells."

They had reached the end of the Naval Headquarters.

Beyond the ironore doors were the courtyards leading to Godhallem. Rain was lashing down full force upon the Blue Fort when they emerged, the wind whipping mercilessly against buildings and trees. Within seconds, Ana's clothes were soaked.

Ana squinted through the night, doing a quick sweep of the courtyards around her for blood. By her side, Ramson cut a striking form through the rain: tall, lean, and long-limbed, Bregonian doublet all sharp lines and hard edges.

He turned to her then, rainwater carving tracks down his cheeks. The only light came from the lamps burning through the windows of the buildings across the courtyard.

Ramson grasped her arms. "Ana," he said, his voice rough. "I don't know how all this is going to end."

She closed her eyes briefly, relishing the way his hands were at once firm and gentle on her, his touch searing heat through the soaked fabric of her shirt. Time trickled away from them, eddying into a distant future where the path of the world split between their success and failure. But right now, in this moment, it was just the two of them.

Lightning flashed overhead, and thunder rumbled as Ramson closed the gap between them. Rainwater dripped down the sharp planes of his face. There was something new to his gaze, something wild and untamed that sparked a fire inside her. His grip tightened. "I'm sorry," he said. "I'm sorry for anything that I've done to hurt you." His wet hair was plastered to his face, his expression open and vulnerable in a way she had rarely seen it. "I'm sorry that I lied to you; I'm sorry that I used you; I'm sorry if I ever made you feel unsafe, I—" His voice caught. "I'm sorry, all right?"

She shook her head. "Don't say that. No matter how this ends, Ramson, I'll be with you."

He was looking at her in a way that left her breathless. And as another streak of lightning tore across the sky, Ana closed the last step between them. Their lips met with all the hunger and desperation of the winds that howled around them, and she dug her fingers into his hair, tasting the salt and heat of his mouth mixed with rainwater.

He made a sound deep in his throat and pulled her against him. The hard planes of his body pressed against hers through the fabric of their shirts and the burning of his skin ignited a fire deep in her soul. He was water and ocean and rain twining around her fierce flame of a heart, and as she kissed him, she had the sensation that she was falling into a bottomless abyss.

When Ramson drew back, he was panting, his hair tangled and dripping water down his face. Ana had never seen his eyes so clear and so bright, his face so open and so confused. His hands trailed heat across her skin as he held her.

In another life, in another story, Ana found herself thinking, they would have all the time in the world to spend with each other, to talk through the confusing tangle of desire and emotions that burned between them right now.

But such tales were for storybooks, and this was not one.

She took a step back. If she stayed with him any longer, she feared she would not have the strength to leave.

But Ramson leaned forward and, this time, pressed a gentle kiss to her lips. There was a clarity to the way his eyes came to rest on hers. "You ready, Witch?"

Ana nodded, and their fingers clasped tightly together. "Try to keep up, con man," she said, and, turning, pulled him into a full sprint toward Godhallem.

45

The main waterway to Godhallem was rushing and roiling like the ruthless currents of a river in flux. Some of it had flooded onto the marble walkway leading to the entrance. Ramson gripped Ana's hand more tightly in his as they began to wade through the torrents of water. Once or twice, she slipped, and even Ramson stumbled in the tides several times, correcting his balance with the trained instincts of a Bregonian sailor that he'd honed long ago.

The first warning sign Ramson came across were two ships smashed against the huge pillars that held up the structure of Godhallem. They were eerily empty, hulls bared and broken, strewn across the marble pavement like bones. Gone were the magen who had controlled the flow of water. Gone were the guards who had lined the steps leading to the Godhallem.

Ramson found them piled at the door, bodies slashed, their blood streaked violently across the floor and the walls. He could guess at the culprit.

Sorsha.

The ancient ironore doors to Godhallem stood half-open, unmoving even in the winds that howled through the walkway.

A sliver of yellow light fell across the pavement. Ramson and Ana inched up to the doors, flattening themselves against the wall.

Ramson drew a deep breath and peered in.

The scene was more dire than he'd imagined.

The courtiers of the Bregonian Three Courts were scattered in a loose ring around the edges of the hall. They were all on their knees, their heads bowed, their bodies rigid.

At the center of the hall, Nita stood before the searock dais, her fists clenched, her eyes narrowed in concentration. She was holding the Three Courts hostage.

By her side was Sorsha. A cord tightened within Ramson at the sight of his sister. She wore her weapons like ornaments: daggers studding the belt at her hips, boots that curved and ended in the tip of a blade, knives dripping blood in both hands. Her auburn hair had come loose and framed her sharp face—where, like a foggy reflection in glass, he saw traces of his own.

Sorsha grinned as she looked around the hall at the men bent at her feet. Her black eyes glinted dangerously as ever, yet there was something different about them, something unchained. If Sorsha had danced around the edges of madness before, she was now locked inseparably with it.

And, sitting on the throne, rings of precious stones glinting on his fingers, was Alaric Kerlan. Ramson had seen many different expressions on his old master's face, but now, there was only unbridled triumph in Kerlan's eyes.

Ramson's gaze roved behind the dais. "Kerlan's men," he murmured in Ana's ear, nodding to the figures who stood in the shadows. Some of them were from the group he'd encountered earlier tonight at Sapphire Port. Others were unfamiliar—meaning Kerlan had had to have planted them in the Blue Fort in the days before. Unease stirred in his stomach as Ramson realized there were more of Kerlan's men roaming around the Blue Fort. There were definitely some ex–Order members whom he thought he'd glimpsed earlier tonight who weren't here among these men.

"I see twenty," Ana whispered.

Ramson did a quick count and nodded. "Some were my fellow Order members," he said with a grimace. "Some, I don't recognize—they could be Affinites."

Ana's eyes narrowed, and he thought he saw the faintest stirrings of red in her eyes. "Shouldn't be a problem," she muttered back.

She was tense, pressed against the wall in front of him, and Ramson felt a sudden sense of panic at the thought of something, anything, happening to her. "I think you should stay back," he began, but Ana turned and pinned him with a glare.

"Not a chance, con man," she hissed, swiping rain from her face. "What are you going to do? Shovel water at them?"

He frowned at her. "Is that all you think I'm good for?" he whispered back, but Ana prodded him into silence. She jerked her chin back at Godhallem, her face suddenly paling.

Sorsha was pacing the dais, a maniacal smile curling her lips. Metal spikes hovered behind her, crowning her head like a twisted black halo. "Who's next?" she shouted, and only then did Ramson see the bodies at her feet. Rivulets of red ran across the smooth floor. The gossamer curtains lining the open wall behind them, leading to the cliff and the precarious plunge to the oceans far, far below, twisted like phantoms as the storm outside continued to slash at them. "Oh, this feels *so good*!"

Kerlan wasn't going to attempt to convince the Three Courts to support him. He was simply going to eliminate those who didn't.

Ramson glanced up. The War Bells hung above the hall, wind swirling through their great metal rims and filling the hall with a low, melodic humming tone. Almost like a warning.

He wasn't here to take down all of Kerlan's forces, Ramson reminded himself. He was just here to ring some bells.

He shifted his angle so that he was looking at the wall to his right, where the stallion symbol of the Earth Court gleamed from the wall. Beneath that was a giant brass lever.

All he needed to do was to get to that lever.

He narrowed his eyes, took measure. Twenty, maybe thirty steps—and he'd have to get there without anyone spotting him. Otherwise, Nita would seize him like a rag doll, Sorsha would riddle him with iron-spiked holes, and his plan would be over before it even began.

"Ana," he said, his tone urgent. "I'm going to ring the War Bells. Once I do that, I'll be discovered, and all hell's going to break loose. I'll need your help to fight Kerlan and his Affinites. And if something happens to me . . ." He drew a breath and looked straight into her eyes. "I need you to ensure that those bells ring at all costs."

There was rain running down her cheeks, but her gaze was like fire. She remained stubbornly silent, staring at him, ensnaring him with those eyes.

Ramson reached out and brushed back a strand of her hair. "Promise me," he said.

"I thought promises weren't your thing," she said quietly.

"I'll take that as a yes, then," he said just as softly, then turned and slipped into Godhallem.

Immediately, Ramson dropped into a squat, and the dais—along with Kerlan, Sorsha, and Nita—disappeared from view. Behind the rows of kneeling courtiers, he wasn't visible to anybody.

Sorsha continued to speak, her voice twisted in bitterness. "For my entire life, all of you have been watching my father use me, experiment on me, and then clap that vile collar back around my neck once he was done with me." She gave a sharp laugh. "Today, it's finally *my turn*! My turn to watch the expressions on your pathetic faces as I destroy this perverse legacy my father and previous men before him have created."

Ramson could sense the ripple of fear even as the courtiers' bodies were held frozen by Nita's Affinity.

Quickly, quietly, he shifted his belt, turning it so that his dagger and Sorsha's blackstone collar were at his back. He couldn't have them dragging by his side.

"Enough." Kerlan's voice rang out. "Well done, my daughters. You and I—we are paving the way to the future."

Ramson could imagine the sick little smile playing about Kerlan's lips. Drawing another deep breath, he gathered his wits, dropped to his hands and knees, and began to crawl toward the Earth Court.

"Bregon. Three Courts." Kerlan's tone turned magnanimous, echoing slightly indoors. "It is time for change. For so long, we have been sat on stale waters. Admiral after Admiral, Court after Court, with no big changes, no show of our true strength to the world.

"Tonight, all that will end. Tonight, Bregon will declare its allegiance to Her Glorious Majesty Morganya of the Empire of Cyrilia. And it will be my absolute *honor* to serve . . . as your Admiral, and as your new King."

There was a ripple of tension across the hall from the courtiers. Ramson froze in his progress, holding his breath. The searock floor was cool, shimmering torchlight weaving between streaks of aquamarine and navy blue. If he pressed his cheek to it, he could pretend he was underwater.

He took a moment to glance back at the entryway, the heavy doors that remained open despite the lashing rain outside. Beyond, there was only darkness. Ana was nowhere in sight.

"In just a few moments," Kerlan continued, "we will be joined by King Darias, who will pass his position to me. Those who join me will be reappointed as officials of our new kingdom." He snapped his fingers. "Nita, loosen their control a bit. Let us see what they have to say."

A shout immediately rose up, somewhere in the area of the Sky Court. "You are nothing but an exiled criminal come to take your vengeance upon this kingdom," the courtier declared. "I would rather die than serve under you."

A rumble of conversation began as others prepared to call out their answers.

But Kerlan held up a hand, and Ramson's veins turned cold when his old master said calmly, "Then your wish shall be granted."

A whizzing sound, a cry, a thud of a body on the stone floor. Godhallem fell into an ominous silence.

Ramson gritted his teeth. *The bells,* he thought, and lifted his head to look at the brass lever on the wall ahead. *Focus on the bells.*

"Delicious," Sorsha purred. Ramson heard the clinks of her iron spikes. "More—give me more!"

Ramson shinnied forward faster. He was so close, just eight or nine steps away. They felt like the length of an ocean. The brass lever gleamed in front of him.

"I am generous, you see," Kerlan continued. "I would not deny you a choice, provided that you make the *correct* choice."

Five steps. Crawling had never seemed more torturous. Sweat beaded on Ramson's forehead. In the background, he could hear his sister speaking.

"Oh," Sorsha said happily. "But I think we're about to have even *more* fun, Lord Kerlan."

Two steps. The lever hovered overhead.

"Won't you show yourself," Sorsha cackled suddenly, and Ramson's blood froze, "oh Brother Dearest?"

46

The rain was lashing down in torrents by the time Linn and Kaïs reached the research wing of the Naval Headquarters. It took them each several seconds to take down the guards, and they were struggling to catch their breath by the time they reached the interior of the research wing.

It was pitch-black in the hall. There was the flare of a flame, and a torch burned to life. Kaïs raised it, and the shadows peeled away.

Linn looked up at him. Rainwater slicked his hair, trickling down the carved edges of his jaw and running down his neck in rivulets.

He motioned to her and began to make for the door to the research dungeons. This time, when he opened it, the light from his torch flared into the darkness beyond. Linn followed him through, and they began to descend.

"What happens to your mother if you help us?" she asked quietly.

"She's the strongest woman I know." Kaïs held the fire high, the outline of his shoulders tense. His voice was distant, as though clouded in memories. "She would never hesitate to do the right thing. I've been focused on surviving and finding her for so long that I had begun to forget what she was like."

"Sometimes," Linn said, "I feel as if I have been away from my family for so long, I would not know them if I saw them again." Her voice caught. How many nights had she spent sleepless, trying to conjure up her mother's face, filling in the details with her imagination where her memory failed?

Kaïs's steps slowed; he turned to look at her. "But we hold on to the spirit of their memories, and we do the best that we can to honor them," he said.

No one had ever phrased it more perfectly, as though stringing the words from her soul and breathing them to life, sparking and bright and warm.

"The night we arrived, Sorsha came to me and showed me my mother's shawl. I recognized it at once—she has kept it all these years we have been apart. They'd spotted me at Goldwater Port; they were waiting for me." Kaïs continued steadily, his steps echoing in rhythm as he made his way down the stairs. "I almost lost it then. I was prepared to do anything and everything to save her. I'd always thought it didn't matter how many people I killed or whom I hurt, if that meant I would get her back. But now I realize . . . I realize I have been dishonoring her memory by doing so. Tonight, I fight for her."

They were nearing the bottom of the steps; Linn could see the arch of the doors that led into the room of her nightmares. Kaïs drew his sword and turned to her. His eyes blazed. "Who do you fight for, Linn?"

Names, faces, and memories flooded her mind. Enn, free as a sparrow, his life cut too short. Ama-ka, still waiting for them back at home. Ana, the friend who had helped her search for her destiny; Ramson, who had started all this the night he'd shown up at the Playpen and handed her the keys to her freedom.

And me, she thought. The girl who had staggered onto the cold, icy shores of a foreign empire. Who had been worked and chained and beaten to within an inch of her life, but who had held on stubbornly, doggedly, through it all. Against all odds.

There were so many others out there like her, still waiting for their chance to fight back.

Linn drew her daggers. "I fight for freedom" was all she said as she wrenched open the doors and stepped inside.

The chamber was longer than she remembered; she saw now that it stretched farther back, the walls interspersed with alcoves. When Kaïs lifted his torch, figures stirred in the far corners of the room.

The gold-haired girl Linn had watched Sorsha experiment on earlier was still sprawled in the same spot. Linn flitted over to her. Her body was cold, and when Linn touched a finger to her neck, she found nothing. She looked up, met Kaïs's gaze, and sadly shook her head.

He held up the set of keys he'd taken from the scholar back in the library and motioned her forward.

As they approached the back of the room, Linn saw that there were more prisoners chained to the walls, their wrists and ankles bound by blackstone manacles. They squinted against the torchlight and shrank away as they approached.

Linn raised her hands. "Do not worry, we are here to free you," she said as Kaïs began unlocking their chains one by one.

There were twenty of them, and they each fell forward with cries of relief as they were released. A few were just as emaciated as the gold-haired girl from earlier, but most were in better shape. They pulled themselves to their feet, helping those who could not to stand. Linn realized that not all of them bore distinctive Cyrilian looks; there were several who looked to be from the Aseatic Kingdoms, and one or two who resembled the people of the Southern Crowns.

Had they all been tricked to go to Cyrilia, only to find themselves being trafficked to a second foreign kingdom as human experiments? The thought made her sick. She needed to tell them that they were safe. That they would never come to harm again. Looking at their haunted expressions now, Linn felt as though she were looking into a mirror of her past self.

It gave her courage. It gave her inspiration.

"I am an Affinite," she said quietly. "And like you, I was trafficked to the Cyrilian Empire, and bound under a work contract against my will."

They were silent, watching her. Waiting.

"Tonight, a battle is taking place—one that will decide the course of history. Anastacya Mikhailov, the Red Tigress of Cyrilia, is putting a stop to the plans of the man who did this to you—Alaric Kerlan. She fights against the exploitation of people like us. But she cannot do it alone." Linn looked around, meeting each of their gazes. "I am choosing to fight for freedom. I am choosing to fight so no other Affinite needs go through what I did.

"You are free to do as you wish now. You may leave if you like. But if you wish to fight by our side—if you have the strength to fight with us—we need your help."

She had no idea where the words had come from, nor how she was able to deliver them so succinctly. She had always shied away from attention, preferring her shadows and wind, but as she looked around the room, Linn felt emboldened by the sight. She had saved twenty lives tonight. She had made a difference.

A dark-haired man in the back raised a hand. "I fight."

Another Affinite, a boy several years younger than Linn, spoke, too. "I'll fight."

One by one, the Affinites spoke, their words ringing loud and clear in the chamber and filling Linn with courage. Ten of them were strong enough to volunteer.

Linn raised her blade and motioned to them. "We must make haste."

As she turned to leave, she caught Kaïs's eyes. He was smiling at her. "Your mother would be proud."

Linn grinned back. "As would yours."

He looked forward, and Linn recognized the emotion dancing across his face with the torchlight.

It was hope.

47

Ramson scrambled to his knees and lunged forward. For a moment, he thought he might actually reach the brass lever; it gleamed in the torchlight as he arced through the air, his arm stretched as far as he could—

He saw movement at the corner of his eye. There was a whizzing sound and he could only watch, as though time had slowed, as a metal blade lodged in his right wrist.

Blood spurted, and a moment later, pain exploded.

Ramson's hand fell on the lever, limp, the tendons in his wrist sliced neatly through.

He scrambled, reaching with his left hand, but something rammed into his back, slamming him onto the floor, knocking the air from his lungs. He thought he heard one of his ribs snap.

"You're *weak,*" Sorsha hissed in his ear. She grabbed his right arm and pushed the blade in deeper. Stars burst in Ramson's vision; his head grew fuzzy with pain as the tip of Sorsha's blade protruded through the other side of his wrist. Blood dripped, hot and thick, down his arm. "For years, I've lived in the unworthy shadow of you and your like. Our father used my body as an experiment. So I killed him." Sorsha tilted her chin back, her eyes catching the bloodred glow of the torch, and Ramson wondered whether she had completely tipped into madness. "I will *destroy* all of you."

"Enough," Kerlan called. "Sorsha, bring him over. I'm going to kill him with my bare hands once I finish with the King." He bared his teeth at Ramson in a smile. "Third time's the charm, right, my son?"

Ramson had escaped death twice at Kerlan's hands.

He suspected Kerlan would not let it happen again.

Sorsha yanked Ramson up by his arm and jabbed a dagger into his side. "Move," she growled.

Ramson's head swam. His right arm alternated between searing pain and hot numbness. *Ana,* he thought, doing a quick search of the hall as he limped forward. It swam before his sight, but beyond the sea of courtiers, he could barely see the door, let alone whether she was still there. *Stay where you are,* he wanted to tell her. *Whatever you do, don't be stupid. Don't be the heroine. Don't do anything rash.*

He could only pray to the Three Gods, at this point, that she would remember her promise to ring the bells.

"It's time," Kerlan declared, and snapped his fingers at Nita. "Bring in the King."

There was a brief silence as Nita leaned in to whisper to him, and Ramson looked up to see displeasure spreading on Kerlan's face. As Sorsha shoved Ramson toward the front of the rows of courtiers, he caught snatches of their conversation.

"What do you mean," Kerlan hissed, "you don't know where he is?"

A small spark of hope flickered in Ramson's chest. It lasted only a brief second, before he felt Sorsha's boot in his back.

Ramson's breath left him as he slammed against the foot of the dais. Pain exploded over his injured right wrist.

A shadow fell over him.

"My dearest guests!" Kerlan spread his hands in a benevolent gesture, his rings flashing as he descended the dais. "It seems there has been a delay on my end. I apologize for the confusion." He flicked a glance at Ramson, and it promised retribution. "So, first, a little demonstration of what happens to traitors of this new regime."

The first blow sent his head cracking against the floor. The world went dark for a moment. When he resurfaced, he found himself gazing into the cold, ruthless eyes of Alaric Kerlan.

His old master was saying something, but it didn't matter anymore. Ramson's thoughts were scattering as he coughed up blood. For some reason, his eyes wouldn't focus on Kerlan's face in front of him. Instead, all that Ramson saw were the strangely bright metal rims of the bells of Godhallem looming overhead, blurring in and out of focus.

Suddenly, they began to move.

And the hall of Godhallem filled with the low, somber calls of its War Bells, echoing far and deep into the night.

48

Ana gripped the lever and straightened. Overhead, the bells sounded, their sonorous tones filling the entirety of Godhallem and reverberating within the searock walls. She spread her Affinity, the heat of the freshly spilled blood within these halls stirring nausea at the pit of her stomach.

It had taken every ounce of her self-control to hold back her Affinity when Sorsha had cut Ramson with her dagger, when Kerlan had slammed his head to the rock so hard that she heard the crack across the hall.

He'd made her promise to ensure that the bells rang, and Ana intended to keep her promise.

But now, looking at him lying on the floor, his hand in a pool of blood puddled beneath him, fury closed in around her.

"Let him go," she snarled, reaching for Kerlan with her Affinity.

A woman stepped in front of him. Ana recognized her as his Deputy. She raised her hands, hair flashing dark with a sheen of blue, and Ana reached for her blood—

Their Affinities hit each other at the same time.

A wave of exhaustion slammed into Ana, her muscles loosening and giving way. Her heart slowed and her lungs grew heavy. Her thoughts turned sluggish. As the other woman's Affinity squeezed tighter, Ana sank to her knees. Spots burst before her eyes. She couldn't see. Couldn't breathe.

But she still had her Affinity.

Ana closed her eyes, grasped the girl's blood, and tore.

The Affinite's cry cut off sharply. She stumbled back, clutching her side as a trickle of blood wound down her chin. Ana twisted again, and the other Affinite collapsed, her eyes fluttering shut as she lost consciousness.

The hold on Ana's organs and muscles receded. Drawing in deep breaths, she pushed herself back to her feet.

Kerlan sat on his throne, no longer smiling. His forces closed in around him, several of whom, Ana noticed, had called on their Affinities. One man held orbs of water hovering over his palms, droplets coalescing from the streams that encircled the dais. Another twined a cloud of sand over her shoulders like a glimmering shawl.

They waited for their master's command.

If that was how they wished to play, Ana would give them the fight they wanted. She swept her Affinity around the hall, navigating through the moving bodies to the open pools of blood cooling around the bodies of the courtiers Kerlan had murdered. The blood began to rise in streams of twisting red ribbons. They coalesced into crimson spheres beneath the light of the chandeliers. And then they began to lengthen, shifting and hardening into blades.

At Ana's beckoning, the blood daggers turned and pointed

at Kerlan and his Affinites. "Surrender, Kerlan," Ana called. "The War Bells are rung. Bregon's Navy will set sail at any moment to foil your attack on the Blue Fort."

Kerlan watched her, his expression cold. The War Bells had fallen silent by now, but echoes of their great, sonorous tones continued to hum in the air.

"The Admiral may be dead," Ana continued, "but as long as I live, I will never allow your plan to succeed."

But there was something different in Kerlan's expression as he straightened to look at her. It wasn't fury or failure that twisted his face.

It looked like . . . triumph.

As Ana skimmed her gaze over the group of Affinites encircling him, she realized something.

Sorsha was gone.

Too late, she caught the flash of movement. Too late, her Affinity picked up on the blood signature cutting amid the crowd and moving *toward* her instead of running away.

Ana had barely turned when Sorsha slammed her fist into Ana's neck.

A sharp pain pierced her flesh, and then blood exploded across Ana's senses. Not in the normal way that it did when her Affinity returned to her, but magnified tenfold, a hundredfold.

She could sense *everything,* as though she had cleaved the world apart and saw from the greatest heights of the skies to the deepest parts of the oceans, churning beneath the waves. Every fleck of blood, every drop of crimson.

Everything was red, everything was burning, the blood so bright that it seared. Her mind and body were afire, the pain electric, tearing into her very bones. As though from a distance, she could hear someone screaming—or perhaps it was her own voice, entwined with the sound of maniacal laughter.

Amid the blazing red were coils of darkness, small at first, and then closing in on her. It paralyzed her. She reached and reached, but her Affinity was rapidly spiraling out of her control, shifting and morphing as though it had taken on a life of its own. As though someone else held the reins now.

And then, abruptly, the crimson receded and her world faded to black.

49

Godhallem had become a scene of massacre.

In the distraction and amid the fleeing courtiers, Ramson had heaved himself away from the dais toward the end of the hall. He could only stare now, his mind frozen in disbelief. The floor was littered with bodies and soaked in an ocean of blood. Puddles formed beneath each corpse, staining the skin red and pooling quietly. A breeze blew in from the open-air end of the hall, stirring the pools of blood.

The few living clustered around the walls on either side of Godhallem. Ramson heard a courtier to his left lean over and retch.

Was this the fate that awaited his kingdom? The world?

A long, drawn-out scream echoed across the hall, and Ramson's world narrowed into sharp focus. He recognized that scream. It pierced his heart like a blade. Unleashed his worst fears.

He turned just in time to see Ana crumple to the ground, blood smearing her neck.

Beneath the emblem of the Earth Court, Sorsha straightened. She clutched her wrist bearing the siphon. The stone glistened with a dark liquid, but even as Ramson watched, the liquid seemed to be absorbed into the band until there was none left.

Something was happening to the skin underneath. Darkness spread across Sorsha's veins, like fissures across a surface. She shuddered, her mouth parted in ecstasy as she held up her hand and began to laugh and laugh and laugh. "Oh, this feels *good,* this feels so *good*!" she shrieked.

No. A part of Ramson was numb with disbelief that the worst they had imagined had happened.

Kerlan was on his feet now, the smug triumph wiped clean from his face. "What have you done?" he hissed.

In response, Sorsha only smiled at him and raised her bloodied blade to her face. Lovingly, she ran her tongue down the length of it.

Kerlan's expression was tight in a way that Ramson had learned to recognize meant the utmost displeasure for his old master. He looked around him, aware of all the courtiers watching them, and reined in his anger. He held out a hand. "Come here, Sorsha."

Sorsha sneered at him. "I don't think I will."

Kerlan's face darkened. "If you don't—"

"You're going to what? Kill off the only successful siphon bearer in the world? The one your empress needs? I'd like to see you *try.*" Sorsha cackled as she began to pace to the center of the hall, casually swinging her blade. Her iron spikes had shifted into flat discs, the edges sharp enough to slice. They orbited her like small gray stars. "You see, this is the problem with men. They're shortsighted and vain and will let their egos get in the way of strategy." She stopped and faced Kerlan, her expression turning ugly. "This is why I don't work for *you.* I work for your empress."

Ramson's mind was hurtling forward. Sorsha had complicated the situation with her series of betrayals, but in the chaos she'd sown, perhaps there was an opening for him. Across Godhallem, with the absence of Nita, courtiers had shifted to huddle behind the seats at the very edges of the court, clearing a space in the middle.

"*Enough.*" Kerlan's features were twisted in a way that made Ramson think of the worst bouts of fury his old master had ever thrown. He watched Kerlan signal at the rest of his men, who had remained behind the dais all this time. "Bring the bearer to me," he snarled. "I want her *alive.* And I want the siphon!"

"I think not," came a new voice, and the entire hall turned to the double doors at the entryway.

Kaïs stepped inside, cutting a massive shape against the night as he drew his swords. Rain slicked his hair, running rivers down his skin. By his side, like a shadow to his flame, stood Linn, daggers drawn. And, behind them, a slew of figures emerged from the rain. They held a much more diverse array of looks than Bregonians, skin tones ranging from pale to fawn and hair from white-gold to ochre. Several held up their hands, and various elements swirled over their upturned palms: water, fire, stone, marble, steel.

Were these the Cyrilian Affinites whom Kerlan had trafficked into Bregon? Hope flickered in Ramson's chest, and for the first time that night, he thought he could feel the tides of the battle turning.

At the dais, a shadow of doubt crossed Alaric Kerlan's face.

It vanished quickly, contorting into fury. He motioned to his forces, then pointed at the new arrivals. "Attack!" he shouted.

Commotion exploded in the hall as a swirl of wind, water, sand, and fire met in the middle of Godhallem, shaking the very foundation of the hall. Overhead, the bells hummed with urgency; sections of searock debris rained down from the ceiling.

Ramson hauled himself to his feet. On either side of him, courtiers had begun fleeing, clearing a path along the walls.

He found his gaze drawn, inevitably, to the spot beneath the brass lever of the War Bells.

Ana's lifeless form lay crumpled on the floor. From here, beneath the roaring sigil of the Earth Court, she looked so small, so helpless. There was nothing Ramson wanted more at that moment than to go to her, to pick her up in his arms and get her out of here.

And yet . . .

He cast his gaze about the hall, searching. It was only when he heard a sharp scream of laughter that he found her.

Sorsha had leapt into the fray of battle, iron and fire whirring in rings around her. She cackled as she shot fire at the sand Affinite, wheeling through her different Affinities to try on him. His half sister wasn't even fighting for any one side; she was merely enjoying being able to wield her powers in her newfound freedom.

Perhaps, then, she would enjoy a game.

Ramson picked up a discarded sword on the floor. "Sorsha," he called.

Sorsha paused in the midst of torturing the sand Affinite

and looked at Ramson. Her gaze widened. She dropped her quarry and began to stalk toward him.

"Brother *Dearest,*" she crooned, spreading her hands.

"I'll play a game with you," Ramson said, and tossed the sword across the floor. It skidded toward her and stopped at her feet. "You injured one of my arms. See if you can get the other one." It sickened him to say those words, to think of what might happen if she won. But he had nothing more to lose. "And," he added as a smile began to bloom across his half sister's face, "no Affinities. We settle this the old-fashioned way."

Sorsha's lips parted with glee. "I never say no to a good game," she said, bending down to pick up the spare sword. "I'm going to savor this, Brother Dearest. I'm going to chop you into so many little pieces that there won't be anything left of you!"

With that, she launched herself at him.

Ramson palmed his own weapon with his good hand, tucking his injured arm to his side. He clung to the folds of his shirt, rooted himself in his center of gravity, and watched his half sister charge toward him, counting her rapid-fire steps. *Fourteen-twelve-ten-eight . . .*

When she lifted her sword to strike, he dropped his, and sprang at her.

The motion must have caught her off guard, for within that split second as he reached for her, he saw confusion twist her features. That was all he needed.

With his good arm, he unhooked the blackstone collar from his belt and snapped it around her neck.

Click. The sound seemed to reverberate across space, across time. Sorsha's face was frozen in surprise. Her sword struck the floor.

Ramson landed several feet away. Pain exploded in his injured shoulder as he used it to break his fall, tucking and rolling. He skidded to a stop against the foot of the dais.

Even amid the chaos, he could hear his half sister's shrieks filling the hall. She tore at her collar, leaving bloody gashes in her neck. Looking at her like this, Ramson almost felt sorry for her. But the blackstone did not budge.

She turned to him then, her features twisted beyond recognition, teeth bared like a wild animal. "*You!*" she howled, snatching her sword. "*I'll kill you!*"

He didn't have time to react. His sword was a dozen feet away, where he'd dropped it. As Sorsha charged at him, spittle foaming at her mouth, her face red with fury, Ramson prepared himself for the inevitable.

And then came a stir of wind, and it felt as though a shadow had slipped before him.

Linn brought up her blades and met Sorsha's sword head-on. The sound of metal on metal reverberated through the hall.

"Go," Linn gasped. "Get Ana!"

Ramson didn't need to be told twice. He scrambled to his feet and made directly for the emblem of the Earth Court. Godhallem had emptied now. The ones remaining were Kerlan's forces, and Linn and Kaïs and the Affinites they had rescued. Bodies littered the hall, blood and ice and other elements of battle smeared against the floor, but Ramson barely saw any of that.

He fell to his knees before the girl lying against the wall of the Earth Court. "Ana. *Ana.*" Her name dropped from his lips like a prayer as he gathered her against his chest. Her normally fawn skin was ashen, and there were dark shadows under her eyes. Her lips were almost gray, as though someone had leached all the life and color from her. She was cold, too cold. "Ana, please." His voice broke.

Love made me weak, his father hissed in his mind. *Love made me a fool.*

Ramson held Ana's limp form in his arms, and as he buried his face in her shoulder, he understood the true meaning behind his father's words.

Love destroys *us.*

50

It felt as though she were fighting her way out of a darkness that kept pulling her down, like the churning waters of a river: cold, biting, and heavy. In that maelstrom, though, a single voice cut through, as though from very far away. Calling her name.

Ana tethered what she could of her consciousness to that voice, and fought to find it.

Gradually, she began to hear sounds: shouts, the clang of swords, a rushing and roaring sound that filled the space around her. Feeling spread back into her limbs, the sensation of the world moving around her, of warmth enveloping her.

Ana's eyes fluttered open. All around, the world was seeping back in a confusing blur of colors and commotion, but here, for some inexplicable reason, she felt safe. Someone held her tight.

"Ramson?" Her voice was a rasp.

He looked at her, his eyes clouded with grief, which then shifted to disbelief, and wonder. In the flickering lamplight of Godhallem, the flashes of fire and the light of battle, he looked as though he had aged years, the skin pale and drawn around his face, cuts and scratches on his cheeks and forehead.

For the first time, she realized that she was seeing him clearly, smelling the sharp scent of swordmetal and fire and sweat on his skin, taking in the way his hazel eyes were flecked with bits of dark brown, the cleft to his chin. It felt as though her world had stilled, emptied of something else, bringing her other senses into sharp focus.

It took her a moment to realize what it was she was missing.

"My Affinity," Ana whispered. "It's gone."

There was an emptiness to her where it had once resided: a chasm so vast, an ache so deep, she thought it would be akin to drowning. Ana gasped, gulping in heaving breaths. Tears burned her eyes as she clawed her hands in front of her, searching for anything to cling to.

Fingers twined around hers; a firm grip trapped her hand. The panic ebbed slightly, and her vision focused.

Ramson was still bent over her. Her nails had raked four long scratches across his neck; beads of blood pooled, but he seemed not to notice. His eyes were heat and pain, searing into hers as he held her. "It's all right," he said, gently shifting her into a sitting position. He pressed her fingers to his lips, his gaze never leaving hers. "You can rest now. The Navy is on its way—thanks to you."

She followed his gaze, taking in the scene in Godhallem. It was nearly empty. There were bodies strewn all around in pools of blood. Kerlan had retreated to the back of his dais, hiding behind the throne. He was utterly alone, and the lack of his men around him made him look defenseless, naked.

A few people were scattered across the hall, panting, nursing various injuries. They wore ragged gray smocks, and they looked . . .

"Affinites," Ramson said, following her gaze. "Linn and Kaïs rescued them from the dungeons."

Ana found Kaïs, bearing down upon the last of Kerlan's men. And then there was Linn, moving so fast she was a blur of shadow, sparring with Sorsha.

Sorsha looked unhinged. Her eyes were so wide that they seemed to bulge from her cheeks; her face was splattered in the blood of the people she had murdered.

Linn lunged. Her blade sliced through the air in an arc, and at first, it appeared as though she had missed. But then she darted back, revealing a long gash across Sorsha's abdomen.

Sorsha whirled around and screamed. "You pathetic little bitch!" she shrieked, and lashed out.

Linn stumbled back, but Ana caught the flash of pain across her face. She dropped to her knees, pressing a hand to her breast. Her fingers grew crimson, and blood began to drip down her wrist.

Sorsha's eyes found Ana from across the hall. "Choose now, Blood Bitch!" she screeched, triumph twisting her face as she staggered to the edge of Godhallem, clinging to the wall that held the Blue Fort over hundreds of feet of cliffs. The wind whipped at her hair. "Stop me, or save your friend?"

Linn's lips had turned pale; a small red puddle had formed on the floor in front of her. She collapsed to the floor as her strength gave way. She was going to bleed to death.

And there was nothing Ana could do about it. "Sorsha," she croaked, climbing to her feet with Ramson's help. "Don't do this. We choose our paths in life."

Sorsha's face was cracked in a leer. Her teeth were bared, froth dripping down her chin. "You fool," she hissed. "We could have been great together. Together, we might have wreaked chaos upon those who imprisoned us, who abused us."

There was so much hate, so much anger burning in Sorsha's face as she snarled at them. But Ana saw something else. A half girl, half monster.

I'd like to think we're not so different after all, you and I.

Was this how she had once looked to the world? Was this what she might have become without Luka and May and Yuri? All Sorsha had needed was for someone to reach out a hand. To tell her that she was wanted, that she was human.

Ana reached out a hand. She glanced to Sorsha's wrist, where the siphon gleamed against the night, and to her belt, where the second one rested. "It isn't too late. You can choose to be good."

Sorsha looked at her and blinked. For a moment, Ana dared to hope that her words had gotten through to the girl, that she had caught her at the brink of the abyss, before the fall.

But then Sorsha's lips curled into a vicious grin. "This is just the beginning, Blood Bitch," she shouted, two daggers appearing in her hands. "The next time we meet, the world will fall at my feet."

And, with a tip of her head, she somersaulted off the edge of the cliff.

By Ana's side, Ramson gave a shout. Something else at the back of Godhallem had caught his attention.

While they had been focused on Sorsha, Kerlan had crept from the dais to where Linn lay, strugglng to stay conscious. In his hands was a piece of searock that had fractured from the floor. Before Ana could even cry out a warning, Kerlan raised the rock over his head and brought it down on Linn's arm.

The *crack* echoed, followed by Linn's scream.

Ana shouted; she heard Kaïs roar in fury and charge forward.

But Kerlan moved fast. In the space of two breaths, he had hauled Linn across the floor until she was balancing precariously at the edge of the drop to the cliffs below.

Panting, he looked up. A slow, crazed smile spread across his face as he met Ana's eyes.

"Nobody move," Kerlan said softly, his voice echoing over the dead silence of the hall, "or she dies."

51

The pain in her arm was like fire. Spots bloomed before her eyes, and her mind was clouding over, fighting to stay conscious. Even the bells had fallen silent.

Dimly, she felt herself being hauled along the floor, her legs dragging limply behind her. Her wound continued to bleed, her arm trailing uselessly by her side, bent at an oddly distorted angle. Each small movement, each tiny shift of gravity was excruciating.

She was only aware that she had reached Godhallem's edge when she felt the cold brush of winds against her skin. They swirled against her face, snatching at her hair and burning her cheeks, as though to whisper: *wake up, wake up.*

Someone was shouting her name. *Linn.*

She knew that voice, knew its owner. His fate had been tangled with hers since they'd met atop the walls of the Salskoff Palace.

Linn met Kaïs's eyes, and the grief in his expression struck her, hard. He lifted his gaze to Kerlan, his face morphing into cold fury.

She looked down. The searock floor of Godhallem ended

where she lay; beneath her was a chasm of darkness, the sound of the ocean rushing up in whorls of cold, salt-tanged air. One wrong move, and she would plunge into the depths below.

"Release her." Someone else had spoken, the words a feral growl. Linn searched along the hall until she found the speaker. *Ana.* A faint sense of relief calmed Linn. Ana was all right. She was alive. She had pushed herself to her feet, Ramson supporting her, her forehead slick with sweat. "Release her, or I'll . . . I'll—"

Kerlan's smile looked more like a mad grimace. "Or you'll what?" he crooned, then turned to the remaining Affinites in the hall, scattered throughout. "If anyone tries to hurt me, I will fling her off. All it will take is a little, tiny . . . *tip,*" he said, and held up her broken arm. Pain seared across Linn's awareness again. "A broken warrior . . . why, she'll hit the rocks below like a ton of bricks."

A broken warrior.

Somehow, those words hurt more than the thought of dying.

"Call off the Bregonian Navy," Kerlan ordered, and he reached back and gripped a fistful of Linn's hair, jerking her head up and baring her throat. "Or, would you prefer to see her pretty face smashed bloody on the rocks below?"

Ana's expression tightened. She gave another snarl but remained where she was.

"What are you waiting for, Blood Witch?" Kerlan said. There was a mad glint to his eyes. "The choice is yours. Call off the Navy, or she dies. I won't ask again."

Linn's head spun. In the span of a single night, Kerlan had murdered nearly half the entire leadership of Bregon, and he would continue to take the kingdom for Morganya if he wasn't stopped.

He had to be stopped.

She dangled at the edge of the drop. She imagined the sea roiling below, waves clawing at the cliffs and receding over sharp rocks. Once, a long time ago—a *lifetime* ago—she might have reveled at the sight, with the winds at her back and her chi strapped to her arms.

Now, she could only look down, watching her arm hang loose beneath her, blood running in rivulets down her skin.

A wingless bird.

Tears blurred her vision. If she fell now, she wouldn't survive. She could barely move with her wound, and the smallest shift of her arm felt as though she were being pricked with a thousand hot needles. She didn't know if she had the strength to even summon her Affinity.

She took in the scene around Godhallem. There were bodies and blood everywhere, but the Affinites she and Kaïs had rescued remained standing. Ana, Ramson, and Kaïs were alive. And the Bregonian Navy was on their way.

They were so, so close.

Ana was shouting something at Kerlan, her face twisted in fury and anguish, but Linn was no longer listening. A faint wind blew in from the outside. Linn looked to the sky. The storm had broken; the stars were out, the silver of their light tinting the black expanse of night. She closed her eyes briefly, thinking of how her mother had said once that no matter where one was in the world, they looked at the same moon and stars.

Linn drew a breath. She knew what she had to do.

"Kill him," she said, her voice a wisp of air. And then, stronger: *"Kill him!"*

Kerlan's blow came out of nowhere. It left her reeling.

"Shut up," he roared, and then he hit her again. Linn tasted blood. "You think I've done all I can do to you? I can break you over and over again, an infinite number of times for my own pleasure."

His voice, the pain, they fell away from her. Tears warmed her cheeks, but Linn focused on the brush of wind against her face, the susurrus of the ocean below that seemed to open its arms to her, wrapping around her like a mother's embrace.

My daughter, they whispered. *Choose . . . to be brave.*

Linn reached deep into the hollow cave of her chest, and found the last of her voice there, still fighting. The last drops of water in an emptying river. "Ana," she gasped. "Kaïs." *Louder.* She spoke so that her voice echoed in the halls, high and thin, but powerful nevertheless. "Kill him and end it. I'd rather die than let him live."

Ana's eyes shimmered behind her tears. Kaïs's eyes were clouds of grief as he raised his swords.

Linn held Kaïs's gaze and nodded. One life, in exchange for thousands of others, was a small price to pay. She would use her life to buy safety for those she loved. For in her final moments, it wasn't hate or anger that filled Linn's thoughts.

It was love.

Love, in Ama-ka's midnight-black eyes, in Enn's laughter that echoed between vast, empty mountains, in the gift of a life she had been given, however brief.

Linn only wished she had just a little more time.

But she would face death as a warrior, as a windsailer. She would be brave.

Linn turned to Alaric Kerlan.

For a moment, they stared at each other, Linn's eyes black

steel, Kerlan's face contorting with the wild wrath of a man condemned.

And then the fury in his expression ebbed. "All right," he said calmly. "Then die."

And he shoved her off the edge.

52

Kaïs didn't even stop to think.

When he saw Linn disappear over the ledge, his mind turned blank, and his body moved by some primal instinct.

He flung his swords aside and took off at a sprint.

Past the bodies. The dais. The throne.

Two, three steps.

The edge of Godhallem drew near.

Kaïs leapt, and for a moment he was airborne with nothing but the rain and the wind and the ocean unfurling beneath him.

Then gravity took over, and he dove after Linn.

53

As Ana's scream reverberated through the hall, Ramson was on his feet, running, blade drawn. Out of all the people whom Kerlan had hurt and all the twisted things the man had done in the past, it was what he had done to Linn that Ramson could not forgive.

He would never forget the sight of the girl, sitting at the edge of life and death, her face a mask of defiance.

Nor the way she had looked at him the night they had first met in Novo Mynsk, her head tilted away from him like a frightened animal, her liquid black eyes betraying the faintest wisp of hope within her.

Ramson had seen his former master deliver death too many times to count, and he'd always thought that the moments before revealed the true character of a person. He'd witnessed mothers shielding their children with their own bodies before Kerlan cut them down; he'd watched Affinites die with their heads held high. Throughout all of it, Alaric Kerlan had always been less man than monster.

But now, on the precipice of defeat, Alaric Kerlan looked no more than a frightened child. With no henchmen to come to his rescue and no bindings holding his opponent back, he cowered against the wall.

Ramson plunged his dagger into his old master's chest.

It was a surprisingly smooth stroke, the feeling akin to gutting a pig. Kerlan put up no resistance. His screech stopped, his mouth going slack, and with an exhale, he slumped against Ramson. A puddle of yellow had formed around his shoes.

Alaric Kerlan, the greatest criminal mastermind of the Cyrilian Empire, had died pissing himself.

It was only then that Ramson let out a breath he didn't realize he'd been holding. With a violent lunge, he pulled himself away from the body of Alaric Kerlan, slumping against the wall of Godhallem, right next to where it ended and open air and cliff began.

Behind him was a scene of massacre, with over two-thirds of the Three Courts slaughtered. The survivors had either fled the scene or cowered in the corners, too stunned to move.

The storm had passed. The rain had cleared and the sky had turned bright with the silver glow of the moon. That was when Ramson saw them. Silhouetted against the horizon were the outlines of hundreds of ships, small at first, but then growing larger, their sails blooming against the sky.

Kerlan's fleet.

They approached fast, and Ramson began to make out the shapes on their sails: Morganya's sigil of the Deys'krug and the crown.

Desperately, Ramson searched the shorelines below for movement, for a sign—*any* sign—that the Bregonian Navy had launched.

And then he heard it.

Somewhere, between the whistle of wind and crash of waves against the cliffs below, Ramson thought he heard music. A strange, rhythmic, and repetitive melody that was almost soothing.

It sounded like . . . bells.

And as Ramson watched, the night lit up with a hundred, a thousand flames. They soared into the air, arcing in a perfect curve, before descending in a shower of fire toward the enemy ships.

Arrows. *War* bells, from . . .

The first Bregonian Navy warship appeared nearly right beneath the cliffs where he stood. Even high up, he could see the tips of flaming arrows being lit, the shape of a bell clocking back and forth as it rang out the commands for war.

Flamed arrows shot into the sky, and under their light, the colors of the ships' flags rippled bright: navy-blue sails, flashing the gold of a roaring, triumphant Bregonian seadragon.

The Bregonian Navy was here.

Ramson sank to his knees.

The first Cyrilian ship went up in flames, and the rest followed suit. Arrows peppered the sky, arcing like comets, carving blazing paths across the night, finding more and more targets.

And still, Bregonian warships kept coming, more and more of them. Their arrows lit the sky so bright that it looked like day.

In the distance, Morganya's fleet burned, the light from their fires reflected in the lingering clouds, lighting the sea and the sky a triumphant, violent crown of corals and golds.

54

At first, there was nothing but the shriek of wind, pummeling her like fists and threatening to tear her apart as she plummeted. In the distance, Linn heard the splash of waves.

And then, in the darkness of her mind she felt hands wrap around her.

A familiar presence: liquid silver, cold-blooded hunter, fierce warrior in one.

"Look at me." His deep voice was in her ear. They were spinning, tumbling, free-falling. *Look at me.* He'd said those exact words to her, back at the prison. It had been her and this soldier and the vast emptiness of night all around them.

She sensed his Affinity on hers, yet instead of clamping down, he pulled hers up. Out of the haze of fear clouding her mind, up and up, until she opened her eyes to the sight of a silvering sky and darting waves below her.

"Look at me," he commanded again, and she did. There was nothing but firm resolution in his eyes. "Now, fly."

With his steady grip on her, Linn closed her eyes.

And called on her winds.

55

The day broke clear and blue, the air golden with the early-morning sun. In the distance, the sea lapped at the sky, always touching yet never meeting. Ana strolled through the courtyard of the Blue Fort, her white linen shirt tucked into navy breeches and a Bregonian blue cloak.

She walked slowly, sometimes pausing to clutch her side. She felt hollow; the world had not been quite right since the Battle of Godhallem three days ago.

Since her Affinity had been siphoned.

She'd spent one day in the medical wing burning with fever, her world an alternating swirl of searing red and churning black, roiling with nightmares. When she'd woken again, everything had become a little duller. The colors, the sounds, the scents . . . she experienced it all as though from behind a tinted glass window.

The healers hadn't been able to determine anything wrong with her physically, and had attributed the symptoms to an adjustment period after losing her Affinity.

It still felt . . . wrong. Sometime throughout the sleepless nights, as she'd tried to reach out in her dark room for a trace, a hint, of her power, she'd realized that this was what she had always wanted. Since her Affinity had manifested, she'd wanted it gone. How many lonely days had she spent before the mirror of her chambers back at the Salskoff Palace, scratching until her arms were covered in trails of red, hoping to dig it out of her? How many nights had she woken to nightmares and tear-soaked pillows, sobbing for her father?

And yet . . . she had seen, repeatedly, evidence that her Affinity could be used for *good.* That, all along, Luka had been right: it wasn't her Affinity, but how she wielded her power, that defined her. She had harmed, she had murdered—but she had also fought against the wicked and the cruel of this world, had learned to heal and strengthen. Kaïs had taught her that her Affinity was a double-edged sword, and he'd been right.

She had just realized it too late.

Ana paused to lean against the pillar of a stone archway. She forced her thoughts to the present, grounding herself in the slow hum of activity as the Blue Fort began to wake all around her.

Though the Bregonian Navy had decimated Morganya and Kerlan's forces, Sapphire Port had been hit hard, its quays destroyed, parts of the town reduced to rubble. Bregon had pulled together its resources to begin reconstruction of their capital.

The Blue Fort had miraculously survived unscathed. In part, it was due to the resilience of its structure, built atop cliffs with impenetrable defenses. King Darias had locked up the research dungeons and was getting to the bottom of all those involved in the siphon scheme. Thus far, they had discovered that of the three leading scholars involved in the research, two had died—including Tarschon—and one, a so-called Scholar Ardonn, had not been found.

Sorsha, too, was still missing.

The courtyards were relatively empty as Ana made her way toward Godhallem, the alder trees still fresh with the scent of rain. A few walkways over, by the small, man-made streams that tinkled through the courtyards, two Affinites sat enjoying the early morning peace. She recognized them; they belonged to the group Linn had rescued from the dungeons and had fought valiantly at the Battle of Godhallem. Bathed and fed and dressed in fresh clothes, they looked young, almost like children. One drew water from the streams in a curling ribbon and flicked droplets at his friend, who summoned twigs and leaves from nearby trees and twisted them into beautiful figurines.

The sight brought an ache to Ana's throat, and she was reminded of a memory once upon a time, when she'd looked upon a small girl sitting in the dead of winter, blowing life into a flower in a snow-covered field. She was reminded, too, of the world she fought for, the one she sought to build after this was all over.

Smiling faintly to herself, Ana turned down the open-air arches that led to the side entrances.

Guards saluted her as she passed by. Most of the Three Courts, Ana had learned, had attributed the survival of their government to her and her allies. At the entrance of Godhallem, she found herself face to face with Captain Ronnoc of the King's Guard. He gave her a deep bow.

Ana inclined her head and stepped into the great halls of Godhallem.

It was impossible not to think of what had happened here, three days earlier. With the bodies removed and the rubble cleared, Godhallem looked restored to some semblance of its former self.

She came to a stop before the dais.

Sunlight filtered in through the back of Godhallem. It swept gold across the various courtiers who were already seated at their respective courts. It pooled at the throne on top of the dais, outlining the figure sitting there.

King Darias sat straight, his crown glinting as he turned his attention from several courtiers to Ana.

In just three days, King Darias seemed to have become a different person. Gone was the child with the flushed cheeks and fever-wet eyes and vacant stare. He sat straight and calm, his hair combed back neatly, dressed in a tailored Bregonian royal uniform. The crown rested on his head, its bronze band cut in the shape of waves and woven through with searock so that it glittered like water and sunlight as it moved. His gaze was bright and intelligent, and Ana suddenly saw a cunning, resourceful boy who had done everything he could to survive the complex politics of a corrupt kingdom. Within days, he'd arrested those involved in his drugging, a scheme that Admiral Farrald and Sorsha had upheld for years. The former Captain Ronnoc had been promoted to Commander of the Royal Guard, tasked with reexamining his personnel and rooting out those who had been loyal to Sorsha Farrald's orders to the detriment of the King.

King Darias's eyes turned to Ana, and this time, they were the sharp gray of swordmetal. He stood and descended the steps, crossing over the narrow square of water separating his dais from the rest of the hall. Ana inclined her head, but the next moment, his hands were at her elbows. "There is no need for that between friends," King Darias said. They stood almost at the same height, and his gaze hovered over her face. Concern creased his brows. "Are you feeling better?"

The words tightened a grasp of panic around her. She'd made sure to layer creams over the dark circles beneath her eyes and brush powders over her face to hide the new pallor to her skin, the sharpness to her cheeks.

"I'm fine," she said. The words rang hollow to her own ears.

King Darias looked at her with knowing eyes, but he didn't press for more. "We take it day by day."

Ana nodded.

"Now," he said, letting her go and stepping back, "we get on with the formalities. Are you ready?"

"Yes." She watched as he returned to his throne. At once, a hush fell all around the hall as the remaining members of the Three Courts turned their attention to their king. The Sky and Earth Courts sat in their respective seats, and standing in rows near the entrance, directly facing the throne, soldiers stood in attendance, dressed in navy-blue livery and bearing the bronze seadragon sigil of the Sea Court.

Commander Ronnoc and several members of the King's Guard stood on either side of the throne, and Ana couldn't help but look at the empty space in front of the dais, which had been occupied by Admiral Farrald just days ago. On either side of the hall, there were unfilled seats, a reminder of the loss that Bregon had taken. But as King Darias stood atop his dais and looked over his Three Courts, hope seemed to fill the room like winds at a ship's sails.

"Three Courts of Bregon," King Darias began. "We have

fought and won against foreign invasion and treason within our very own Courts. Today, I am glad to address you as your king."

A thundering round of applause rose from the Three Courts.

"As you well know, our victory was not easy, and it certainly would not have been possible without certain people." King Darias nodded at Ana. "The Red Tigress of Cyrilia and her allies have been instrumental to saving Bregon. On behalf of my Three Courts and the entire Kingdom of Bregon, I thank you, Anastacya Mikhailov, Red Tigress, for fighting on our side."

Red Tigress. She'd almost forgotten that name. Yet as she stood, letting the words soak in, there was a flurry of movement on all sides of Godhallem as the Three Courts rose to their feet. And Ana could only watch in astonishment as King Darias Rennaron of Bregon turned to her and sank into a deep bow.

They'd spoken about this meeting beforehand during her many visits to his chambers in the aftermath of the battle, but he hadn't mentioned this part of his speech. An ocean breeze stirred through the open-air doorways of Godhallem.

"We have not found Sorsha Farrald's body," King Darias continued. "We will continue looking. We need to ensure that Sorsha Farrald—if she is alive—does not reach Empress Morganya with our last siphon."

There was a somber hush in the room, every single pair of eyes focused on their king.

"Therefore, I would like to declare an alliance with the Red Tigress of Cyrilia." A grin curled the King's lips as he turned his gaze to Ana. "I would like to pledge one thousand Bregonian troops to set sail with the Red Tigress to launch a counterattack against the current Cyrilian regime."

Ana matched his smile and gave a single nod. King Darias had discussed this with her privately in the days past, but it had to be formally voted upon by the Three Courts.

Now, the King's clear gray eyes swept across the hall. "All those in favor, stand and say *aye.*"

At first, there was only silence.

And then, somewhere in the area of the Sky Court, a courtier stood. "Aye."

"Aye!" another shouted from the Earth Court.

"Aye." A captain of the Navy spoke from directly behind Ana.

Ana stood very still, holding her breath, as all around her, courtiers from the Three Courts of Bregon made their stand, cries of "aye" filling the air. Outside, the wind and the waves seemed to roar in triumph, and above, the bells of Godhallem hummed, as though the gods themselves murmured in agreement.

"Anastacya?"

She blinked and turned her attention back to King Darias. He was smiling widely at her. "The Three Courts of Godhallem have unanimously voted in favor of an alliance," he said, and as she turned to look all around, Ana saw that all the courtiers of the Three Courts were standing, facing her. She thought of the first day she had arrived here, of the sneers and jibes these men had given her as she stood beneath them in her ragged clothes.

Now, their expressions held only respect.

Perhaps, Ana thought, change was not so impossible after all.

King Darias spread his arms. "Well, Red Tigress of Cyrilia?" he asked. "Do you accept?"

Courage filled her, a surge of hope. She had lost her Affinity, but here . . . *here* was proof that she did not need it to lead.

That her Affinity was not what made her capable, that it did not define her after all.

She was the Red Tigress of Cyrilia, and that would be enough.

Ana drew a deep breath, threw her shoulders back, lifted her chin, and stepped forward. "King Darias and the Three Courts of Bregon," she said, her voice ringing loud and clear in the halls of Godhallem, "I accept."

56

The sun had risen higher in the sky by the time she left Godhallem. The Blue Fort was now bustling with activity, the courtyards surrounding Godhallem crowded as messengers, courtiers, and soldiers of the Blue Fort hurried to and fro. There was a Succession Ceremony to take place at noon as King Darias sought to refill the seats in his government left vacant by Kerlan's massacres during the Battle of Godhallem.

Ana walked away from the direction of the crowds. She followed a familiar path that wound through the alder trees. People around her grew sparser until at last, she turned the corner of a building. Ana parted the curtain of vines and ascended the steps.

The old guard tower was haloed in sunlight, its outcrop of rock carving a private, intimate space over the ocean below. Outlined against the sky was the young man she sought.

Light glistened on his sandy-brown hair and lit up the gold emblazoned on his navy-blue tunic. He tapped an impatient rhythm with his knee-high boots. A sword hung at his hips, its hilt the proud, roaring sigil of a seadragon.

He turned at her approaching footsteps, and his expression

softened. The bruises on his face had been carefully covered in powders, but she saw the stiff way he carried himself, the bandages on his hands and arms.

She'd barely seen him in the past two days, which he'd spent under extensive supervision in the medical ward of the Blue Fort, surrounded by healers. Her heart opened as she drank in the sight of him now, and she couldn't help but think of the way he had kissed her that night in the storm, of how gently he'd held her back at Godhallem.

"You look better," Ramson said. His expression was smooth, closed, his gaze cool and clinical as he surveyed her. Ana's steps faltered, the flickers of warmth within her turning cold. Why did it feel as though a strange new distance had opened up between them?

"Thank you," Ana said. They hadn't spoken about her Affinity; she'd found it easier if he didn't bring it up. It felt like a wound, and each mention or thought only served to reopen it. "I just met with the King and the Three Courts." This, she had told him about, in the brief moments they'd exchanged words.

A shadow crossed his eyes. He turned his gaze to the ocean. "How did it go?"

"The alliance is approved. We leave this afternoon."

Ramson continued to stare out at the sea, as though he hadn't heard her. The waves crashed onto the shores far below the cliffs.

Finally, he spoke. "I'm not going with you." The words were so quiet, they might have blended with the wind.

The world seemed to slow around her then. She could swear she felt a piece of her heart cracking. "What?"

Ramson turned to look at her at last, and she knew him

well enough to understand the shuttered expression that he had carefully constructed. He'd been hiding something from her, and she'd been too caught up in her own affairs to catch it.

"King Darias offered to reinstate me in his Navy as a commander," Ramson said tonelessly. "I turned down the offer."

She stared at him, her lips parted, her breathing becoming unsteady.

"So," Ramson continued, "he offered me an unofficial appointment, as captain of a special fleet of the Navy, tasked to hunt down the remainders of Alaric Kerlan's allies in Bregon."

The space and the silence stretched an ocean between them now, filled with the churning of waves in a storm-tossed sea.

For your path, Little Tigress, I see an ocean. And, as Ana took in the sight of him, outlined against a vast blue of sky, she began to have an inkling that Shamaïra's words held one more facet of meaning to them than she'd known.

"And you accepted." The words fell cold from her mouth.

He inclined his head in confirmation. "I am to attend the Succession Ceremony today as an unofficial guest."

Seeing him now, watching her with a gaze that made her feel as though they were the only two people left in this universe, Ana couldn't stop the thoughts she'd been keeping out.

She wanted to kiss him. She wanted to be with him. She wanted . . . she wanted him.

"You never asked me." Her voice was tight, if only so that she could steady the maelstrom of her thoughts.

"I never thought I had to," he replied, and she had the impression she was speaking to a stranger. She'd expected a quip, a teasing glimmer in those hazel eyes, a wicked curve of his mouth.

But the man standing before her was no longer the Ramson Quicktongue she'd met in that prison in Cyrilia, with his quick grin and cunning words and beguiling smile. Sometime, in the course of their journey, he had become Ramson Farrald, con man and commander of a Navy fleet.

She tore her gaze from his. Her chest felt tight, the wounds on her heart still raw from the loss of her Affinity. This, though, was an ache she had never experienced before: the sensation that her heart was being torn completely in two.

He had made his choice.

And she had made hers.

Deny it, she thought. *Say you'll stay with me.*

But even as she leaned against the sun-warmed rock, the susurrus of waves and the cries of seagulls tiding over them, she knew what was meant to happen.

A day will arrive when you will be asked to sacrifice that which you hold dearest for the good of your empire.

Had Shamaïra seen this moment? Had she been trying to warn Ana, back then?

Had she known how it would feel to have her mind wanting one thing and her heart another?

"So this is the end," Ana said quietly. The sentence hung in the air, half question, half statement, lingering. Waiting for his response.

He had been watching her with a small crease to his brows. And then the tension seemed to leave his body and he exhaled. "Ana." Her name sounded like a supplication coming from his lips. "I . . ." He shut his eyes briefly, and she thought of that day in the storm, when they had held each other at the cliff's edge and he had kissed her.

It had felt like the start of something back then. Not the end.

"Will I see you again?" The words slipped from her lips before she could help herself.

Ramson was quiet for a long moment, watching her carefully, and she wondered whether he would respond with a cruel truth or a kind lie.

At last, he spoke. "I don't make promises."

She heard the second part to his sentence, almost as clearly as he'd spoken it to her that day on the ship, when the moon had shrouded them in silver and the sea had glittered azure. *So I don't have to break them.*

"Well, then." The distance between them stretched, a gaping abyss, an uncrossable ocean. Her voice threatened to break, but Ana forced the words out. "I have another appointment. I suppose this is good-bye."

He said nothing, only watched as she turned and walked away, each step taking an eternity, widening the chasm between them until she turned a corner and he disappeared between the rock and the sky and the sea.

Ana crossed to the guest quarters of the Blue Fort. The searock walls seemed somehow muted, the danger and mystery of their edges shaved off with the changes of the past few days. She remembered coming here less than a week ago, and the place had seemed like an impenetrable fortress to her.

Now, it still was, only it had taken Ramson with it, too.

Kaïs waited outside the chambers as she reached them; he hadn't left for the past two days. His eyes flickered as he watched her approach.

"Are you all right?" His voice was deep, somber.

Ana had grown to dread that question. She wondered whether he was reaching for her Affinity with his, and whether he found only emptiness where it had once been. "I'm fine," she replied. It was simply another pain she would grow numb to. Her gaze flicked down Kaïs's face, and she thought of the promise she had made Shamaïra. It seemed like a lifetime ago. "Your mother would be proud of you," Ana said quietly.

He bowed his head. "I cannot return to Cyrilia. If Morganya's troops catch me alive when all of Kerlan's troops are dead, they will know of my betrayal. They will hurt my mother. And so I have a favor to ask of you, Kolst Imperatorya."

"Call me Ana," she replied. "You needn't ask anything of me. Do you really think me so heartless as to leave your mother behind, when she saved my life? I promised to help Shamaïra find her son, and now that I have, I promise I will not rest until she is safe and out of harm's way." Tentatively, she reached out a hand and rested it on his shoulder. He grew very still, but did not flinch away. "I will find her, Kaïs."

He lifted his eyes, and for a moment, they looked at each other. Something had shifted between them, like ice beginning to thaw. He had made mistakes in his past—as had she—yet now, their choices had led them to different paths. Ones that had begun to converge.

Ana looked past him, to the open doors of the chamber beyond. "Is she inside?"

He nodded.

She felt the change as soon as she entered the chambers: winds, sweet and balmy with a tint of salt, stirring at her hair and tickling her exposed skin. The chamber was drenched in sunlight, the balcony doors thrown wide open, the white gossamer curtains fluttering gently. Outside, far below, the ocean whispered.

A figure was propped up on chairs on the balcony outside. Ana's heart clenched at the sight of her friend's slender silhouette. She stepped outside. "Linn."

Linn glanced up from her chair. Her face was paler than Ana remembered; dark circles shadowed her eyes, and her cheeks jutted out more sharply. Ana put her hands around her friend's shoulders. Had they always been this bony?

"Hello," Linn said quietly. Ana tried not to look at Linn's right arm, wrapped in bandages and bound to her chest. Her eyes flicked to Linn's stomach, and against her will, she recalled the storm that night, the wild look on Kaïs's face as he'd stumbled back, Linn clutched to his chest like a small, broken bird. Her vest and undershirts had been soaked through with crimson, yet Ana had only been able to watch as healers rushed to her friend's side, desperately trying to stem the flow of blood.

The bones in Linn's arms had been utterly shattered, with some muscles severed completely. The healers at the medical ward had done the best work they could on Linn, and said that she would no longer feel the pain. But that was all they had promised.

They had disposed of Kerlan's body, Ramson supervising as it was carted off to a remote site to be buried where no one would find it, and where it would not soil the burial sites of those around him.

Ana only wished she had found a way to make him suffer. To make him *pay*.

To Linn, she said, "You look good. The healers will take care of you. You'll return even stronger."

Linn turned her face to Ana. "My arm may heal," she said, "but your Affinity . . ." She choked and squeezed her eyes shut. "I should have stayed with you."

"No," Ana said. "You helped us win the battle, Linn."

Linn's dark eyes glistened. "King Darias came to see me. He said they are finding out everything they can about the siphons. We will get through this, Ana. *Together.*"

"Together," Ana whispered, and leaned against her friend, their arms interlinked, their heads resting together. They stayed like that for a long time, holding tightly to each other.

After a while, Linn spoke. "I will never stop fighting," she said. "I have been searching for my path all this time, but I know it now, Ana. I felt it when I freed those Affinites from the research dungeons." She looked up, her eyes fierce. "I am going to make sure not a single Affinite in this world goes through what I went through."

Ana's throat closed. Linn's words held the echoes of another brave young girl; perhaps, Ana thought, the bravest child she'd known. The one who'd had enough hope to spark a revolution.

May had wanted to bring hope to every Affinite. And Ana would never stop fighting until that was true.

She squeezed Linn's hand. "And where will you go?" she asked. Linn had declined to return with her to Cyrilia, but she hadn't mentioned what her plans would be.

Her response surprised Ana. "I will go back," Linn said. "To Kemeira. If Morganya sent her forces to Bregon, then there is nothing stopping her from crossing the Jade Trail to the Aseatic Isles. I must prepare my empire." She paused, and her face hardened. "The issues of Affinite trafficking have long run deep in the fabric of my empire, and the rest of the Aseatic Kingdoms. It is, in part, the inaction of our governments that has brought suffering to my people. It is time we fought back."

A sudden idea struck Ana, so logical that she wondered why she hadn't thought of it earlier. "Linn, will you be Cyrilia's ambassador?"

Linn blinked, curiosity opening her features.

"Our empires have long existed in a state of war," Ana pressed. "But I think together, we can reconcile our nations, our peoples."

Linn's face lit up, and it felt like watching the sun rise. "Ana, I would be honored to serve as ambassador between our empires."

Ana threw her arms around her friend again. For the first time in days, a laugh bubbled from Linn's lips, sprinkling the air like spray from a summer sea. "The honor is mine," Ana said. "Thank you."

"I will return to Kemeira," Linn said. "I will warn my leadership—and all of the Aseatic Kingdoms—of the turmoil in Cyrilia. And . . . I will try to bargain for an alliance between our empires and gather support for the great war to come."

Together, they turned to admire the sea. The world seemed to unfurl beneath their gazes, the enormity of their task held at bay with the whispering waters, rising and receding into eternity. Ana allowed herself to enjoy this moment, basked in the warmth of the sun and wrapped in the coolness of the breeze, arm around her friend.

And then, beneath the brilliant blue skies of Bregon, the bells of Godhallem began to toll for the Succession Ceremony.

57

It was a beautiful day to set sail. The waterways to the Blue Fort were lined with ships, and as Ana descended the steps of Godhallem, she noticed that the Bregonian warship awaiting her below had been reoutfitted. It flew a different flag: a roaring Cyrilian tiger, but instead of its usual silver-white, it was painted red.

Bregonian Royal Guards and members of the Navy lined the steps; they held up their hands in salute as Ana passed by. When she reached the gangplank, a familiar figure was waiting for her.

Daya gave her a full-on grin and clicked her heels together in a salute. She'd changed into a brand-new outfit, complete with polished brass buttons and high leather boots, fitting for her new role as captain of Ana's fleet. On the back of her dark gray coat was the symbol of a woman with hair like flames. King Darias had specially commissioned the coat for her, out of respect for the goddess Amara of Kusutri.

Ana couldn't help but smile back. "Don't salute me," she whispered, giving her friend a nudge. "I can't get used to it."

"Aye, aye," Daya replied, tapping her fingers to her forehead again. Ana laughed, and together they boarded the ship. The wind out here was stronger, and her crimson cloak arced out behind her as she turned to stand at the front of the ship.

At her back, Daya shouted orders, and the members of her new crew sprang to action. There were others on the ship, too, Ana noticed with a surge of pride: the Affinites Linn had freed from the dungeons, who had fought with them during the Battle of Godhallem, were scattered about the deck, dressed in fine Bregonian clothes. Within just several days, the gauntness to their cheeks had filled, and the pallor to their skin had been replaced by healthy flushes. King Darias had promised all the trafficked Affinites safe passage back to their own kingdoms, but several had volunteered to join Ana's cause. They made the sign of the Deys'krug over their chests as they spotted her, and Ana returned the gesture.

The gangplank began to retract, and as the crew began to haul anchor, Ana leaned against the railing and gazed out. A crowd had gathered at the steps now, courtiers and guards and servants and other personnel of the Blue Fort. She caught sight of King Darias at the very top of the stairway. He grinned at her, and she raised a hand to wave back.

Yet there was no glimpse of the person she had most wanted to see. Ana kept searching the crowd even as the sails unfurled with a *whumpf!*, even as the ship began to glide and pick up speed between the massive searock pillars that lined the waterway.

And then they were drawing farther and farther from the buildings of the Blue Fort, and the great ironore doors were opening, the currents on either side of them speeding up as they turned to the waterway that led out to the open sea.

"Ana, look!" Daya shielded a hand to her face and pointed behind them.

Ana turned. Dozens of ships had begun to follow theirs, sails blooming with both the blue Bregonian seadragon and the red Cyrilian tiger.

Red Tigress, Ana thought as the wind around them picked up and the open sea rushed to greet them. Against all odds, she had survived, and she sailed for home with a fleet of the strongest Navy in the world.

She'd wondered, in the days after the Battle of Godhallem, who she was now without her power. She'd looked into the mirror and thought of a time long ago, when a lonely girl had sat in her empty chambers in a great palace looking at her red eyes and believing herself to be a monster.

But, Ana realized, without her Affinity . . . nothing would change. As long as unfairness existed in this world, as long as there were people who upheld cruelty and oppression, she would keep fighting.

She still wore her gloves out of habit rather than necessity, but the hood of her new cloak rested against her shoulders. Ana turned her face to the sun, and breathed in.

Remember who you are, Shamaïra had whispered. *Who the people need you to be.*

She'd been stripped of her title, and she'd been stripped of her Affinity. But, Ana thought, she would not let herself be defined by either.

"Captain," she called. "I'd like to send a message."

Daya turned to her crew. "Scribe!" she called, and a boy came forth, a gray Bregonian seadove balanced on his shoulder, scroll and quill in his hands.

"Your Highness," he said.

Ana reached into the folds of her cloak. With a light tug, the chain around her neck came loose, and she pulled out a silver Deys'krug. Ana unfastened the chain and handed it to the scribe. "Address it to Yuri Kostov, Commander of the Redcloaks."

As the scribe bound the chain to the seadove's leg, Ana quietly tucked the Deys'krug into her shirt pocket. No matter what happened, the pendant was a symbol of a friendship she would forever keep close to her heart. *We will come full circle again,* she thought. *Yuri.*

"What will the note say?" the scribe asked.

Ana looked forward, to the open sea, to the endless horizon. Behind her was the full support of the Bregonian Navy, flying new flags—*her* flags. Ahead lay uncertainty, and a long battle to be fought.

"'Prepare for war,'" she recited. "'The Red Tigress returns.'"

58

Linn watched from her balcony as the oceans of Sapphire Port blossomed silver and blue with the swollen sails of a hundred ships. They sluiced through the glistening, sun-warmed waters, and it wasn't until their outlines painted the horizon that she realized she was smiling.

She closed her eyes and summoned her winds, and in her mind, she was a little bird borne on their currents, dodging and swerving between great masts and swollen hulls and ten thousand liveried soldiers. She sent her winds as far as they would go, twirling and dancing between waves of leaping fish, ballooning the sails and kissing the ships.

May the winds watch over you, my friends, she thought, and for a brief moment, she might have sensed her winds wrap around a familiar presence—fiery as flames and sharp as a steel blade, shrouded in a brilliant red cloak. She thought she felt familiar fingers lift into the air, as though Ana knew that the winds bore Linn's spirit and held out a hand in farewell. And then she was too far gone, beyond the sphere of Linn's reach with her Affinity.

There was a knock inside her room. She didn't have to turn

to sense his presence like rock carving through her winds, firm and strong.

"King Darias sent this for you." Kaïs's voice was quiet. He hadn't left the hallway outside her chambers since she'd been carried here from the healers.

He laid a plain, flat box in her lap. Wordlessly, Linn lifted the cover.

Her throat caught as she unfurled the object within. It was a chi. A chi that was slightly bent, torn in some places and carefully patched up with different material, carefully washed clean. But as she smoothed it out between her fingers, the wing glimmered.

A note was tucked between its folds; it fluttered out like a butterfly with a life of its own. Linn caught it between her fingers.

We all have monsters in our minds, it read, *but it takes courage and perseverance to defeat them. I know you will defeat yours.*

Monsters, she thought, closing her eyes. They all held monsters within them.

A hand clasped her shoulder. She turned to see Kaïs by her side, gazing down at her. "I have not had the chance to apologize," he said quietly.

"There is no need."

"I was not going to." She looked up at him in slight surprise, but he continued. "Someone very wise once taught me this: action, and counteraction." He clasped his hands together in an imitation of the sign Kemeirans made, of yin, and yang. "I will go wherever you will go. I pledge my swords to protect you, my shields to defend you."

"Kaïs—" Her voice caught. "What about your mother?"

"Ana promised me her safety. If Morganya's troops find out that I have betrayed Kerlan and survived, they will hurt my mother." He paused. "Besides, I think my mother would want me to fight back, to make amends for my mistakes of the past."

"To fight back," Linn repeated, and she understood that she and Kaïs walked the same path now. Emotions stirred inside her, and she found words spilling from her lips—words that she had been too shy to speak aloud before. "That day when I freed the Affinites in the research dungeons," she said, "was the first time I . . . no longer felt like a victim. Like I could truly make an impact, in changing the fates of people like me."

He looked at her then, and she had the feeling that those eyes were piercing into her very soul. "My mother has the ability to see Time, and she has always told me she prefers to look to the future instead of the past." A gentle breeze stirred his hair, which fell in waves over his temples. The Bregonian sun had returned a healthy tan to his face. "I cannot change my past, but I can fight for this world's future."

Something flickered between them, deeper than friendship, or even love: the knowledge of a shared experience, a common goal. They had both been brought into the Empire at a young age, exploited and abused for their abilities.

Now, they were free to make their own choices.

"If we are to fight," Kaïs said, his tone shifting to something akin to playfulness, "then we must begin training. You are the best warrior I know; let us make a bet as to whether you can best me with one hand."

Linn's smile turned to a smirk. "I do not think that is even a question," she replied.

Kaïs took the chi from her and grasped her uninjured arm.

With a light tug, he pulled her to her feet and began to strap the contraption to her back. "There," he said when he was done.

A strong gale tossed the curtains of her room into the air, pushing her forward. Linn took a step toward the balustrade. With one arm, she pulled herself up, Kaïs's hands guiding her as she steadied herself.

Looking down, she felt that same fear push against her, the whispers of doubt beginning to cloud her mind.

Wingless bird.

I have broken you.

A breeze snatched the note from King Darias out of her hands. It twirled in the air before her, and she caught a glimpse of the words. *I know you will defeat yours.*

Linn straightened. The wind was stronger now, whistling like the voices of her past come to remind her of what she was made of.

Choose to be brave.

Linn felt a stir of Kaïs's Affinity in her mind, nudging her forward, and she knew what he would say to her in this moment.

Look at me. Those molten silver eyes, the strength of his grip.

The world opened before her, sparkling water and endless sky.

Now, fly.

Linn drew a breath. Summoned her winds.

And leapt.

59

The small town of Elmford lay stretched out along a shore of white sand beaches, its stone houses squat and sturdy along the daily drag of waves. A few dozen steps inland, outside the town, was a little hill that rose from the fine, soft sands. Wild grasses grew on it, and interspersed between were patches of white heather, swaying gently to the wind. Dressed in a gown of summer white, it sat patiently, looking out at the sea like a guardian angel.

Elmford's bare dust roads lay quiet in the early-morning light as Ramson passed through, alone on horseback. His Navy uniform was stiff and new, threaded with golds and silvers. It felt like a dream, to be wearing it.

He'd gone back to Sapphire Port to inspect the ship where he'd found Kerlan's lair. Instead of the makeshift laboratory, he'd found the place swept empty, without a single sign of anyone having ever been there. The spies that Kerlan had stolen into Bregon, ex-members of the Order of the Lily, had disappeared without a trace.

Except there was *always* a trace, and if there was anyone who could sniff it out, it was Ramson Quicktongue.

The opportunity had presented itself when King Darias appeared in his chambers a week ago with the offer to reinstate him in the Navy. They'd reached a deal of sorts. At the Succession, King Darias had announced the launch of a special fleet within the Navy dedicated to track down and destroy what remained of Kerlan's spies in Bregon. Ramson had watched from the shadows.

It was mostly the ocean, here, that brought back so many memories. The waters were warmer in the south of Bregon, and Ramson remembered standing at the edge of his broken-down house by the beach, dreaming of the day that a figure that was his father would return to him and his mother.

His horse's steps were soft in the sand, and it wasn't long before he spotted the hill. His knuckles whitened on his reins. His father hadn't lied; he could make out the white heathers, starkly and vibrantly alive on an otherwise barren shore.

Ramson dismounted and walked to the hill. He carried a small jar tucked carefully beneath his arms.

I suppose you'll die unknown and irrelevant, your unmarked body rotting along the sewage of the Dams.

Just like your whore of a mother.

Ramson knelt by the unmarked grave. He threaded a hand through the fine, soft sands, the clumps of wild grasses and white flowers that covered the hill like a gods-woven blanket.

Before, his greatest fear had been that he would never amount to anything in his life. That he would die a bastard son of a father who despised him, a man made of lies and deceit and forged by trades of blood. He had loathed his birthplace, the shameful secret that had earned him whispers of *packsaddle son* and *illegitimate child* like knives in his back.

It had occurred to him, in the moments after he'd walked out of Godhallem with his new mission, that he could turn his life story around. He could fabricate a tale of his mother as a duchess from a distant town to whoever cared to ask; he could have requested to retrieve her remains and have them buried in the highest burial site in his kingdom.

But, Ramson thought, running his fingers through the little heather flowers, he didn't need that. He'd had enough of lies; he'd had enough of pretending to be someone he simply wasn't.

"I'm back, Mam," Ramson said quietly. "I'm sorry it took so long."

The little white heathers fluttered with a gentle breeze.

Once, a long time ago, beneath a blistering noon sun and with the warmth of a wooden jetty at his back, Jonah Fisher had told Ramson to live for himself. Jonah had spoken the words that would define Ramson's trajectory and haunt his dreams even long after the boy was gone.

Your heart is your compass.

But what happened if your heart pulled in two different directions?

The Whitewaves stretched tauntingly into the horizon. He'd gazed out from the balcony of his private chambers the day she had left, the outlines of Ana's ships seared into his mind long after they'd disappeared.

Ramson shut his eyes and swallowed, and the crashing of the waves thrust memories pounding into his head, flipping faster and faster like the pages of a book. He'd thought he'd made the right choice, but whenever he closed his eyes, *she* was all that he could think of, the fierce glare of her eyes, the stubborn set to her chin, the tilt of her head that beckoned a challenge at him.

He'd let himself go that night, under the torrents of rain and thunder and wind that still raged in his chest. They had clashed like water to fire, and he'd tasted the hunger and conflict on her lips, so close to his own desperation.

She had asked for his help that day, right before the Succession, and it was as close to pleading as he'd seen her come. And Ramson had known he'd made the right choice then—yet that certainty had begun to erode with each passing day.

She was to lead Cyrilia—he believed it—and there would be no space in her life for him. He would not abandon everything he had wanted and worked for his entire life to give way to his feelings.

Ramson ran another hand through the white heather before standing and making his way to the sea.

It was strange, he thought as he stood on the white sands of his past, gazing out at the seas and remembering his most fervent, crazed childhood dreams. He'd wanted to lead the Bregonian Navy. And he'd wanted to stand at the edge of the ocean, watching the sea swallow the sun with his father.

It was as though the gods had granted his wildest dreams with the most ironic twist of fate. He had everything he wanted. And he stood now, watching the waves with the ashes of his father.

But someday, when I am gone, look from the sky to the shining sea, across the magnificence of this kingdom our ancestors have built from the ground. And perhaps, then, you will know a little of how it feels.

The uniform weighed on his shoulders, his new task heavy on his mind. He'd spent his life running away from his father, from Kerlan, from becoming anything those men had ever stood for. But Ramson wondered, as he watched the waves push and pull at the shore, whether he had simply run in a full circle and ended up right back at the beginning, trying to undo the damage those two men had caused in his life, in this world.

Jonah had asked him to live for himself. Ramson wasn't sure he could grasp that meaning yet—not as long as any remnants of his father's or Kerlan's legacy lived on to see another day.

If this was what he needed to do, if this was what he logically thought was the *right* thing to do . . . then why did his heart seem to pull in another direction?

The ocean stretched vast and lonely before him, and in that moment, Ramson knew that he was a man with everything and nothing all at once.

He scattered the contents of the jar, watching as the ashes of his father spread over the ocean breeze and disappeared, swallowed by the endless, empty sky.

EPILOGUE

The snows had stopped when Yuri returned to Goldwater Port. Instead, the world had frozen over in a layer of gray, soot scattered black over ashes.

He wound his scarf more tightly around his neck and held out his hand, igniting a small flame in his palm as he made his way through the city. The once-colorful streets of his childhood town were dark and empty, glass from shattered windows and debris from dachas crunching under his boots as he walked.

It was the first time he'd been back since the day of the Imperial Inquisition four weeks ago, and the sight of his massacred town was something Yuri would never forget. He and the rest of the Redcloaks had hidden in a shelter in the Syvern Taiga, not daring to communicate with Goldwater Port in case the Imperial Inquisition was watching their base. Yuri had been waiting weeks for his mother to send a snowhawk signaling that the town was clear.

When the silence had stretched on, he'd resolved to check on the state of things himself.

Yuri turned a corner and came upon the first body. It was frozen beneath a layer of snow and ice; the light of his fire illuminated the dead man's face, still cast in midscream, the muscles now slack.

He lifted his eyes and found an entire street of corpses.

The fire in his palm sputtered, and for a moment, he couldn't breathe. He recognized the faces of the dead; he'd grown up with them, visited them during his rare trips home from the Salskoff Palace.

The local baker, sprawled in the snow, his limbs bent at odd angles.

The old potato seller, her throat gashed open.

The ironsmith, dead in a puddle of his own blood.

Panic beat a drumroll in his chest, and he began to walk faster, taking long, steadying breaths to calm himself. He had just turned down the street to his dacha when he sensed the shadows around him deepen. From the edges of his firelight, a figure peeled away from the walls. Ice cracked under his boots as he approached.

Yuri could only stare at the figure standing before him. The light from his flames licked at the boy's face: skin the brittle porcelain of a sickle moon, eyes the color of a familiar darkness.

Yuri slowed to a stop. "Seyin? What are you doing here?" Seeing his former Second brought to mind the correspondences they'd had, the strict admonishments Yuri had written. He'd stripped Seyin of his title and stopped short of expelling him from the Redcloaks.

"We need to talk" was all the former Second said.

Yuri couldn't fathom why Seyin had ridden all the way to Goldwater Port. Even more, he couldn't fathom why Seyin hadn't told him about coming. "We can talk inside," he replied, making to move forward.

But Seyin stayed where he was, hands stuffed in the pockets of his cloak, his face half-shrouded in his hood.

A feeling of foreboding crept through Yuri. "Seyin, get out of my way."

The other boy's dark eyes glimmered; shadows warred across his face. "No," he said quietly.

Yuri walked forward. Seyin made to block him, but Yuri shoved him out of the way. He heard Seyin's grunt as he hit the ground, but he didn't care. He began to run.

He could barely breathe from the pounding of his own heart, from the fear that squeezed his throat so tight, he thought he would throw up. No communication from Ma for weeks, returning to a ghost town, Seyin showing up out of nowhere . . . His mind was blank, his steps beating a frenzied rhythm of *no no no no no no no—*

The truth awaited him when he reached the entrance of his home.

The glass of his family's restaurant was broken, the shards buried under layers of snow and ash. The inside was dark, tables overturned and chairs smashed against the walls. Only the moonlight filtered through, illuminating silverware and blankets and personal belongings strewn across the floor, as though someone had gone through the contents of his entire home.

But Yuri's gaze was drawn to a silhouette lying in the middle of the restaurant. Drifts of snow had settled on the floor, but he could make out the shape of a body, the faded red kirtle crumpled where she had fallen. A lock of red hair spilled from her bun, dangling across her back.

Everything inside him broke loose. "M-Ma?" His voice came out in a cracked whimper.

She didn't stir.

Yuri scrambled forward, the world swaying around him. He was vaguely aware that he'd dropped to his knees, the glass and shattered porcelain on the floor slicing through his breeches and his palms as he crawled forward, leaving a trail of blood across the floor.

"Ma?" he gasped, and when he reached out to sweep the snow from her arms, her skin was ice-cold. His hands shook, hovering over her. "Ma," he begged, and then he was sobbing, calling her name over and over again into the silence all around.

Hands closed around his shoulders, pulling him back, speaking his name. Yuri yelled and shook them off, crawling forward to where Ma lay—

And then she disappeared. Where she had been, there was only empty floor, snow lying in drifts across wood.

Yuri turned. Seyin knelt beside him. There was something like anguish on his face. "Yuri," he began, but something cracked in Yuri. Suddenly, the hollow space in his chest was afire, his head splitting from the heat, his vision red.

Yuri yelled and sprang, his hands closing around Seyin's neck. *"Give her back!"* he screamed. *"Drop your bullshit illusions!"*

Seyin gave the barest of nods, and Yuri let go. When he turned around, she was there again, small and hunched against the darkness.

"I'm sorry," Seyin rasped. "I didn't want you to . . ." He trailed off.

Yuri closed his eyes. It felt as though there were a fire burning inside him, the flames threatening to consume his soul. His breaths came hot; his palms glowed red. "Why did you come here?" he demanded without looking at Seyin.

There was a pause. "Novo Mynsk has fallen," Seyin whispered. "Shamaïra's been taken. I believe the Red Tigress is responsible for her capture; while I waited here for your return, I received a note from her pleading for our help." His lips curled.

The flames inside Yuri flickered hotter, higher. A strange sense of detachment descended over him. He drew a deep breath. When he exhaled, fire sparked in the air before him. He could feel his hands catching on fire, his hair beginning to singe. "Seyin," he said calmly. "Get out."

The fire poured from him like lava. It snaked across the floor, jumping onto chairs and tablecloths and crawling up the walls. Yuri breathed in deeply as his Affinity climaxed, and for a moment, he looked in a broken shard of glass and saw himself afire: a twisting, writhing mass of reds and oranges.

He bent down and kissed his mother's cold cheeks. Yuri smoothed out her hair, the beautiful, bright red curls he'd inherited. He removed his cloak and tucked it carefully around her, the way she had tucked him into bed before he'd gone to the Salskoff Palace as an apprentice.

He touched a finger to the cloak and set it on fire.

Seyin was waiting for him outside. The entire street had transformed. Crimson and shadows danced on the gray-bricked walls and frozen streets like the flames of the hells themselves.

A movement in the skies caught his eyes, and Yuri looked up. From the moonlit night, a shadow descended swiftly upon them. The light of the burning dacha tinted its black feathers red.

Yuri held up an arm, and the seadove alighted. Its talons dug into the thick padded sleeves of his coat. A note was tied to its legs. Yuri removed it and unfurled the scroll.

The letter consisted of a single sentence, as vague as the way things had been left between him and the sender.

Prepare for war. The Red Tigress returns.

Seyin read the note and looked up. "War with us, or war against us?" he asked.

Yuri did not answer. He gripped the note so hard that his hands shook. He'd come back to find an entire town massacred at the whim of a monarch. He'd seen what happened when empresses clashed for the throne. For in the great games of kings and queens, it was the innocents, the pawns, who suffered.

Enough. No more sympathy, no more friendships. Those were weaknesses that had cost him his mother's life.

Yuri would wipe the board and create a world in which the pawns ruled.

The tips of his fingers were glowing, and within moments, the note was on fire. Yuri watched the flames consume the scroll, eating away at it until there was nothing left but ashes.

He held out a hand and let them fall to the ground.

"Send out snowhawks to all of our forces," he said. "We begin the revolution. The monarchy must fall, and its followers with it."

Seyin watched him behind cold, clouded eyes. "Dak," he said slowly. "And the Red Tigress?"

Yuri met his gaze. "You'll finish the job you started," he replied, "as my Second-in-Command."

Behind him, his home for nineteen years burned. Before him, the trail of bodies pooled the streets with blood. The colors blended, searing through his vision, and the world was awash in red.

Yuri spread his arms, and the fires at his palms roared to life, curving up his sleeves and flaring behind his shoulders like wings.

"I will remake this world to be right, no matter the cost," he said. He would burn it all down, to rebuild it the way it was meant to be. Fire and blood, death and destruction. "Let it be known that this is the end of their crimson reign."

GLOSSARY

CYRILIA

Affinite: person with a special ability or a connection to physical or metaphysical elements; ranges from a heightened sense of the element to ability to manipulate or generate the element

blackstone: stone mined from the Krazyast Triangle; the single element immune to Affinite manipulation and known to diminish or block Affinities

bliny: a type of pancake made of buckwheat flour and best served with caviar

bratika: brother

chokolad: cocoa-based sweet

contessya: countess

copperstone: lowest-value coin

dacha: house

dama: lady

deimhov: demon

Deys: Deity

Deys'voshk: green poison that affects Affinites and is used to subdue them; also known as Deities' Water

Fyrva'snezh: First Snows

goldleaf: highest-value coin
Imperator: Emperor
Imperatorya: Empress
Imperya: Empire
kapitan: captain
kechyan: traditional Cyrilian robe typically made of patterned silk
kologne: scented perfume
kolst: glorious
kommertsya: commerce
konsultant: consultant
mamika: "little mother"; term of endearment for "aunt"
mesyr: mister
pelmeny: dumplings with fillings of minced meat, onions, and herbs
pirozhky: fried pie with sweet or savory fillings
pryntsessa: princess
ptychy'moloko: bird's milk cake
Redcloak: rebels; a play on the colloquialism "Whitecloak"
silverleaf: medium-value coin
sistrika: sister
sunwine: mulled wine made in the summer with honey and spice
valkryf: breed of horse; a valuable steed with split toes and an incomparable ability to climb mountains and weather cold temperatures
varyshki: expensive bull leather
Vyntr'makt: winter market; outdoor markets usually established in town squares prior to the arrival of winter

Whitecloak: colloquialism for the Imperial Patrols prior to the arrival of winter

yaeger: rare Affinite whose connection is to another person's Affinity; they can sense Affinites and control one's Affinity

BREGON

gossenwal: ghostwhales

ironore: a type of rock with defensive properties mined in the Kingdom of Bregon

magek: magic, or an Affinity

magen: a wielder of magic; an Affinite

searock: a rare type of rock with absorption properties, found only in the Corshan Gulf of the Kingdom of Bregon

Sommesreven: the Night of Souls, when Bregonians commemorate the dead

wassengost: water spirits

ACKNOWLEDGMENTS

"They" say the sophomore book is by far the most difficult to write, and I can now unabashedly add my name to the "They" list. Writing *Red Tigress* was by no means an easy feat, especially while working full-time, but the following people have made it possible.

First, Krista Marino, my utterly amazing and whip-smart editor, whose dagger-sharp insights continue to drive my work to the next level. Thank you for making this book the best that it can be. I remain so incredibly grateful to work with you.

Peter Knapp, my fearless agent, who opened the doors to make all this possible, and who continues to champion me. Thank you for your excitement, your optimism, and your guidance. As well, thank you to the entire team at Park & Fine Literary for the continued support and belief in my work.

The fantastic team at Delacorte Press—this book would not exist without each of you. Beverly Horowitz, our tireless champion; Monica Jean and Lydia Gregovic, whose fingerprints are all over these pages; Mary McCue, publicist extraordinaire; and the entire team at Random House Children's Books, who make the publishing world feel a lot smaller and a lot more like home. I am so thankful to be working with you.

My readers, book bloggers, and people of the book community who have supported this series or sent me messages about my books—no words can describe my gratitude for you. You make all this possible.

My former colleagues, the AM crew at Citi, and in particular, my manager (and future film producer-director), Joan Dsilva—thank you for making work something to look forward to every morning, for supporting my creative endeavors, for the cheerleading and the team lunches. I hope CRM revolutionizes before I return.

My writer friends—thank you for helping me survive Sophomore Book Hell. Cassy Klisch, my first and forever reader, whose sharp critique and unending love for the hot mess of a first draft helped me love this book myself and gave me the strength to work on it in the months thereafter. Francesca Flores, my rock in Revisions Waters, whose critiques were a lifeline throughout that particular level of hell. Molly Chang, whose company (plus many glasses of wine) was a necessity in completion of my first draft (literally on a boat). Katie Zhao and Becca Mix, who came to my rescue with some very early disaster Trash versions—I promise this is now probably Recyclable. Ayana Gray, a rare combination of a fellow writer and F1 fan, whose kind wisdom and reverse-word-count progress truly helped in the toughest writing days. Grace Li, for the cheerleading that made me believe in my stories, and whose words continue to nourish my heart. Andrea Tang, for all the Sophomore Book Crisis panic discussions and note sharing. Lyla Lee, for teaching me about US time zones and for writing the beautiful books my younger self needed.

My evil twin, Amy Zhao, whose gym sessions and cat therapy were much-needed sources of replenishment and rest and who never ceases to show love for all my strange story ideas. Here's to a lifetime of F1 trips together. My bestie, Crystal Wong, for reading the earliest drafts and for all the years of encouragement . . . and for helping me get turnip prices when I was neck-deep in revisions. You make my life better and brighter. Betty Lam, whose cheerleading and excitement over my fantasy ideas make me believe in them myself; Kathlene Nguyen, whose support for me started on the first day I set foot on this continent. I hope by the time this is published, my island will be as pretty as both of yours, and that I will have finished FMA:B. My high school and forever friends, Sara, Jessica, Kevin, Jack, Darren, and Alex, who have tolerated my shenanigans since we were actual teens, and who continue to read about my fictional ones.

All my friends who have shown up for me and this bloody little series over the years, who came to my launch and made it standing room only: I love you all, and I am so grateful for every one of you.

Mom and Dad Sin, whose fighter's spirit inspire the revolution in these books; Ryan, whose higher-class peasant home provided refuge from the pandemic as I worked to revise this book; and Sherry, whose cheesecakes are the crème de la crème.

Weetzy, for those summer days in Beijing spent reading and writing our stories of girls with magical powers. I guess between us, I'm the one who still hasn't grown out of that phase. Thank you for being so generous and understanding at my best and worst times and for cheering me on. Know that I will always be here for you, too.

妈妈，爸爸：感谢你们一生对我的支持，传述的精神。从小到大，你们的努力与奋斗打造出了我们家的一片小天地，创造了我幸福完美的童年。我今天的成就、未来的成功、以及写的每一本书也都是亏你们的。

And, last but not least, my Idiot Fiancé, Clement: No words can describe how perfectly you fit me and how blessed I am to have you in my life. There are some things even the storybooks can't capture. However, Growlithe loves me more, and I make the Best Oxtail Stew. So shush.

THE PRINCESS AND THE CON MAN
RETURN IN THE THRILLING
CONCLUSION OF THE
BLOOD HEIR SAGA:

CRIMSON REIGN

SPRING 2022

ABOUT THE AUTHOR

Amélie Wen Zhao was born in Paris and grew up in Beijing in an international community. Her multicultural upbringing instilled in her a deep love of global affairs and cross-cultural perspectives. She seeks to bring this passion to her stories, crafting characters from kingdoms in different corners of the world. She attended college in New York City, where she now lives. Amélie is the author of *Blood Heir* and *Red Tigress.*

ameliezhao.com
@ameliewenzhao